SHERLOCK HOLMES IS LIKE

SIXTY COMPARISONS FOR AN INCOMPARABLE CHARACTER

SHERLOCK HOLMES IS LIKE

SIXTY COMPARISONS FOR AN INCOMPARABLE CHARACTER

EDITED BY
CHRISTOPHER REDMOND

WILDSIDE PRESS

CONTENTS

INTRODUCTION

Christopher Redmond

The essays in this collection are not an analysis of *what* Sherlock Holmes is like (brilliant, unsociable, hawk-nosed) but rather case studies of *whom* he can be said to be like. Their sixty suggestions range across centuries and continents, and include figures from belief and legend as well as from contemporary fiction and film. Some are household names, while others will be unknown to nearly all readers. In each case, while the author has been encouraged to provide an introduction to the character in question, the ultimate purpose of the comparison is to shed light on some aspect of the character of Sherlock Holmes, whose complexities are far from exhausted more than 130 years after he was introduced to a curious readership.

Other than Watson himself, who met a cold reception in *A Study in Scarlet* when he alluded to Edgar Allan Poe's C. Auguste Dupin and Émile Gaboriau's M. Lecoq, the first person to compare Sherlock Holmes to anyone may well have been the Edinburgh-born author Robert Louis Stevenson. He wrote to Arthur Conan Doyle in April 1893 praising the just-published *Adventures of Sherlock Holmes*: "That is the class of literature that I like when I have the toothache.... Only the one thing troubles me: can this be my old friend Joe Bell?" He meant that in Holmes he saw the style and abilities of medical professor Joseph Bell (1837–1911), whom ACD also acknowledged in a succession of writings and interviews as the source, or at least a source, of his character.

There would be little doubt about Bell's role if it were not that ACD's son Adrian Conan Doyle chose to deny it. It was not Bell whose penetrating deductive ability was reflected in Holmes, Adrian thundered in letters and interviews beginning in the 1940s; it was ACD himself. Most readers since then have been inclined to see in ACD's honest, slightly credulous face not Holmes but Watson. Otherwise, various sources or partial sources for Holmes have been suggested, lately including Manchester-based detective Jerome Caminada (1844–1914), who was hailed in a 2016 biography as *The Real Sherlock Holmes*. Bell's colleague Sir Henry Littlejohn also deserves a nod, and was for a time intended to be the topic of a chapter in this book. Sources of individual incidents in the tales of Sherlock Holmes—or incidents in his career, if the reader prefers to treat the character as historical—have been reported in scores of Sherlockian articles and in such substantial studies as Donald A. Redmond's *Sherlock Holmes: A Study in Sources* (1982). And the great detective would not have his very name were it not for several Sherlocks, some of them cricketers, one of them a great-aunt of the author, and one superlatively important Holmes, the elder Oliver Wendell Holmes of Boston.

But the figures who resemble Sherlock Holmes—who are *like* him—are not all sources for the character by any means. Indeed, it may work the other way round: most historians of mystery fiction see Holmes as a source for Ellery Queen, V.I. Warshawski, and every other detective of the past century. Then there are figures who may have been influenced by the same originals who helped to form Holmes, whether they are already identified in those source studies, or are merely figures in books ACD read and absorbed at some time in his life. The complexities are endless.

So are the comparisons. James Iraldi's 1953 essay in the *Baker Street Journal*, noting how much Sherlock Holmes is like Niccolò Paganini (1782–1840), would not be out of place in this book. In 1958, *BSJ* editor Edgar W. Smith drew attention to a self-portrait by Émile Jean-Horace Vernet (1789–1863), often thought to be the "Vernet, the French artist" mentioned in "The Greek Interpreter" as a great-uncle of Holmes; minus the moustache, Smith implied, that noble profile might well be Holmes's, as portrayed by Sidney Paget. In the 1940s Christopher Morley, founder of the Baker Street Irregulars, drew attention to similarities between Holmes's adventures (and implicitly Holmes himself) and other products of the literature he called "Victorian corn", including Robert Louis Stevenson's *New Arabian Nights*. Barbara Goldfield, an enthusiast of the television series "The Man from UNCLE", wrote to the newsletter *Baker Street Pages* in 1966 to compare its central figures Napoleon Solo and Illya Kuryakin with Holmes. Actor Ian McKellen, who was about to star in "Mr. Holmes", told an interviewer in 2015 that Holmes is "like Santa Claus… he's always been there."

While one character may resemble Holmes in skills or idiosyncrasies, another's resemblance comes in physical appearance or in the position he holds in the public eye and popular culture. Thus there is wide variety in the comparisons the sixty authors of this volume have divined. Few characters other than Holmes can be said to have worn a deerstalker, but there are more significant parallels to be found: devotion to fact and logic, brusqueness in private life combined with unexpected compassion, enjoyment of recreational substances that can be tossed aside in a moment when the need arises, a balance between art and science, the ability to turn a memorable phrase in speaking truth to power, loyalty and devotion to a comrade, and, of course, the charisma to attract enthusiasts over more than a century. Reading these chapters makes it clear that many heroes, rebels, advocates of justice, ascetics, hedonists, and proponents of reason—and Sherlock Holmes was all of these things, among others—have surprising qualities in common.

My own interest in the thought-provoking similarities among disparate characters, or at least characters from different origins, dates back many years to a reading of the 1936 book *The Hero: A Study in Tradition, Myth and Drama* by FitzRoy Somerset, Baron Raglan. Analyzing figures from Moses to King Arthur, many of them supposed gods, Raglan finds a "pattern" of 22 features which frequently recur. Oedipus has the highest score with 21 of those features, and Robin Hood has 13.

Sherlock Holmes, although not a god, and although not included in Raglan's roster, conforms strikingly to the pattern: he can be seen to have about 13 of the features, a higher score than that of, say, Siegfried. He "prescribes laws", for example (*The Whole Art of Detection*), nothing is known of his childhood, nothing is known of his death. He suffers "death" at the Reichenbach and experiences a "resurrection" three years later. (A fall from grace and a mysterious death at the top of a hill are involved in several of Raglan's points.) The spring dates of Holmes's death and resurrection, and the name of the adversary whom he conquers—Moriarty, suggesting *moriar*, "I shall die"—may echo the Christian story of the death and resurrection of Jesus (who would score at least 16 points on Raglan's scale if he were included). But such characteristics are not peculiar to any one faith, fiction, or mythology. Christopher Sequeira, who wrote this anthology's chapter about Superman, wrote to me as the book was in a late stage of editing: "I just realized, Holmes and Superman both were *killed* in their continuities before being revealed months and months later as still alive!" The attentive reader may find the same motif in other chapters as well.

As preparation for this book began, I made a list of the figures I might like to see included. Some were obvious enough: one or two of Raglan's classical figures, beyond doubt, but also Mr. Spock of "Star Trek", who has been part of the Sherlockian discourse since Goldfield's 1967 essay "Did Sherlock Holmes Have Pointed Ears?" King Arthur and Robin Hood, the two greatest figures of English folklore, seemed essential, as were Batman, Gandalf (Goldfield, prolific in her time, had written about him as well), Nero Wolfe, and, once the decision was made to include historical characters, Oscar Wilde. Then the net spread, and soon my list had far more than 60 entries, so that potential authors could be offered many choices. In the end some promising figures did not make the cut, including Dracula, Flashman, Canadian detective John Wilson Murray, Martin Hewitt, the Scarlet Pimpernel, and a character said to be even more universally recognized than Santa Claus, never mind Sherlock Holmes: Ronald McDonald.

On the other hand, some of the figures suggested by potential authors would never have occurred to me, and the book would have been far poorer without them. It is thanks to suggestions from volunteers that this book features Gertrude Stein, Loki, the Gunslinger, Smiley, Sadeq Mamqoli, and Josiah Willard Gibbs, among others. And then there is the final section of the book, "Something Recherché", which it will be best to let the reader discover unaided.

I am profoundly grateful to all the authors represented in this volume, most of whom generously complied with the deadlines and constraints I suggested, and all of whom brought knowledge and insight that no single person, not even an editor, could ever achieve. I hope they have not been too deeply offended by my tinkering with their work, or by my editorial brusqueness at times. This book is the third in what seems to be a series of anthologies, each including the work of 60 Sherlockian authors. Some 33 of its 60 authors are newcomers, while 27 were represented in one or both of the previous books, *About Sixty* (2016) and *About Being a Sherlockian* (2017). The anthology formula seems to be established, and I have again collected a mixture of authors, demographically and geographically varied, diverse in interests and approaches, and incidentally divided roughly equally between the sexes.

My thanks are due to many well-wishers on this and the preceding volumes; to Carla Coupe and her colleagues at Wildside Press; to the nine volunteer proofreaders; and now to those who will read and, with good fortune, enjoy the essays in this book. I hope these writings open new lines of thought and amazement in two directions: about the sixty characters discussed—some of whom will almost surely be new to any individual reader—and about Sherlock Holmes himself, seen in these pages through sixty facets of a bright prism. We never seem to tire of finding new things to say about him.

No royalties from the sale of this volume will be paid to either the authors or the editor. Royalties earned will, with the cooperation of the publisher, be turned over in their entirety to the Beacon Society, a not-for-profit organization of Sherlockians with the purpose of introducing young people to Sherlock Holmes through classrooms and libraries.

Christopher Redmond (Carleton Place, Ontario) is the author of *A Sherlock Holmes Handbook*, *In Bed with Sherlock Holmes*, *Lives Beyond Baker Street*, and other books. He was founder of the website Sherlockian.net, and is a Baker Street Irregular and a member of the Bootmakers of Toronto.

EMINENT VICTORIANS
AND OTHERS

They were of great service to me, and especially
that one incidentally truthful piece of biography.

The Hound of the Baskervilles

A SHREWD PRIVATE INQUIRY AGENT

Sir George Lewis

Donny Zaldin

While Sherlock Holmes was not without predecessors (Edgar Allan Poe's C. Auguste Dupin) and successors (Dorothy L. Sayers's Lord Peter Wimsey and Agatha Christie's Miss Marple), he is acknowledged to be the world's greatest *fictional* consulting detective—the Sherlockian "grand game" notwithstanding. There are, of course, similarities between Holmes and these and other members of the brotherhood and sisterhood of consulting detectives. But this essay will compare Sherlock Holmes to the real-life solicitor who set the bar of the Sherlockian age: Sir George Lewis, the only one of the sixty characters in this volume to appear in the Canon—when he conducted "negotiations... over the Hammerford Will case," in "The Illustrious Client."

George Henry Lewis, born in 1833, twenty-one years before Sherlock Holmes, was bred and reared in the law, following in the footsteps of his accomplished father, to whom he became articled at the young age of 17. Two years later, he tried and won his first case, in which he cleared a man charged with robbing a publican. Notable successes in criminal and financial cases soon followed, making him a favourite of society's powerful and wealthy upper crust, including Edward, Prince of Wales, later King Edward VII—referred to as a "one-man scandal industry for George Lewis"—as well as the lower classes whom he also championed, earning him the sobriquet, the "poor man's lawyer."

But eventually Lewis removed his wig and retreated from the limelight as barrister and litigator to take on the role of solicitor and negotiator, arranging "delicate matters which are to be kept out of the papers," much like Sir James Damery in "The Illustrious Client." Lewis was included in the honours list and knighted in 1893 by Queen Victoria, was made a baronet in 1902 by King Edward VII, and a Companion of the Victorian Order in 1905. Lewis's 1911 obituary in the *Times* described him as "the confidential adviser of many prominent people," relying "upon his great tact," and "priding himself most upon his peculiar success in keeping his clients from coming before the public eye at all."

In *A Study in Scarlet*, in order to ascertain what "work" it was in which Sherlock Holmes was engaged, Dr. Watson completed a 12-point list of subjects which included literature, philosophy, astronomy, politics, botany, geology, chemistry, anatomy, sensational literature, and British law, assessing how well-informed his new roommate was in each of them. In corresponding fashion, a list of *How Sherlock Holmes is like Sir George Lewis* appears below.

Success at his profession: George Lewis was the pre-eminent solicitor of his time—in fact, the only solicitor to achieve the kind of fame bestowed upon the great barristers of his day, whose advocacy skills were showcased in meticulous newspaper accounts of dramatic trials and legal proceedings. Sherlock Holmes was the pre-eminent consulting detective of his time, whose cases and methods were detailed for the benefit of eager and devoted readers by his biographer and friend, Dr. John H. Watson, albeit in a less instructive, more romantic way than Holmes would have preferred. Watson noted in the twelfth and final point of his list that Holmes "has a good practical knowledge of British law," and went so far as to state in "The Five Orange Pips" that Holmes *was* "a lawyer," although neither Watson nor the writers on the writings have ever substantiated that claim. Both lawyer and detective were the first choice in their respective professions for those who required their services.

Clientele: George Lewis's clientele were primarily members of the upper stratum of the English class system. In addition to the King, they included influential politicians such as Charles Stewart Parnell and Sir Charles Dilke; English newspaper editor W.T. Stead, pioneer of investigative journalism who died aboard the *Titanic*; and British-American socialite, actress and producer Lillie Langtry, known as "The Jersey Lily." But Lewis also provided his services to residents of the slums along the dangerous Ratcliffe Highway and the poverty-stricken and crime-infested Seven Dials neighbourhood in London's East End. Sherlock Holmes's clients also included *la crème de la crème* of British upper class society. Like Lewis, Holmes served King Edward VII, as well as a "certain gracious lady" who presented him with "a remarkably fine emerald tie-pin" at Windsor for "carry[ing] out a small commission," and the highest government officials: Lord Holdhurst, cabinet minister and future Premier of England (in "The Naval Treaty"); a twice-Premier, Lord Bellinger, and the Secretary for European Affairs, the Right Honourable Trelawney Hope (in "The Second Stain"). Holmes's clients also included members of the middle and lower classes, including clerks, typewritists, and governesses.

Confidentiality: On September 29, 1907, the *New York Times* wrote: "There is probably no man in England who is the repository of so many scandalous secrets as Sir George Lewis... [of whom] it has been said... he holds the honor of half the British peerage in his keeping... [and]

this astute lawyer is considered to be more proficient out of the Divorce Court than in it" by "keep[ing] out of [it] even more cases than he has carried through it." The *Wanganui Chronicle*, in the antipodes of New Zealand, noted in his obituary that "probably of no other man has society ever made such a confidant, and no man carried so many secrets of other people to his grave." Similarly, Sherlock Holmes does not always share with the official police his deductions and the identities of guilty parties, instead exercising his "private judgment" by allowing several offenders to escape the formal legal process, including James Ryder, Captain Jack Croker, Dr. Leon Sterndale and Lady Hilda Trelawney Hope. Explains Holmes in "The Priory School": "There is no reason, so long as the ends of justice are served, why I should disclose all that I know."

Exhaustive and all-encompassing memory: Lewis's obituary in the *Times* cited his "encyclopaedic memory," which he systematically honed. Realizing that his business was of an "extremely confidential nature," he seldom, if ever, made handwritten notes, destroyed his legal papers and, partly on this account, never wrote an autobiography, in order to ensure that his clients' secrets would die with him. Although he granted a somewhat candid interview in an 1893 issue of the *Strand* magazine, Lewis never betrayed any confidences which his clients revealed to him. Holmes also possessed an eidetic memory, which included a "strangely retentive memory for trifles." He informs Watson in "The Red-Headed League," "As a rule, when I have heard some slight indication of the course of events, I am able to guide myself by the thousands of other similar cases which occur to my memory."

Knowledge of past records and details of crime: The *Dictionary of National Biography*, 1912, Second Supplement, credited Lewis with "an unrivalled knowledge of the past records of the criminals and adventurers of both sexes, not only in England and on the continent of Europe, but in the United States, which was peculiarly serviceable to him and to his clients in resisting attempts at conspiracy and blackmail." Similarly, in *A Study in Scarlet*, Watson assesses Holmes's knowledge of "sensational literature" as immense. "He appears to know every detail of every horror perpetrated in the century," supporting his theory that, "There is nothing new under the sun. It has all been done before." As well, he keeps a detailed catalogue of criminal cases from newspaper "cuttings" in "ponderous commonplace books" ("The Engineer's Thumb").

Types of cases: Lewis's cases involved forgery (the questionable authenticity of an 1887 letter penned by Charles Stewart Parnell regarding the death of a political rival), blackmail (Oscar Wilde's scandalous 1893 letter to "Bosie," the nickname of his lover, Lord Alfred Douglas), poisons and poisoning (to determine whether the 1875 poisoning by antimony of barrister Charles Bravo of Balham was suicide or murder), cheating at cards (regarding the accusation that Sir William Gordon-Cumming cheated at baccarat in the 1890 Tranby Croft affair), and robberies (the Hatton Garden diamond robbery and the 1855 gold bar theft en route from London to Paris). These matters are all reminiscent of Sherlockian themes, including forgers and forgeries (the Conk-Singleton forgery case), blackmail (from "A Scandal in Bohemia" to "The Illustrious Client"), poisons ("The Sussex Vampire" and others), cheating at cards ("The Empty House"), and robberies ("The Blue Carbuncle," "The Beryl Coronet" and "The Mazarin Stone"). A comparison of George Lewis's cases to those of Sherlock Holmes—especially having regard to the dates when they took place—bolsters the argument that several of Sherlock Holmes's cases were inspired by the legal cases of George Lewis.

How he played the game: Lewis's obituary in the *Times* observes that "he was not so much a lawyer as a shrewd private inquiry agent; audacious, playing the game often in defiance of the rules, and relying on his audacity to carry him through"—also an astonishingly accurate description of Holmes and his own methods. In "The Bruce-Partington Plans," Holmes confides to Watson, "I play the game for the game's own sake," and in "Thor Bridge," Holmes tells a member of the local constabulary that if he successfully solves the case, he doesn't ask to have his name mentioned and "need not appear in the matter at all."

The pursuit of justice: In his first compelling case, George Lewis intervened and skillfully cross-examined the widow Florence Bravo at a coroner's inquest on her second husband's death by poisoning, following which the coroner changed his verdict in the death from "suicide" to "wilful murder." This prompted the press to call Lewis an "Avenging Angel." Like Lewis, Holmes did not so much enforce the law as he pursued *justice* (which is "every man's business"), dedicating himself to that ideal "as far as [his]… powers go" in order to ensure that "the sword of justice is still there to avenge."

Renown: Caricatures of Lewis and Holmes, each drawn by "Spy" (Leslie Ward), appeared in the September 2, 1876, and February 27, 1907, issues, respectively, of the British weekly magazine *Vanity Fair*, subtitled "A Weekly Show of Political, Social and Literary Wares." The magazine regularly featured a full-page colour lithograph of a contemporary celebrity or dignitary, totalling over 2,000 images between 1868 and 1914, which are now considered the chief cultural legacy of the periodical, forming a vivid and informative record of the period.

Conclusion: Although George Lewis and Sherlock Holmes practised very different professions, they ran along parallel lines, driven by similar motives: a dedication to their craft and their clients, as well as to a higher mission to pursue and attain justice, each in his own way.

Donny Zaldin (Toronto, Ontario) is a Bootmaker of Toronto, Baker Street Irregular, and ASH, who has been published in the *Baker Street Journal*, *Serpentine Muse*, *Canadian Holmes*, *Magic Door*, and *Explorations*, and contributed as author and editor to BSI series volumes. He is married and devoted to his own "certain gracious lady", Barbara Rusch, and their six children and 15 grandchildren.

VICTORIAN REVOLUTIONARY

Charles Darwin

Alexian A. Gregory

It is with great joy and deep satisfaction that I get to compare two of my intellectual heroes, Charles Darwin (1809–1882) and Sherlock Holmes. For it is precisely their great intellects that spring to mind when viewing these two gentlemen, who shared both historical and ethnic identities. They were both English, and equally they were both Victorians, though Holmes was born in the heart of the era, in 1854, and Darwin was born some 28 years before the Victorian age began.

"I am a brain, Watson. The rest of me is a mere appendix," says Holmes in "The Mazarin Stone." So let's begin with his logic, which he repeatedly calls "deductive." In this, Holmes is quite mistaken. Deductive logic begins with a general principle or a cause and proceeds from there to an effect or a conclusion. When Holmes says in *A Study in Scarlet* that "From a drop of water a logician could infer the possibility of an Atlantic or a Niagara without having seen or heard of one or the other," *that* is deductive reasoning. There Holmes begins with the origin, a single drop of water, and develops it into an Atlantic or a Niagara, the effect.

But when Holmes is on the case, he must always reason backwards from the effect to the cause. Sir Charles Baskerville is dead. Was it satanic supernaturalism or human malignity that snuffed out his life? Holmes follows the clues back to the cause of this mischief, Jack Stapleton. So it is with all of the cases that come to him: Holmes reasons backwards from the effect, the crime, to the cause, the perpetrator.

Here is Holmes in his own words (from *A Study in Scarlet*) on reasoning backwards: "In solving a problem of this sort, the grand thing is to be able to reason backwards…. Most people, if you describe a train of events to them, will tell you what the result would be. They can put those events together in their minds, and argue from them that something will come to pass. There are few people, however, who, if you told them a result, would be able to evolve from their own inner consciousness what the steps were which led up to that result. This power is what I mean when I talk of reasoning backwards, or analytically."

Darwin, who is best known for his development of the theory of evolution by natural selection, similarly reasoned backwards, or inductively, from effect to cause. For example, here are a plethora of avian species. They have many features in common, yet also have serious differences, i.e. speciation. What caused this variation? Ploddingly, patiently, and persistently Darwin gathered his facts. He organized them and worked his way back to the cause of speciation. The ultimate truth he discovered and established for all time is that for allied species there is a common ancestor whose related descendants ultimately diverged into different species and varieties.

So the strongest steel thread that binds Darwin and Holmes is their use of inductive logic, their reasoning backwards from effect to cause. Such reasoning is based on solid and verifiable facts to arrive at the cause, be it criminal or biological.

Some of Darwin's inductive results were no less astonishing than Holmes's. Dave Hone, writing in the *Guardian* on October 2, 2013, tells the story of a particularly striking instance:

> In early 1862, a British orchid grower sent Charles Darwin a series of orchids from Madagascar, which included the beautiful and star-shaped flower of *Angraecum sesquipedale*. This has an exceptionally long nectary (getting on for 30 cm) and in a book on orchid pollination, Darwin suggested that this extreme feature may have evolved alongside a moth with an exceptionally long tongue to pollinate it.
>
> He wrote to a friend at Kew:… "In Madagascar there must be moths with probosces capable of extension to a length of between ten and eleven inches."… Here was a firm prediction and one that has become famous in evolutionary circles, but hard to confirm.…
>
> In 1907, more than 20 years after Darwin's death, a subspecies of the gigantic Congo moth from Madagascar was identified and named as *X. morganii praedicta*.… The moth is large at around 16 cm in wingspan, but the proboscis is truly colossal and can be more than 20 cm in length forming a huge coil in front of the head when not in use. However, while there was now an orchid with a long nectary and a moth with a huge tongue, the question remained: did *X. morganii praedicta* really feed on *A. sesquipedale*?
>
> It wasn't until 1992, nearly a century later, that observations were made of the moth feeding on the flower and transferring pollen from plant to plant with both videos and stills being taken. This was observed in the wild and confirmed further with studies in captivity.
>
> Thus more than 130 years after Darwin first suggested that a large moth pollinated an African orchid, his hypothesis was confirmed.

There is yet another connection between Holmes and Darwin. Holmes was not only aware of Darwin, but clearly he also read and appreciated him highly. The proof appears in Holmes's own words to Watson in *A Study in Scarlet*: "Do you remember what Darwin says about music? He claims that the power of producing and appreciating it existed among the human race long before the power of speech was arrived at. Perhaps that is why we are so subtly influenced by it. There are vague memories in our souls of those misty centuries when the world was in its childhood." So Holmes read Darwin and indeed was a Darwinian!

Darwin's journey aboard the *HMS Beagle* circumnavigated the globe and took him to varied and faraway locales—South America, Australia, Galapagos, and Tahiti. This voyaging gave him scientific knowledge. Holmes's Great Hiatus did the same for him. He traveled very widely: Persia, Arabia, the Sudan and Tibet. On the scientific side during his travels he worked on coal-tar derivatives in Montpellier in southern France.

Darwin published varied works on such subjects as climbing plants, insectivorous plants, vegetable mold, and the expressions of emotions in man and animals, all various facets of biology. Holmes's literary output went much further afield. He produced works on Lassus's motets, tobacco ash, footprints, early English charters, and, of course, bees.

Darwin and Holmes were keenly intelligent men with wide interests. Their intelligence was of a very active nature. They used their brains and applied themselves sedulously to their pursuits and didn't stop until they got results. Each in his own way solved mysteries—one on the mechanism of speciation, and the other on the originators of crimes.

Darwin and Holmes each left deep and indelible footprints on history's path. After Darwin, science was never the same. His discoveries and his reasoning influence and direct scientific thought to this day. Biologists, geneticists, and paleontologists *inter alia* are his scientific descendants and remain in deep debt to him. And Holmes, too, has "descendants." Nero Wolfe, Perry Mason, Ellery Queen, Colombo, Jessica Fletcher, Jane Marple, Hercule Poirot, V.I. Warshawski and so many other detectives who reason backwards are his children and grandchildren. They are indebted to him no less than scientists are to Darwin. The detective story is no longer the same because of Holmes's arrival.

If Darwin revolutionized scientific mysteries by observation and analysis, then Holmes revolutionized murder mysteries scientifically by observation and analysis. Both of their revolutions still resonate strongly and shape their respective genres to this day. That's a rather impressive, nay, extraordinary historical legacy for these two Victorian gentlemen. We are happily in deep debt to them both.

Alexian A. Gregory (Verona, New Jersey) is a retired mailman. He is appropriately invested in the Baker Street Irregulars as The Grimpen Postmaster, and is also a member of the Adventuresses of Sherlock Holmes. He enjoys architectural history, Byzantine history, linguistics, and shopping on eBay, and his favorite relaxation is doing the *New York Times* Sunday puzzles with co-conspirator Julie Gonzalez.

MAKING THE AIR OF LONDON SWEETER

William Thomas Stead

Peter Calamai

He was last seen alive "alone... in silence, and, what seemed to me, a prayerful attitude or one of profound meditation."

That could well be a description of Sherlock Holmes, awaiting his final confrontation with the embodiment of evil at Reichenbach Falls. Instead it is a survivor's memory of William Thomas Stead (pronounced "sted") on April 15, 1912, standing on the listing deck of RMS *Titanic*. Travelling first class, the 62-year-old passenger had already given his lifejacket to a fellow passenger and helped women and children into lifeboats.

Had Sherlock Holmes been a passenger on that White Star liner, I do not doubt that he would have emulated the selfless actions of W.T. Stead. After all, in "The Final Problem" he assured Professor Moriarty that he would "cheerfully accept" his own destruction "in the interests of the public" if his actions also resulted in the professor's destruction. Holmes might even have spent the initial chaotic minutes in the *Titanic's* first-class smoking room, as did Stead, although Holmes likely would not have chosen a penny Bible as his final reading material, and might have smoked a pipe while Stead favoured cigarettes.

After Stead's death the *Daily Mail* hailed him as "one of the most remarkable personalities of our time—a brilliant mind, an apostle of many causes, an essentially great journalist, a man of devasting sincerity and rigid principle, yet with interests as wide as the world and an inexhaustible love of adventure."

Omit (temporarily) the journalist reference, and the rest of that tribute rings true for Sherlock Holmes, does it not? Yet there is also a striking parallelism between the career paths of the two men. As Holmes explains to Watson in *A Study in Scarlet*, he created his own unique calling as a private consulting detective. He was *sui generis*.

So too was W.T. Stead. Starting out in journalism, he confidently proclaimed that he would use the power of the press to "smite the powers of darkness in high places" and to plead "for the fallen and weak everywhere." Stead invented the idea of government by newspaper and practised it so successfully that Lord Esher, Edwardian *eminence grise* and professional confidant, proclaimed that between 1884 and 1888 "Stead came nearer to governing the U.K. than any other man." Stead also invented the concept of trial by newspaper and pioneered investigative journalism. Like Holmes, he had seen a need in society and crafted his own unique calling in response.

The parallels between the two men are manifested in many other ways large and small. Both were lifelong advocates for justice. Again in "The Final Problem," when his own death was very much in his thoughts, Holmes sums up his career: "The air of London is sweeter for my presence. In over a thousand cases I am not aware that I have ever used my powers upon the wrong side." That was May 1891, and W.T. Stead would have been justified in making the same claim. Consider:

In August 1883 Stead had become chief editor of the *Pall Mall Gazette*, a sedate Clubland afternoon daily with a circulation that seldom went above 6,000. (The *Telegram*'s was 200,000.) He had been offered the post on the basis of his nine years as the crusading editor of *The Northern Echo*, a daily serving County Durham and Teeside in northeast England.

In his first 22 months as editor, Stead launched at least six "escapades" which made the *Pall Mall Gazette* into a paper which everyone of influence had to read. That included Holmes, who lists the *Pall Mall* as one of the newspapers for the advertisement in "The Blue Carbuncle." Stead's nimble pen and social conscience produced an explosive series, "The Truth About the Navy," which led to a doubling of defence spending; parlayed a church report on slum housing into a Royal Commission and sweeping legal reforms; sent General "Chinese" Gordon to his death at the hands of rebels in Sudan; and played a decisive diplomatic role in a clash over Afghanistan between Russia and Britain.

Yet Stead's claim to journalistic fame—perhaps his most striking parallel with Holmes—was his campaign against child prostitution and legalized pedophilia in late Victorian London. Under the modest heading "The Maiden Tribute of Modern Babylon," Stead revealed in July 1885 how he arranged to buy a 13-year-old girl from the country for £5. He then had her examined by a madam to obtain a certificate of virginity that would satisfy the eventual purchaser of the girl in a London brothel. In four installments the *Gazette* detailed, without euphemisms, the leather straps, padded rooms and smothered screams when such maidens were regularly raped by wealthy Victorian gentlemen.

"The Maiden Tribute" exposed the corruption of several of London's elite groups, who either profited from or indulged in the procurement, sale and eventual abuse of young, under-privileged girls. Though never going so far as to name people, Stead revealed how the trade was "winked at by many administrators of the law," how it was "practiced by some legislators" and even how one "well-known member of Parliament [was] quite ready to supply... 100 maids at £25 each." Perhaps not surprisingly, MPs had for years been blocking passage of an amendment to the criminal law that would raise the age of consent for women from 13 to 16.

The "Maiden Tribute" articles caused an uproar that has never been equalled in British journalism. Northumberland Street outside the newspaper's offices was packed sidewalk-to-sidewalk with people. Riots broke out at the *Gazette*'s offices as news vendors and would-be purchasers laid siege to obtain copies. At one point the press ran for 36 hours without stopping, printing 100,000 copies a day instead of the usual 12,000. The fourth and final installment in the series was produced by Stead overnight, dictating to three shorthand secretaries in relay. At the end, he managed only by wrapping his throbbing head in wet towels.

Reaction was immediate. By the end of the week the stalled amendment had been rushed through second reading at Westminster; before the year end the age of consent was legally raised to 16. The next year Parliament went on to repeal the Contagious Diseases laws, which legalized prostitution in garrison towns.

So Stead would certainly have been justified in claiming that the air in London (and elsewhere in England) was sweeter for his presence. His reward, instead, was three months in jail, convicted on a trumped-up charge of abduction.

Like Stead, Holmes was regularly involved with matters of public morality. Think of the lecherous Mormon demands in *A Study in Scarlet*, followed unabated by the "adventuress" Irene Adler in "A Scandal in Bohemia," adultery in "The Cardboard Box," abduction for forced marriage/rape in "The Solitary Cyclist," the multiple blackmail-worthy marital indiscretions in "Charles Augustus Milverton" and so on. Christopher Redmond concludes (*In Bed with Sherlock Holmes*) that sex figures in all but a dozen of the 60 canonical stories.

The strongest Holmes parallels with Stead, however, occur in "The Illustrious Client" and "The Disappearance of Lady Frances Carfax," with which Redmond deals at length in his first chapter. In the former story Baron Gruner was almost certainly involved in the white slave trade, recording details in his "lust diary"; a strong case can also be made that "Holy" Peters and his wife were brothel-recruiters, with Lady Frances shipped back to England naked in a coffin. In both adventures, Holmes appears to be emulating Stead's "Maiden Tribute" campaign.

Stead continued to "smite the powers of darkness in high places" and to plead "for the fallen and weak everywhere." In February 1887, a peaceful rally of unemployed men in Trafalgar Square was charged by mounted police. Part of the crowd broke away and began a series of riots in Pall Mall, St. James's Street and fashionable Mayfair. Stead's nimble pen rushed to defend the Radicals and Socialists who had organized the rally.

Yet the *Gazette* began losing circulation and advertising in a backlash from its male establishment readers—not because they favoured the buying and selling of underaged virgins but because they favoured the sexual double standard. And even more so because these men of power and influence were aghast that people previously considered powerless could force MPs to take actions they personally opposed when backed by what poet Matthew Arnold dismissed as the "New Journalism." The paper's proprietor blamed Stead for the drop in circulation, and he was out of a job by 1890.

Not yet out of causes. Stead joined George Newnes, of *Strand* magazine fame, to found an influential weekly, the *Review of Reviews*, where he threw his considerable energies into promoting world peace through arbitration. In fact, it was to attend a peace congress in New York that the grizzled and down-at-the-heels journalist took passage on the *Titanic*.

As a crusader for social justice, Stead was *sui generis*. Both he and Holmes left their stamp upon their professions for posterity. The great journalistic crusades of the British press can all be traced back to Stead, such as the thalidomide exposés in the *Sunday Times* under Harold Evans, who also started his career on the *Northern Echo*. So too, however, can the worst excesses of the tabloid press, such as when a detective working for the *News of the World* in 2011 hacked the mobile phone of a murdered schoolgirl.

And while Holmes is—horrors!—fictional, some investigative techniques such as fingerprints, footprint casts and the standard use of a microscope were introduced to the public in the stories long before they were widely adopted by the professional forces. Detectives today still strive for his degree of ratiocination.

The parallels never end. Indeed, Holmes could have been invoking the muckraking side of Stead's journalism when he proclaimed that "my business is to know what others don't know."

Perhaps the most poignant comparison is how the two men are remembered today. The fictional Sherlock Holmes strides as a colossus among the icons of modernity with new adventures of varying literary skill abounding in print and in electronic fan fiction, two television series, and movies almost yearly. Serious studies of the original 60 stories fill bookcases and there are at least a dozen "biographies" or character studies. Statues of Holmes adorn Baker Street tube station in London, Conan Doyle's birthplace in Edinburgh, the Sherlock Holmes Museum in Meiringen, Switzerland, and the embankment in front of the British Embassy in Moscow.

Not so for W.T. Stead. W. Sydney Robinson, author of the most recent Stead biography (after a 90-year hiatus), writes: "In the light of his contemporary relevance, it is surprising that Stead is not more widely acknowledged as a maker of modern Britain." The biography *Muckraker: The Scandalous life and Times of W.T. Stead* explores the reasons why "many of his closest friends and admirers willfully allowed his memory to fade."

And yet, in a foyer of the Peace Palace which houses the International Court of Justice in The Hague are displayed the busts of renowned peace campaigners. William Thomas Stead is there. The inscription on the bust cites his campaigning for peace conferences but also his courage as an editor in exposing child prostitution and legalized pedophilia in late Victorian London.

Peter Calamai (Stratford, Ontario) worked in daily newspapers for 45 years as a reporter, editor and foreign correspondent. A member of the Baker Street Irregulars, he co-edited *Canada and Sherlock Holmes* in the BSI Press International series. In 2014 he was made a Member of the Order of Canada in recognition of his science journalism and advocacy for adult literacy.

UNKNOWN TO THE GENERAL PUBLIC

Josiah Willard Gibbs

Christopher A. Zordan

The name J. Willard Gibbs will probably generate one of two re-sponses. For most readers that response is "Who?" Many scientists or engineers reading this, on the other hand, are probably familiar with the name Gibbs, and likely grumbled about him during their education. And here we have the first similarity with the great detective: a genius who is as unknown to the general public as he is renowned in his profession, to borrow a phrase from *The Valley of Fear*. But whether you know of Gibbs or not, it falls to me to convince you, the reader, that Sherlock Holmes is like Josiah Willard Gibbs.

I intend to make the case by discussing Professor Gibbs's life and career. Born in New Haven, Connecticut, in 1839, Gibbs would spend almost his entire life there, associated with Yale College, and becoming one of the most significant scientists America has ever produced. At the time of his birth, the Gibbs family had been producing clergymen and academics of distinction since the 17th century. Gibbs was a diligent student and intended to continue his studies at Yale College, where his father was on the faculty as a professor of sacred literature. The cus-tom at Yale in the 1850s was that the examinations were *viva voce*, and young Gibbs, being of a shy and retiring nature, viewed the admittance examinations with some trepidation. He sought the advice of a family friend, a Professor Thatcher, who was on the Yale faculty. At that meet-ing, Thatcher quizzed Gibbs on a variety of topics and at the end of the interview notified him that he was admitted to Yale College.

Gibbs's undergraduate career was distinguished, including winning prizes for mathematics, Latin composition and Latin oration; he would be selected to give the Latin oration at his commencement ceremony. He spent his time as a student at Yale focused on his studies, rarely partici-pating in the social activities of the school except in an occasional *pro forma* manner. He would go on to earn a PhD in 1863, the first awarded for engineering in the United States, and only the fifth PhD awarded in the United States in any discipline. His dissertation focused on the application of mathematics to practical problems of the time.

His teaching career began as a lecturer in Latin and natural philosophy, what we now call physics. Between August 1866 and June 1869 Gibbs spent time in Europe, where he met many of the foremost scientists of the day, including chemist Robert Bunsen, the inventor of, among other things, the Bunsen burner, a device that Sherlock Holmes used at his laboratory bench at 221B Baker Street.

For Gibbs, this sabbatical was important for two reasons. First, in the 19th century the world's center for science was Europe—especially Germany, France, and England. Gibbs's education benefited from exposure by broadening the scientific and technical tools he would apply to his later work. Second, this trip introduced Gibbs to the world-wide scientific community and put him on the map, as it were. His ability was recognized early, and major scientific figures in Europe would go on to translate his work into German and French to make it accessible to the Continental scientific community, a recognition of the significance of Gibbs's talent.

During his first semester in France, he worked such long hours teaching and in study as to cause a nervous breakdown, and consequently he wintered in the south of France to regain his health at the end of 1866. He later traveled to Berlin and then to Heidelberg before returning home, in all a three-year hiatus from New Haven. Back at Yale, Gibbs would become a professor of mathematical physics and dedicate himself to his research, rarely leaving New Haven again except for regular holidays to the Adirondacks or the White Mountains.

The phrase "his research" is a feeble way to describe the breadth and significance of Gibbs's contributions to science. To say that he changed the face of science is not an understatement. His innovations spanned all manner of scientific endeavor:

- Mechanical engineering: his doctoral dissertation focused on optimizing mechanical gears, and shortly after finishing school he patented a new railroad brake mechanism, a significant invention at this time because rail travel was growing at a rapid pace in post-Civil War Reconstruction America.
- Vector calculus, vector analysis, and probability: important to mathematics, many fields of engineering, and game theory into the current day.
- Optical physics: There is a family story that having troubles with his sight, Gibbs correctly diagnosed astigmatism, calculated the correct lens properties for glasses and had lenses ground to his specifications. It would not be an easy exercise even today.
- The behavior of charged particles near semi-permeable membranes: all manner of phenomena in biology and biochemistry rely on charged particles at the surface of, or moving across, biological membranes.

Gibbs's most important contributions, however, came in the field of thermodynamics—the study of energy and its interaction with matter. He applied mathematical rigor and systematic thought to many of the problems facing scientists of the day: how to predict if a reaction is spontaneous, how mixtures of solids, liquids and gases reach equilibrium with each other, and the statistical treatment of the interaction of matter and energy.

For more than 100 years now, undergraduate scientists and engineers have taken courses grounded in the work of Gibbs's life. That's *courses*, plural. As a physicist, chemist or engineer, one cannot escape the influence of Gibbs in one's professional education. His work on thermodynamics is familiar in our everyday lives, from why your air conditioning bill is high (it takes a lot of electrical energy to make heat go against its equilibrium) to how to design and operate refineries, chemical plants, even a car engine, and why living things need a lot of energy to survive. His work also helps explain why perpetual motion machines or 100-percent efficient mechanical engines are impossible.

Sherlock Holmes's intellectual accomplishments, from detection to the study of polyphonic motets and the Buddhism of Ceylon, are well known and no doubt pervade many people's reasoning process every bit as much as Gibbs's. However, the two men have similarities that go well beyond the products of their work, as they were alike in how they lived. Both were averse to social interaction outside a small group of people, were life-long bachelors, and maintained single residences for much of their lives—in Gibbs's case he lived with his sister and brother-in-law in New Haven during his long career.

Gibbs was also known to love long walks and was a master at steering a horse and carriage, frequently seen around New Haven driving his sister's carriage. One difference, however, is that Gibbs was willing to accept accolades for his professional accomplishments. In addition to a number of honorary doctorates from institutions in the United States and Europe, he was made a member of the National Academy of Science in 1879 and received the Rumford Prize from the American Academy of Arts and Sciences in 1880, was made an honorary member of a number of European learned societies, and was elected a Foreign Member of the Royal Society in the United Kingdom.

In 1901 he was honored with the Royal Society's Copley Medal, then the most prestigious award in the sciences. The Copley Medal was first awarded in 1731 and is still awarded to this day. The Nobel Prize, first awarded in 1901 did not, at the time, have the prestige that it now has or the Copley Medal did at the time. Had Gibbs lived even a few more years, he would likely have also been awarded a Nobel Prize. Any scientific honors awarded to Sherlock Holmes have now been forgotten, although it is on record that he was offered a knighthood for his achievements in various fields.

Gibbs died in 1903, having lived the quiet academic life he desired, and left a legacy that is the foundation for modern day physical chemistry and chemical engineering and which influenced the early pioneers of quantum mechanics.

So here we have two men of intellect who literally changed the world thanks to their genius, their focus on their work, their ability to see and describe what others did not or could not. They lived the lives they wanted; and accordingly, Sherlock Holmes is like J. Willard Gibbs.

Christopher A. Zordan (East Brunswick, New Jersey) is a chemist who regularly encounters the science of Professor Gibbs. He is a Baker Street Irregular (with the investiture of "Bunsen Burner") and an Adventuress of Sherlock Holmes, and can be found at many New York area Sherlockian gatherings.

HE JUST KNEW

Charles Sanders Peirce

Leah Cummins Guinn

The young man's eyes burned. Hours upon hours he'd spent, poring over photographic enlargements of Silvia Ann Howland's signature—42 examples of it, yielding 30 different downstrokes. Of 25,830 possible comparisons, he had found 5,325 coincidences, making the relative frequency of such less than 20 per cent. However, all of these coincidences had to show up not twice, but three times, to account for the will's second page codicil and its two copies. The probability of this occurring was, according to his calculations, one in 5 to the 30th power. It was, frankly, much easier to believe that Henrietta Howland Robinson had traced those signatures, hoping thereby to invalidate her aunt's most recent will. Although she had inherited half of the estate, Robinson wanted the entire $2 million for herself.

She lost her case on a point of law, rather than powers of 10, but the man's time had not been wasted. If genius was, indeed, the capacity for taking pains, he'd just been given a lesson in how such reasoning—and mathematics—could be applied to real problems. And if he ever read in the *American Law Review*, how, compared to this case, "the curious stories of Poe will be thought the paltriest imitations," he might even have fancied himself a bit of a Dupin.

The next time the man played detective, he was a decade older, in New York City for a scientific conference. He had long been prey to various neurological conditions and when, soon after his steamship docked, he began to feel "fuzzy-headed," he disembarked so quickly that he left behind his overcoat and, more importantly, an expensive Charles Frodsham watch and chain, which actually was the property of his employer, the United States Government. He ran back to his stateroom, only to find the coat and watch had vanished.

Most people would complain to the purser, but he wasn't most people. Instead, confident in his ability to ferret out the culprit, he gathered up all of the ship's waiters and proceeded to question them, Columbo-style, careful to leave the impression that he was a bit thick. Once he reached the end of his impromptu line-up, however, he realized that, after all of the fuss, he still had—literally—no clue who the thief might be. But he had to find his watch—he couldn't afford the shame, or the penalty he might face for losing it. So he whipped around and—suddenly—*he just knew*.

The waiter denied everything, wouldn't even accept $50 for returning the items, and so he was forced to turn to Pinkerton's for assistance. George Henry Bangs, the head of Pinkerton's New York City branch, rather doubted the man's statement that he knew Mr. —— would leave the Fall River steamship at 1 p.m., and (immediately) go to pawn a stolen watch for $50. That held up the investigation for a day. The detective assigned to his case even followed another steamship employee. But our amateur was vindicated when his timepiece turned up at a pawnshop and (it turned out) the ticket *had* been made out to the man he'd first accused. All that remained was to retrieve the coat and chain, which he did by going to the thief's house and—over the protests of both the detective (they had no warrant) and the women living there—searching until he found both. The thief was arrested and remanded for trial.

Did the victim ever attend any of his conference? We don't know. But "The Case of the Stolen Watch," like that of the Howland will, left a tremendous impression on Charles Sanders Peirce. When in 1867 he and his father, acclaimed Harvard mathematician Benjamin Peirce examined page after page of those signatures, he was looking for evidence to prove or disprove the hypothesis, "Henrietta Robinson has forged a codicil." He was using the process of induction; quite straightforward. But the incident on the steamship—that was something entirely different. He hadn't any theory, beyond the notion that a waiter had been involved. Nor had he any clues. But he had, suddenly, for no obvious reason, been certain which man was the thief. This sort of thing, he realized, happened too frequently in science and human thought in general to be purely coincidental. Out of myriad possibilities (someone had run onto the boat and stolen his watch, for example... or a giant bird... or a vengeful ghost), he had quickly hit upon the most likely ones: it was a waiter, and it was *that man*. Human beings, he concluded, were good guessers, and there had to be both a reason for this—and a way to improve the process.

And when it came to thinking, Charles Peirce was all about improvement. In his lifetime, he would invent the quincuncial projection of the globe, conceptualize an electric switch-circuit computing machine, produce the bulk of the *Century Dictionary*, create the theory of the economy of research, and originate the philosophical theory of Pragmatism. His "theory of signs" gave rise to the modern field of semiotics. A natural teacher, he taught logic both to Harvard students and to ambitious learners via correspondence. His wide-ranging intellect devoured all it encountered—chemistry, mathematics, literature, philosophy, religion, biology, meteorology, medicine, psychology, metaphysics—and produced accordingly. In the age of professionalization, he was one of the last true polymaths, and his life's ambition was to formulate a "theory of everything." Not a very few believe he came close.

Yes, yes, you say, tapping impatiently on the arm of your chair, *this is all very interesting, but how was he like Sherlock Holmes?*

Well, aside from solving crimes (of which, admittedly, Holmes did much, much more), there are other similarities. Holmes, with his knowledge of sensational literature, chemistry, mathematics, history, linguistics, apiculture, the theatre, music, botany, and criminology (among other subjects) was himself a polymath, and he published his own collection of monographs and books on a variety of topics, notably a *Practical Handbook of Bee Culture, with some Observations upon the Segregation of the Queen,* and a textbook on "the whole art of detection". Like Peirce, the son of a Harvard professor and a U.S. senator's daughter, he—the scion of "Yorkshire squires"—enjoyed an upper-class background and education. Peirce suffered from trigeminal facial neuralgia, a fantastically painful condition which kept him from working for weeks at a time, while armchair psychologists who have not personally treated either man have nonetheless diagnosed them with bipolars 1 or 2, depression, anxiety, or any number of other psychiatric conditions, in an attempt to account for their wide swings from feverish activity to utter lassitude. Whatever their afflictions, both men were enthusiastic and skillful self-medicators, artfully juggling the stimulants and depressants (cocaine and morphine for both; nicotine for Holmes and alcohol for Peirce) readily available in their time. They were both confident (arrogant) enough to violate the law when they believed it suited a higher purpose, be it burgling or compounding felonies—or conducting an unconstitutional search of another's property. Finally, because apparently real people *do* have them, both men had archenemies. Sherlock Holmes was dogged by James Moriarty (criminal, scholar, author of *A Treatise on the Binomial Theorem* and *The Dynamics of an Asteroid*), until the Professor met his death at Reichenbach. Peirce (albeit unknowingly) had his dreams of academic success and significant publication repeatedly quashed by astronomer Simon Newcomb who, despite his own research on asteroid orbits, was not a criminal, but instead driven by personal envy and puritanical morality.

We do not know if Peirce and Holmes ever met—by book or in person—but there is no doubt that, had they done so, they would have recognized in each other kindred spirits. Both well-dressed, articulate gentlemen (with high voices) who, nonetheless, were fairly slovenly when it came to household order, they might have traded stories of their devoted companions—Holmes had his Watson, and Peirce his Juliette.

While Holmes typically passed on the credit for his work to others, and Peirce craved fame and wealth, I suspect they would both appreciate the fanatic followings they've inspired in the 20th and 21st centuries. Not one to avoid the "grit in the lens," Peirce would likely take full advantage of his female devotees, while Holmes might find them bewildering at best. Over brandy by the fire, they would share thoughts and theories they could rarely discuss with anyone else, inspiring (perhaps) even more papers to fill the box in the attic of 221B and the piles of writing bequeathed to Josiah Royce. Then, they would both relax—Peirce on the settee, Holmes in his basket chair—and silently visit their brain attics (Holmes), allowing the play of musement (Peirce) to spark even more theories and solutions.

No, we do not know—for sure. But there is at least one suggestive bit of evidence. Let's go back to Peirce's desire to improve our ability to guess—to come up with better hypotheses, better theories—to which we could apply our powers of induction or deduction. He succeeded, and called it "abduction." Through this process, he believed, people could better sort the facts and theories available to them, to come up with the best possible solutions to their questions—which could then be tested. Here are two definitions for "abduction." Which came first, I'll leave you to decide:

Facts cannot be explained by a hypothesis more extraordinary than these facts themselves; and of various hypotheses the least extraordinary must be adopted. (Charles S. Peirce)

Which, being translated:

> "It is an old maxim of mine that when you have excluded the impossible, whatever remains, however improbable, must be the truth."

Leah Cummins Guinn (Fort Wayne, Indiana) is a writer and stay-at-home mother. A member of the Illustrious Clients of Indianapolis, she is the author of many Sherlockian pieces, among them (with Jaime N. Mahoney) *A Curious Collection of Dates: Through the Year with Sherlock Holmes*. She blogs at wellreadsherlockian.com.

THE DRAMATIC REVEAL

Harry Houdini

Doug Elliott

One man is synonymous with prodigious feats of detection, the other with miraculous escapes. At first blush they could not have been more different, the languid, remote, genius detective and the brash, energetic showman. Yet they were alike in many important ways.

Let's start with a brief biographical note. Houdini was born Erich Weiss in Budapest in 1874, making him twenty years younger than Sherlock Holmes. His family immigrated to America in 1876, settling in Appleton, Wisconsin. Fascinated with magic at an early age, young Erich, or Harry as he Americanized himself, set himself up as a conjurer, traveling around with various sideshows, initially with his brother Dash and later with his wife Bess.

Struggling to make ends meet as a sleight-of-hand magician, he started doing escape tricks and at last hit the big time in the Orpheum and Keith's chains of vaudeville theatres. In 1900 he took his handcuff act to Europe. He challenged anyone to lock him up in a pair of cuffs—including the BYO variety—and he would quickly free himself. He also had the inspiration to challenge local police forces to lock him in their cells. These stunts garnered massive publicity, and he always escaped, sometimes following his captors out of the room seconds after the key was turned to lock him in.

Harry returned to America in triumph, and from then on Houdini was a sensation, "The Original Handcuff King and Jail-Breaker." In subsequent years Houdini's escapes became bigger, more elaborate and apparently more dangerous: locked upside down into a glass tank of water, nailed handcuffed into a packing crate and thrown into a river, hanging upside down in a straitjacket high above a busy street.

It is no surprise that drama and suspense were the bread and butter of Houdini's profession. He learned that to simply free himself was not enough: he had to keep the crowd waiting, let the tension build. Suitably manacled, he would step into a tall wooden cabinet and the orchestra would strike up the first of many tunes. He would finally reappear as much as an hour later, sweating, dishevelled and exhausted but smiling, waving his restraints triumphantly in the air. The crowd went crazy. This was magic as theatre, and Houdini was the master.

Sherlock Holmes also proved to be an expert at the dramatic reveal. Perhaps the best example of this occurs in the climax of "The Norwood Builder." "Holmes stood before us," recalls Watson, "with the air of a conjurer who is performing a trick." And, having assembled an audience of five, he materializes with great fanfare the missing and presumed dead Mr Jonas Oldacre of Lower Norwood.

Indeed, the sudden and unexpected revelation was somewhat of a trademark for Holmes. In "The Second Stain," he arranges for an important letter to be returned miraculously to the same locked dispatch-box from which it had been stolen. "Mr Holmes," exclaims the European Secretary, "you are a wizard, a sorcerer!" In another incident, Holmes restores an important government document to Mr Percy Phelps in a similarly dramatic manner: presented on a covered tray which Phelps thought carried his breakfast.

Then there's the big finale of the story of Hugh Boone:

> Holmes stooped to the water jug, moistened his sponge, and then rubbed it twice vigorously across and down the prisoner's face.
>
> "Let me introduce you," he shouted, "to Mr Neville St Clair, of Lee, in the county of Kent."
>
> Never in my life have I seen such a sight. The man's face peeled off under the sponge like the bark from a tree. Gone was the coarse brown tint! Gone, too, the horrid scar which had seamed it across, and the twisted lip which had given the repulsive sneer to the face! A twitch brought away the tangled red hair, and there, sitting up in his bed, was a pale, sad-faced, refined-looking man, black-haired and smooth-skinned, rubbing his eyes and staring about him with sleepy bewilderment.

And the famous black pearl of the Borgias is dramatically revealed after Holmes shatters—with evident enthusiasm and not a word of explanation—a bust of Napoleon. So it goes throughout the Canon: the magical appearance performed with impeccable timing and just the right audience. "Surely our profession would be a drab and sordid one," Holmes confides to a fellow detective in *The Valley of Fear*, "if we did not sometimes set the scene so as to glorify our results."

Houdini and Holmes are also alike in the way they respected their professional forebears. Or failed to do so. The seventeen-year-old Erich Weiss took his stage name from the French conjurer Jean-Eugène Robert-Houdin (1805–1871) and at first heaped praise on the great magical innovator. Yet a mere ten years later he concluded that his magical inspiration was a fraud who stole or bought most of his tricks, fictionalized his autobiography and hired a ghost-writer to pen his memoirs. "The master-magician, unmasked, stands forth in all the nakedness of historical proof, the prince of pilferers," he wrote in his mean and angry book, *The Unmasking of Robert-Houdin* (1906).

Holmes is similarly dismissive of his investigative predecessors, though with less vitriol. In one of his first meetings with Watson, Holmes scoffs at Edgar Allan Poe's ground-breaking detective C. Auguste Dupin: "Dupin was a very inferior fellow. That trick of his of breaking in on his friends' thoughts with an apropos remark after a quarter of an hour's silence is really very showy and superficial. He had some analytical genius, no doubt; but he was by no means such a phenomenon as Poe appeared to imagine." He takes a similar potshot at Émile Gaboriau's detective M. Lecoq: "Lecoq was a miserable bungler… he had only one thing to recommend him, and that was his energy. That book made me positively ill."

Both Houdini and Holmes stood unique in their professions, but they nevertheless had rivals. Holmes believed himself superior to his fellow private detectives. "Here in London we have lots of government detectives and lots of private ones. When these fellows are at fault, they come to me, and I manage to put them on the right scent."

Similarly, Houdini was quick to take offense if another magician seemed to be doing a similar act, going so far as to take out newspaper ads to denounce his rivals and threaten lawsuits, such as the following in the London newspapers:

> STOP THIEF! I, Harry Houdini do hereby give notice that I have fully patented my handcuff act or show, according to the laws of Great Britain, and I will positively prosecute any and all manager playing infringements or colorable imitations.

Both men were skeptics in matters of the supernatural. Houdini dedicated much of his later years to investigating and denouncing fraudulent spiritualist mediums. He was enraged by the false hopes that these charlatans gave to the bereaved, while smugly taking their money. Holmes, too, had no time for the supernatural. "This agency stands flat-footed upon the ground," he emphasized to Watson, "and there it must remain. The world is big enough for us. No ghosts need apply."

When Sherlock Holmes remarked that "The Press, Watson, is a most valuable institution, if you only know how to use it," he might have been quoting Houdini. Both men expertly used the media of their day for their own purposes. As far back as *A Study in Scarlet*, Holmes placed the following ad in every morning paper:

> FOUND: In Brixton Road, this morning, a plain gold wedding ring, found in the roadway between the White Hart Tavern and Holland Grove. Apply Dr. Watson, 221 B, Baker Street, between eight and nine this evening.

And in another incident he capitalizes on having taken a beating to give the public—and the villain—the impression that he was on death's door. After ensuring that the newspapers covered the attack with the lurid headline "Murderous Attack Upon Sherlock Holmes," he advises Watson to "exaggerate my injuries… Put it on thick, Watson. Lucky if I live the week out. Concussion. Delirium—what you like! You can't overdo it."

And of course there's this, in "The Blue Carbuncle":

> "Here you are, Peterson, run down to the advertising agency and have this put in the evening papers."
> "In which, sir?"
> "Oh, in the *Globe*, *Star*, *Pall Mall*, *St. James's*, *Evening News*, *Standard*, *Echo*, and any others that occur to you."

In a pinch, Holmes was not averse to placing false clues in the press. Through reporter Horace Harker he places an article giving a misleading impression of his conclusion on a case:

> It is satisfactory to know that there can be no difference of opinion upon this case, since Mr. Lestrade, one of the most experienced members of the official force, and Mr. Sherlock Holmes, the well-known consulting expert, have each come to the conclusion that the grotesque series of incidents, which have ended in so tragic a fashion, arise from lunacy rather than from deliberate crime.

Of course if you have a tame reporter, it's also helpful to have a gossip columnist in your pocket. Holmes had the inimitable Langdale Pike, "his human book of reference upon all matters of social scandal". But sometimes keeping news *away* from the papers is the best way to use them. Holmes was instrumental in preventing news of the affair of "The Missing Three-Quarter" from becoming public, no small feat in the febrile press environment of Victorian London.

Houdini also proved himself to be a master at manipulating the media. He invited local reporters to attend his shows and made sure they were tantalized in advance with hints of an impossible escape challenge or a controversy in the making. "Most of my success in Europe," he wrote, "was due to the fact that I lost no time in stirring up local interest in every town I played." In some cases the press responded by issuing counter-challenges. Following one celebrated challenge issued by the *London Daily Illustrated Mirror*, he was able to paste into his press scrapbook at least 75 separate news stories about his successful escape from their specially-made handcuffs.

Both men had a direct connection with the great writer Sir Arthur Conan Doyle. Houdini and Conan Doyle met in 1919, three years after Sir Arthur had whole-heartedly adopted the spiritualist cause. The believer and the skeptic became fast friends before falling out over Spiritualism in 1922. As to the well-known and highly significant Sherlock Holmes-Conan Doyle connection, I will leave that as an exercise for the reader.

Perhaps the single most important nexus between the two men is their degree of fame. George Bernard Shaw is said to have identified the three most famous people in the history of the world, real or imagined, as Jesus, Sherlock Holmes and Houdini. (This well-known quote is nonetheless much disputed, as no one seems to be able to identify its origin. It may have been invented by sportswriter Bert Sugar in 1976. We may never know for sure.) It is a measure of this fame that they are universally known by a single name. Say "Houdini" or "Sherlock" and everyone knows whom you are talking about.

In 1926 Harry, still on tour and at the peak of his fame, died from peritonitis after a punch to the stomach by an over-eager fan ruptured his appendix. I have been unable to unearth any reliable reports of the death of Sherlock Holmes. In this, the two men are not at all alike.

Doug Elliott (Sydney, Australia) has been writing about Sherlock Holmes and Arthur Conan Doyle for almost forty years. A member of the Baker Street Irregulars and the Sydney Passengers, he is also a founding member of the Friends of the Arthur Conan Doyle Collection of the Toronto Public Library. Some of the material about Houdini in this essay is derived from Ruth Brandon's *The Life and Many Deaths of Harry Houdini* (1993) and Kenneth Silverman's *Houdini!!!: The Career of Erich Weiss* (1996).

HOLMES IS A HOLMES
IS A HOLMES

Gertrude Stein

Laura Sky Brown

If you're reading this book, I'm betting you know a certain story already: Emotionally complex person who has just survived a life-altering trauma arrives in a European capital, feeling at loose ends, and almost immediately encounters a quirky but compelling genius who will make life monumentally exciting from now on. *Coup de foudre!* Adventures ensue.

That person's name, with its somewhat mysterious middle initial, is one intimately familiar to you, I believe. I speak, of course, of Alice B. Toklas, who left San Francisco after the great earthquake and fire of 1906 and headed for the Continent where, on her second day in Paris, she met the genius who became her life partner, Gertrude Stein (1874-1946). It's interesting how closely their relationship's origin story parallels that of Dr. John H. Watson, who met Sherlock Holmes in London shortly after being invalided home from... well, you know the rest. These two pairs have more in common than their meet-cute back-stories, but it all definitely starts there.

Let me start by saying I'm no literary critic, no academic expert, merely a fan in whose personal life Sherlock Holmes and John Watson, and Gertrude Stein and Alice B. Toklas, have been important characters. So much in my own life started when I met these four unforgettable people. To the young sexual-orientation self-questioner of the 1970s, looking to stock her brain with the building blocks of a happy life in a pre-Internet, pre-gay-rights world, there not only weren't healthy examples of happy grown-up same-sex couples in everyday life; there weren't any examples at all. To want a same-sex partner seemed very much like a solitary, secretive, and often shameful quest destined to end in loneliness.

Consider that discouragingly blank backdrop, and then imagine the balm it was to discover Arthur Conan Doyle's pair of utterly devoted men living the bohemian life together in central London. Whether or not you, presumably a Sherlock Holmes aficionado, have ever leaned toward thinking of the Holmes/Watson relationship as sexual, it would be a mean-spirited reader (and a wrong one) who tried to deny that these two men were devoted to each other all their lives. They had, on whatever physical plane you put them, something I had never seen but longed for: a happy same-sex domestic life. (Don't even say "but they weren't real," because if believing Holmes and Watson are real is wrong, I don't want to be right.)

A close second among literary discoveries of my youth was the influential, avant-garde, and fascinatingly crackpot pairing of Gertrude Stein and Alice B. Toklas, who led an even more bohemian life in central Paris than Holmes and Watson enjoyed in central London. Nobody has tried to suggest *they* were just friends; but then, they lived a few decades later. I saw the parallels between the two couples immediately and organically, and from that day to this, some four decades later, I look to them as the very archetypes of devotion, cheerful tolerance of each other's quirks and eccentricities, and, I guess, a sort of permission to live as messy and unconventional a life as one wants—with a partner of the gender of one's choosing.

With that back story of my own, I am delighted to share a few reasons that I believe Sherlock Holmes is like Gertrude Stein (and John H. Watson is like Alice B. Toklas).

Holmes and Stein made similar first impressions. As we've already established, an upper-crust, educated, yet extremely socially divergent genius meets a forgiving, admiring, but rock-solid "regular person," and the rest is history, whether it's Alice Babette Toklas with Stein or John Hamish Watson with Holmes. In Stein's *The Autobiography of Alice B. Toklas*, here's how that meeting is described: "I may say that only three times in my life have I met a genius and each time a bell within me rang and I was not mistaken." Compare that with Watson's comments when he realized what kind of brain his new friend brought to the relationship:

> "Oh! a mystery is it?" I cried, rubbing my hands. "This is very piquant. I am much obliged to you for bringing us together. 'The proper study of mankind is man,' you know."

Adding to the similarities, both were scientists, after a fashion: Stein had begun medical school in the United States before decamping to Paris, declaring herself bored with the idea; Holmes, of course, was described by Watson as having "Knowledge of Chemistry: Profound." With familiarity came the increasing understanding that each of the two geniuses was basically lazy and indolent and expected (and got) others to do the drudgery, leaving Holmes and Stein free to do the intellectual heavy lifting (from a comfortable chair). Watson and Toklas both fully accepted this as their lot, according to the written record of Watson and Toklas (that latter's autobiographical material was actually written by Stein, but then I am told Watson didn't actually do his own writing, either).

They had two famous addresses. They set up housekeeping at what became two of the Western world's most famous literary addresses: 27, rue de Fleurus in Paris, and 221B Baker Street in London. From the turn of the century till shortly before the outbreak of World War II, up-and-coming artists and assorted hangers-on could be found as guests at the Stein salon, while visitors from royalty to street urchins climbed the 17 steps at Baker Street to consult with Holmes. To this day, tourists and fans can approximate the experience, but the rue de Fleurus location is private (there's a plaque, though), and the Baker Street location is a for-profit museum (there's a statue nearby, though). (Spoiler alert: I've made pilgrimages to both.)

They both had mental processes that were hard to "get." Let's talk about the way both Holmes and Stein struck the casual observer in their lifetimes and right up to the present day: they're weird. They don't behave or think like "normal" people. They're preternaturally gifted in seeing what other people never do. Until and unless more explanation of their methodology is proffered, their logic is impenetrable to those they encounter—and in basically the same way. Which of the two does this sound like? "Does it make any difference if a dog does not know the difference between a rubber ball and a piece of paper?" You're not sure, are you, until you read the sentence that follows: "No not any why he does." (It's Stein, from *The Geographical History of America*.) Or, put another way (John Watson's way, in "A Scandal in Bohemia"):

> I could not help laughing at the ease with which he explained his process of deduction. "When I hear you give your reasons," I remarked, "the thing always appears to me to be so ridiculously simple that I could easily do it myself, though at each successive instance of your reasoning I am baffled until you explain your process. And yet I believe that my eyes are as good as yours."

They had important but annoying brothers. The older brother who is reputed to be smarter but who is way less interesting, and who serves a useful purpose: each had one. Stein's art-collector brother Leo actually lived with Stein and Toklas until the siblings famously fell out and stopped speaking to each other. Holmes's love-hate relationship with his more conventional and also more diabolical brother, Mycroft, is more imaginatively documented in the BBC TV series and fanfiction than in the Canon, but he is still a presence. There's even a less well understood, even older brother in both histories, Michael Stein and Sherrinford Holmes. Sherrinford may have just been a rough draft, but Michael, by staying home in California and managing the family's financial interests, was more of a bank draft for his artistic younger siblings.

They were all about relationships, especially with their muses. They may have been two of history's most famous one-offs, but Stein and Holmes were actually all about relationships. We think about Stein's salon and her championing of then unknown and unappreciated painters.

We think about Holmes's (usually) warm interdependence with Scotland Yard, with his Irregulars, and even with Mrs. Hudson. In that vein, the most striking thing about the books by and about both of these figures is how they reveal the characters' relationships with others while ostensibly being about their own exploits. Watson was writing about Holmes but actually painted a portrait of their life as a pair; he was the biographer who revealed himself as much as he revealed his subject. The same can be said about *The Autobiography of Alice B. Toklas* and other works, which may have been by (and mostly about) Gertrude Stein but which were portraits of the two of them.

But these portraits weren't without a certain tension. How arrogant, you might say, that Gertrude Stein writes her partner's "autobiography" and then talks about herself most of the time. How self-centered, you might say, for Holmes to seem to ignore the many contributions of Watson to his success as a detective. You'd be right, but you'd also miss the near obsession they had for each other that led to the diarizing of their lives in such detail. One reason I think these couples will never leave the popular imagination is that they were so colorfully and memorably described and memorialized, especially in the words they used to describe each other.

And they both had endlessly interesting mind palaces. Of all the many fascinating things about Sherlock Holmes, the most compelling to me is the idea of his making a voluntary choice of what to keep and what to discard inside his head—"the mind palace," as the TV series *Sherlock* memorably depicted it, an actual place with rooms to be furnished (and demolished) at will. I prefer to see it as it's described in *A Study in Scarlet*: like a dusty attic at the top of the house into which private stuff can be crammed. "I consider that a man's brain originally is like a little empty attic, and you have to stock it with such furniture as you choose," as he put it.

Gertrude Stein's published works have been criticized as nonsensical; she has just as often been exalted as visionary. She wrote seemingly off the top of her head, and a lot of what she wrote is what you'd charitably call nonlinear. Yet I see her as a person who, just as Holmes did, stocked her brain with such furniture as she chose and discarded a lot that ordinary writers would have kept in stock in their brains. How else did she take such an experimental path in her writing, one that that either brightly illuminated or irritatingly misdirected the later course of literature, depending on your point of view? If Holmes had decided to experiment with words rather than chemicals or blood (or unpleasant sounds on the violin), would he have come up with similar innovations? I mean, "Depend upon it, there is nothing so unnatural as the commonplace."

If only they could have met sometime, perhaps on a rainy evening in London or Paris on a case. Picture the two of them surrounded by pipe smoke and butting heads, completely discombobulating the detectives of the Quai or the Yard or annoying the hell out of Hemingway and Picasso.

There is definitely a whole lot of *there* there. Not to put too fine a point on it, Stein and Holmes are both kind of obnoxious. I get that. Seen in a certain light, they're a pair of intolerable asses, really. But they're *my* intolerable asses. Life would be so dull without them.

Laura Sky Brown (Ann Arbor, Michigan) is an editor and a lifelong devotee of the world of Holmes and Watson, who are at least as real to her as most of the people she comes across. Having spread her appreciation for the Canon in greater or lesser degrees to each of her four children, she has done her duty to future generations.

THE CASE OF THE TWO BACHELORS

Sir Isaac Newton

Lee Vann

Living three hundred years apart, and as different as a consulting detective and a pioneering mathematician can be, Sherlock Holmes and Isaac Newton nevertheless offer some remarkable parallels. A well-known scientist who lived 1643–1727 and spent most of his career at the University of Cambridge, Newton had significant impact on the foundations of our understanding of mathematics; he laid the groundwork in fields from classical mechanics to calculus. But both he and the figures of London-bound Sherlock Holmes have helped shape people's view and understanding of their respective professions. The two characters also had many similarities in their professional and personal lives.

Sherlock Holmes is presented as an isolated figure, highly protective of his personal life. Despite the range of interactions that he has with clients and associates, he shares little about himself with others, even with Dr. Watson, at least during their initial association. It is not until after Watson questions Holmes regarding his techniques that Holmes becomes progressively more open with him. Similarly, Isaac Newton shared these tendencies towards secrecy and was, according to the Newton Project, "a deeply introverted character and fiercely protective of his privacy."

Holmes and Newton shared a deep interest in science and chemistry—"alchemy" in Newton's time—and were driven towards research and discovery. Newton's skill with discovery is well documented. Among his many achievements, he created an understanding of gravity, the laws of motion, and calculus. Holmes similarly pursues new knowledge and achieves his own discoveries, a trait established as part of the initial introduction of his character (when he has just developed a chemical test that detected blood in materials) and reinforced with mentions of other work, such as his monograph about varieties of cigar ash.

Strikingly, both Newton and Holmes assisted in finding those who committed crimes. Holmes's skill with what he described as deduction and his ability to find the truth behind crimes is well illustrated throughout the descriptions of his adventures. Newton was also involved with investigators and, like Holmes, was highly successful in his efforts. In 1696 Newton was appointed as Warden for England's Royal Mint and was in charge of the detection and prosecution of counterfeiters during a time when England was facing an economic crisis caused by widespread forgery. In *The Death Penalty as Monetary Policy: The Practice and Punishment of Monetary Crime*, Carl Wennerlind describes the crisis as a "counterfeiting plague" and states that Newton's work at finding and prosecuting counterfeiters was "performed with great vigor and success."

Both of these characters gained their professional positions through unconventional means. Holmes is depicted in the stories as being the only consulting detective in the world, a position he claims to have created. Newton gained his position as a professor of mathematics through means that were unconventional for his time. In 1669, professors of mathematics were required to be ordained as priests of the Church of England, but Newton gained special permission from King Charles II to be appointed without being ordained.

Neither Sherlock Holmes nor Isaac Newton ever married or showed any apparent romantic interest in women; their strongest and most significant personal relationships were with other men. Both are situated during eras where homosexuality was forbidden, with dangerous consequences should an individual be revealed as gay. Yet despite those risks, and based on their interactions with others, the possibility of homosexuality exists. According to Natalie M. Rosinsky in *Sir Isaac Newton: Brilliant Mathematician and Scientist*, in 1689 Newton spent most of the year in London, where he began an intense relationship with the Swiss mathematician, Nicolas Fatio De Dullier. Rosinsky points out that in the letters between them, the emotions expressed were of a romantic nature. Indeed, Newton pleaded with Nicolas to move in with him. When De Dullier said that he needed a stronger reason than his health to move, Newton wrote that he could not go into detail regarding the reasons in a letter, and continued: "I wish sir to live all my life, or the greatest part of it, with you, if it was possible." The two continued a close relationship until 1693, when De Dullier departed and Newton fell into a state of deep depression. Newton's breakdown was variously blamed on an assortment of causes, including mercury poisoning, but the context of the situation reported also suggests the possibility of emotional trauma related to the ending of a relationship.

Isaac Newton had given Nicolas Fatio De Dullier money in addition to offering to share rooms with him. Holmes, mirroring this incident, offered Watson an opportunity to live with him and made some effort to gain his agreement to cohabitation. In "The Norwood Builder," a certain Dr. Verner purchased Watson's practice at the highest price asked, which enabled Watson to resume sharing rooms with Holmes. It was not until later that Watson discovered Dr. Verner was a relative of Holmes, and in fact Holmes himself had provided the money. This story was published directly after "The Empty House," in which Holmes returns from his apparent death and a three-year absence. By that point in the stories the two men are both well established and living within their means, so had no financial need to move in together as they did in earlier stories. Holmes had a steady stream of clients and Watson a well-patronized practice. There was no need for either to room with another individual, yet Watson was still willing to sell his practice to move back in with Holmes, and Holmes had made significant effort in contacting family to help facilitate Watson's move, in addition to personally financing the exchange.

As with Newton and De Dullier, while there is no explicit confirmation of a romantic entanglement between Holmes and Watson, several aspects of the stories pointedly suggest that such a relationship existed. Additional examples include an unexplained letter mentioned in *The Hound of the Baskervilles*. Watson has written a series of reports to Sherlock Holmes, and when Holmes returns the letters to Watson, he withholds one. There is no explanation given for what was in the letter or why it was kept, yet it was considered significant enough to be mentioned in the story. It is not used for the case or mentioned again. It is possible to consider that the letter could have been romantic in nature and that is why Holmes might have desired to keep it. Holmes had a very close relationship with Watson and was more open with him than with any other individual. Holmes even laments his absence in one of the few stories where Dr. Watson was not featured, "The Blanched Soldier": "It is here that I miss my Watson." Holmes sought and invited Watson's company, and his state of disarray and instability during times of his extended absence could be attributed to pining.

Sherlock Holmes and Isaac Newton are both highly intelligent, influential, and hotly debated individuals. While it is unlikely that the full truth about either will ever be known, they have significantly impacted history and the global community. They both continue to be important figures today.

Lee Vann (Tri-Cities, Washington) maps their way through life with Geographic Information Systems. They hold a degree in geography from the University of Washington and are a member of the Sound of the Baskervilles and the John H Watson Society.

THE OBSERVATION OF TRIFLES

Sigmund Freud

Robert Stek

What names still ring true and remain familiar in the minds of the general public all over the world more than a hundred years after their introduction? Sherlock Holmes and Sigmund Freud. How could a fictional character be as well-known as the man who explored the human mind more thoroughly than any other who came before him? They were a lot alike!

For followers of the Great Detective there is clearly a relationship between Holmes and Freud. The most obvious connection: things go better with coke. Even without the brilliant juxtaposition of Holmes and Freud in the much-loved 1975 novel *The Seven-Per-Cent Solution* by Nicholas Meyer (later a film starring Nicol Williamson as Holmes and Alan Arkin as Freud), Freud's research on cocaine and Holmes's use of the stimulant were well known. Freud's early published cocaine research spurred medical journal articles touting cocaine's use in treating everything from indigestion and flatulence to tuberculosis and morphine addiction before its more addictive properties dampened enthusiasm for its general use. Holmes reached for his needle and vial of a seven-per-cent solution whenever he became bored from a lack of interesting cases on which he could focus his superb investigative mind.

A closer examination of Sherlock and Sigmund reveals more than their shared fascination with cocaine. Even in Meyer's novel when Freud states that he is no detective but merely "a physician whose province is the troubled mind," Watson notes "that the difference was not that great." There are certainly similarities in their methods of observations and inferences, and both owe a great deal to an Italian art historian and critic named Giovanni Morelli.

Morelli (1816–1891) became an expert in detecting the works of copyists, students, and imitators of established painters. His method did not depend upon similarities of composition, theme, subject content, or other broad categories. He learned to identify the "fingerprints" of painters through careful observation of distinguishing features that indicated an artist's barely conscious habits of portraying details. He observed small clues from trifling details. For example, he noted how the artist renders "earlobes, fingernails, shapes of fingers and toes" in secondary figures in a painting.

Both Holmes and Freud based their respective methods "upon the observation of trifles," though with some differences. Holmes, of course, was looking for any and all clues to solve a mystery or a crime. Freud was looking for subtle clues from a patient's experiences and history in order to uncover the past source of some current problematic thoughts or behavior.

Any observant Sherlockian attaches great importance to the statement that Holmes makes in "A Scandal in Bohemia": "You see, but you do not observe." Both he and Watson have climbed the steps to their sitting room in Baker Street hundreds of times, yet only Holmes knows there are seventeen steps because he has seen *and* observed. Intuitively we understand the distinction. Holmes is sharing with Watson his own observation that seeing is just the first step. In seeing some trifle, Holmes has learned to filter out less of the background data presented to all his senses. In searching for clues to a crime he immediately and automatically relates the smallest of details to the context in which it occurs, references that information to his vast knowledge of other crimes and human nature, analyzes it within that context, recognizes the significance of a trifling detail and organizes his thoughts so as to make use of that information for his purposes. Holmes uses his methods and "strangely retentive memory for trifles" in uncovering just how a crime has occurred. He might generate several hypotheses about how a crime was committed, but he relies upon data, these *trifles*, to formulate his specific hypotheses. "It is a capital mistake to theorize before one has data. Insensibly one begins to twist facts to suit theories, instead of theories to suit facts."

Sigmund Freud developed a universal structural theory of the mind (psychoanalytic theory) and a procedure (psychoanalysis) to cure his patients of their troubling symptoms. Psychoanalytic theory seeks to explain the complex relationship between the body and the mind and furthers the understanding of the role of emotions in medical illness and health. It is a general theory of how the mind works and especially recognizes the importance of unconscious mental activity. From years of carefully listening to patients' reports of their own thoughts, their dreams, their free associations and their parapraxes (slips of the tongue or "Freudian slips"), Freud also recognized that early experiences, even events experienced before a child had developed language to describe them, contributed to his patients' behaviors and symptoms. In the process of psychoanalysis, Freud would note the specific associations, dream symbols, the verbal slips, the emotions of a patient—the trifles to which Freud paid attention—and then form hypotheses about what happened to the patient in the past and what was currently happening to them in their daily life. Freud acknowledged his debt to Giovanni Morelli in his essay *The Moses of Michelangelo* when he wrote:

> It seems to me that [Morelli's] method of inquiry is closely related to the technique of psychoanalysis. It, too, is accustomed to deduce secret and concealed things from despised or unnoticed features, from the rubbish-heap, as it were, of our observations.

And then there is the science of deduction. Holmes is often described as the master of deduction. Yet while he uses both deductive and inductive reasoning in making inferences and coming to conclusions, he astounds us and is at his best when he uses abductive reasoning: he starts with an observation or combination of observations (often incomplete) and then attempts to find the simplest and most likely explanation. Unlike pure deductive reasoning, the premises do not guarantee the conclusion, but the inference is the best explanation available. Holmes sometimes states that he has a number of possible hypotheses which explain the known facts. Abductive reasoning is often used by doctors who make a diagnosis based on test results and by jurors who make decisions based upon the evidence presented to them. A Sherlockian example might be:
Curiously, the dog did nothing in the night-time.

> If the hypothesis *the dog knew the person passing by* is true, then the dog doing nothing makes sense.
> Therefore, there is reason to believe that the dog knew the person who passed by in the night-time.

Freud used the same type of reasoning:

> Some specific unconscious material is revealed through a slip of the tongue or dream symbols.
> If the particular psychoanalytic explanatory hypothesis is true, then the dream symbols or slip of the tongue makes sense.
> Therefore, there is reason to believe that the slip of the tongue or the dream symbols reveal specific unconscious material.

Or more specifically:

> The patient is anxious and depressed and has no energy; in nightmares he chased by a giant green monster threatening to devour him.
> If the psychoanalytic principle *everything frightening in a dream represents an unwanted aspect of the dreamer and must be actively repressed* is true, then being afraid of what these symbols represent as a part of the dreamer makes sense.

Therefore, some unconscious, unwanted, hidden part of the patient is causing his depression and anxiety and is using up his psychic energy to defend against these thoughts.

Both Holmes and Freud used the power of their superbly analytic minds to uncover that which others could not see. Holmes always revealed to Watson his reasoning in solving a case. Watson would frequently exclaim something like "How absurdly simple!" and Holmes would respond, "Quite so. Every problem is absurdly simple when it is explained to you." Freud also explained his reasoning; he wrote voluminously about psychoanalytic theory, created the technique of psychoanalysis, and over the last century influenced millions of physicians and psychotherapists who applied his theories in their attempts to help others.

The similarity of their thinking, their penchant for observing the smallest detail, their initial interest in, and then abandonment of cocaine, their noticeable presence in late Victorian and early Edwardian popular press, and their longevity in the minds of the general public all attest to their similarity. Did their communalities develop independently? Consider: Freud admits to reading the stories of Sherlock Holmes. One of Freud's most famous patients, the Wolfman, in *My Recollections of Sigmund Freud*, recalled:

> Once we happened to speak of Conan Doyle and his creation, Sherlock Holmes. I had thought that Freud would have no use for this type of light reading matter, and was surprised to find that this was not at all the case and that Freud had read this author attentively. The fact that circumstantial evidence is useful in psychoanalysis when reconstructing a childhood history may explain Freud's interest in this type of literature.

Freud himself likens his own work to that of a detective:

> If you, as a detective, are involved in investigating a murder, then do you really expect to find that the killer has left his photograph and address at the crime scene, or will you not necessarily be content with weaker and more indistinct traces of the wanted personality?

And finally, in a letter to Carl Jung, Freud wrote:

> I responded in an extremely wise and ingenious way, by seemingly guessing the facts out of quiet signs in a Sherlock-Holmes-like fashion.

I conclude that both men were master detectives—Holmes, the master of detection in the world at large, and Freud, the master of detection in the inner world of the mind. But Holmes was there first, and therefore, Freud was like Holmes!

Robert Stek (Magnolia, Delaware) is a retired psychologist. A member of the Baker Street Irregulars and the Adventuresses of Sherlock Holmes, he attends most Sherlockian society meetings within a 100-mile radius of his home. When not speaking about Conan Doyle and spiritualism, he enjoys all things Lewis Carroll.

THE IMPORTANCE OF BEING SHERLOCK

Oscar Wilde

Michael J. Quigley

Arthur Conan Doyle may have repeatedly insisted that his character, Sherlock Holmes, was entirely based on Dr. Joseph Bell, and some
contemporary commentators believed that Holmes was the man Doyle
himself aspired to be. But it is near impossible to ignore the evident
and profound similarities between Sherlock Holmes and a very different
figure: Oscar Wilde.

As with many moments of creative genius, the unlikely friendship
between Doyle and Wilde has its genesis in an accidental encounter—a
blind date. On August 30, 1889, Joseph M. Stoddart, an American
publishing agent, played host to two of the brightest new stars in
London's literary scene, Arthur Conan Doyle and Oscar Wilde, at dinner
at the Langham Hotel. Stoddart had come to London to commission
new fiction for *Lippincott's Magazine*. Not only did Wilde and Doyle
not know one another, but they came from different worlds and different
literary genres. One was a champion of the aesthetic movement and
self-described bohemian poet and playwright; the other, who would later
be knighted for his services to the Empire, was a staunch proponent of
that empire and was a practitioner of romantic adventure, almost Gothic
fiction. Nevertheless, the two writers got on fabulously and charmed each
other with mutual flattery and respect for their literary accomplishments.
For all their seemingly opposite personas, Wilde and Doyle both shared
the stigma of being Anglo-Irish at a time when Britain was suspicious
and often contemptuous of the Irish. Both men were unusually tall and
large-framed. And both came from middle-class artistic families.

By the end of the meal, Stoddart had secured commitments from
Doyle and Wilde that each would write a short novel for *Lippincott's*.
Wilde produced *The Picture of Dorian Gray* and Doyle the second appearance of Holmes and Watson, in *The Sign of Four*. Despite its being
the second Sherlock Holmes novel, it was this work that truly established
the character the world would come to know, and would lead to two

additional novels and a series of no fewer than 56 short stories featuring the famous detective.

So much did Doyle admire Wilde, or at least the Wildean persona, that he fictionalized him as Thaddeus Sholto in *The Sign of Four* and, ultimately, drew upon Wilde's character and persona in his creative evolution of Sherlock Holmes. After his first two Sherlock Holmes novels, the first of which was written before his meeting Wilde, the other written after meeting him and with Wilde appearing as a supporting fictional character, Doyle succumbs to Wilde's influence upon him, as a writer—culminating in the evolution of Holmes, himself, as a Wildean character.

In his memoirs, Doyle recalls that "golden evening" and Wilde's enthusiasm about *Micah Clarke*, which Doyle had recently published. Wilde's conversation left an "indelible impression." Doyle had nothing but praise for Wilde, both personally and as a playwright, calling him "the champion of the aesthetic" with "delicacy of feeling and tact... a delicate sense of humour... happy and curious." This is astonishingly high praise for a man whom Doyle had only just met, and the admiration he expresses exceeds the critical acclaim Wilde received in both life and death. It would be little wonder if Doyle went on to give his character a gradually more Wildean personality. While it may sound trivial, he even gave Holmes the same birth year as Wilde (1854). One scholar (Angela Kingston in *Wilde Imaginations*, 2003) declares that "the strong impression made by Wilde upon Doyle compelled the latter to try to capture something of Wilde's essence in fiction." Others note that Doyle actually did a very poor job of "fictionalizing" the real-life aesthete, as he simply transposed Wilde into the novel, changing little but his name. The description of Thaddeus Sholto closely approximates that of Wilde, according to his contemporaries: "Nature had given him a pendulous lip, and a too visible line of yellow and irregular teeth, which he strove feebly to conceal by constantly passing his hand over the lower part of his face."

But by the time of *The Adventures of Sherlock Holmes*, Doyle no longer introduces Wildean secondary characters into his works, but attaches a number of Wildean characteristics to Holmes himself, allowing him, as a fictional character, to evolve and grow. Inspired by Wilde, Doyle finds expression of his own aesthetic voice through Holmes.

Prima facie, Holmes seems an absurd messenger of aestheticism, "art for art's sake," the idea that art did not have any didactic purpose; it needed only to be beautiful. But Holmes is the master observer, and therefore sees beauty as well as evidence, and evidence of beauty. There are many quotes attributed to Holmes that seem to channel Oscar Wilde peppered throughout the Canon, including the famous words from "The Naval Treaty" about a rose as "assurance of the goodness of Providence.... This rose is an extra. Its smell and its colour are an embellishment of life, not a condition of it. It is only goodness which gives extras."

That Sherlock Holmes recognizes intrinsic "goodness" without any further qualification, and that there can be "extras," is to recognize that it is what it is for its own sake, without being indicative of anything but its nature. That he finds hope in things of beauty speaks to his character as an aesthetic. Compare these words from Oscar Wilde: "Those who find ugly meanings in beautiful things are corrupt without being charming. This is a fault. Those who find beautiful meanings in beautiful things are the cultivated. For these there is hope. They are the elect to whom beautiful things mean only Beauty."

However, even the aesthetic Wilde recognized that beauty could shield something more sinister, not because the beauty was tainted, but rather because it was a distraction: "Behind every exquisite thing that existed, there was something tragic." We see a similar line of thought from Holmes: "The lowest and vilest alleys in London do not present a more dreadful record of sin than does the smiling and beautiful countryside."

Aestheticism was not the only thing for which Oscar Wilde drew fame or notoriety. Many now view Wilde as the first example of the modern homosexual gentleman. This is an arguable point, but it is an uncontested fact that Wilde was homosexual—though not openly so, it being a criminal offense in those days. But neither did he hide his affection for youth and the male form, claiming the Platonic love of the Greeks. He relished the reputation he acquired as a result. Wilde's flirtations with homosexuality presented Doyle with a literary problem, especially after Wilde was obliged to flee to France for safety, after a long two years at hard labor in jail in England for the crime of "gross indecency," a lesser charge than sodomy, but one that conveyed the same social stigma.

Doyle did not want to impose that reputational burden upon Holmes. Victorian England was a conservative histo-cultural era wherein models of masculinity and femininity were defined in their minutest details. Wilde, riding the waves of his aesthetic movement, clashed with Victorian sexual identity and the very mores of sexuality, not simply by practicing homosexuality or assigning women and men roles that transgressed the Victorian gender norms, but by positing a philosophy "in which gender was perceived as rather more fluid," as D. R. Piso writes in *Victorian Representations of Crime and Masculinity* (2016).

Doyle could not impose the very heavy burden of homosexuality upon Holmes and, by extension, upon himself. Thus Holmes emerges as an asexual character. Society, however, had already interpreted the relationship between Dr. Watson and Sherlock Holmes as quasi-sexual, despite Doyle's continued efforts to prove otherwise by having Holmes often refer to Watson as a ladies' man and, indeed, having Watson married. Popular perception of the two men as lovers was undoubtedly sharpened when Watson found his way back home to Holmes after his marriage ended under some sad circumstance. It was a bold literary statement, but it reflected who Arthur Conan Doyle had become. As his literary social circle expanded, Doyle came into contact with several homosexuals and was always the first to step up in their defense.

The impression that Wilde made on Doyle then found expression in various characters, including Holmes himself, who became progressively more epigrammatic in some of Doyle's other Sherlock Holmes stories—something noted as early as 1975 in the Sherlockian classic *Naked Is the Best Disguise* by Samuel Rosenberg. In "The Red-Headed League," an effeminate Duncan Ross and John Clay appear, echoing the names of two of Wilde's close friends, Robert Ross and John Gray. Further complicating these associations is the fact that "Duncan Ross" is the alias of a character named William Morris!

Doyle's views about homosexuality were based more in compassion than in the progressive values of Wilde. For Doyle, homosexuality was never a question of morality, but rather a mental illness that could be treated. As abhorrent as that may seem today, it was a radical departure from societal norms that considered homosexuality the behavior of a deviant criminal. Within this particular matrix, it is hardly a great leap of the imagination to consider that Doyle was defending homosexuals, and their lifestyles, as proxies for Oscar Wilde. It is unsurprising that when conventional readers were attacking Wilde for the implicit homosexual theme in *The Picture of Dorian Gray* and pointing to passages which they found completely immoral, Doyle stepped up to the defense of his friend, stating that he found nothing immoral in the work.

Doyle's acute sense of justice was awakened again in 1916, compelling him to rise to the defense of another friend, Sir Roger Casement, an Irish diplomat accused of being "the foulest traitor who ever drew breath." Doyle might have succeeded in saving the convicted Irishman's life, on grounds of insanity, had it not been for the discovery of Casement's diary, which chronicled in detail his homosexual escapades. Indeed, Doyle's feelings about homosexuality were more liberal than the norm. It seems evident that Doyle's impassioned defense of homosexuals, such as Casement, can be traced back to Wilde, who was his first homosexual friend, a man he understood and respected, whose literary artistic compositions he appreciated beyond measure.

Critics, among them Irene Rubio ("Sexuality in Arthur Conan Doyle's *The Sign of Four*," 2016) and Louise Jensen (*Representations of Sherlock Holmes*, 2014), maintain that by his having integrated so much of Wilde's personality and characteristics, Doyle unwittingly assimilated much of the public homosexual persona which Wilde wore very well, and imposed it upon Holmes. The implication here is that Doyle did not intend to portray Holmes as homosexual but, as he developed this character by borrowing from Wilde's own, nevertheless did exactly that.

While Wilde had been able to function as bisexual for a period of time, even marrying and fathering two children, by 1894 he could no longer pretend an interest in women. He enjoyed their gossipy conversations but found them undesirable as sexual partners. Wilde had, in fact, expressed disgust at the sight of his pregnant wife. At precisely the same time, Doyle wrote "The Greek Interpreter," in which Holmes is portrayed as having an "aversion to women." This cannot be dismissed as coincidental. Doyle had acted upon his need and gave shape to Wilde in the form of Holmes.

In "The Greek Interpreter" Holmes and Watson go to the Diogenes Club to spend some time with brother Mycroft. In its non-sexual meaning as "strange," the Diogenes Club is described as "the queerest club in London, and Mycroft one of the queerest men." But by 1894, "queer" had already acquired its modern connotation. The Marquis of Queensberry, whom Oscar Wilde later sued for criminal libel, had referred that year to "the Snob Queers like [Lord] Rosebery." The words "earnest" and "languid," used in other stories and applied to Holmes, also had homosexual connotations. It is an ironic coincidence that Wilde's most notorious detractor and antagonist, the Marquis of Queensbury, who was the father of Wilde's most public lover, was named John Sholto Douglas.

Wilde had a reputation for staying at gentlemen's clubs and associating with strange characters. He was a self-confessed bohemian. Possibly because, like Doyle and Holmes, Wilde was a member of the middle class, the high society in which he was frequently seen and sought was little more than material for his satirical works. He had shed his skin a long time ago and only wore his carefully crafted aesthetic persona, but he was forgiven because he came from the middle class. It takes Holmes a little while longer to unleash the bohemian within; when he eventually does, he is similarly forgiven because of his social status. Thus readers are made privy to Holmes injecting himself with cocaine, using young street boys to spy for him, taking a young teenage boy to serve as his valet and page, and, as Piso writes, ultimately, throwing Victorian upper-class social norms and conventions to the winds.

Arthur Conan Doyle was a typical Victorian English gentleman and initially portrayed Holmes in that light as well. Then Holmes began to gradually change, with Watson reporting that his friend was "transformed," suggesting that Holmes was undergoing what K.C. Smith calls "animal transformation" with "animal-like characteristics" ("Forming and Protecting the Middle-Class Ideal," 2008). Finally, in the words of Watson, Holmes "loathed every form of society with his whole Bohemian soul." In short, after meeting Wilde, Doyle wrote a collection of short stories in which the façade of respectable Victorian gentlemanly mores, values and norms seems to dissipate.

Holmes first appears in print two months after the Labouchere Amendment which made "gross indecency" a crime. *The Sign of Four* was published in February 1890, during the fevered publicity about the Cleveland Street scandal. After Wilde's death, Doyle published "The Empty House," in which Holmes asks Watson to accompany him to the Continent after nearly losing his life in Vere Street—another location associated with homosexual scandals. It further depicts an attempt by

Holmes to foil his own murder by having a wax image of himself—a second self, as with Dorian Gray and his painting—sculpted by *Oscar Meunier*. Rosenberg lists, among many ingenious parallels, the murderous Irish "wild beast," an outcast whose name is Sebastian Moran, the initials "S.M." evoking Wilde's pseudonym, "Sebastian Melmoth," adopted after his release from prison.

Doyle's view of homosexuality as a mental disorder may have also found expression in other aspects of the Sherlockian Canon. What we are to make of Professor Moriarty, given the "dark rumours" that forced him to resign his university job and the "hereditary tendencies of the most diabolical kind" that he supposedly suffers from? But perhaps that is a tale for which the world is not yet prepared.

Inasmuch as it is nearly impossible to imagine Sherlock Holmes without his Boswell, John Watson, it would be only natural to ask whether Lord Alfred "Bosie" Douglas was Watson's counterpart for Oscar Wilde. Like Watson to Holmes, Douglas is inextricably connected to Wilde. The two men had a contentious love affair as early as 1891 and off and on until Wilde's imprisonment. Douglas wrote some of the most loving and touching poems and letters for Wilde. But he could also be cruel and petty. Ultimately, Wilde's love for Douglas proved more genuine than Douglas's love for Wilde. For this reason, I don't think that Lord Alfred qualifies to be Wilde's Watson. That isn't to say that Wilde didn't have a Watson. I would argue that Robert "Robbie" Ross was "the one fixed point" for Oscar Wilde—apparently Wilde's first male lover, and a steadfast and true friend even after their love affair had ended. Following Wilde's imprisonment in 1895, Ross went abroad, but he remained loyal to Wilde and was with him when he died on 30 November 1900.

A final, if sad, epilogue to the Holmes/Wilde comparison is that both the detective and the playwright finish their days in self-imposed exile. For the former, this exile is in the form of a well-earned retirement to Sussex. Before his retirement, Holmes himself adopted the alias of Sigerson and traveled throughout the Far East, Near East, and parts of Africa during his great hiatus following his supposed death at the Reichenbach Falls. For his part, Wilde spent his last three years in impoverished exile in France. He took the name "Sebastian Melmoth," after St. Sebastian and the titular character of *Melmoth the Wanderer*, a Gothic novel by Charles Maturin, Wilde's great-uncle.

Whilst many may resist the argument that Holmes, as he evolved, became a Wildean, there is no other way to describe the drastic, albeit somewhat gradual, change which overcame Holmes after Doyle met Oscar Wilde. As influenced and as in awe of Wilde as was Holmes's creator, it is impossible to consider that the creation was not similarly influenced. It was. Whilst stopping short of stating that Holmes was the mirror image of Wilde, it is difficult to counter this concluding statement: Holmes was a composite character, influenced by the personalities of his creator, and certainly of Dr. Bell, but much more than doubly so by Oscar Wilde.

Michael J. Quigley (Arlington, Virginia) is a naval intelligence officer serving in the office of the United States Secretary of Defense. He is a Baker Street Irregular and the founder of the Diogenes Club of Washington, DC. He holds master's degrees from Georgetown University and the U.S. Naval War College, and has been published in the *Baker Street Journal* and *The Watsonian*. A fuller version of this study has appeared in the *BSJ*.

LEGENDS AND IMMORTALS

The writer was so carried away by his own story
that he imagined himself at the
supreme moment to be the hero.

"The Three Gables"

UNDER THE EYE OF ATHENE

Odysseus, King of Ithaca

Adrian Nebbett

The Great Hero, after the defeat of his enemy, is driven into exile. After wandering through many lands, and languishing in a distant country in the arms of an alluring nymph, he finally returns to his own country. There, he discovers that in his absence many pretenders to his title have emerged, whom he must overcome before he can finally retire to a farm in the country.

This is the story of Odysseus (Ulysses), who, after the defeat of King Priam and the fall of Troy, was driven into exile by the gods, sailing to many lands, experiencing many adventures, before finally being held captive in the embrace of the nymph Kalypso on her distant isle. In his absence, as Homer's *Odyssey* has told readers for some 2,800 years, his palace is overrun with suitors, each eager for the hand of his supposed widow, Penelope. Finally, after twenty years, with the help of the goddess Athene, he is brought home by the Phaiakans, and left, in his sleep, on the strand of his home country, Ithaka, his return ushered in by the hostile hounds of his faithful old servant, Eumaios. After defeating the suitors, Odysseus returns to the farm of his father, Laertes.

And this might also be the story of Sherlock Holmes. After the defeat of Professor Moriarty at the falls of Reichenbach (and it is worth noting at this point that "Ex-Prof. Moriarty" is an anagram of "Priam Rex of Troy") he was driven into exile, wandering through many lands, experiencing many adventures during his Great Hiatus, before reappearing in the *Strand*, where his arrival was heralded by the hostile *Hound of the Baskervilles*. (As a sleeping Odysseus was returned to his home by the Phaiakans, perhaps it is not too far a stretch to think of a "sleeping" Holmes in *The Hound*, absent for much of the story, being presented in a case from before his disappearance and still not confirmed alive.) At the end of his career, Holmes retires to his bee-farm in Sussex.

But what of the lady in whose arms he languishes during his final absent years? Or the many suitors attempting to take their place on his throne? Is there evidence for these in the Canon? Well, perhaps not, but if we look at Holmes's place in the world outside the Canon during his years of absence, we see many pretenders to the Holmesian mantle, both in parody (Picklock Holes, Thinlock Bones, Herlock Sholmes, and the rest), and in the slew of detectives (including Martin Hewitt, A.J. Raffles, and Loveday Brooke) appearing in his place in the *Strand* and its competitors, whom he had to out-detect on his return, to maintain his reputation as the greatest of the great detectives.

But the lady across the seas? In October 1899, in the final years of his absence from the public eye, far across the ocean, the character of Holmes reappeared in authorised form in William Gillette's stageplay, *Sherlock Holmes*, unwillingly ending every performance in the loving embrace of the heroine, Alice Faulkner. The play was a hit, and this was Holmes's "life", at least in the public eye, for the next two years. But, as Kalypso was persuaded by the goddess Athene to return Odysseus to his homeland, so, in 1901, Gillette was persuaded to return Holmes to London. These events arguably led to his genuine reappearance in the *Strand* that same year.

It was Athene who watched over and protected Odysseus throughout the Trojan War and during his exile, and there is evidence that the same was true for Holmes. In one of his more perilous adventures, when he and Watson make their foray into the home of the blackmailer Charles Augustus Milverton, a bust of Pallas Athene stands on the top of Milverton's bookcase, watching over them. As the pair face the prospect of discovery after Milverton's inopportune return, a mysterious unnamed woman appears and shoots Milverton dead. Athene is presented as a mistress of disguise throughout the *Odyssey*: could the identity of Milverton's murderess finally have been uncovered?

Of course, it is not just Athene who uses disguises as a matter of course. Amongst Holmes's own many disguises throughout the Canon, in "The Empty House" he reappears after his long absence disguised as an old bookseller, fooling even his closest friend Dr Watson. Odysseus, likewise, on his return to Ithaka appears to those closest to him, including his wife, Penelope, and son, Telemachos, in disguise as an old beggar. It is worthy of note that he strengthens his disguise with claims to having heard rumours about himself, including that "Odysseus had gone to Dodona, to listen to the will of Zeus, out of the holy deep-leaved oak tree for how he could come back to the rich countryside of Ithaka". It should be remembered that one of the books that Holmes carries to strengthen *his* disguise is *The Origin of Tree Worship*.

But what of Odysseus's most famous adversary during his wanderings, the Cyclops, Polyphemus? I know of no one-eyed men in the Canon, but I would argue that we can see his equivalent in Moriarty's lieutenant, Colonel Sebastian Moran, in "The Empty House". In the *Odyssey*, Odysseus and his men encounter Polyphemus in his cave, where they are held captive before ambushing and blinding him. In "The Empty House" Holmes, Watson, and Lestrade's men ambush Moran in the cavelike emptiness of Camden House. But what of that single eye, and the blinding?

I would suggest here that we can read Moran's air-rifle as the equivalent of the Cyclops's single eye. Whether we take the rifle's sights as a symbolic eye, or simply recognise that the shooter must close one eye to accurately aim, it is undeniable that Watson, in his description of the moment of shooting, describes how he saw "his *eye* gleam as it peered along the sights". A veritable description of a cyclopean Moran if ever there was one! The symbolic blinding of Moran occurs after his capture, when Watson explicitly states that "Holmes stepped up to the window, closed it, and dropped the blinds".

To further cement the comparison, Homer tells us of the Cyclops throwing rocks at Odysseus's ship as he attempts to escape the island. In "The Empty House" we are told of Moran employing identical tactics as Holmes lies on a ledge above the falls after the demise of Moriarty at Reichenbach: "A huge rock, falling from above, boomed past me, struck the path, and bounded over into the chasm. For an instant I thought that it was an accident; but a moment later, looking up, I saw a man's head against the darkening sky, and another stone struck the very ledge upon which I was stretched."

It is also in "The Empty House" that we learn that Holmes's faithful landlady, Mrs Hudson, has maintained the rooms at Baker Street in the same condition they were in when Holmes set off on his pursuit of Moriarty. She also participates actively in his capture of Moran, moving the wax bust to make it appear more lifelike. In the *Odyssey* we learn that Odysseus's faithful housekeeper, Eurykleia, watches over the storeroom of his palace, filled with gold, bronze, clothing, olive oil and wine, "for the day when Odysseus might come home even after laboring through many hardships", while upstairs, Odysseus's spears still stand in their racks. Like Mrs Hudson, Eurykleia participates in the plot against the suitors, not only ensuring that the women are detained inside the palace while Telemachos hides the weapons, but even volunteering to carry the light for him when he does so.

Perhaps as renowned as his duel with the Cyclops is Odysseus's encounter with the Sirens. Of course, it would be tempting to link these alluringly deadly songstresses with the sopranic adventuress Irene Adler, but I believe that the parallels go deeper than this. Holmes's distrust of women is well-documented, but we should also remember his passion for their music, whether this be the aforesaid Adler, or the splendid bow-work of Mme Norman-Neruda (*A Study in Scarlet*), or Carina, whose singing so entranced him that he was willing to put his investigation on hold to hear her perform at the Albert Hall during the events of "The Resident Patient".

Odysseus has his men lash him to the mast of his ship so that he may hear the sirens yet not yield to their allurements. We can imagine Holmes's equivalent torment as his heart is moved by the music of women and yet he is forced by his distrust to remain cold and distant. In the disguised Odysseus's reaction to Penelope when she reveals her distress to him, we may see a parallel to Holmes's customary response to his female clients: "His eyes stayed, as if they were made of horn or iron, steady under his lids. He hid his tears and deceived her."

When we recall that Odysseus instructs his men to block their ears with beeswax so that they will not hear the song of the temptresses, we wonder whether Holmes's retreat into the Sussex countryside to keep bees may have been as much an escape from his tormented attitude to women as it was a retirement from the work of a detective.

A more general love of music is shared by Holmes and Odysseus, and it is while he is listening to the singing of Demodokos that we first see Odysseus wearing "a great mantle dyed in sea-purple". Later we hear of him wearing a "woolen mantle of purple" and a "double cloak of purple". We cannot help but be reminded of Holmes's famous purple dressing-gown, worn in "The Blue Carbuncle".

But ultimately it is Holmes's detective work, his plotting and counter-plotting, that brought him public renown, and here again we see direct parallels in Odysseus. Early in the Odyssey he is described as "he who is beyond all other men in mind" and is "known beyond all men for the study of crafty designs". Athene says that "it would be a sharp one, and a stealthy one, who would ever get past you in any contriving."

It is of course the idea for the Wooden Horse of Troy that is Odysseus's most acclaimed and audacious scheme: a seemingly innocent gift taken into the enemy stronghold, but concealing a hidden danger to bring about their downfall. Holmes imitated his predecessor's scheme on any number of occasions, whether it was smuggling himself into Irene Adler's home disguised as an injured priest or sending Watson into the lair of Baron Gruner in the guise of Dr Hill Barton bearing the distraction of a rare Ming saucer. His awareness of Odysseus's plot also enabled him to readily identify similar plots on the part of malefactors, for example the deadly ivory box received from Culverton Smith in "The Dying Detective", a case Holmes brings to a conclusion through a "crafty design" worthy of Odysseus himself.

It is Odysseus too who must ultimately take the credit for Holmes's most renowned deduction. In "Silver Blaze", Holmes famously deduces that the abductor of the racehorse Silver Blaze must have been a member of Colonel Ross's staff because of "the curious incident of the dog in the night-time", when the Colonel's dog did not bark at the intruder, indicating that it was someone familiar to it. A classic piece of detective work, no doubt, but also one pre-empted by Odysseus some three thousand years before. When he first returns to Ithaka, Odysseus stays with an old family servant, Eumaios, in a farmhouse close to the beach on which he was left by the Phaiakans (a farmhouse that bears more than a close resemblance to Holmes's Sussex villa, it might be added). Shortly thereafter, Odysseus's son, Telemachos, arrives. Hearing only footsteps, Odysseus is able to tell that the visitor is known to Eumaios: "Eumaios, someone is on his way here who is truly one of yours, or else well known, since the dogs are not barking."

Adrian Nebbett (Mantin, Malaysia) has spent the last twenty years on his own odyssey, leaving his home in England to teach drama and English in Malaysia, Vietnam, Sri Lanka, and the United States. He is the owner of the Sherlockian pastiche and parody website schoolandholmes. com.

TALE OF THE TRICKSTER

Loki

Angela Misri

The first time I made the connection between the characters of Sherlock Holmes and Loki, Norse god of mischief, was when I watched the first Robert Downey, Jr. *Sherlock Holmes* movie (2009). Before you purists leap out of your chairs brandishing your sword-canes, you should know that my response to that realization was to do my research: to return to the Canon to find out if Arthur Conan Doyle's original sketch of the detective we know and love actually held these trickster characteristics I usually associate with Loki.

The answer was yes. A trickster is someone who enjoys misleading others, and I believe that is a shared trait of the original ACD character of Sherlock Holmes and the Loki of ancient Norse mythology.

Introductions: The first description we get of Sherlock Holmes in *A Study in Scarlet* comes from Stamford, the old friend of Watson's who arranges their introduction as a way to provide both men with a roommate.

> He is a little queer in his ideas—an enthusiast in some branches of science. As far as I know he is a decent fellow enough.

Right away we know that Holmes is abnormal: decent but decidedly not normal.

Loki makes his appearance in one of the central documents of Norse mythology, the 12th century series of poems called *Poetic Edda*. He figures in six poems of the *Edda*: "Völuspá", "Lokasenna", "Þrymskviða", "Reginsmál", "Baldrs draumar", and "Hyndluljóð".

The first time he is mentioned by name is verse 35, by a völva (wise woman) whom Odin has asked to speak of the past, the present and the future. In translation from Icelandic:

> One did I see | in the wet woods bound,
> A lover of ill, | and to Loki like;
> By his side does Sigyn | sit, nor is glad
> To see her mate: | would you know yet more?

This first description tells us a few things—that Loki is "a lover of ill," that he is bound in "the wet woods" and that he has a faithful but unhappy wife sitting at his side. Also it seems pretty clear that that is not the end of their story. Later in the series of poems, Loki is portrayed as sneaky, intelligent, and often in opposition to authority. Loki is by turns playful, malicious, and helpful, but he's always irreverent and nihilistic.

Both Loki and Sherlock Holmes are described as outside the norm, though one is described as "decent" and the other "a lover of ill" which could hardly be a synonym for decency.

So far, the bare minimum of similarities, but we press on.

Intelligence. "Lokasenna" is made up almost entirely of Loki taunting the rest of the Gods, who are assembled at a peaceful dinner. Again, Loki's outsider nature seems to be the driving force for his aggressive behaviour. He gets jealous of a server who is praised by the gods, kills the server, and is tossed out of the dinner. Loki talks his way back into the party (basically the "parley" argument made by various characters in *The Pirates of the Caribbean* series) and goes through the gods one by one, insulting each in turn. The gods do their best to reply in kind but fail against Loki's superior wit and delivery.

> Why, ye gods twain, | with bitter tongues
> Raise hate among us here?
> Loki is famed | for his mockery foul,
> And the dwellers in heaven he hates.

Loki's intelligence is part of why he is tossed out of the party. Yes, he deploys his intelligence in spiteful, mean ways, but surely in part because he has a huge insecurity about being an outsider to every party. He responds to this insecurity by striking out at his closest family, sometimes in mischief and sometimes with malice.

Holmes, meanwhile, is often described as cold, and seems to find particular joy in making the local constabulary feel stupid in comparison to his superior intellect. This habit can also be seen as mischievous because I don't think it comes from a place of malice, nor is it mean to detract from the solution of a crime.

In "A Scandal in Bohemia", refuting the idea that Holmes had any romantic feelings for Irene Adler, Watson writes: "All emotions, and that one particularly, were abhorrent to his cold, precise but admirably balanced mind." Some other descriptions of Holmes's coldness:

- He rose from his chair now with a cold sneer upon his pale face.
- Holmes was cold and stern and silent.
- That cold, incisive, ironical voice could belong to but one man in all the world.

His coldness is often defended by his best friend and chronicler as necessary for the kind of work he does. Holmes must turn off all his emotions in order to focus on the important clues in a crime. But that rationale does not justify Holmes's arrogance and dismissiveness of people he considers of lesser intelligence. Take a read of this sarcastic remark to a police inspector:

> "Yes, Lestrade, I congratulate you! With your usual happy mixture of cunning and audacity you have got him."

And this arrogant remark by which Sherlock elevates himself in the context of his Scotland Yard counterparts:

> "I flatter myself that I can distinguish at a glance the ash of any known brand, either of cigar or of tobacco. It is just in such details that the skilled detective differs from the Gregson and Lestrade type."

There are many such examples to be found in the Canon:

> "What do you think of it?" [Gregson and Lestrade] asked.
> "It would be robbing you of the credit of the case if I was to presume to help you," remarked [Holmes]. "You are doing so well now that it would be a pity for anyone to interfere." There was a world of sarcasm in his voice as he spoke.

Holmes and Loki share an intelligence—and an arrogance about it—that they are not careful to hide from others. Holmes is perhaps tempered by his best friend's personality (and to be honest, might not be fully revealed because Watson could be tempering his coverage of their case books to protect the Great Detective's image), but Loki, untrammelled by any friends, is free to release his malicious intelligence on the world, except when his brother gets involved, not unlike Sherlock's brother, Mycroft.

Conflict with brothers. Loki's relationship with Thor is admittedly more violent and adversarial than the one described between Mycroft and Sherlock Holmes, but there are commonalities nonetheless.

Mycroft Holmes makes an appearance in four canonical stories: "The Greek Interpreter", "The Final Problem", "The Empty House" and "The Bruce-Partington Plans." In "The Greek Interpreter" Sherlock Holmes says of his brother:

> "He has no ambition and no energy. He will not even go out of his way to verify his own solutions, and would rather be considered wrong than take the trouble to prove himself right. Again and again I have taken a problem to him, and have received an explanation which has afterwards proved to be the correct one. And yet he was absolutely incapable of working out the practical points."

This description is proved true in the other stories where Mycroft makes an appearance although he's not an active member of the team, preferring to leave all the actual work of solving a mystery to his younger brother. I have a feeling that if Thor and Sherlock met in a bar they'd find a lot of similarities between their bossy brothers. These siblings should be their closest allies, but both come across as necessary evils in their lives, to be avoided as much as possible.

Thor is on the side of the right, or at least the side of the majority. He plays by the rules, and is the favourite of their father and mother, Odin and Frigg. In fact, in many of the stories where Loki starts some kind of trouble, Thor is left to clean it up. Thor's method is invariably to kill someone or something, not to use his brain, but it once again makes Thor the son whom Odin and the rest of the gods value, while Loki is left very much on the outside. Mycroft is also the favoured son, working with the British government on the "side of the light" in a much more acceptable profession than that of Great Detective.

An interesting side note about compass directions: in the poem "Lokasenna", Thor threatens Loki with Mjöllnir, saying he will throw Loki "up on the roads to the east." So, the East is a bad place, one must assume, according to Thor. In "His Last Bow" Holmes says to Watson:

> "There's an east wind coming all the same, such a wind as never blew on England yet. It will be cold and bitter, Watson, and a good many of us may wither before its blast. But it's God's own wind nonetheless, and a cleaner, better, stronger land will lie in the sunshine when the storm has cleared."

Holmes is referring to the onset of the first World War, but it's an interesting parallel with the threat Thor makes against Loki. In the BBC *Sherlock* series, Mycroft threatens Sherlock the same way, warning that "an East wind is coming."

Back to the trickster part of both these characters: there are so many opportunities in both these men's stories where they could have just solved the problem they were up against with kindness and in full transparency to the people around them—but they chose not to. I believe that disregard for "getting along" and that mischievous spark they get from being different makes them so alike, and also makes Loki's case all the more sad. If he had had his own Boswell, to perhaps temper his intelligence into helping more than harming, he might have had a very different end. Ragnarök, the end of the gods' world, is much worse than Reichenbach—but that's a whole other story.

Angela Misri (Toronto, Ontario) is an author, journalist, designer, and podcaster. She is the creator of the Portia Adams Adventures, a popular pastiche series featuring a 19-year-old detective in 1930s London who inherits 221 Baker Street.

THE SPIRITUAL POWER AND THE FLYING HAIR

Lord Shiva

Susan E. Bailey

Have you ever wondered how Holmes manages to survive his confrontation with Moriarty at Reichenbach Falls when his adversary does not? Or how he obtains his incredible powers of mental facility and observation? Could it be said that Holmes is an intellectual superhero, or somehow greater than other human beings? Or, for that matter, why is he so attractive to generations of women and men alike?

I have the solution to all these questions. The answer is that Holmes is like the Hindu god Shiva.

Lord Shiva is the patron deity of many of the longstanding monastic orders of Hinduism. As such, many Hindu ascetics revere Shiva as their exemplar. He also is the god of *yogis*, or practitioners of yoga, and is considered by many traditions to be yoga's founder. In the *Yoga Sutras* of Patanjali (c. 100 BCE–500 CE), the practice of yoga includes not just the postures, or *asanas*, which discipline the body, the physical forms that we see students in yoga classes practicing today. It is also about ethical behavior, self-control, and meditation. Patanjali describes two types of meditation: *dhyana*, or abstract meditation, and *dharana*, meditation on a fixed point, object, or concept. We see Holmes perform something akin to *dharana* meditation many times in the Canon. Take for example the scene in "The Man with the Twisted Lip," which was so evocatively portrayed by Jeremy Brett. Holmes prepares himself for an all-night meditation session by arranging an "Eastern divan" of pillows. He seats himself in silent, motionless contemplation, haloed by pipe smoke, until he reaches his conclusion as to the location of Neville St. Clair.

Patanjali writes that along the path to spiritual liberation, the yogic adept may acquire *siddhis*, which are spiritual attainments or accomplishments. These attainments include what we might describe as superhuman or "magical" powers. Watson, in comparison to Holmes, often appears unable to perceive or reason with the same capacity. Perhaps there is no deficit in Watson in particular—perhaps no normal human would be able to perform on Holmes's level. Perhaps through achievements gained from yogic practice he is able to function on a higher plane.

Consider some of the *siddhis* listed in the *Yoga Sutras* that Holmes could have put to good use: seeing and hearing things from great distances, extraordinary strength, foreknowledge of one's death, freedom from hunger and thirst, freedom from bodily awareness or physical pain, exceptional physical health, the ability to heal oneself. If Holmes had advance knowledge of when and how his death would occur, it would allow him to take greater physical risks in pursuit of criminals. Being unaffected by hunger and thirst could allow him to work for long periods without ceasing, only to consume food and drink again once he had concluded his case. Only a few times do we see Holmes fall ill. At the beginning of "The Reigate Puzzle," Watson is summoned urgently to his bedside in France, only to discover upon his arrival that Holmes has already recovered from his illness. In the beginning of "The Devil's Foot," Watson writes that Holmes's doctor has recommended physical rest to restore his health, but "the state of his health was not a matter in which he himself took the faintest interest, for his mental detachment was absolute." This signifies to me that Holmes's meditative practice allowed him the ability to persevere despite repeated physical exertions that would have laid lesser men low.

In addition to the attainments described by Patanjali in the *Yoga Sutras*, the *Bhagavata Purana* (c. 500–1000 CE) lists further powers that a practitioner can accrue through yoga and meditation. These include the ability to know the minds of others, the ability to check the negative effects of poison, and the ability to assume any form one desires. By the potential use of telepathic powers, Holmes could easily determine if he was being deceived, such as when the King attempts to pull the wool over his eyes in "A Scandal in Bohemia." Holmes could also be able to avoid an attempt at infecting him with a virulent tropical disease, as in "The Dying Detective." If Holmes had the ability to actually alter his physical form, it would immensely aid in him in his many undercover disguises. It no longer seems strange that Holmes could fool even his best friend by hiding his true appearance such as he does in "The Empty House."

For one who strives to emulate Lord Shiva, a thorough spiritual discipline, or *sadhana*, could also consist of ascetic practices which generate spiritual power, as Shiva is the patron god of renunciants, monks, and ascetics. In fact, in "The Missing Three-Quarter," Watson describes Holmes as having an ascetic appearance. Such practices might consist of sleep deprivation, fasting, seclusion, chastity, and not cutting one's hair. How many times have we seen Holmes work tirelessly without food or sleep? Aside from his time rooming with Watson, Holmes spends long periods of time living alone, not speaking to others, and avoiding social engagements. In addition, Hindu renunciants frequently remove themselves from populated areas and retreat to isolated places to focus on their spiritual practice without disruption, much as Holmes retires to the Sussex countryside at the end of his active career.

Holmes's interest in baritsu or bartitsu could also be viewed in this light as a variety of spiritual practice. The *Atharva Veda* (c. 1200–1000 BCE) describes bands of warrior ascetics who practiced martial arts and were skilled with weapons. From approximately 1100 to 1800 CE, a number of Hindu warrior ascetic movements arose in response to Muslim invasions into India, the members of which also developed their own techniques of martial arts. In contemporary Kerala state in southern India, there are still monastic orders which engage in such practices.

It is often assumed that Holmes adopted many of these yogic or meditative practices during his visit to Lhasa, Tibet, during the Great Hiatus. However, if we are to use Baring-Gould's chronology, almost all of the behaviors I have described were observed by Watson prior to Holmes's fall from Reichenbach. I conclude that Holmes's conversations with the lamas in Lhasa were for the purpose of refining or augmenting his practice, or comparing it with others of like mind. It is still correct to see similarities between elements of Tibetan Buddhism and Holmes's practices which I have identified as Hindu. There is a strong and direct historical connection between the Buddhism of Tibet in particular and the traditions of worship of Lord Shiva. The Tibetan alphabet was based on Sanskrit, the sacred language of Hinduism. Many Hindu religious texts that have been lost in the original Sanskrit are extant today in Tibetan translation. And Lord Shiva is a part of the Tibetan pantheon. However, I think it is more appropriate to identify as Hindu the yogic, meditative, and ascetic practices we see in Holmes, because that is their historical origin. Remember, before the historical Buddha became enlightened, he was first a Hindu ascetic. As Buddhism became a new religion, whatever Hindu practices were found to be fruitful or productive were retained.

In Holmes's case, the spiritual practice of chastity or sexual abstinence is noteworthy. In Victorian society, it would not be unusual for a man of Holmes's status to marry. However, he could not do so, I would argue, due to his ascetic spiritual practice. In fact, it would behoove him to avoid more than a casual association with women. It is not surprising that Holmes would state in "The Second Stain" that women are never to be entirely trusted, nor for him to disdain Watson's choice to marry at the end of *The Sign of Four*. In light of Holmes's asceticism, I view the sentiment he expressed in "The Second Stain" to be not so much a commentary on the nature on women, but a warning that engaging with them could be dangerous for him. If Holmes were to marry or have a romantic relationship, then the spiritual power that he accrued through his practices would be depleted and thus his spiritual attainments could be lost, and with it his significant advantage over the ranks of criminals.

There is special importance to one of these ascetic practices, namely, avoiding cutting one's hair. One of the essential characteristics of Lord Shiva as he is pictured in Hindu iconography is his long, flowing, matted locks of dark hair. He is shown with it piled on his head and cascading over his shoulders as he meditates. When Shiva dances, his hair flies about him. His unkempt locks indicate that he is unbound by societal norms and exists beyond vain care for his appearance. It shows that his focus is on spiritual goals, not worldly ones. I think it is important to mention this characteristic given the amount of attention that is paid to Sherlock's hair in BBC's *Sherlock* by both the production staff and the audience. The actor who plays Sherlock, Benedict Cumberbatch, was specifically asked to grow his hair long as a part of portraying the character, and it has become a part of Sherlock's distinctive appearance that resonates with fans of the show. When I see Sherlock's profusion of dark, wavy hair, it reminds me of Shiva's hair.

Lord Shiva's hair and Sherlock's hair also signify their prodigious mental or spiritual powers. It visually suggests that the brain is a fertile place. This idea is actually borne out by ancient Hindu understandings of the body and how it is affected by yogic, meditative, or ascetic practice. Through sexual abstinence, spiritual energy is retained within the body and drawn up the spinal column to bathe the brain so that it becomes increasingly powerful. Physiologically, this is how it was understood that spiritual attainments could be made manifest by the yogic practitioner. Thus one who is full of spiritual power is simultaneously suffused with restrained eroticism.

In her book, *Shiva: The Erotic Ascetic*, Professor Wendy Doniger explains how in Hindu mythology Shiva can be both the ideal husband and the ideal ascetic. In fact, the two do not contradict each other. It is Shiva's persistent asceticism that imbues him with the erotic prowess that draws women to him. Much like Shiva, I would argue, we should consider Sherlock Holmes to be an erotic ascetic.

Susan E. Bailey is the 2017 winner of the Morley-Montgomery Memorial Award and is a former Gasogene of Watson's Tin Box of Ellicott City, Maryland. She holds master's degrees in religious studies from Harvard Divinity School and Duke University.

THE ADVENTURE OF THE MISREMEMBERED KING

Arthur of Britain

Margie Deck

The search for the historical King Arthur is fraught with problems. Little historical evidence exists. From what is available, some scholars believe he was a minor king or war leader of Celtic Britons who led the defense of Britain against Saxon invaders in the late 5th and early 6th centuries AD. The earliest documentary accounts of Arthur are found in the Historia Brionum, composed by the Welsh *Nennius* (c. 796) and the *Annales Cambriae* (c. 954); many early poetic sources and Welsh legendary tales mention an Arthur. The first extended history of Arthur's exploits is found in the *Historia Regium Britanniae*, written by Geoffrey of Monmouth about 1140—although it is more than likely that Geoffrey found it necessary to augment his reporting with a bit of fancy.

There is no one canonical version of Arthur's history. The themes, events, and characters of Arthurian legend vary, and are set across Brittany, Cornwall, Wales, Cumberland, Scotland, and, by the middle ages, France, Germany, Italy, and Spain. The real King Arthur and how he truly fits into "the Matter of Britain" remains an entangled mystery.

But it hardly matters. Ask anyone about King Arthur and out will pour whimsical tales of a round table with noble knights, Excalibur, Merlin, and the Holy Grail. This idea of Arthur is found in the metrical romances composed by the French poet Chrétien De Troyes (1160–1186), and is most firmly seated in the *Morte d'Arthur*, first published in 1485 by Sir Thomas Malory. *Morte d'Arthur*, a retelling of the legends of Arthur in a single work, is considered by many to be one of the finest romantic works in English literature. Malory appears to dispense with what one critic dubbed "pseudo-historicity," landing solidly on the side of myth. But, again, it hardly matters. The Queried-Anyone knows that Arthur existed, was a king, and had a round table as surely as they know that Sherlock Holmes always wore a deerstalker and always said "Elementary, my dear Watson."

Except, of course, he didn't. But, yet once more, it hardly matters.

An eager (or perhaps weary) Sherlockian may attempt to explain about the Sherlock Holmes Canon, the sleuth's cloth traveling cap worn only on certain expeditions, and Holmes's exact use of the word "elementary." The Queried-Anyone will listen politely (or perhaps impatiently), nod, and then walk away, promptly ignoring the explanation. King Arthur and Sherlock Holmes are interwoven into contemporary thought with identities that are larger than any one canonical view. Stories about them are told again and again, appearing in literature, television, film, and endlessly on the Internet, in a myriad of genres. The king and the consulting detective are legends with qualities, true or not, which continue to resonate through generation after generation.

When the child of the sister of Vernet, the French artist, and the descendant of country squires brought Sherlock Holmes into the world in 1854, they certainly would have been aware of the myth of Arthur. The 19th century brought reawakened interest in medievalism and Romanticism, and especially the medieval version of King Arthur. The high point of this interest perhaps is found in the *Idylls of the King* by Alfred, Lord Tennyson, a poetic treatment of the Malory Arthurian legend, comprising twelve long poems published between 1859 and 1885. This retooling of Malory's tales for the Victorians proved immensely popular, selling thousands of copies.

The Arthur of the Victorians is an epic hero, but not one who is flawless. This Arthur has fears, exhibits jealousy, and sometimes suffers doubts. Yet he is still a symbol of courage, honor, honesty, and the chivalry of Camelot. In spite of his imperfections, he remains a warrior willing to accept a challenge and defend the honor of his court. The medieval version of the king and his court is a myth the Victorians could look upon as symbolic of a golden age lost to England. "In the Victorian age," writes historian Stephanie L. Barczewski, in *Myth and National Identity in Nineteenth-Century Britain: The Legends of King Arthur and Robin Hood*, "people continued to contrast the harsh, workaday realities of modern life with the gentler, romanticized world of the Middle Ages. As change threatened to sweep away everything familiar, Britons turned to the medieval past, which seemed to possess the comforting security and stability their own world lacked. Medievalism has often been interpreted as a reaction to industrialization."

These dreaming-of-a-better-age Victorians accepted Sherlock Holmes wholeheartedly when he came into their consciousness in a small way with the publication of *A Study in Scarlet* and *The Sign of the Four*, and in a big way when the adventures began appearing in *The Strand*. Certainly they did not view Holmes as a king from a golden past but as a modern gentleman and hero, perhaps even as a man before his time, considering his methods. This contemporary man, however, exhibited many of the traits they found comforting in their myth of King Arthur: he sometimes feels fear, jealousy, and doubt, and yet he is a symbol of courage and honor. He is a warrior, the first to accept a challenge, and he is willing to die for the good of his kingdom.

To see his commitment, one needs to look no further than his response when threatened with destruction by Moriarty for interfering in the activities of the master criminal: "If you are clever enough to bring destruction upon me, rest assured that I shall do as much to you.... I would, in the interests of the public, cheerfully accept [my own death]." Fortunately, Moriarty failed.

As the Victorian age passed by, the canonical exploits of Sherlock Holmes and Dr. Watson continued to be published into 1927. But it did not take hundreds of years of retelling their stories for their Victorian age to come to be considered a golden time. Writing in volume 1, number 2, of the *Baker Street Journal* in 1946, Edgar W. Smith described the mythic view of Sherlock Holmes in the Victorian Age with his editorial, "The Implicit Holmes," opening with: "What is it we love about Sherlock Holmes? We love the times in which he lived, of course: the half-remembered, half-forgotten times of snug Victorian illusion, of gaslit comfort and contentment, of perfect dignity and grace." In the same piece, Smith goes on from the golden age to the mythic Holmes who "stands before us as a symbol of all that we are not, but ever would be... the fine expression of our urge to trample evil and to set aright the wrongs with which the world is plagued."

Seventy-plus years on from Smith, interest in the mythic Holmes and his illusionary world shows no sign of abating. Recent searching with Google for "Sherlock Holmes" returned more than 3,830,000 possibilities—an almost unimaginable number to contemplate for a storybook character from the late 1800s. The mythic Holmes is now universal.

For many, universal Holmes is also touchingly personal, as Cambridge-based Holmesian author Morton George beautifully described: "Sherlock Holmes pops up like the one fixed point in the changing ages. He saw the Victorian era become Edwardian, took soldiers through the Great War and [World War II], and gave those at home the benefit of his presence. Holmes sat in our homes through the post war shortages and the new age of 1950's TV-owning. He was there in the eighties, [with] dear Jeremy Brett and Co., while there was an inequality to fight. When there is a need for Holmes to return he does. There'll always be an England while there is Sherlock Holmes."

A similar Google search for King Arthur returns more than 12,000,000 possibilities—obviously the king is universal, and interest in him continues unabated as well. Does the interest in the universal Arthur touch upon the personal too? Certainly, yes, as Tyler Tichelaar, author of *King Arthur's Children: A Study in Fiction and Tradition*, succinctly explains: "Scholars will debate for centuries to come whether Arthur ever lived, but either way, Arthur is in our genes—if not in our actual DNA, then in our human nature to dream of a better world. Arthur is remembered because he strove to create an idyllic world, a Round

Table—an early form of democracy where justice prevailed—and for a short time, he succeeded. In the end, we might fail like he ultimately did, but we cannot aspire to anything grander ourselves, and so we carry on Arthur's legacy of hope."

Arthur's legacy of hope is some 1,400 years older than Holmes's, but the similarities are there. Dr. Watson's greatest words about Holmes, "him whom I shall ever regard as the best and the wisest man whom I have ever known," could easily have been said of the once and future king.

Ask anyone.

Margie Deck (Spanaway, Washington) is a long-time member of the Sound of the Baskervilles; she is a past recipient of the Footprints of a Gigantic Hound award for service to the organization. She is also a member of the Dogs in the Night, a frequent visitor with the Stormy Petrels, and a charter member of the John H Watson Society, where she currently serves as Treasure Hunt Master.

TAKING THE LAW INTO HIS OWN HANDS

Robin Hood

Mark Hanson

Sherlock Holmes is like Robin Hood in so many ways. They are similar in terms of their places of residence, whom they associated with (including their rivals), the methods they used to be successful, and their underlying social consciences.

Since we are all fans and scholars of Sherlock Holmes, allow me to begin by describing my vision of Robin Hood, since his history is so long and varied. (One of the most enduring figures of English folklore, he is first mentioned in a poem from 1377; the most common version of his story sets his exploits during the rule of Prince John, about 1190, while King Richard I was away from England crusading.) I'm picturing a Robin Hood at his very best—energetic, brave, honest, courteous, skilled, with a kind heart and an overruling vision of social justice. Note: I am also picturing Sherlock Holmes at his best—an engaged, motivated, working Holmes.

Sherwood Forest, in Nottinghamshire, was the hidden sanctuary for Robin Hood, his Merry Men, and their community, according to the consensus of the stories. He and his band would lure pursuers—chiefly the Sheriff of Nottingham's men—into the greenwood, but then whistle for their comrades, armed with bows and arrows, to surround and capture them. As Sherlockians, we cannot help but think of "The Dying Detective", where Holmes set the perfect trap to capture the diabolical murderer Culverton Smith in his own rooms. "The parallel is (again) exact."

Well, of course, Sherlock Holmes's sanctuary was his residence at 221B Baker Street. Insulated and cared for by the devoted Mrs. Hudson, he also had a friend and confidant there for many years in Dr. John Watson. Famous for not leaving his lodgings for days or weeks at a time, Holmes also trapped culprits in his rooms ("The Blue Carbuncle") and even directly across the street ("The Empty House").

Robin Hood's best friend was identified variously as Little John, Will Scarlet, or Alan-a-Dale. Sherlock Holmes, of course, had his beloved

Watson. Robin Hood had his Merry Men as his allies and army. To conduct his work, Sherlock Holmes employed, besides revolver-carrying Watson, the intrepid and infallible Toby, his Baker Street Irregulars, and lastly, the police. The London force had authority, manpower, and reach: Inspector Lestrade was "as tenacious as a bulldog when he once understands what he has to do."

Robin Hood, while fighting social injustice and tyranny, was pitted against the Sheriff of Nottingham (and his force) and ultimately, Prince John (in the absence of his brother King Richard the Lionheart). Sherlock Holmes had to battle thieves, murderers, assassins, criminals, and their agents—and ultimately London's criminal mastermind, Professor James Moriarty. On occasion, even the police and justice system were obstacles or contrary to Holmes and his methods.

A large part of what endures about both Robin Hood and Sherlock Holmes is their skill. The chief of Sherwood Forest is legendary for his ability as an archer, but he was also highly skilled in personal combat with a longstaff or sword. Throughout the Canon, we also see Holmes's skill at defending himself with boxing, "baritsu, the Japanese system of wrestling", or even his walking stick—indeed Watson in *A Study in Scarlet* calls him "an expert singlestick player", something that could have been said of Robin Hood.

Holmes's main weapon, of course, was his mind: his powers of observation (such as his skill in examining physical evidence at the crime scene), keen intellect, and his ability to use reasoning and logic. His imagination was key, as well, and he was constantly critical of the lack of imagination and vision in almost all the police detectives he encountered. Holmes's education in chemistry only enhanced his capacity as a detective, and his pioneering work in the field of (literary) criminal forensic science can hardly be overstated.

Both Sherlock Holmes and Robin Hood were energetic, highly motivated men, confident in their abilities. Being literary characters, both, of course, possessed a flair for the dramatic and a sense of showmanship. Splitting an arrow already on the bull's eye, indeed!

Both characters were also skilled at using disguises to operate unnoticed and unimpeded. And both were known to use complicated, strategic plans to flush out and capture their enemies.

Robin Hood, operating in a harsh and unjust society, was driven to be an outlaw by the (according to tradition) unchecked and corrupt Prince John and his right hand, the Sheriff of Nottingham. His commitment to robbing from the rich and giving to the poor varied in degree among his iterations over the centuries, but served to illustrate the motivation of the character, not to mention creating timeless, universal appeal for readers and audiences worldwide.

Taking the law into his own hands was not unknown to Sherlock Holmes, either. From concealing or withholding evidence from the police, to breaking and entering into buildings and homes during his investigations, the great detective had his methods and his moral code. "It's every man's business to see justice done," he says in "The Crooked Man". Just as his upright gentleman companion John Watson was always willing to join him in breaking the law for a just cause, we the readers remain always right beside him, as well.

Watson even described Holmes as refusing cases if the cause was unjust, and his moral code even allowed him to let guilty parties escape the law. One thinks mainly of jewel thief James Ryder in "The Blue Carbuncle": "I suppose that I am commuting a felony, but it is just possible that I am saving a soul."

At their best, both Robin Hood and Sherlock Holmes are generous, courteous, and even chivalrous. The master of Sherwood Forest followed a code that specifically outlined never harming women, and while Holmes's focus was always on the facts of each case, one thinks of the consideration and sympathy he does display for his young female clients, whether named Violet or otherwise. A striking example is Holmes's outrage at the potentially forced marriage of Violet Smith in "The Solitary Cyclist". Ever the observer of the human condition, Holmes does recognize the power, complexity, and subtlety of the fairer sex. He is a Victorian gentleman, after all.

Along with King Arthur, surely Robin Hood and Sherlock Holmes make up the three most iconic and enduring characters in all of British literature, and the latter two certainly share common characteristics. Their legends persist.

Mark Hanson (London, Ontario) is a devotee of old movies, a denizen of Twitter, and a founding member of the Cesspudlian Society of London.

MAN OF STEEL

Superman

Christopher Sequeira

"Don't you mean Batman?" you say. You know, the other cape-wearing, universally recognised DC Comics character dating back to the World War II era? After all, Batman's the non-super-powered world's greatest detective; his persona is thus something like, say, that of a masked version of Holmes (indeed, DC has leveraged off that several times over the years, with Batman even combining his investigative efforts with Holmes's a few times in DC's continuity).

Well, yes, Sherlock Holmes is like Batman. But, far more interestingly—because it's less obvious, but just as true—he's also like Superman.

Lifestyles, occupations, environments. The lean, angular Baker Street sleuth created by Arthur Conan Doyle might not reflexively be likened to the powerfully muscled "man of steel" created by Jerry Siegel and Joe Shuster, but when we think of the characters' personal profiles, similarities aplenty emerge.

Both are independent, professional guardians of the law, who accept or decline to get involved in matters at their own discretion and are not motivated by money. Superman takes no fees, and Holmes, we well know, has an esoteric attitude to remuneration—seeming to accept it only to pay his way in life, and eventually having been so well rewarded it doesn't concern him in his later years.

Both characters evolve in their continuities to the point they are universally famous, and a neat little fact is that we recognise them by their sobriquets as much as by their formal names: Superman (a.k.a. Kal El, a.k.a. Clark Kent) as "the Man of Steel"; and Holmes as "the consulting detective".

Both characters have made life choices to support their life's work: Holmes eschews friends, sentiment generally, and romantic attachments particularly (lest they "bias my judgement"), and Superman has repeatedly had to avoid a permanent on-going relationship with women he has loved, like Lana Lang or Lois Lane, because of the supposed risk of his enemies striking at him through a wife. (Well, so much is true for the vast majority of the character's history at any rate; a de facto relationship or marriage to Lois Lane has occurred more than once and been undone more than once.) This apparent monastic tendency makes them both very focussed, and engenders an additional nobility to their life's work of opposing crime.

Both characters are long-term residents of perhaps the largest, most variegated and seemingly sophisticated cities in their contemporaneous worlds: Holmes in London, and Superman in Metropolis. They spend most of their years at quiet, unglamourous apartments with an alphabetic numeration (Holmes at 221B Baker Street; Superman, in his Clark Kent guise for the longest time living at 344 Clinton Street, in the third floor apartment numbered 3-D). They are very much contented with these big-city lives: Holmes interacting as cases and interest strike him, but enjoying the music, dining, and culture that attract his attention when he is not at work, and Superman as Clark Kent fully immersed in his city's activities, especially as a major news outlet's reporter. Both characters have documented associates and contacts in the press (Superman more so than Holmes via his job at the *Daily Planet*) and government law enforcement services (Holmes more so than Superman via his work with Scotland Yard).

Family. Both men have almost no family when they commence their careers. Holmes has a brother (whom he interacts with so rarely his flatmate, Watson, knew nothing of his existence for years), deceased parents we know almost nothing of, and an unspecified distant relative, Doctor Verner. Superman has one cousin (Kara El, or Supergirl) but the world of Kal El's origins—Krypton—is as dead and gone from his primary daily concerns as is Holmes's parents' squiredom. Note, too, that the sole relative each hero has in their current lives is a bastion of virtue themselves, worthy of a series of their own adventures, possessing powers on a scale of their relative. Indeed, Supergirl has had her own comic-book series, movie, and TV shows; and Mycroft has proved popular enough to sustain frequent appearances in Holmes visual media and solo literary pastiches, and may even have been the thinly (no pun intended) disguised original of the Martin Hewitt mysteries by Arthur Morrison, published in the 1890s. We probably can't determine whether nature or nurture was responsible, but both the Holmes and the El clans produced more than one outstanding champion of good.

Friends and romantic interests. Apart from their relatives, both men have two significant, non-adversarial relationships. Holmes's relationship with Irene Adler begins as adversarial in nature but is reversed to profound, professional, and more-than-professional regard. Compare this to Superman's relationship with Lex Luthor, which began when the two were teenagers and great friends before transforming into deadly enemies. It is significant to note how these two figures in each man's life share and swap different symbolic and psychological attributes when placed into context with their respective lead series character.

Both men have a primary male friend, valued above all others and permitted to engage in the hero's professional career in ways no other person is (for Holmes, Watson; for Superman, Jimmy Olsen). Both men have one woman of true emotional and psychological import in their lives (for Holmes it's Irene Adler; for Superman it's Lois Lane). In the lives of the heroes, one of these relationships is absolutely necessary; the other is important, but we could see them managing their lives happily without that relationship. In Holmes's case Watson is his most important relationship, whereas in Superman's case it is his relationship with the woman, Lois Lane.

Watson and Lane are both journalistic presences! They each repeatedly base a career on writing about the hero, even writing about the cases in which they aid or are involved in cases *with* the hero. Both these writers provide the world with the best viewpoint of the hero: the honest, sincere, and up-close look at their selfless efforts, their dedication, and their courage in the face of adversity. Jimmy Olsen and Watson are, however, also comparable, as only Olsen (a photo-journalist) is accorded the classic Superman Signal Watch; he alone can summon Superman when trouble is afoot in Metropolis.

Irene Adler, although in only one canonical Holmes story, is an absolutely pivotal character; she is painted as an investigator/operative of the highest order (just like Lane).

And one final trivial, yet mesmerising, detail about the two secondary characters, Jimmy Olsen and Irene Adler: Both were repeated and successful transvestites. I mean no insult at all to those who adopt the garb and persona of a gender other than that first assigned to them when I say "successful"; in this context, I simply mean they adopted such identities avowedly as disguises, according to the original texts, and these appearances in the identities were carried off so well as to engender (ouch!) no suspicion as to the person's real identity.

James Olsen, in completely canonical Superman adventures, was a frequent wearer of female garb (supposedly disguising himself—*gee, just relax and come out, JO, we're here for you!*—as a woman to get scoops). We know of Irene Adler's successful forays into male attire and identity.

(Additionally, both men have one significant friend from their youth who knew even then the reality of their amazing powers: In Holmes's case it is Victor Trevor from the *Gloria Scott* affair, and in Superman's case it is Pete Ross, who knows Clark Kent's secret from their childhood in Smallville, but who hides that knowledge even from Clark.)

Associates. Both men are also members of what might be termed law enforcement fraternities. Holmes is an independent but maintains a slowly strengthening friendship over the years with the Scotland Yarders, who we know (from Lestrade's words in the matter of "The Six Napoleons") eventually hold the view that "we're not jealous of you at Scotland Yard. No, sir, we're very proud of you, and if you come down tomorrow there's not a man who wouldn't be glad to shake your hand." Superman, for his part, often assists with the cases of the Justice League of America, and most often works with league member Batman and (his associate) Robin—who might be likened to Lestrade and Gregson because of that. Interestingly, the Batman-Superman relationship over the decades of DC continuity has varied from them seeming like drinking buddies to them being actively hostile teammates. The Lestrade comparison might be more apt with this in mind—he didn't always respect Holmes's powers completely, as when he was "indifferent and contemptuous" in "The Boscombe Valley Mystery".

Adversaries. Great heroes of course demand great opposition to make us judge them as worthy of distinction, and both Superman and Holmes have that requirement checked off. It is beyond dispute that Holmes's unparalleled nemesis, the one who categorically causes the greatest threat to his entire world, is of exactly the same occupation as Superman's greatest arch-foe: Professor James Moriarty and Lex Luthor are both scientists. They head huge, complex organisations, have accumulated vast wealth which still is not enough for them, and lead public lives pretending to be benevolent citizens. Luthor's chronology began with him as a science-terrorist, before settling on the captain of industry (and sometime political figure) he uses as cover since the 1980's stories, which has since carried over to all media incarnations of him.

Indeed, DC Comics, let me at the word processor if you ever want to have Luthor and Moriarty meet! Although one could not avoid the literary possibilities in speculating that Moriarty's *Dynamics of an Asteroid* contained the theorems that the late Isaac Asimov believed it did (the short story "The Ultimate Crime", 1976) and that the Professor could have concocted a means for blowing up the Earth; but that—horror of never-before-revealed horrors—Moriarty's work might get into evil, *alien* hands and lead to the planet Krypton's demise!

There are other villains in both men's rogues' galleries, too, although some of these are less well known. Where Superman battles the animalistic, brutal Doomsday, whose sheer might makes him a deadly threat, Holmes must withstand the slavering jaws of the Hound of the Baskervilles. While the Man of Steel must grapple with the works of the inhuman, scheming Brainiac, who lives to enslave people in domed containers like bottled ants, is he that different from the consulting detective's enemy, the monstrous master blackmailer, Charles Augustus Milverton, who seals his victims in prisons of compromise? And while the Baker Street sleuth must contend with the mercenary assassin Colonel Moran, does the Colonel twirl a moustache any less devilishly than the ruthless confidence trickster John Corben, alias the human armoured tank, Metallo, who hides his lethal kryptonite heart from sight in his chest cavity as easily as Moran conceals a lethal firearm in his walking cane?

Their place in history. We've considered and compared the narrative mechanics of the Superman and Sherlock Holmes fictional series, and seen much that is alike, but there is a final, more important way these two figures mirror one another.

They are both characters who went on to become literary, even visual, templates: exemplars for a century of fictional series concepts. Holmes was not the first fictional detective, but he is the perfect embodiment of all the attributes of a series scientific-investigating hero. His skills, his demeanour, his occupation, all established him as a private detective character with a single-minded obsession with rooting out crime for the right reasons with superlative skills. He was the best in his field, so why wouldn't we want to keep seeing his work, in the original and in pastiche, from 1887 until the current day and beyond? And why wouldn't he spawn countless followers, from the obviously derivative to the fresh and unique?

Likewise, Superman wasn't the first costumed hero with a concealed identity (that would probably be Zorro in prose or the Phantom in comics), but he was the best, properly distilled, version, with a moral compass and a purpose, as well as astonishing meta-powers.

You can't draw a character with a magnifying lens without invoking the name Sherlock Holmes, and you can't draw a stick figure in a cape without people saying "Superman". These two typify their entire genres; they are world-famous, decades-long-loved pop culture figures who command the adoration of vast audiences, and they could not do so without sharing the most important of all their traits. Their vocation—seeking justice—is their purpose, and it always outweighs other concerns, even their own safety, security, and personal happiness. This is not only why they stand highest, but why they still stand tall, fictional characters though they be, in the minds and hearts of billions.

Christopher Sequeira (Sydney, Australia) is a long-time member of the Sydney Passengers and a horror, mystery, science fiction, and superhero writer and editor. He is editor and a contributor for Echo Publishing's anthology *Sherlock Holmes: The Australian Casebook.*

THE CASE OF THE
EMPEROR'S MOUSTACHE

Raja Birbal

Meghashyam Chirravoori

As I grew up, I consumed a nourishing diet of stories about Birbal—one of the best-known figures in India's rich folklore—and Akbar, the emperor he served. I first read them in a comic book (probably in Grade 4), then in a book of stories in Hindi (in Grade 5), and then in English and Hindi textbooks.

The stories alongside are a perfect blend of history, myth, and fiction. No one really knows which parts are true and which aren't. The historical Birbal lived from 1528 to 1586 and was one of the *navratnas* (nine gems) in the court of the famous Mughal emperor, Akbar (ruled 1556–1605). Honoured with the title of Kavi Priya (poet laureate), Birbal advised the emperor on matters of religious, spiritual, and military significance.

The Birbal I will talk about here, though, is the Birbal of the folktales, the witty and intelligent Birbal whose presence of mind enthralled me as has only one other character. For it was three years after coming across Birbal's fascinating stories that I met Sherlock Holmes, in Grade 7. As I look back now, it is almost scandalous that I didn't think of Holmes and Birbal in the same vein. Maybe the two different cultures they came from made me put them in two different boxes.

But now, as I look back, I see that the similarities between the two just don't seem to end. Almost every unique quality of Holmes pops up in some way in an Akbar-Birbal story. Let's start with the quality that every reader associates with Sherlock Holmes: observation and deduction skills. Holmes, of course, showcases these skills in full measure in every story from the "dog in the night-time" deduction in "Silver Blaze" to the masterful deduction about why the body was found on the roof of a train in "The Bruce-Partington Plans".

While Birbal isn't a consulting detective (he is more of a consulting judge-cum-king's-advisor-cum-witty-guy), his brain has the same skills in ample measure. In the Akbar-Birbal story involving a pantomime, two men are imitating a bull's movements. Only their feet can be seen under a bull's costume as they walk, eat, and charge exactly like a bull. Everyone claps, but Birbal watches quietly. When the show is over, Birbal throws a pebble at the bull, and the actors twitch exactly the way a bull would reflexively twitch. That's when Birbal cheers loudly. His logic is that any actor can act like a bull, but to twitch impulsively like a bull—that's top-notch acting. One could easily replace Birbal with Holmes in such a setting and have Holmes clap exactly like this, then explain why to the bamboozled Watson.

Birbal often settles issues with his keen observation. In one story, a villager and an oil merchant are quarreling over a bag of coins, each claiming the bag is his. Birbal asks to have the bag placed in a bowl of water. Soon, oil starts floating in the water, confirming that the bag's owner is the oil merchant. Simple, almost silly in retrospect, just like many of Holmes's deductions, this solution looks obvious once you're told about it.

In another story, when asked to find out who the guest and who the employees of a rich man are, Birbal immediately singles out the guest, based on how emphatically the employees laugh at the rich man's joke. Sherlock Holmes could have done the same.

Holmes never really cares about how he's perceived by others—the work is his reward. In "Thor Bridge", "The Norwood Builder", and "The Cardboard Box", among other stories, he absolutely refuses to take any credit. In "The Blue Carbuncle" and at least six other cases, he lets the criminal go, even if others think he hasn't been able to solve the case.

Birbal shares the same trait of not caring how he's perceived. In one anecdote, a man says to Birbal, "I have walked 20 miles to see you, and all along the way people have said that you are the most generous man in the country." Birbal sees through his sycophancy. He asks the man, "Are you going back the same way?" When the man says yes, Birbal quips as he walks away, "Will you do me a favor? Please deny the rumor of my generosity all the way back to your house." Not caring two hoots about how they're perceived is probably one reason that makes both Holmes and Birbal successful. They're not wasting precious brain power figuring out what others think of them.

Then there's Holmes's famous out-of-the-box thinking. He looks beyond the obvious in tale after tale. In "Silver Blaze", he creatively reconstructs the sequence of events that led to the disappearance of the horse. In "The Boscombe Valley Mystery" and "The Beryl Coronet", he turns the cases on their heads by coming up with innovative explanations that show the accused are innocent.

Birbal is not far behind. When Akbar asks him to show him a person who is both the *noblest* and the *lowest*, Birbal brings in a beggar. How is he the lowest? He is a poor beggar with clothes in tatters. And the noblest? He is a beggar who has been granted an audience with the emperor himself.

When Akbar asks Birbal exactly how many crows there are in the kingdom, Birbal immediately answers: 95,463.

"What if there are fewer?" asks Akbar.
"The rest have gone on a vacation to some neighboring kingdoms."
"Or if there were more than that?"
"Other crows are visiting your kingdom, *Huzoor*."

Birbal is cleverly hinting that Akbar's question is foolish and that there's no need to pursue this whim.

Admittedly, Birbal's creativity is more of the "let's show you how 2 plus 2 is 5" type. It's different from Holmes's brand of creativity, which is about coming up with ingenious explanations for bizarre events. But Birbal's and Sherlock Holmes's right brains would light up by the same amount in a brain scan.

While in observation, deduction, and creativity I would still rate Holmes slightly ahead of Birbal, when it comes to his way with words, Birbal is the unmatched winner.

To be sure, Holmes has his way with words, too. In "The Cardboard Box", he knows exactly how to empathize and extract info. "Quite so, madam," he says in his soothing way. "I have no doubt that you have been annoyed more than enough already over this business." In "A Scandal in Bohemia", Holmes coaxes all the information he wants out of the "horsey men". In "Charles Augustus Milverton", he wins a maid with his words and becomes engaged to her to extract info about Milverton.

But Birbal is at another level altogether, probably because he *needs* to be good with words for his survival. After all, his companion is not a sycophantic Watson, but Emperor Akbar himself! He needs to be spoken to in a diplomatic way: "Yes, you are great, Almighty King, but make sure you don't mess it up!"

When Emperor Akbar asks Birbal what he would choose if he were given a choice between justice and a gold coin, Birbal chooses the gold coin. As the shocked emperor grimaces, Birbal says, "Your Highness has already ensured that justice is accessible to every single person in the kingdom, but since I'm perennially short of money, I chose the gold coin."

In another tale, the emperor asks his courtiers, "What punishment should be given to a person who pulls my moustache?" The other courtiers suggest that such an offender should be beheaded or flogged. Birbal says he should be given sweets. Why? The only person who would dare to do this would be the king's grandson!

Just like Sherlock Holmes, Birbal loves challenging problems and solves them in a way that makes you whistle in appreciation. When Akbar's ring falls into a dry well, Birbal throws a ball of fresh cow dung onto the ring and then throws down a stone with a string tied to it. He lets the dung harden, and then pulls out the stone and ring with the string.

This reminds me of Sherlock Holmes's craftsman-like solution to the problem of how the pistol shot was fired in "Thor Bridge".

While all these are pretty palpable similarities, the two characters also share a more subtle trait. I believe Holmes is a compassionate man at heart. Not, admittedly, one who would say to someone, "Oh, I'm so sorry this happened. I understand," but the kind of compassionate man who lets the thief go in "The Blue Carbuncle" with two powerful words: "Get out!"

Among his other kind words: in "The Boscombe Valley Mystery", "I will keep your confession, and… it shall never be seen by mortal eye." In "The Three Gables", "I suppose I shall have to compound a felony as usual. How much does it cost to go round the world in first-class style?" Birbal exhibits the same subtle streak of kindness.

There are many stories where people who have been wronged (sometimes by the emperor himself) approach Birbal for help. When a gardener is sentenced to death just because the emperor fell down in the garden, Birbal interferes. He asks the gardener to spit at the emperor's throne. After he does so, Birbal then says to the emperor, "There could be no person more loyal than this unfortunate gardener. Fearing that you ordered him to be hanged for a trifle, he went out of his way to give you a genuine reason for ordering him to be hanged." Why does Birbal butt in? Because he has a heart.

Similarly, when the emperor threatens an astrologer who tells the emperor that "your relatives and friends will all die before you," Birbal consoles the astrologer. He then reinterprets the astrologer's prediction: "You will live longer than any of your friends and relatives." This gets the astrologer out of trouble. Such instances—where there's no personal gain or fanfare, but only basic human empathy at work—exist as subtle undertones in both Holmes and Birbal stories.

By the by, talking of fanfare, have I mentioned Sherlock Holmes and Birbal's flair for drama yet? While they may not make a big deal of their kindness, Holmes and Birbal both love to create a ruckus once in a while. Look at the way Holmes breaks open the final bust in "The Six Napoleons": "A flush of colour sprang to Holmes's pale cheeks, and he bowed to us like the master dramatist who receives the homage of his audience."

Or look at the way he actually sets fire to a portion of the building to expose the hiding culprit in "The Norwood Builder". He could have solved the case in a more nonchalant way, but then that wouldn't make you say "wow", would it?

Birbal does no less! In one story, a man is challenged to stand in River Yamuna's cold waters for a night and will get 100 gold coins if he succeeds. He does it, and when asked how, he explains that he had focussed his attention on a lighted lamp post 50 yards away. That's it—the emperor denies the man the prize because the fellow might have received some heat from the lamp-post. Birbal is outraged, and his penchant for drama takes over. Mr. Drama King doesn't turn up in court the next day. When Akbar is concerned and reaches Birbal's house with his courtiers, he finds that Birbal is cooking *khichdi* (a dish of rice and legumes) with the pot high up on a tree branch and a low fire burning far below.

The amused Akbar asks, "How can the *khichdi* be cooked if it's so far away from the fire?"

Birbal quips, "Why, *Huzoor*, the same way a freezing fellow can draw heat from a lamp post 50 yards away."

Of course, not every aspect of Sherlock Holmes is duplicated in Birbal. The times in which they lived were different. Birbal is the imperial poet laureate; Holmes is at best into reading poetry (he owns a "pocket Petrarch") but surely not into writing it. Birbal is more about witty comebacks while Holmes is more about clinical deductions. And no, Birbal is never mentioned using a seven-per-cent solution of anything. Or solving problems with three pipes. Or getting immensely bored. Or writing superb monographs.

All in all, here's how I'll sum it up. Strip away the superficial mannerisms and cultural differences between Holmes and Birbal and you'll find two people who would immensely enjoy each other's company and probably say to each other as they parted, "We should catch up again, real soon."

> Once Birbal met Holmes at a party,
> And they had a warm heart-to-hearty.
> They discussed deductive reasoning
> And wordplay full of seasoning
> About Akbar, Irene and Moriarty!

Meghashyam Chirravoori (New Delhi, India) runs Sherlock-Holmes-Fan.com, a site that focuses on Sherlockian trivia and facts. He teaches English in an interesting way (at least he thinks so) to children in India along with his wife, Krupa. He is also a part-time computer science enthusiast.

WHILE THE STARS WHEELED OVER

Gandalf the Grey Wizard

Tatyana Dybina

It is with a mischievous smile that I tap the keys on my keyboard to write these few words about a well-known character, famous for his pipe, wisdom, weird sense of humor, and enormous love for explosive stuff. Known under various names, he travelled far and wide, appearing on friendly doorsteps at the least expected hour (mostly inconvenient). He persuaded his friend to start on a journey to an unknown destination, just like that, at once. He was sent abroad to spy on the enemy and he did that job quite well. Standing alone on the edge of a deep chasm, he faced his enemy and disappeared with him into the deep. He was supposed to be dead, yet returned, clad in shabby attire.

Am I talking about Sherlock Holmes? No, not exactly, although the description sounds quite familiar. Rather, this brief introduction is dedicated to Gandalf the Grey, wizard of Middle-earth. Yes, that same Gandalf, who, according to *The Hobbit* by J.R.R. Tolkien, was the man who used to make such particularly excellent fireworks and was responsible for so many lads and lasses going off into the blue for mad adventures. There was even something about some magic diamond studs that fastened themselves. But that's enough for now.

Doesn't sound like Holmes so far, right? And yet I'm going to show Gandalf's striking resemblance to the famous sleuth of 221B. Or vice versa.

I'm tempted to say that the first glimpse of the wizard in his wide-brimmed hat could be dated to 1911, when, according to Tolkien's biography by Humphrey Carpenter, the author of Middle-earth adventures bought a postcard labelled *Der Berggeist* somewhere in Switzerland. The word "Switzerland" already rings a bell, yet perhaps misleadingly this time. Six years after the publication of the biography, Manfred Zimmerman discovered that the postcard with Tolkien's inscription "origin of Gandalf" is actually a reproduction of an artwork by German artist

Josef Madlener, who painted Der Berggeist ("The Mountain Spirit") in the second half of the 1920s.

Whether from Switzerland or not, Gandalf appears in *The Hobbit* (published 1937), where he persuades his friend to accompany him to some remote destination. The corresponding scene in "The Final Problem" immediately comes to mind, with only one difference: Holmes apologized for being late. Yet the real fun starts in *The Hobbit: An Unexpected Journey* (2012), where Gandalf, played by Ian McKellen—a Sherlock Holmes of the modern screen, by the way—whisks away Bilbo Baggins, acted by Martin Freeman, who is John H. Watson to another Holmes.

Speaking of Gandalf already whisking away Bilbo Baggins, I almost forgot to mention one more curious fact from the non-trivial career of the wandering wizard. The point is that he wasn't born in Middle-earth at all. According to *Unfinished Tales*, he was sent there among others who were "forbidden to reveal themselves in forms of majesty... but coming in shapes weak and humble were bidden to advise and persuade Men and Elves to good, and to seek to unite in love and understanding all those whom Sauron, should he come again, would endeavour to dominate and corrupt". In a word, Gandalf was sent to Middle-earth as a secret agent in the perfect disguise. Of course, there was no need for Gandalf to graduate in an Irish secret society at Buffalo or to give serious trouble to the constabulary at Skibbareen as Holmes did. He just spent some 2,000 years "gaining knowledge of Middle-earth and all that dwelt therein". And so good was his disguise "that only those that knew him well glimpsed the flame that was within". Here comes Watson's description of Holmes in "The Final Problem": "For an instant the wrinkles were smoothed away, the nose drew away from the chin, the lower lip ceased to protrude and the mouth to mumble, the dull eyes regained their fire, the drooping figure expanded." No resemblance? There is some, I believe. But that's not all.

Omitting such trivial things like smoking habits, though both Holmes and Gandalf smoked like steam trains, the multiplicity of names under which both were known (Gandalf has thirteen at least; Holmes has at least six), and their love for music (at this point Gandalf has something in his pockets to challenge Holmes playing violin: as one of Ainur, spirits created before the world was even conceived, he played his part in Music of the Ainur), I'm getting closer and closer to my favorite point of this strange comparison.

Next, I'm going to tell how the fantasy wizard and Victorian detective both faced their enemies, both undertook a perilous climb after that, and for some time were both supposed to be dead. Here is Holmes's account of events at Reichenbach Falls: "He rushed at me and threw his long arms around me.... We tottered together upon the brink of the fall.... I slipped through his grip, and he with a horrible scream kicked madly for a few seconds, and clawed the air with both his hands. But for all his efforts he could not get his balance, and over he went. With my face over the brink, I saw him fall for a long way. Then he struck a rock, bounded off, and splashed into the water."

Gandalf wasn't that lucky at the Bridge of Khazad-dum. Here is a third-person account: "With a terrible cry the Balrog fell forward, and its shadow plunged down and vanished. But even as it fell it swung its whip, and the thongs lashed and curled about the wizard's knees, dragging him to the brink. He staggered and fell, grasped vainly at the stone, and slid into the abyss. 'Fly, you fools!' he cried, and was gone."

Looks like there is no chance for a character to give a first-person version of the events after such a fall. And yet there he is, the same wizard in shabby clothes, telling his friends the rest of the tale: "He brought me back at last to the secret ways of Khazad-dum: too well he knew them all. Ever up now we went, until we came to the Endless Stair.... From the lowest dungeon to the highest peak it climbed, ascending in unbroken spiral in many thousand steps, until it issued at last in Durin's Tower.... Out he sprang, and even as I came behind, he burst into new flame.... A great smoke rose about us, vapour and steam. Ice fell like rain. I threw down my enemy, and he fell from the high place.... There I lay staring upward, while the stars wheeled over."

What about Holmes? He climbed some sort of stair after his encounter with Moriarty as well. That's what he told Watson after his rather dramatic reappearance: "I stood up and examined the rocky wall behind me.... A few small footholds presented themselves, and there was some indication of a ledge.... On the whole, then, it was best that I should risk the climb.... At last I reached a ledge several feet deep and covered with soft green moss, where I could lie unseen, in the most perfect comfort." The resemblance between the two accounts is quite impressive.

Moreover, after an appropriate hiatus, both characters returned definitely changed: Gandalf the Grey turned to Gandalf the White. As far as Sherlock Holmes is concerned, he changed so much that some scholars even called him an impostor. (The idea of Holmes as impostor isn't as exotic as it seems. Among sources that have suggested as much is "His Last Arrow" by Christopher Sequeira, published in the anthology *Gaslight Grimoire*, which presents a theory explaining Holmes's impressive abilities. Holmes is, in fact, not human at all. He is a sort of demon, a creature of antiquity brought to England by Watson. Even at this point Holmes is like Gandalf, who just pretends to be human. Well, it was a part of his mission in Middle-earth, after all.)

Summing it up, I can say without doubt that Victorian detective Sherlock Holmes is like wizard Gandalf of Middle-earth: both whisk their unfortunate friends to dubious adventures, both smoke pipes, and both return from the dead to give a full account of the event. For there is no story without its listener.

Tatyana Dybina (Moscow, Russian Federation) is a freelance photographer and writer. She is also a proud member of several assorted Sherlockian Facebook communities, but claims that she has done nothing remarkable yet. She shares her den with a huge gray cat.

HE SEEMS TO HAVE POWERS OF MAGIC

O.Z. Diggs, the Wizard

Beth L. Gallego

There was once a boy who ran away from home to join a circus. His name—Oscar Zoroaster Phadrig Isaac Norman Henkle Emmannuel Ambroise Diggs—was far too long (and the last seven initials formed a rather unflattering acronym), so he cut it down to just the first and second initials, which he painted on all his possessions, including his hot-air balloon. A stray air current carried him in that balloon to a land populated with talking animals, enchanted objects, and witches both good and wicked, where the inhabitants were surprised to see, in large letters on the side of this flying contraption, the name of their own country: O.Z.

Meanwhile, in the city of London, Sherlock Holmes was a young man creating a career for himself, meeting a fellow who would become his closest friend as well as his biographer, and becoming known as the one who could solve mysteries no one else could untangle. As different as these two men appear on the surface, Sherlock Holmes is like Oscar Diggs, the Wizard of Oz, whose existence was made known to the world in L. Frank Baum's book *The Wonderful Wizard of Oz* in 1900.

Born on opposite sides of the Atlantic Ocean, they are contemporaries, products of the latter half of the nineteenth century. Neither man ever specifies his exact age, but there are clues scattered throughout their respective narratives. The Wizard tells Dorothy, "I was a young man when the balloon brought me [to Oz], and I am a very old man now." While he might have considered himself old by the time Dorothy discovered him, he was probably no more than about fifty. He states that he was born in Omaha, a city that was only officially recognized as such in 1854. Holmes, too, is cagey about his age, referring to himself as "middle-aged" in two separate stories. If we accept the oft-suggested year of Holmes's birth—1854, the same as that of Omaha's incorporation—he would have been approaching age fifty at the close of the century.

The Wizard is secretive about his past, sharing that he made his living performing sleight-of-hand magic and ventriloquism, but not revealing even his full name until the fourth book of the series. Holmes is equally reticent with details about his family life; it is not until several years into their acquaintance that Watson learns Holmes has a brother.

Alone, stranded in an unknown land, the Wizard finds that he has knowledge and skills those around him do not understand. His hot-air balloon is thoroughly unfamiliar technology to the inhabitants of Oz. The ability to fly must come from some kind of magic, so the man in the balloon must be a sorcerer. With no apparent way to get back home, he opts to let the assumption go uncorrected and uses the skills in stagecraft that he has developed over his years with the circus to make a pleasant, if lonely, life for himself.

Sometime before meeting Watson, Holmes lived on his own in rooms in Montague Street, whiling away his hours of "too abundant leisure time" at the British Museum, pursuing an eclectic course of scientific study and solving the occasional mystery. In those early days, he was figuring out how to support himself with what Reginald Musgrave calls "those powers with which you used to amaze us."

His "powers" of observation are not magical or superhuman, though they strike a number of others that way. Mrs. Ferguson of "The Sussex Vampire" says that he "seems to have powers of magic," and Mary Holder in "The Beryl Coronet" says, "Why, you are like a magician." Such comments are not always complimentary. When Stanley Hopkins finds the silver "stolen" from the Abbey Grange exactly where Holmes suggests he look, the frustrated Inspector says, "I believe that you are a wizard, Mr. Holmes. I really do sometimes think that you have powers that are not human." More often, though, the reaction is simple astonishment, as it is for James Dodd, who remains impressed after Holmes explains his chain of reasoning:

"You see everything."
"I see no more than you, but I have trained myself to notice what I see." ("The Blanched Soldier")

Holmes has spent years honing a skill that others let go undeveloped. And, in truth, he is a bit of a showman, well aware that opening his conversation with Dodd with the conclusions drawn from his observations is a way to impress.

The Wizard also knows how to impress an audience with a projected image. Literally so, in some cases: he presents himself as "a great Head" to Dorothy, "a lovely Lady" to the Scarecrow, a "terrible Beast" to the Tin Woodman, and "a Ball of Fire" to the Cowardly Lion, then confronts them all as a disembodied voice in an apparently empty room. It is only when Toto knocks over the screen shielding the man that the illusion is shattered, and the Wizard admits, "I have been making believe."

"Making believe!" cried Dorothy. "Are you not a Great Wizard?"

"Hush, my dear," he said. "Don't speak so loud, or you will be overheard—and I should be ruined. I'm supposed to be a Great Wizard."

"And aren't you?" she asked.

"Not a bit of it, my dear; I'm just a common man."

"You're more than that," said the Scarecrow, in a grieved tone; "you're a humbug."

"Exactly so!" declared the little man, rubbing his hands together as if it pleased him. "I am a humbug."

At heart kind and well-meaning, the Wizard is all too aware that his magic isn't magic at all. And, as feared, once his "humbuggery" is discovered and he reveals how the tricks were done, his former audience is disappointed to discover that he is only a man, after all.

Holmes recognizes his own flair for the theatrical when he says in *The Valley of Fear*, "Some touch of the artist wells up within me, and calls insistently for a well-staged performance." Holmes is apt to don a disguise or perform a little sleight of hand in the course of solving a case, slipping the Mazarin stone into Lord Cantlemere's coat pocket for instance, or presenting Percy Phelps with his missing naval treaty on a covered breakfast dish. Watson makes the comparison explicit when Holmes stages a scene to force Jonas Oldacre out of his hiding place: "Holmes stood before us with an air of a conjurer who is performing a trick." Now and then, Holmes perhaps takes things a bit too far, as when in "The Empty House" he casts off his disguise in an "unnecessarily dramatic appearance" that causes poor Watson to faint.

Upon the entirely different dramatic (re-)appearance of a missing letter in a dispatch-box, Lord Bellinger exclaims, "Mr Holmes, you are a wizard, a sorcerer!" Holmes is nothing of the sort, and this is no more real magic than the Wizard's sideshow trick of making one small white piglet turn into nine tiny white piglets. Holmes could probably recognize, if not quite empathize with, the Wizard's concern that "people would soon discover I am not a Wizard, and then they would be vexed with me for having deceived them."

Holmes might not use his talents to deliberately deceive others for his own gain, but he enjoys the admiration he receives. Early on, Holmes tells Watson, "You know a conjurer gets no credit once he has explained his trick; and if I show you too much of my method of working, you will come to the conclusion that I am a very ordinary individual after all." Later, Watson is amazed by Holmes's observation that Watson has recently recovered from a summer cold, until Holmes explains his thought process: an analysis of the scorch marks on the soles of Watson's new slippers. Holmes's chagrin is evident: "'I am afraid that I rather give myself away when I explain,' said he. 'Results without causes are much more impressive.'"

Some of those who seek out both Holmes and the Wizard are desperate for results, however attained. "How can I help being a humbug," the

Wizard asks in a moment of introspection, "when all these people make me do things that everybody knows can't be done?" In their separate interviews with the Wizard, the Scarecrow says that "no one else can help me," the Woodman claims that "you alone can grant my request," and the Lion claims that among "all Wizards you are the greatest, and alone have power to grant my request." Dorothy braves the dangers on the way to the Emerald City because "only the Great Oz could help her get to Kansas again."

Hoping to solve a problem with speed and discretion, Hilton Soames pleads with Holmes as "the one man in the world who can help me." John Openshaw warns Holmes that his case "is no ordinary one," and Holmes replies, "None of those which come to me are. I am the last court of appeal." Faced with the mysterious deaths of the Tregennis siblings, Mr. Roundhay declares, "We can only regard it as a special Providence that you should chance to be here at the time, for in all England you are the one man we need." Holmes, like the Wizard, is a man to whom people come to ask the impossible.

With a bit of wordplay and a dash of stage magic, the Wizard is able to grant the impossible wishes of the Scarecrow, the Tin Woodman, and the Cowardly Lion. When it comes to getting Dorothy home to Kansas, though, his good intentions fail him. He loses control of the ropes holding the balloon back from launch, and he can do nothing but wave goodbye as the balloon carries him away from Oz without her. Holmes, despite his reputation, makes the occasional blunder as well, sometimes with devastating consequences.

Stepping outside of the stories, Holmes and the Wizard are also similar on an extra-textual level, each standing out as something new in literature upon his earliest appearances. While there were a few detectives in fiction, a recurring character featuring in a series of stand-alone short stories was different, and Holmes was immediately popular with the readers of the *Strand* magazine. In writing *The Wonderful Wizard of Oz*, Baum set out to create "a modernized fairy tale, in which the wonderment and joy are retained and the heart-aches and nightmares are left out." Stories for children with magical creatures and strange lands already existed, of course, but Dorothy's tale was different, and it was beloved by children from the start.

Both Holmes and the Wizard, once released into the world, refused to disappear. Baum sent the Wizard off in his balloon from the Emerald City in that very first book with the words, "And that was the last any of them ever saw of Oz, the Wonderful Wizard, though he may have reached Omaha safely, and be there now, for all we know." Doyle sent Holmes over the Reichenbach Falls with Moriarty in "The Final Problem":

> An examination by experts leaves little doubt that a personal contest between the two men ended, as it could hardly fail to end in such a situation, in their reeling over, locked in each other's arms. Any attempt at recovering the bodies was absolutely

hopeless, and there, deep down in that dreadful cauldron of swirling water and seething foam, will lie for all time the most dangerous criminal and the foremost champion of the law of their generation.

Yet, despite these efforts, neither the Wizard nor Holmes could be disposed of so easily. The "humbug wizard" and the "scientific detective" appeared again and again in new adventures, and they continue to live in the popular imagination to this day.

Beth L. Gallego (Los Angeles, California) is current "Boy in Buttons" (leader) of the John H Watson Society, an open and inclusive worldwide online Sherlockian society. She is a member of the Curious Collectors of Baker Street and the Sub-librarians Scion, and she talks about yarn, tea, and Sherlock Holmes (not necessarily in that order) at thistangledskein. com.

CHARACTERS OF LITERATURE

I found my attention wander so continually
from the fiction to the fact.

"The Boscombe Valley Mystery"

IF SHERLOCK HOLMES
WAS IN SERVICE

Reginald Jeeves

Lee Eric Shackleford

You're walking down the street, minding your own business, when someone you know rushes up to you. "Help me," this acquaintance pants. "I'm trying to think of the name of an iconic English figure, a colossal genius who solves other people's problems. Tall, dark, poised—people come to him in their greatest hour of need—you know who I mean!"

You smile your tolerant Sherlockian smile. "You're thinking of the great consulting detective—" you begin, but this person stops you with a dismissive gesture.

"No, no, this one's a *butler*."

And you suppress a wince.

"He is not a butler. That is a mistake frequently made in America. He is a *valet*, a gentleman's personal gentleman, and his name is Jeeves."

"Jeeves!" this person cries out triumphantly, as if they had done all the work themselves. And off they cheerfully bound, with not so much as a by-your-leave. You continue on your journey, now pondering the similarities between these two cerebral titans.

You begin with the superficial: for example, that Holmes and Jeeves are both known to the world thanks to eager chroniclers who share their adventures: respectively, Dr. John H. Watson and Bertram Wilberforce "Bertie" Wooster. You further muse that Holmes and Jeeves are alike in that they are almost exclusively referred to by their last names alone. You recall being surprised by the moment in "The Greek Interpreter" when Mycroft Holmes calls his brother "Sherlock." Then you smile in recollection of the equivalent moment in *Much Obliged, Jeeves* when the disgraced valet Bingley cheekily greets Jeeves as "Reggie," because you had shared narrator Bertie's feelings at that moment: "I froze in my chair, stunned by the revelation that Jeeves's first name was Reginald. It had never occurred to me before that he *had* a first name."

Holmes and Jeeves both quote freely from books written in other tongues, you recall, and both are capable of quickly winning the hearts of manor-house cooks and scullery maids. But are those the only other similarities, you wonder? Surely not.

You think of the physical images of the two men, and you recall that Holmes and Jeeves are both described by their chroniclers as habitually stoic, even statue-like. In "The Naval Treaty," for instance, Watson describes Holmes as displaying "the utter immobility of countenance of a red Indian." And again you smile as you recall Bertie's less flattering description in *Jeeves and the Feudal Spirit* of Jeeves standing respectfully apart from a conversation and looking "like a stuffed frog."

As a professional valet, Jeeves is of course fastidious in his attention to the personal appearance of a proper gentleman. And, you remember, so is Sherlock Holmes. You recall how, in *The Hound of the Baskervilles*, Watson marvels that even though Holmes was camping on the moors, he "had contrived, with that catlike love of personal cleanliness which was one of his characteristics, that his chin should be as smooth and his linen as perfect as if he were in Baker Street." You equate this with the often-quoted exchange in "Jeeves and the Impending Doom," where a distraught Bertie Wooster wails, as Jeeves attempts to properly tighten his master's bow tie, "What do ties matter, Jeeves, at a time like this?" To which Jeeves calmly replies, "There is no time, sir, at which ties do not matter."

Now that you consider the matter fully, you realize you are overlooking the obvious. The most important similarity between Holmes and Jeeves is that they are courts of last appeal, the person sought out when all other methods have failed. Time and again hand-wringing clients drop into the chair at Baker Street and pour out their troubles to Sherlock Holmes and are soon gratified by his solution to their problem. And when Bertie Wooster gets himself into trouble (this happens with alarming frequency), sooner or later the shimmering intellect of Jeeves will offer a way out.

In fact, the brilliant solutions offered by Jeeves are, you say to yourself, suggestive of a Sherlock Holmes who had chosen a life in service.

So how else are they similar? You recall that they are both men of physical reserve but capable of violence when necessary. You think for a sad instant of Holmes at Reichenbach (forgetting somehow that it turned out all right after all), but counter it with the happy thought of Jeeves in "The Inferiority Complex of Old Sippy," sending Sippy into unconsciousness (for his own good) with one well-placed stroke of a golf club. You smile as you consider that those two adventures rid the world of Professor Moriarty and a lurid Chinese vase.

Then the truth flashes before your eyes like St. Elmo's Fire. Holmes and Jeeves are capable of violence, yes, but the truest evidence of their common genius is in *manipulating affairs at a distance*. No debasing physical contact is necessary. While men of lesser intellect might dirty their own hands while preventing someone from upsetting a well-laid plan, Holmes and Jeeves will instead, for example, arrange for that person to be marooned in the proverbial Middle of Nowhere.

Your favorite example of the "stranding tactic" for Holmes is in "The Retired Colourman," in which Holmes sends Watson off on the train to the sleepy village of Little Purlington in the company of the quarrelsome Mr. Josiah Amberley. Holmes knows, but does not tell Watson, that by the time they learn their trip has been pointless, the last train of the day will be long gone. So they are forced to spend the night in what Watson calls "the most primitive village in England." All of this, of course, to give Holmes time to make a thorough search of Amberley's house and to prove Amberley to be the perpetrator of the murders he himself called on Holmes to investigate.

And immediately the equivalent "stranding tactic" for Jeeves leaps to your memory. In "Jeeves and the Old School Chum," Jeeves is tasked with restoring the domestic tranquility of the Bingo Little household, threatened by the arrival of Mrs. Little's childhood friend Laura Pyke, who is now an annoying diet-fanatic. Jeeves accompanies the family and friends to the Lakenham races, many miles from the Little home, and deliberately leaves the group's picnic basket behind. When this apparent oversight is revealed, the female members of the party at first claim they can easily do without food for hours. But then, on their return trip, their car runs out of petrol (Jeeves at work again) on a long and lonely road, making it impossible for the ladies to be home in time for tea. The result: the tempers of the two young women burst into full fury, bringing a definite end to the reign of terror perpetrated by the woman Bingo calls "the Pyke."

This new line of thought has intrigued you more deeply than you had expected. Holmes and Jeeves, you now realize, are indeed remarkably similar. In fact, had they been born at the same time, they could easily have changed places, like the heroes of a Gilbert and Sullivan operetta. But no, they are denizens of different eras; if for Holmes it is always 1895, then for Jeeves it is always 1925. (And as always, you marvel that Jeeves could have remained so resolutely in the Jazz Age throughout the stories presented by P.G. Wodehouse, starting in 1915 and continuing all the way to 1974.) So for Jeeves to be at the height of his powers in the 1920s, he would have to have been born fully thirty years after Holmes. So much for their being brothers.

But, the thought strikes you, they could be father and son. This realization is so powerful it literally stops you in your tracks, creating an obstacle for your fellow pedestrians. ("Tourist!" someone behind you snarls.)

No. You shake your head, dismissing the *père et fils* idea and continuing on your way. "Absurd," you mutter. "Nonsense."

But as you arrive at your destination (a bookstore, of course, but you knew that) you wonder why this possibility has not been the subject of more frequent speculation. Has not practically everyone else been proposed as a son, daughter, or other descendant of Sherlock Holmes?

You dismiss the notion as ridiculous. But before abandoning it forever, you do consider the undeniable truth: if Sherlock Holmes were to have a son, surely that child would have grown up to be that brilliant, stoic, endlessly resourceful solver-of-insoluble-puzzles Reginald Jeeves.

Lee Eric Shackleford (Hickory, North Carolina) teaches for the University of Alabama at Birmingham and is the author of the play *Holmes & Watson*, the creator of Herlock (www.herlock.us), and the artist behind countless Sherlockian cartoons. Once upon a time, he helped Cmdr. Data play Sherlock Holmes on *Star Trek: The Next Generation*.

THERE WAS METHOD
IN HIS MADNESS

Hamlet, Prince of Denmark

Wendy Heyman-Marsaw

So many accomplished actors have portrayed both Sherlock Holmes and Shakespeare's Hamlet: John Barrymore, Christopher Plummer, Ian Richardson, Nicol Williamson, Benedict Cumberbatch, John Gielgud, David Warner, Derek Jacobi, Ian McKellen, Orson Welles, Peter O'Toole, Cedric Hardwicke, Jeremy Brett, Basil Rathbone. All of these actors had a commanding presence and enjoyed some critical success in playing both parts, which suggests that there must be some significant similarities between the two characters.

But this rather superficial commonality goes much deeper. Although Dr. Watson initially describes Holmes's literary skill as "Nil", Holmes quotes the Bard 14 times in his various cases. A Sherlockian scholar is known to have stated that the 56 stories and four novels that make up the Sherlockian Canon are filled with more wisdom and quotable lines than any other collected works aside from the Bible and the canon of, yes, William Shakespeare. Thus I attempt here to explore how Hamlet and Sherlock Holmes share significant similarities in behaviours, thought processes, and speech.

Though written about 1600 (and based on earlier sources), a time that significantly predates the concept of the formal detective story, "Hamlet" is first and foremost a detective case describing a murder investigation conducted by Hamlet, Prince of Denmark, into the death of his father, the late King, also apparently named Hamlet. Holmes and Hamlet exhibit similar character traits: they are men alienated from common society, ratiocinative, perceived by some as "mad" in their behaviours at times, with depressive symptoms and reliant on the devoted friendship of a lone man. They also share a sense of purpose, justice, and duty which directs their efforts. Now let us look more deeply.

When we meet Hamlet he is in a state of deep mourning over the untimely death of his father. Hamlet laments, "How weary, stale, flat, and unprofitable seem to me all the uses of this world." Sherlock

Holmes—who when lacking a case to challenge his faculties, would lapse into morose moods and the comfort of a seven-per-cent solution of cocaine—similarly observes: "But is not all life pathetic and futile? We reach. We grasp. And what is left in our hands at the end? A shadow. Or worse than a shadow—misery" ("The Retired Colourman"). Clearly both Hamlet and Holmes suffer from severe bouts of depression.

Hamlet has but one true friend to whom he can confide his feelings—Horatio. Similarly, Holmes's only deep and enduring friendship is with Dr. John H. Watson. Horatio and Watson do their utmost to demonstrate their support and loyalty and share a deep concern for their respective friends' welfare. When Horatio makes a self-deprecating comment about his own "truant disposition", Hamlet will not allow his friend to disparage himself in this way. It is very evident that Sherlock Holmes would not tolerate such self-criticism from his friend Watson, either. The devotion of both pairs of friends is strikingly poignant. After the death of Hamlet, Horatio says "Now cracks a noble heart. Good night sweet prince, and flights of angels sing thee to thy rest." An equally shattered Watson, upon the assumed death of Holmes at Reichenbach Falls, refers to Holmes as "the best and the wisest man whom I have ever known."

The play begins when Hamlet is confronted by the ghost of his father (whom Horatio and two officers also see). The late monarch states that he was murdered by his brother, Claudius. Hamlet must have some doubt regarding the ghost's allegations because he decides to stage a play whereby he can observe for himself whether his uncle exhibits self-incriminating reactions. Whilst Holmes's view on the subject of apparitions is more pointed—"The world is big enough for us. No ghosts need apply"—he also comments that "if the matter is beyond humanity it is certainly beyond me" ("The Devil's Foot"). As for gaining insight into an allegation, Holmes makes himself very clear: "It is a capital mistake to theorize in advance of the facts." He also famously states that when one gathers sufficient data, "once you have eliminated the impossible, whatever remains, however improbable, must be the truth". Therefore, what some view as inaction by Hamlet can be argued to be valid ratiocination. Hamlet's use of a play to be an instrument to draw out the truth, would also be viewed as a positive by Holmes: "My old friend will tell you… that I can never resist a dramatic situation…. Watson insists that I am a dramatist in real life. Some touch of artist wells up in me and calls insistently for a well-staged performance" ("The Mazarin Stone", *The Valley of Fear*). Hamlet's use of the drama proves to be an invaluable tool for ascertaining the truth of the ghost's allegations. Further, Hamlet swears to his father that he will wipe all "trivial" interest and pursue his father's commandment and that "it alone shall live within the book and volume of his brain." This is totally comparable to Holmes's approach to problem-solving and his references to his brain "attic".

The tension within Hamlet continues to build, and he experiences great difficulty coping with the status quo in court. At one point he asks

Guildenstern, one of the courtiers, "Do you think I am easier to be played upon than a pipe? Call me what instrument you will... you cannot play upon me." Holmes, too, has no tolerance for people who try to manipulate him.

Hamlet simulates madness to enable him to draw out the truth behind the machinations and murderous acts of his uncle—now stepfather—King Claudius, and the king's incestuous or adulterous affair with his mother, Queen Gertrude. He also uses this assumed madness to extricate himself from a previous romantic understanding with the Lord Chamberlain Polonius's daughter, Ophelia, which has become untenable. Again Holmes demonstrates a parallel with Hamlet: "Love is an emotional thing, and whatever is emotional is opposed to that true cold reason which I place above all things." Polonius also notes "Though this be madness, yet there is method in it," an expression so applicable to Holmes that it is actually echoed in "The Reigate Squires" by Inspector Forrester: "Some folk might say there was madness in his method."

The famous "To be or not to be" soliloquy is judged by some to be evidence of Hamlet's indecisiveness and inactivity. However, I contend that he is turning the matter over in his head, much as Holmes says, "I am never precipitate in my actions" ("Charles Augustus Milverton"). Indeed, Hamlet is challenged by problems which could easily immobilize Holmes for hours on end as he seeks a way to come to terms with the facts of a case.

Hamlet arrives at a firm resolution—to seek revenge for his father's murder—but finds that his choice is to kill or be killed when exile is forced upon him by Claudius. This is reminiscent of the way Holmes springs into action when the game is afoot. Hamlet turns the tables on Rosencrantz and Guildenstern, who are prepared to have him killed, and has them disposed of first. The action heats up: Laertes returns to avenge his father's death and his sister Ophelia's suicide. He challenges Hamlet to a duel and uses a poisoned tip on his sword. He cuts and poisons Hamlet, but Hamlet picks up the weapon and kills Laertes. Holmes, it must be remembered, is an expert swordsman too.

The final bloodbath occurs when the queen drinks from the poisoned cup Hamlet intended for the king. Hamlet runs the king through with the toxic sword and forces him to imbibe from the tainted cup as well. It is possible to imagine Hamlet, say, as Holmes does, that "I think there are certain crimes which the law cannot touch, and which therefore... justify private revenge.... Violence does, in truth, recoil upon the violent, and the schemer falls into the pit which he digs for another" ("Charles Augustus Milverton", "The Second Stain").

Wendy Heyman-Marsaw (Dartmouth, Nova Scotia) is the author of *Memoirs from Mrs. Hudson's Kitchen,* a member of the Spence Munros (Halifax), a Master Bootmaker in the Bootmakers of Toronto, and a member of the Sherlock Holmes Society of London. Her Mrs. Hudson website and blog are at www.mrshudsonskitchen.com.

THE TRUTH, THE WHOLE TRUTH, AND NOTHING BUT THE TRUTH

Fitzwilliam Darcy

Mary Miller

Two of the most iconic male characters in 19th century literature are known for the truths that surround them. The first truth concerns Mr. Fitzwilliam Darcy, expressed in the first sentence of Jane Austen's 1813 novel *Pride and Prejudice*: "It is a truth universally acknowledged, that a single man in possession of a good fortune, must be in want of a wife." The second truth is expressed by Mr. Sherlock Holmes: "How often have I said to you that when you have eliminated the impossible, whatever remains, however improbable, must be the truth?"

Now let's take a closer look to see just how, at first blush, these two characters are more alike than one might think.

They are both men of the 19th century, when the term "gentleman" meant a certain level of decorum, appearance, and responsibility. Their education was most likely taken at one of the two main universities of the day, Oxford or Cambridge. They both have been portrayed in appearance as tall, dark-haired, lean, with the air and deportment of the aristocracy.

But where they are more alike than most might realize is in the level of responsibility they both display. While Darcy appears brooding and condescending through a good portion of the novel, we come to realize that he is actually a caring and true gentleman when wrongs need to be righted. Holmes is portrayed similarly throughout the Canon but with many more examples of his caring and doing the right thing.

They both are the saviors of young women in need, even when some of the young women didn't either realize they needed to be saved or truly appreciate it.

In Darcy's corner we have his actions in saving his younger sister Georgiana from the grips of Mr. Wickham, when a planned elopement to Gretna Green was discovered. But his more important rescue is saving Lydia Bennett, who had also fallen under the spell of Mr. Wickham. Darcy makes sure Wickham marries Lydia and settles Wickham's debts, at considerable cost to himself. Darcy does all this not for Lydia's sake (she is clueless about what she has done or how it affects her family) but for Elizabeth, whom he loves even after she refused his first offer of marriage.

The number of young women for whom Holmes comes to the rescue is much longer, but let us just focus on three Violets and one Helen. Both Violet Hunter and Violet Smith are young women of strong character who find themselves in need of advice and ultimately protection by Holmes. They both find themselves in mortal danger from evil men who want to use them for their own purposes and advancement—not unlike George Wickham. Helen Stoner is another strong young woman who has suffered great loss and humiliation and yet knew enough, when the situation presented itself, to seek the counsel of Holmes. However, not unlike Lydia Bennett, a third Violet, Miss de Merville, does not seek help from Holmes. Her Wickham comes in the form of Baron Gruner, an alleged abuser and killer of women. Holmes puts himself in grave danger helping her. One would hope that this Violet realized at the end that she owes a debt of gratitude to Holmes, unlike Lydia Bennett, who never realized how Darcy saved her.

On the subject of women, we can't proceed any further without discussing The Women of Darcy and Holmes. The love story of Fitzwilliam Darcy and Elizabeth Bennett has continued to be read and studied around the world for the past 200 years. Their journey from disdain of each other to understanding and eventually to true love has become the baseline of romance novels to this day.

The love story involving Sherlock Holmes is much more complex. The only woman in the Canon that Holmes has ever given proper respect and regard to is the well-known adventuress, Irene Adler. Darcy and Elizabeth's courtship goes on for months with each learning about the other and, more importantly, about themselves. Holmes and Irene were only together for a few days. And Holmes was the one who learned about Irene as he observed those around her. The two times they interacted with each other, Holmes was disguised as a groom and a clergyman. Irene only knew of Holmes by reputation, not by appearance. Yet at the end when Irene bested him and left with her husband, Holmes could not help but admire and, perhaps, love a woman as clever as him.

As gentlemen of the 19th century, Darcy and Holmes both respect the social order of things. They understand the written and unwritten rules of rank and privilege. However, neither of them will tolerate those of rank and privilege abusing their positions, especially when it affects those they love and care about. In Darcy's case, the crisis is his aunt Lady Catherine De Bourgh's abuse toward Elizabeth in the famous scene where she demands that Elizabeth pledge never to enter into an engagement with her nephew. It embarrasses him as a gentleman to have a close relative of rank who is so crass and rude. Similarly, Holmes's involvement with the King of Bohemia as the King tried to hide his affair with Irene made Holmes realize the honor of Kings is laughable.

In their domestic lives, Darcy and Holmes are blessed with two of the most famous housekeepers of their century. Darcy's Mrs. Reynolds oversees the running of Pemberley and serves as a surrogate mother to both Darcy and his younger sister Georgiana. When Elizabeth visits Pemberley with her aunt and uncle Gardiner, she hears from Mrs. Reynolds how caring and considerate Darcy is to his staff and tenants. This makes Elizabeth realize, as she learns more about Darcy, that she has continued to misjudge him. Holmes's housekeeper is the long-suffering Mrs. Hudson. She tolerates his scientific experiments and visitors at all hours of the day and night. She serves as a doting mother, especially when Holmes abuses his body as he tries to solve cases and neglects himself.

Up to now, we have discussed mainly women and their relationships with Darcy and Holmes, but let us not forget their wingmen. Mr. Darcy's boon companion is one Charles Bingley. Darcy sees himself as the older and wiser one in the relationship and tries to protect Bingley from bad influences and those he presumes to be designing women. Bingley ultimately stands up for himself and declares his love to Jane Bennett. As both Darcy and Bingley marry Bennett sisters, their friendship grows stronger as brothers-in-law.

Sherlock Holmes has one of the most famous and long-lasting friends in literature in Dr. John H Watson. The relationship of these two men develops as they solve mysteries and crimes together even as Watson marries and sets up his medical practice. They start out as men needing a roommate to make ends meet. They evolve into a friendship that many feel goes beyond a pair of crime fighters to an example of two men who truly care, respect, and love each other until their dying days. They may be the first example of the modern-day "bromance."

A final example of how Darcy and Holmes are alike is their continued popularity in today's pop culture. Thanks to movies and television, Darcy and Holmes live on. While their written stories have been around since the 19th century, the ability to see their stories come to life has introduced many to these characters that the written word cannot.

For some actors, portraying either Darcy or Holmes has become the defining achievement of their acting careers. When you hear the name Colin Firth, the picture of a wet Mr. Darcy in a clinging white shirt comes to mind (even though this scene is not actually in *Pride and Prejudice*). While many actors have portrayed Sherlock Holmes, these three are probably the most famous in the modern era—Basil Rathbone, Jeremy Brett, and Benedict Cumberbatch. Each has brought a unique perspective to Holmes: Rathbone, the wartime Holmes; Brett, the Victorian Holmes; and Cumberbatch, the 21st-century Holmes.

In conclusion, the evidence shows that Mr. Fitzwilliam Darcy of Pemberley has much in common with Mr. Sherlock Holmes of Baker Street—and that's the truth.

Mary Miller (Indianapolis, Indiana) is a lifetime member of the Jane Austen Society of North America and serves as its Indiana Regional Co-ordinator. She is also a member of the Illustrious Clients of Indianapolis and the Amateur Mendicant Society of Detroit.

BETWIXT TWO THINGS

Huckleberry Finn

Rob Nunn

Arthur Conan Doyle was one of the most popular British authors of his day, and his contemporary, Mark Twain, held the same distinction in the United States over roughly the same time period. Doyle downplayed his most popular character, Sherlock Holmes, in favor of what he termed more serious works, while Twain, on the other hand, famously said, "High and fine literature is wine, and mine is only water; but everybody likes water."

Different though these two authors may be, they are almost always remembered first and foremost for a single character. Doyle will forever be remembered as the creator of Sherlock Holmes, and Twain will always be linked to Huckleberry Finn. While both of these characters' tales begin with "The Adventures of..." and feature a character named Watson who chafes at the titular character's bohemian lifestyle, Huck Finn's great adventure down the Mississippi River has important parallels to the cases of Sherlock Holmes—more than one might first imagine.

Right off the bat, Huck Finn is quick to recap his adventures with Tom Sawyer in a previous book with the famous line, "You don't know about me, without you have read a book by the name of *The Adventures of Tom Sawyer*." Dr. Watson frequently begins his stories by referencing Holmes's other cases, both published and unpublished.

The Adventures of Huckleberry Finn, published in 1884, is mostly remembered for its tale of a boy traveling down the river, and we often forget that the story starts off with a local tale, a structure very similar to the early chapters of *The Valley of Fear* and *The Sign of Four*. We see Huck irritated with his position in polite society, chafing at the Widow Douglas's prayers before meals and Miss Watson's spelling lessons, reminiscent of Holmes's views on cultural invitations: "This looks like one of those unwelcome social summonses which call upon a man either to be bored or to lie."

Even though Huck Finn's bare feet and corncob pipe will never be mistaken for Holmes's evening wear and black clay pipe, clear similarities can be found in Huckleberry's dealings with his own Professor

Moriarty: his father. Pap confronts Huck in his bedroom one night, just as Moriarty met with Holmes in Baker Street. Pap hounds Huck through the next few chapters, similar to the ways that Moriarty's henchmen followed Holmes in "The Final Problem." Another parallel comes from Huck's description of Pap: "There warn't no color in his face, where his face showed; it was white; not like another man's white, but a white to make a body sick, a white to make a body's flesh crawl—a tree-toad white, a fish-belly white." Anyone who has recently read "The Blanched Soldier" will immediately recognize that phrase from when Dodd described the pallor of Godfrey Emsworth. "His face was—how shall I describe it?—it was of a fish-belly whiteness."

But the biggest similarity between Pap's and Moriarty's stories happens when Huck fakes his own death to escape his tormenting father, a strategy very reminiscent of Holmes's battle with Professor Moriarty at the Reichenbach Falls. Both characters led the world to believe that they had met their ends in a watery grave. Even though both heroes reemerge, they are no longer bothered by their nemeses, as both Pap and Moriarty have died off-page.

And once Huck is away from Pap, the meat of his story begins. Huck meets up with Jim, Miss Watson's runaway slave, as they are hiding out on Jackson Island. Just like everyone else from town, Jim believes Huck Finn to be dead. And when Huck shows up, Jim has a hard time believing what he sees, just as Watson has a hard time with the fact that Holmes is actually alive when he returns in "The Empty House." Throughout the Canon, Holmes is often described as having a mischievous smile or a mischievous twinkle in his eye, and the reader can imagine the same look on Huck's face as he repeatedly plays tricks on Jim throughout the early part of their partnership. One such trick results in Jim being bitten and poisoned by a snake, similar to how Holmes put Watson at risk during their vigil at Stoke Moran.

As Huck and Jim leave Jackson Island to begin their new lives, their raft becomes a floating version of 221B Baker Street. Fog swirls around their traveling home base while adventures seek them out. Slave-hunters, dangerous riverboats, and treacherous thieves are drawn into Huck and Jim's lives like clients and Scotland Yard detectives to Holmes and Watson's doorstep. Huck says, "What you want, above all things, on a raft, is for everybody to be satisfied, and feel right and kind towards the others." This sentiment could just as easily apply to Holmes and Watson's abode on Baker Street.

While Huck and Jim travel, they find themselves needing information, and Huck is quick to take on different personas to learn what he needs, even posing as a young girl at one point. Any fan of the Great Detective will quickly see the parallels between Huck's disguises and Holmes's Captain Basil, drunken-looking groom, and elderly woman. Holmes is also adept at playing foolish to learn information, as he does in "The Reigate Squires" or *The Sign of Four*, a skill that Huckleberry Finn uses to a masterful degree.

Huck and Jim later land on a grounded steamboat, come across a gang of thieves, and overhear two of the thieves talking about killing the third. No matter what country our heroes may be in, America or England, you can always count on thieves turning on one another. Holmes's own run-ins with back-stabbers occur in "The Boscombe Valley Mystery," "The Musgrave Ritual," "The Crooked Man," "The Resident Patient," and "The Solitary Cyclist."

Later on, Huck and Jim find themselves separated in the fog of the river at night. Once they are reunited, Huck's impish habit of practical joking leads him to convince Jim that he dreamed up the whole event. Jim falls for Huck's trick for a while, but soon figures out that it really did happen. Jim gets upset with Huck's behavior, causing Huck to apologize profusely to Jim, as we see Holmes do to Watson in "The Devil's Foot" and "The Empty House," although those were much more serious matters.

In Twain's manuscript of *The Adventures of Huckleberry Finn*, he had originally included a chapter describing the waters of two rivers mixing and the similar blend that made up life on the river. When Twain set the manuscript for *Huckleberry Finn* off to the side for a time, he used this piece of writing as a chapter in another project, *Life on the Mississippi*. He had intended to insert this chapter back into *Huckleberry Finn*, and some versions of the book have included it, causing the casual reader some confusion, just as does Holmes's mind-reading episode when it appears in both "The Cardboard Box" and "The Resident Patient."

As Huck and Jim continue down the Mississippi, Huck finds himself in the middle of a long-running feud between two families. Just as in "The Boscombe Valley Mystery," the two children of warring families have fallen in love unbeknownst to their fathers. In both stories the young lovebirds end up together, although horrific violence falls upon the warring families in each tale.

Huck escapes the feud, and he and Jim are soon back on their trip. Just as in "The Three Students" and "The Reigate Squires," our heroes' relaxing travels can't last long. Huck and Jim are soon saddled with two on-the-run grifters, the so-called duke and king. These two con men attempt to turn quick scores at each town they land. Their get-rich-quick schemes are very similar to those of Roaring Jack Woodley, Killer Evans, and James Windibank, and at one stop they deploy a religious scam that would make Holy Peters proud. Once Huck has had his fill of their antics, he sets a trap with their latest victim, Mary Jane Wilks, to expose the frauds, rather like Holmes's ploys in "The Naval Treaty" or "The Norwood Builder." But Holmes's tricks work much better than Huck's do, Huck finding himself trapped with the king and the duke while handwriting is analyzed à la "The Reigate Squires."

Of course, Huck eventually escapes and makes his way back to Jim and the raft. After their adventures on the river, Huck and Jim find themselves in another exploit on the farm of Silas and Sally Phelps. Just as with the beginning experiences in the early chapters of the book, this episode isn't what first comes to mind when people remember their reading. In fact, it feels very similar to the second half of *A Study in Scarlet*, a story tacked onto another one that tangentially relates to the main narrative, yet feels very out of character with the rest of the story.

While Huck Finn is the epicenter of action in his story, Jim is a steady and reliable companion. Jim is left behind frequently during Huck's adventures, just as Watson is when Holmes is off collecting information for a case. But our two heroes always come back. Over the course of sixty stories, we see Holmes and Watson's friendship grow, and Huck and Jim's development is just as prominent in their own story. Many readers focus on Huck's growth as a friend towards Jim, but what often goes unmentioned is Jim's steadfastness throughout the story. Jim is Huck's protector and moral compass from the beginning of their journey and proves to be more intelligent than many people would give him credit for. The same thing could be said about John Watson.

Although details in the course of life for Sherlock Holmes and Huckleberry Finn have many parallels, loyalty may be the similarity that is most prominent. Once Huck admits to himself that he is friends with a slave, one can imagine Huck standing up for Jim the way Holmes does when the King of Bohemia tries to dismiss Watson: "It is both, or none." Huck is willing to earn eternal damnation for his loyalty to his friend and never looks back from that point on. Both Holmes and Huck have these feelings reciprocated. Although Jim and Watson use different words, Jim saying, "Jim won't ever forget you, Huck; you's de bes' fren' Jim's ever had; en you's de *only* fren' ole Jim's got now," is very reminiscent of Watson's words on Holmes: "whom I shall ever regard as the best and the wisest man whom I have ever known."

Rob Nunn (Edwardsville, Illinois) is the author of *The Criminal Mastermind of Baker Street* and blogs his thoughts on Sherlockiana at InterestingThoughElementary.blogspot.com. He is the head of The Parallel Case of St. Louis, and a member of the Noble Bachelors of St. Louis and The Harpooners of the Sea Unicorn.

ADVENTURE FOR ALL, AND ALL FOR ADVENTURES

Charles, Comte d'Artagnan

Karen Ellery

Reading a good story is like spending time with a good friend. Reading a good adventure story is like having an adventure with a friend. And reading a good adventure story that features good friends is like finding yourself invited to accompany your favorite people on the journey of a lifetime, whether it's crossing the city or crossing the channel. We read to spend time with our literary friends, and there are no finer friends than Holmes and Watson... or the Four Musketeers. And that is why I believe that Sherlock Holmes is like d'Artagnan.

I don't exactly mean Charles Ogier de Batz de Castelmore, Comte d'Artagnan (1611–1673), Musketeer, spy, governor, and adventurer. The historic Comte does have one important thing in common with Holmes: his adventures were so numerous and so legendary that they inspired writers to turn them into popular stories, to the extent that many people consider d'Artagnan himself to be fictional. It is not for the historical count but for his fictionalized persona, the fantastic fighter and faithful friend d'Artagnan of *The Three Musketeers* (1844), *Twenty Years After*, and *The Vicomte de Bragelonne*, that I wish to make my case and comparison to Holmes. There are too many parallels in their stories and too many friendly connections to be overlooked; so please join me as I look them over.

The process of fictionalization is perhaps the first common element. Almost everything we know (or think we know) about the character of Holmes comes to us through the medium of two writers: Dr. John H. Watson and Sir Arthur Conan Doyle. Almost everything we know about the character of d'Artagnan comes to us via French novelist Alexandre Dumas, *père*, who in turn took his material from an earlier writer, Gatien de Courtilz de Sandras, who wrote *Mémoires de Monsieur d'Artagnan* in 1700, based (perhaps loosely) on the life of the Comte d'Artagnan. Both characters were brought to the loving attention of the reading public in installments, stories told over time in the popular press. Holmes is closer to us in period and language, while d'Artagnan's stories face the hurdles of translation and a few extra centuries, but our appreciation for them both is timeless.

Many have told these stories and added to them over the years. The Holmes pastiches seem as numberless as the stars, and the d'Artagnan romances are not without their unofficial sequels. However, because of the adventurous nature of the tales, they are perhaps best known to the public through their dramatic adaptations. From plays to films to television, these characters are presented in a bewildering variety of periods and situations, with many actors appearing in both storylines. Christopher Lee, Charlton Heston, and Bill Paterson have all played characters in both Holmesian and Musketeerian productions, and Michael York, a fine actor who remains, to many, the quintessential personification of d'Artagnan, also played Sherlock Holmes (in the 2010 animation "Tom and Jerry Meet Sherlock Holmes"—thanks to Howard Ostrom for this tidbit). Yes, Sherlock Holmes *is* like d'Artagnan, who is like Michael York.

In their stories, both d'Artagnan and Holmes come to us as young men—brilliantly talented, iron in will and constitution, possessed of healthy egos, but still just starting to make their way in their chosen professions. Both are experiencing a want of funds, driving d'Artagnan to seek his fortune in Paris, and Holmes to seek a roommate for his lodgings in London. And so their adventures and their legendary friendships begin.

Dr. John H. Watson, Athos, Porthos, and Aramis are the best friends anyone could want. They are older than our two heroes, but less extraordinary: appreciative of their young friends' brilliance, yet possessing sterling qualities of their own. D'Artagnan earns the friendship of the Inseparables, the Three Musketeers: Athos, the soul of honor, the perfect French gentleman; Porthos, a fiercely loyal man of action, if less agile of brain; and Aramis, a romantic and a writer, with a wide experience with women. Holmes's companion Watson combines all of these qualities in his own person: gentleman, man of action, romantic, and chronicler. These men and their friendships humanize their extraordinary companions.

In fact, these friendships are as important to their stories, and to our continuing love of them, as the adventures themselves. Holmes is lost without his Boswell: he's the most perfect reasoning and observing machine that the world has seen, but before Watson, he was cold, relatively friendless, and subject to devastating enervation when bored. D'Artagnan, throughout his long story arc, often laments that he is at a loss when not supported by his friends. His fine sensibilities absorb and reflect the qualities of his friends, which ennoble, make him more ambitious, and ultimately more successful. When Watson abandons Holmes for a wife (or two, or three, or five), Holmes does not stop detecting, but we hear less about him; he becomes less of a presence. When Porthos leaves the service to marry, Aramis to become an abbé, and Athos to go back to his estate at Bragelonne, d'Artagnan remains a musketeer and soldier but never advances, never truly succeeds in his projects until he regains the company and support of his friends.

Ah, but when our friends are united, they bring us along on such adventures! With the help of his friends, d'Artagnan travels to England on two important adventures: the first to save the reputation of the Queen of France, Anne of Austria, wife to King Louis XIII (the "affair of the diamond studs"); and the second in an attempt to save the life of King Charles I of England (*Twenty Years After*). During the latter adventure, the Musketeers are made privy to the location of the English crown jewels, which are eventually restored to King Charles II as he fights to gain the throne. Obviously Charles doesn't tell them everything, because several centuries later, Holmes finds a few more pieces of the treasure when he solves the mystery of the Musgrave Ritual.

Holmes and Watson also cross the channel for adventure, albeit in the opposite direction. There is the tracking and arrest of Huret, the Boulevard assassin—an exploit which wins for Holmes an autograph letter of thanks from the French President and the Order of the Legion of Honour; also the investigation of Mme. Montpensier, which frees her from the charge of murder which hangs over her in connection with the death of her step-daughter, Mlle. Carère. If only Watson had had the time to tell us more about these Gallic escapades!

For a truly exciting adventure, you need a good villain, and our two groups of friends have two of the best. Holmes's arch-enemy is Professor James Moriarty, the Napoleon of crime. D'Artagnan, Athos, Porthos, and Aramis must contend against Cardinal Armand Jean du Plessis, 1st Duke of Richelieu and Fronsac, who is... well... the Cardinal of France. Both antagonists are masters of strategy who control far-flung networks of agents and spies. These agents provide further adventures: Col. Sebastian Moran tries to kill Holmes for revealing his card-sharping scheme and his murder of the Hon. Ronald Adair; the Comte de Rochefort (a.k.a. the Man of Meung) is responsible for, among other evils, the abduction of Mme. Constance Bonacieux, the love of d'Artagnan's life. No matter how powerful, brilliant, or fierce their antagonists, however, our heroes best them all.

In mentioning Constance, I open the door to romance. Watson writes of Holmes: "As a lover he would have placed himself in a false position. He never spoke of the softer passions, save with a gibe and a sneer." And while it is true that the young d'Artagnan is very much affected by his stronger passions (we hear of at least three of his mistresses), he really only has one romance: Constance, the wife of his landlord, abducted first for her role in assisting her Queen to meet with the Duke of Buckingham, and later out of revenge for d'Artagnan's interference with the Cardinal's plot. She is killed before d'Artagnan can rescue her, and their love is never consummated. Later in his stories, d'Artagnan himself gibes and sneers at romance and the mad motivation it provides to others. So while both our heroes may be figures of romance, neither man is a romantic.

All these adventures take place in times and societies in which men are the movers and shakers; however, both storylines do feature remarkable women. We learn of the haughty and lovely Violet de Merville; the haughty and lovely Anne of Austria; the fiery and vengeful Kitty Winter; and the fiery and adoring Kitty-the-soubrette (alas, we never learn her surname). Both storylines feature grateful Queens who reward our heroes with gems and graciousness. But there are two especially strong and memorable women who oppose our friends and feature so vividly in their adventures that they may be called adventuresses.

To Sherlock Holmes, Irene Adler is always *the* woman. She has a soul of steel, the face of the most beautiful of women, and *the mind of the most resolute of men*. Holmes approaches her disguised as an amiable and simple-minded Nonconformist clergyman and surprises her secret from her—the location of her romantic portrait with the King of Bohemia. When she realizes she has been found out, she decamps, leaving Holmes with nothing but a picture and the memory of being bested by a woman.

To d'Artagnan, the adventuress is always Milady, a.k.a. Milady de Winter, a.k.a. Milady Clarik, Countess of Sheffield, a.k.a. the Comtesse de la Fère, a.k.a. Charlotte Backson, a.k.a. Anne de Breuill. This woman of many aliases has an indomitable will and a face that men would (and do) die for. D'Artagnan approaches her disguised (by the shades of night) as the Comte des Wardes, and surprises her secret from her—the brand of a fleur-de-lis on her shoulder, showing her to be convicted as a prostitute. When she realizes she has been found out, she decamps, leaving d'Artagnan with nothing but a ring and the fear of a truly terrifying opponent. In the end Adler wins and Milady loses, but both are worthy antagonists, respected and remembered by our heroes and their friends as well as countless fascinated fans.

I could go on, but I'll merely note one more link between Holmes and d'Artagnan, and this one is tangible. When d'Artagnan saves Queen Anne, she presents him with a ring containing a magnificent diamond. He is later forced to sell the diamond to finance another adventure. The Queen discovers this and buys back the ring for herself. Twenty years later, during the conflict of the Fronde, she is pressed by her lover (possibly her secret husband) Cardinal Mazarin, to name the person who had saved her in earlier times. She names d'Artagnan and his friends, and gives Mazarin the famous diamond to give to them as a reward for serving her again. Mazarin, being a miser and inordinately fond of brilliants, teases d'Artagnan with a glimpse of the diamond, but then keeps it for himself. This diamond is never described beyond "very fine," but I believe I know it: a great yellow stone that becomes known by the name of the man who inveigled it from the hand of Anne of Austria. This diamond, once in the possession of d'Artagnan, is the Mazarin Stone!

"Let us remain friends. Ministers, princes, kings, will pass away like mountain torrents; civil war, like a forest flame; but we—we shall remain; I have a presentiment that we shall."

These wise words from Athos prove prescient: our heroes remain in our hearts and memories, ideals of friends and adventurers, Sherlock Holmes and d'Artagnan.

Karen Ellery (Minneapolis, Minnesota) is a longtime member of the Norwegian Explorers of Minnesota, the Stage Manager of the St. John's Wood Accomplices, co-translator of the Klingon "Blue Carbuncle," and proprietor of 221T Teaware & Press.

DEERSTALKER OR BUSBY

Brigadier Etienne Gerard

John Baesch

Sherlock Holmes is like Brigadier Etienne Gerard, at least in certain ways. Holmes having a French grandmother may have meant that Gerard and Holmes had some relatives in common. After all, "Art in the blood is liable to take the strangest forms."

Let us establish our dates. Gerard, military hero in the service of the Emperor Napoleon, first saw print in Arthur Conan Doyle's story "How the Brigadier Won His Medal" in 1894, and is generally considered to have been born in the early 1780s. Sherlock Holmes is conventionally believed to have been born in 1854. Napoleon lived from 1769 to 1821, while Holmes's Queen Victoria lived from 1819 to 1901. There is just one more character: Baron Jean-Baptiste-Antoine-Marcellin de Marbot, a noted French light cavalry officer during the Napoleonic Wars who was very much like Gerard in appearance and temperament. Baron de Marbot wrote a thick, two-volume memoir, *The Memoirs of Baron de Marbot*, translated from the French by Arthur John Butler and published in London by Longmans Green (1892–1897). If he is not the "original" of Gerard, he at least has some remarkable similarities.

With Brigadier Gerard, Doyle was trying to bring a new character and new hero to the literary stage. Enter Gerard. The first anthology of his stories was *The Exploits of Brigadier Gerard*, most of the stories having first appeared in the *Strand* in the very memorable canonical year of 1895.

Peace had prevailed since the Congress of Vienna, held after the 1815 Battle of Waterloo, and brought relative stability to continental Europe for 81 years. The other actions during that time—Queen Victoria's "little wars" (Crimea, Boer War, the Franco-Prussian war, various colonial conflicts)—were notable exceptions. *Pax Britannica regnat:* British peace rules.

The Napoleonic Wars of 1803–1815 had inspired changes in all the military sciences and defined how new weaponry and tactics would be deployed. Napoleon himself was an artillerist; Gerard was a Hussar. For the artillery, new weaponry meant more accurate guns. Infantry would spread out to avoid getting in the open and caught in the bursting radius of the cannon balls. Meanwhile, while all this was going on, the Hussars would be deployed on the flanks to protect the rear formations. Armor units (tanks) now performed the sort of missions formerly performed by horses.

Sherlock Holmes was at least reasonably educated about Napoleonic history. In the story "The Abbey Grange," he remarks: "We have not yet met our Waterloo, Watson, but this is our Marengo for it begins in defeat and ends in victory." Brigadier Gerard participated in all Napoleon's European campaigns. His first action was at Marengo in Italy in 1800. He served in Spain, Portugal, Italy, Germany, and Russia.

Conan Doyle prepared extensively for writing stories about such a character. He not only read Marbot's memoirs but studied military science and listened to old soldiers. He made Gerard dashing... dashing just before the arrival of the gendarmerie or the military provosts who are seeking to arrest (at best) or summarily execute him for espionage. He is exceptional in military skills and exceptional in his devotion to his Emperor.

Where Holmesian scholarship has identified some of Holmes's most gnomic sayings as examples of "Sherlockismus," we might also claim to have identified the more self-important "Gerardianism," as when Maréchal André Masséna, Duc de Rivoli, Prince d'Essling, one of Napoleon's most talented officers, engages Gerard for a secret and dangerous mission. (By the way, as we go through their little skits, please keep in mind that laughter is not only permitted but also encouraged.)

> "Colonel Etienne Gerard," said Masséna, "I have always heard that you are a very gallant and enterprising officer."
> It was not for me to confirm such a report, and yet it would be folly to deny it, so I clicked my spurs and saluted.
> "You are also an excellent rider."
> I admitted it.
> "And the best swordsman in the six brigades of light cavalry."
> Masséna was famous for the accuracy of his information.

The Brigadier's horse is shot while he is behind the English lines and he himself is captured by guerrillas. But he unwittingly accomplishes his mission. Later, in another incident, Gerard steals an English horse. He encounters a group of Englishmen holding a fox hunt. Gerard knows nothing about English foxhunting, so he joins the "hunt," runs down the fox, and kills the animal with his sabre. This does not go well with the English hunting party. Sometime later, the story continues:

> But one officer of Masséna's force had committed a crime which was unspeakable, unheard of, abominable; only to be alluded to with curses late in the evening, when a second bottle had

loosened the tongues of men. The news of it was carried back to England, and country gentlemen who knew little of the details of the war grew crimson with passion when they heard of it, and yeomen of the shires raked freckled fists to heaven and swore. And yet who should be the doer of this dreadful deed but our Friend the Brigadier, Etienne Gerard, of the Hussars of Conflans, gay-riding, plume-tossing, debonair, the darling of the ladies and of the six brigades of light cavalry. ("How the Brigadier Slew the Fox")

In Holmes's case, it was the German espionage service who cursed his name. With Holmes, all is drama; with Gerard, most is comedy. His escapades could bring up memories of a good Wodehouse story with Jeeves and Wooster.

The adventures of Etienne Gerard are like the comedy plays of Titus Maccius Plautus, the Roman playwright who wrote plays about 200 years before Christ. The funniest (at least in my opinion) is *Miles Gloriosus, The Bragging Soldier*. In English, in the play or movie version, it is called *A Funny Thing Happened on the Way to the Forum*.

Both Holmes and Gerard are good at disguises. Holmes's numerous disguises are familiar to all; Gerard's success at disguise was crucial—he borrows his beloved Emperor's gray coat and distinctive black hat to act as a decoy for the Emperor and save him from the distracted Prussians in the retreat from Waterloo.

In their public and literary life, both Holmes and Gerard were ardent patriots for their country, and they were recognized for their service. Dr. Watson relates that "My friend spent a day at Windsor, whence he returned with a remarkably fine emerald tie-pin. When I asked him if he'd bought it, he answered that it was a present from a certain gracious lady [Queen Victoria] in whose interests he had once been fortunate enough to carry out a commission. He said no more. More publicly, the Emperor decorated Brigadier Gerard with the Ordre de la Légion d'honneur. (The President of France awarded Holmes *his* Order of the Legion of Honour for services in the matter of Huret, the Boulevard assassin.)

Both Holmes and Gerard are good at speaking truth to power. Sherlock Holmes is always self-assured, unimpressed by wealth and social standing of the client or the police. Gerard's close association with Napoleon means his qualifications are well known to the Emperor as "one who is all spurs and moustaches, with never a thought of anything beyond women and horses." Holmes at least had a countryman's familiarity with horses, which stood him in good stead whether he was mingling with ostlers or racing patrons. Women were perhaps another matter.

Gerard, like Holmes, has the ability to think fast. However, it's clear that Holmes achieves his successes through brilliance, hard work, and logic, while Gerard's narrow escapes are mostly due to luck. He often misunderstands the situation around him, but always ends up all right.

Still, it must be admitted that Holmes and Gerard are remarkably different in a lot of ways. For example, in the well-loved story "How the Brigadier Slew the Fox" mentioned above, Gerard singlehandedly caused an international incident, while Holmes was frequently hired to avert just such contretemps. How would Holmes have dealt with Gerard, one wonders? Like he does Lestrade?

In fact, while sharing some characteristics with Holmes, Gerard shares others with Watson. Watson served his country as an army physician, even wounded in the service, a wound he carried (one place or another) all his life. Watson, too, was a gallant gentleman, claiming an experience of women "over many nations and three separate continents." Holmes himself called Watson a man of action.

Perhaps the closest analogy turns out to be between the two sets of paired characters, in each case the great thinker and the man of action: Holmes and Watson with Napoleon and Gerard. Each pair animates the stories. Each pair piques our imagination. We want to observe them in action together again and again. And so we continue to turn the pages.

John Baesch (Baltimore, Maryland) grew up watching trains and spent his working life with the Baltimore & Ohio Railroad, Amtrak, and several engineering firms. His exposure to Sherlock Holmes began at the library of Baltimore's Loyola High School; he is now a member of the Baker Street Irregulars and other societies.

LIKEABLE EVEN WHEN LEAST REASONABLE

Professor Henry Higgins

Fran Martin

"He is of energetic, scientific type, heartily, even violently interested in everything that can be studied as a scientific subject, and careless about himself and other people, including their feelings. His manner varies from genial bullying when he is in a good humor to stormy petulance when anything goes wrong; but he is so entirely frank and void of malice that he remains likeable even in his least reasonable moments."

A fairly accurate description of Sherlock Holmes? Those studying the great detective and his methods are familiar with many of the traits stated above and would agree. However, in this case, the man described is, in fact, Professor Henry Higgins, who is featured in George Bernard Shaw's play *Pygmalion* (1913) and later (1956) in the well-known musical based on it, *My Fair Lady*. Both Holmes and Higgins are confirmed bachelors living in London, each tended to by their devoted housekeeper and keeping company with a new-found friend and colleague, Dr. Watson and Colonel Pickering respectively, who keep them "flat-footed upon the ground."

Let us dissect, step by step, Shaw's precise description of Henry Higgins to demonstrate the similarities between the two men.

Higgins is described as energetic. This can also be said of Holmes, as Watson tells us that "Nothing could exceed his energy when the working fit was upon him" (*A Study in Scarlet*).

Both men are energetic in the pursuit of their professions. Holmes is "brilliant, articulate and most passionate about his work", which is also how Shaw describes Higgins.

Holmes, like Higgins, is of the scientific type. Detection to Holmes was an exact science. Each case was viewed as a scientific exercise. When we are first introduced to Holmes, he is in a chemical laboratory at St. Bartholomew's Hospital. Higgins has a laboratory in his house. Besides a desk and cabinets, we see various instruments such as a phonograph, a laryngoscope, a row of tiny organ pipes complete with bellows, and burners. Higgins uses his client, Liza, as an experiment in phonetics. He refers to it as "the science of speech."

Shaw states that Higgins was "careless about himself and other people, including their feelings." Watson tells us that Holmes was just the same. In "Thor Bridge", we hear that he "took little care for his own safety once his mind was absorbed in an investigation." As for other people's feelings, Higgins had to be reminded by his colleague, Colonel Pickering: "Does it occur to you, Higgins, that the girl has some feelings?" To which Higgins replies: "Oh no, I don't think so."

How many times has Holmes reproached Watson about his writing? About his help in a case? Holmes: "I cannot at the moment recall any possible blunder which you have omitted" ("Lady Frances Carfax"). Watson announces his engagement to Mary Morstan only to have Holmes say, "I really cannot congratulate you." Watson admitted that he was somewhat hurt by this statement.

We see many instances of bullying on the part of Higgins. His client, Liza, exclaims that Higgins is "a great bully, you are." After all, he has referred to her as a creature, baggage, a squashed cabbage leaf and dirty, and if she does not behave and do as she is told, she will "be walloped by Mrs. Pearce (the housekeeper) with a broomstick."

Holmes really can't be described as a bully, but when confronted by an adversary, he does display a certain harshness, which his profession can call for, such as threatening a visitor with a hunting crop in "A Case of Identity". He demonstrates impatience with those who are on a lower intellectual plane than himself ("The Blue Carbuncle") and Watson explains: "He was angry when crossed or thwarted, but his innate good humor usually reasserted itself quickly in that half comic and wholly philosophical view which was natural to him when his affairs were going awry" ("The Missing Three Quarter"). Holmes also displays a "somewhat sinister cheerfulness" in "Thor Bridge".

To Holmes "The man is nothing, the work is everything" ("The Red-Headed League"). We see the same thing in the way Higgins treats his client Liza. The only thing that matters is the end result. When Higgins is asked by his client "What did you do it for?" he replies: "Why, because it was my job."

Holmes, like Higgins, displays a love of attention and the applause that accompanied it. For Holmes we see this in *A Study in Scarlet* and in "The Six Napoleons". Both men liked to impress those around them.

Holmes was told that he might have made a fine actor, and in *The Hound of the Baskervilles* he states that "Some touch of the artist wells up within me, and calls insistently for a well staged performance." When Higgins displays his impressive talent to others by deducing where they were from based on their speech, he is asked: "Do you do this for your living at a music hall?" To which he replies: "I've thought of that. Perhaps I shall one day." Both men enjoy making deductions in their own way and are delighted upon seeing the reactions of their audience.

Neither is a very sociable fellow, as Holmes himself admits to Watson in "The Gloria Scott". In "The Noble Bachelor" he comments on his correspondence: "This looks like one of those unwelcomed social summonses which call upon a man either to be bored or to lie." Higgins, similarly, admits that he is not comfortable in social gatherings and comments on a recent party: "I felt like a bear in a cage, hanging about doing nothing. The whole thing has been simple purgatory."

Attitude towards women? Henry Higgins tells us that "Women upset everything" and admits, "I am a confirmed old bachelor and likely to remain so." Holmes tells us that "Woman's heart and mind are insoluble puzzles to the male" ("The Illustrious Client") and announces that "I should never marry myself, lest I bias my judgement." (*The Sign of Four*).

About life in general? Henry Higgins: "What is life, but a series of follies?" Sherlock Holmes: "Life is full of whimsical happenings" ("The Mazarin Stone").

Unfortunately, the creator of Professor Higgins, George Bernard Shaw, was anything but a fan of Sherlock Holmes, describing him as "a drug addict without a single admirable trait." In turn, Arthur Conan Doyle, a neighbour of Shaw when he resided in Hindhead, once said of him, "I have known no literary man who was more ruthless to other people's feelings. And yet to meet him was to like him."

Holmes and Higgins: two men could not be more alike. Each displays a dual nature. Each, at times, is depicted as being short-tempered, arrogant and egotistical to the point of rudeness. Yet we love them both. We love their passion and dedication to their work. We admire their devotion to their closest friend and family. We would be hard-pressed to find two men more alike.

Fran Martin (Vancouver, British Columbia) is a retired administrator, a grandmother, a Master Bootmaker, and president of the Stormy Petrels of British Columbia as well as keeping up links with Sherlockians on the west coast of the United States.

ALWAYS ACROSS THE DESERT

Roland Deschain of Gilead, the Gunslinger

Jaime N. Mahoney

The man in black fled across the desert, and the gunslinger followed. (*The Dark Tower: The Gunslinger*)

"There he goes," said Holmes, as we watched the carriage swing and rock over the points. "There are limits, you see, to [Moriarty's] intelligence. It would have been a coup-de-maître had he deduced what I would deduce and acted accordingly." ("The Final Problem")

"Am I supposed to like Roland?" I asked my mother this question by text—my way of letting her know that I had finally acquiesced to her years of increasingly insistent suggestions that I give Stephen King's epic fantasy series a try. I thought she would be pleased. "I'm having trouble with this story."

"Of course you're supposed to like him," she replied, after a significant pause. I'm never sure if she struggles with my questions, or just with texting. "He starts out rough, but he evolves as the story goes along. He has a clear code of morality, and always does what needs to be done, no matter what. Where are you in the book? What did he just do?"

He had just massacred an entire village, that's what he had just done, and it sat poorly with me even if all the villagers *had* been possessed. Call me squeamish. "Am I *really* supposed to like him?"

I believe I heard my mother's exasperated sigh and following snort, even through her text message. I could replicate the sound exactly. "I don't know, Jaime. Am I *really* supposed to like Sherlock Holmes?"

No matter how old you are, it is *very annoying* when your parent has a point.

I thought about Roland Deschain, this character I wasn't sure if I liked, and whom my mother had been reading about since before my very existence. Then I thought about Sherlock Holmes, whom I was certain I had loved from the very first word of *A Study in Scarlet*. These stories have consumed both of our lives. We both have found ourselves pulled along by characters who are bigger than their pages, bursting at the bindings of their books.

I meditated on my mother's words, as the gunslinger would have. I thought about the man on a journey, single-minded and focused, whose first steps were unsure even as they knew their direction. The man in pursuit of an elusive quarry who is always one step ahead of him and is the center of all that is wrong with his world. He's a haunted man, a man of no friends and who neither desires nor pursues them—until the right companion enters his life and completely upends it. In both instances, the companion is named John.

It's a steady name, a sturdy name: John. A name with mileage, that has seen the best and worst of the world. While the gunslinger's young companion prefers to go by Jake, it is really no different from the fact that Holmes seems to know his doctor exclusively as Watson. On their first meeting, Jake tells Roland, "I didn't ask to be here," indicating that their meeting was predestined and unavoidable. Likewise, Watson is eager to meet Sherlock Holmes: "I am the very man for him. I should prefer having a partner to being alone." He is hellbent on being taken to his destiny in that St. Bart's laboratory, despite Stamford's repeated warnings and misgivings, the opportunities to turn back.

As I sat in thought, the commonalities continued to present themselves. Roland is in pursuit of his enemy, the man in black, from the very first words of the story. The gunslinger's conflict with his enemy carries back to even before the narrative began. Their hatred is deep and layered, their animosity bitter and nuanced. On the other hand, it takes Sherlock Holmes some time to meet Professor Moriarty. Although pastiche, film, and television do love to theorize on some history that the two might share, "The Final Problem" is actually the 24th short story in the Canon. One wonders if the detective wasn't off-page all the while, looking at his pocket watch and waiting for some *real* conflict to arrive while he dealt with red-headed men. Once he does, the Professor's spectre lingers, as though he had always been there—and will never leave. There is no canonical wrongdoing that Sherlockians do not try to link back to him, whether with theory or conjecture, or just a very big hammer and force of will. For there is no story without a struggle, no hero without a villain. Who is Roland if he does not have someone to direct his guns at, and who is Sherlock Holmes without a target for his massive intellect?

The gunslinger appears to be on a single journey with one goal, one that takes place over the course of eight books, totaling more than four thousand pages. But even as the last book closes, Roland's journey goes on, with the message that everything ends as it begins. Sherlock Holmes, on the other hand, gets four novels and fifty-six short stories (and that's not even considering the incalculable amount of pastiche and scholarship that has been written about the great detective). An impressive body of work to be sure, but it's a *finite* body of work. Each case has a clear beginning and a conclusion (even if it's not a satisfying one), and there are few references and plot points that carry over from story to story (even fewer that carry over consistently).

Or, like the gunslinger, does Sherlock Holmes go on? As Sherlockians we know, of course, that Sherlock Holmes "never lived and so can never die," but more than that—we also "hear of Sherlock everywhere." The cartoon character wearing the familiar checked hat and smoking a pipe, the alien who speaks of "eliminating the impossible," the song that references Baker Street between the ribbons of a saxophone's refrain— all are continuations of the detective's story. If somewhere the gunslinger still follows the man in black across the desert, then Sherlockians can say with confidence what year it always is, and know what they will find in front of the fire at 221B.

As Jake says to the gunslinger, "Go then, there are other worlds than these."

I asked to write about Roland Deschain for my mother, who is not a Sherlockian, and who suppresses an expression approaching mild indigestion whenever I mention my hobby to her. More than anything else, that is what the gunslinger and Sherlock Holmes have in common: my mother and me. My mother is not a Sherlockian, but she is the great reader of my life, who taught me to appreciate the written word. And she loves Roland Deschain, loved him from the very first word that brought him to life, in the same way that I love Sherlock Holmes. The gunslinger's journey moves with the beat of her heart and flows through her veins. I understand that, because the echo of my heartbeat is the sound of a carriage moving down Baker Street.

Such is the nature of these characters. Such is the power of a story. They bind us together, her and me—invisibly but irrevocably. These characters are footprints across the desert, and the echo of the climb up seventeen steps. They go on, and what is there for us but to follow?

So we go then… to other worlds than these.

Jaime N. Mahoney (Gaithersburg, Maryland) is co-author of *A Curious Collection of Dates: Through the Year with Sherlock Holmes*, proprietor of the Sherlockian blog "Better Holmes & Gardens," and a member of Watson's Tin Box.

SOULLESS IN LONDON

Alexia Tarabotti

Courtney M. Powers

I had quite the time trying to think of a historical figure or fictional character who I thought was anything like Sherlock Holmes. After all, he's the only one in the world, right? But then it came to me in the form of Alexia Tarabotti, the main character in author Gail Carriger's Parasol Protectorate Series. The series consists of five books; *Soulless, Changeless, Blameless, Heartless,* and *Timeless.* It is also available in two omnibus volumes, in case you wanted to treat yourself to something out of this world... literally.

The first book in the series, *Soulless,* was released October 1, 2009, to rave reviews and spent some time on the *New York Times* best-seller list as well as some other fancy lists of best books for 2009. I didn't discover the books until 2012. By that time the final book in the series, *Timeless,* had been published, and it turned out I had been following the author on Twitter for some time. And speaking of following Ms. Carriger on Twitter, I reached out to her through that medium to ask if a comparison between Holmes and her creation had ever been done. She responded: "Nope. But I'm honored by the thought." Having the blessing of the author herself, more or less, I pressed on.

Gail Carriger is the pen name of Tofa Borregaard, who was born in California. She is an archeologist and lover of tea. As to her age, she has said that "it isn't nice to speak on a woman's age," but Google does offer some clues.

Parasol Protectorate and a subsequent series fall under the genre of science fiction and the subgenre of Steampunk. This subgenre is typically set in an alternate Victorian England and often is described as "what history would look like if the future happened sooner." Steampunk can include fiction with science fiction, fantasy, or horror themes. I will tell you, Parasol Protectorate offers a bit of all three.

The series focuses on Alexia Tarabotti (later Maccon), a spinster, whose only duty is to marry and leave her mother and stepfather's home as soon as possible (please and thank you). But this is not something Alexia is after doing. She has her own issues with the local vampire hive and werewolf clan to deal with, thank you very much. Carriger describes her main character thus: "Many a gentleman had likened his first meeting with her to downing a very strong cognac when one was expecting to imbibe fruit juice—that is to say, startling and apt to leave one with a distinct burning sensation." It's fair to say the same could be said about Sherlock Holmes.

Alexia is also like Holmes in that they both are living in London during Queen Victoria's reign. Their appearance could also be considered similar: Alexia is described as having a prominent nose and a slight curl to her hair, and being very tall in stature. Sound familiar? Her personality is also aligned to our favorite detective in that she is often no nonsense, blunt with everyone (this includes her—later—long-suffering spouse, and even Her Majesty Queen Victoria, if you can imagine that). Above all else, her pragmatism in finding resolutions to each novel's core problem seems to echo Holmes's effectiveness.

Alexia even has her own Watson in her best friend Ivy Hisselpenny (later Tunstell). Ivy fills this role rather nicely. But Ivy, like Watson, serves as Alexia's conscience—dare I even say her soul at times? That's necessary, of course, because Alexia doesn't actually have a soul, which makes her alien to most emotional experiences. Holmes, too, exhibits signs of soullessness, but we have also seen hints in the other direction when he opens up to clients. Such is not the case with Alexia, who literally has no soul to guide her in any situation. She is "a preternatural," someone who is born with the ability to neutralize a supernatural's ability through maintained contact with the supernatural creature. For example, should she touch a werewolf, he or she would lose all supernatural abilities for the duration of their contact.

In the London where Alexia dwells, science and steam technology are the state of the art. The books themselves usually involve Alexia and her band of irregulars (what else would you call a Wolf Pack, a Vampire with a penchant for the latest fashion, an eccentric inventor, and her Watson?) somehow getting in the middle of one mess or another and eventually working it all out to reach some sort of resolution by the end. In fact, almost every book has someone trying to kill Alexia or someone close to her. While this has not been the case in most of Holmes's adventures, it is not unknown, as in "The Illustrious Client."

Unlike Holmes, who turns down virtually every accolade, even from royals, Alexia does accept Queen Victoria's request to be her Muhjah on what is known as the Shadow Council. This role makes her the deciding vote when there is a stalemate between the Vampire Potentate and the Werewolves Dewan. In this instance she seems more like Mycroft Holmes and his "minor role in the British government," when we all know he is, in fact, the British government. Her role as Muhjah to the Queen, wife of the head of the largest werewolf clan in London, and mother, keep her rather busy, as one might imagine.

Were I to pick a favorite or best book of the series, it would have to be *Blameless*. In this entry in the series, Alexia finds herself back with her parents, tossed off the Shadow Council, and pregnant. Since it is widely known that her partner is a supernatural and that humans and supernaturals cannot have children together, there is no way the child is his... or is there? Obviously, her marriage and the later birth of the child makes her less like Holmes, despite their resemblances in mannerisms, appearance, and talents. However, were they to ever cross paths in London, I do believe Alexia would leave Holmes with the most profound headache he has ever had. Perhaps she would even be lauded as "*that* woman," unlike Ms. Adler, who was always "The Woman."

Courtney M. Powers (Albany, New York) is the founder of the Sherlock Holmes society the Avenging Winters of Albany. She enjoys spending her free time with her husband and toddler.

TINKER TAILOR SHERLOCKIAN SPY

George Smiley

Clarissa Aykroyd

In his introduction to *The New Annotated Sherlock Holmes* (2005), John le Carré wrote: "With no Sherlock Holmes, would I ever have invented George Smiley? And with no Dr Watson, would I ever have given Smiley his sidekick Peter Guillam? I would like to think so, but I doubt it very much."

Since the 1960s, John le Carré's books have explored espionage and current affairs with unusual psychological acuity. Most famous of all are his books about a short, pudgy Cold War spy named George Smiley, who first appears in *Call for the Dead* (1961) and later in *The Spy Who Came In from the Cold* (1963), *Tinker Tailor Soldier Spy* (1974), and others. Self-effacing and apparently unremarkable, Smiley seems very different from Arthur Conan Doyle's tall, striking, overtly brilliant Sherlock Holmes. But a close examination of the George Smiley novels and the Sherlock Holmes stories reveals countless parallels between the characters. Smiley becomes a more well-defined and specific extension of aspects of Holmes's character, making Holmes the pattern or archetype on whom Smiley is based.

The opening chapter of *Call for the Dead* is titled "A Brief History of George Smiley". In this chapter, there are several interesting similarities between him and Holmes. Smiley is "without school, parents, regiment or trade", and throughout the Smiley novels, we never learn about his family. Prior to meeting Sherlock's brother Mycroft, Watson says: "I had never heard [Holmes] refer to his relations, and hardly ever to his own early life.... I had come to believe that he was an orphan with no relatives living" ("The Greek Interpreter"). Smiley enjoys his profession of intelligence officer, or spy, because it offers him "academic excursions into the mystery of human behaviour, disciplined by the practical application of his own deductions". In *Call for the Dead* and particularly in its sequel *A Murder of Quality* (1962), Smiley takes up a very Holmesian role, often more detective than spy as he solves mysteries. In "The

Speckled Band", Helen Stoner appeals to Holmes by saying, "I have heard... that you can see deeply into the manifold wickedness of the human heart." Holmes himself writes in one of his monographs about "the Science of Deduction and Analysis... which can only be acquired by long and patient study" (*A Study in Scarlet*).

Smiley and Holmes both embody a duality of character. While Holmes is a logician above all, he is not quite the "calculating-machine" that Watson accuses him of being in *The Sign of Four*. Not all of Holmes's decisions throughout his career are those of a cold reasoner. In "The Blue Carbuncle", for example, Holmes lets a thief go free and says: "I suppose that I am commuting a felony, but it is just possible that I am saving a soul". As for Smiley and his recruiting of new agents: "His emotions in performing this work were mixed, and irreconcilable. It intrigued him to evaluate from a detached position what he had learnt to describe as 'the agent potential' of a human being; to devise minuscule tests of character and behaviour which could inform him of the qualities of a candidate. This part of him was bloodless and inhuman.... By the strength of his intellect, he forced himself to observe humanity with clinical objectivity.... But Smiley was a sentimental man" (*Call for the Dead*). Smiley is constantly troubled by this duality, although he seems to be both more sentimental and colder than Holmes. (The stakes are usually higher in the Smiley books: Smiley makes decisions which result in the deaths of others, even former friends, but which are also portrayed as necessary.)

There are elements of Smiley's life which resemble paths Holmes could have taken but shrank from in order to guard his powers. Smiley is more easily swayed or confused by emotion, and especially by his version of "The Woman", his wife Ann Smiley. Women who directly or indirectly bring men to untimely downfalls are a theme of le Carré's work. In the Karla Trilogy (*Tinker Tailor Soldier Spy*, *The Honourable Schoolboy* [1977] and *Smiley's People* [1979]), this is a recurring theme in each novel, affecting both heroes and villains. Ann Smiley is repeatedly unfaithful to Smiley, who can never quite give her up. His blind spots regarding Ann are sometimes near-fatal, particularly in *Tinker Tailor Soldier Spy*, where the Russian arch-enemy Karla engineers one of Ann's infidelities in order to distract Smiley as much as possible in his hunt for a traitor within the Circus (their name for the British intelligence service).

There are no exact parallels between Ann Smiley and Irene Adler, "The Woman" to Holmes. In "A Scandal in Bohemia", there is no relationship between her and Holmes, despite the wishful thinking of a million screenwriters and pastiche writers. And yet, just after Watson introduces her, he says: "It was not that [Holmes] felt any emotion akin to love for Irene Adler," and instantly the reader wonders why he would say this if there was truly nothing there. Portraying Holmes as an emotionless man uninterested in "the softer passions", Watson says: "Grit in a sensitive instrument, or a crack in one of his own high-power lenses, would not be more disturbing than a strong emotion in a nature such as his." As for Smiley, his marriage introduces turmoil into his life. In *Tinker Tailor Soldier Spy*, the unmasked traitor says to Smiley: "You had this one price: Ann. The last illusion of the illusionless man." Smiley resolves to leave behind "emotional attachments which have long outlived their purpose. *Viz* my wife" (*Tinker Tailor Soldier Spy*), but he never quite can.

Holmes nips all of this in the bud when, in *The Sign of Four*, Watson announces his engagement to Mary Morstan. After stating that he cannot congratulate Watson on his upcoming marriage, Holmes says: "Love is an emotional thing, and whatever is emotional is opposed to that true cold reason which I place above all things. I should never marry myself, lest I bias my judgment." These seem like the words of a man who resists emotional attachments because he fears them and because he sees vulnerability as a threat. (Interestingly, a recurring theme in "A Scandal of Bohemia" is that of the mask or disguise. Holmes and Irene Adler meet only when one or the other is in disguise: Holmes as a groom and then as a priest, and Irene Adler in male dress. This hints at the building of walls against strong emotions, even if unconsciously. It also suggests the methods of spies.) One wonders if Smiley is, in his relationship with his wife, another aspect of Holmes led to its natural conclusion—that is, if Holmes had taken a different path and resisted marriage less successfully. Smiley's feelings about Ann are not so dissimilar to Holmes's feelings about love in general, but Smiley is already in too deep.

Smiley, like Holmes, has an arch-enemy. Karla is a powerful and shadowy figure in the Russian intelligence services. He is even more distant from Smiley than Professor Moriarty is from Holmes, and his downfall seems even more unlikely. Smiley's colleagues also recognise the parallels. In *Smiley's People*, Saul Enderby (the head of the Circus) warns Smiley about consequences: "When you and Karla are stuck on your ledge on the Reichenbach Falls and you've got your hands round Karla's throat, Brother Lacon will be right there behind you holding your coat-tails and telling you not to be beastly to the Russians." The furtive Sam Collins suggests that Karla is "sitting in Moscow waiting for Holmes or Captain Ahab to catch up with him" (*Smiley's People*).

Smiley meets Karla only twice; Holmes meets Moriarty only twice. Seen at a distance by Watson in "The Final Problem", Moriarty appears as "a man... walking very rapidly" and a "black figure"; Karla, before his final confrontation with Smiley, is a "solitary black figure start[ing] his journey" (*Smiley's People*). Even more persuasive are the parallel descriptions of the Reichenbach Falls in "The Final Problem" and Smiley's impressions in the closing pages of *Smiley's People*. Watson describes the Reichenbach Falls with these words:

> The torrent, swollen by the melting snow, plunges into a terrible abyss, from which the spray rolls up like the smoke from a burning house. The shaft into which the river hurls itself is an

immense chasm, lined by glistening coal-black rock, and narrowing into a creaming, boiling pit of incalculable depth, which brims over and shoots the stream onward over its jagged lip. The long sweep of green water roaring forever down, and the thick flickering curtain of spray hissing forever upward, turn a man giddy with their constant whirl and clamor. We stood near the edge peering down at the gleam of the breaking water far below us against the black rocks, and listening to the half-human shout which came booming up with the spray out of the abyss. ("The Final Problem")

In *Smiley's People*, as Smiley is about to meet Karla for the second time at a bridge in Berlin and possibly win the long battle, he thinks of the damage caused by their conflict and wonders whether the cost was worth it. Then he has a kind of vision, both physical and moral: "Like a chasm, the jagged skyline beckoned to him yet again, the swirling snow made it an inferno. For a second longer, Smiley stood on the brink at the smouldering river's edge." The atmospheric parallels between these two passages, and the similar vocabulary used, are remarkable—but Smiley's struggle is more internal, and he invests the landscape around him with feelings of doubt and fear. Ultimately, his struggle with an arch-villain has a greater moral complexity than the Holmes-Moriarty duel. If Holmes has regrets or doubts over the death of Moriarty, he never shows them. As so often, it is left to readers to develop Holmes's emotions further.

More parallels emerge throughout the Smiley novels, showing that le Carré had Doyle's stories in mind as he developed his own. In *Tinker Tailor Soldier Spy* we learn that Bywater Street in London's Chelsea, where Smiley lives, is "a cul-de-sac exactly one hundred and seventeen of his own paces long", and that "he knew how many stairs there were to each flight of his own house." This recalls Holmes in "A Scandal in Bohemia": "I know that there are seventeen steps [from the hall in 221B Baker Street up to the sitting-room], because I have both seen and observed." Smiley, who despite his solitary nature is surrounded by fellow spies, has a few Watsons at different times, including Inspector Mendel (who also has the Holmesian characteristic of being a beekeeper) and particularly Peter Guillam, of whom the narrator Ned in *The Secret Pilgrim* (1990) says: "Peter had played Watson to George's Sherlock Holmes in the long search for the Circus traitor."

In many of his stories, Smiley has to come out of retirement. In "His Last Bow", Holmes comes out of retirement to play a double agent as World War I begins. In that story, Watson says to him: "We heard of you as living the life of a hermit among your bees and your books in a small farm upon the South Downs." In *A Legacy of Spies* (2017), an aging Peter Guillam tracks down an even older Smiley in a library in Freiburg, Germany. (There is a charged nature to this flight to Europe which is reminiscent of "The Final Problem", and Guillam goes via Basel, like

Holmes and Watson. Climactic, emotional moments in the Smiley stories often take place during or after a flight to Europe.) This could be Smiley's equivalent of the cottage on the Sussex Downs: he says to Guillam, "An old spy in his dotage seeks the truth of ages."

The English poet laureate Ted Hughes once said of his forerunner Edward Thomas: "He is the father of us all." Smiley could easily have said this of Sherlock Holmes. In some respects, Smiley is a more finely drawn Holmes, a natural conclusion to some of Holmes's strongest tendencies. Beyond this, there are many episodes and other characters in le Carré's books where an echo of Doyle is heard, or where the atmosphere conjures up a particular story. In paying tribute to Sherlock Holmes and Sir Arthur Conan Doyle, le Carré created his own works of distinctive genius, which is surely one of the greatest compliments of all.

Clarissa Aykroyd (London, England), originally from Victoria, British Columbia, works as a publisher. She first encountered Sherlock Holmes in childhood and has been a Sherlockian for more than 30 years. Her published writings include poetry on Sherlock Holmes and other subjects, and a blog about poetry, thestoneandthestar.blogspot.co.uk.

LOST BOYS

Peter Pan

Bob Coghill

A silhouette. That's all it takes.

Almost universally, this literary character can be identified simply by a silhouette, often just head and shoulders and of course with his unusual hat, and often with a pipe in his mouth.

The author, Sir... well, let's just say the author, who, to those who know and love him can be identified by just the use of his three initials, was born in Scotland, but he and his character will forever be identified with London. His address changed over the years, but when he first moved to London, he was located not too far from the British Museum.

But I am ahead of myself. Let's go back to Scotland, where our author grew up and from where he eventually graduated from the University of Edinburgh. It was in Scotland that he learned so much of his art from his mother. You could say that our author was inordinately fond of his mother. He wrote her many letters, and she often provided feedback to her son. She had told him story after story and helped him to become, like her, an excellent storyteller: indeed, one of the most eminent storytellers of his day.

And he did tell stories. Many of them. It probably would surprise him greatly to discover that in 2018, he and his character were still as popular as ever. It might even upset him a little that the one character for which he is most famous is not what he considered among his best. He wrote many articles, stories, novels, and even plays, but almost all of them have been obscured by that one creation of his, the one who still appeals, well after a century since his creation. In his lifetime, his works were translated to many languages in many countries, and they continue to be published around the world. But as one biographer lamented, "despite his hugely successful literary output in his lifetime, the one character has so eclipsed his other writings, that many people today know this alone of all his works."

A quick glance at the index of any of the many biographies of our author show his associations with many of the other authors of his day, such as H.G. Wells, George Bernard Shaw, Rudyard Kipling, A.A.

Milne, P.G. Wodehouse, Thomas Hardy, and E.W. Hornung, to give only a few. Also found in the indexes are some of the literary magazines and publications with which he was connected. There were *The Bookman, Cornhill Magazine, McClure's, The Scotsman*, the London *Times, Tit-Bits, Punch*, and others. There are also politicians connected with our author: Prime Ministers H.H. Asquith, Arthur Balfour, and David Lloyd George, President Theodore Roosevelt, even Queen Victoria. He was actively involved in many clubs, including the Athenaeum, the Authors' Club and the Idlers. There are a significant number of listings under such causes as the Copyright Act, pirated copies of his writings, particularly in the United States, playing cricket with a team called the Allahakbarries, and to the amusement of some, quite a bit about fairies.

Many scholars continue to keep alive the memory of both character and author. For example, eminent literary scholar R. Lancelyn Green wrote a great deal about both. There are significant university archives in England and Scotland devoted to both, but many of the manuscripts and related materials are held in American universities so that British scholars need to plan a trip to North America to do complete research. In Toronto there are even, in the special collections department of the Toronto Public Library, a significant number of titles devoted to the character.

The character lives on, not just in the books, but also in television shows, films, plays, and musicals. Many actors have portrayed the character, and you can almost give the age of the devotee depending on which actor they feel is the definitive one, the one who really personifies the character. From the Victorian age through to the present, our character has become an instantly recognizable symbol that has endured over time.

All of the above accurately describes our beloved Sir Arthur Conan Doyle and his creation, Sherlock Holmes. But, in fact, it is all, of course, about that other Scotsman, Sir James Matthew Barrie (1860–1937), and his creation, Peter Pan.

ACD and JMB did not just live parallel lives. Their lives intersected often, and they knew each other well and developed a lifelong friendship. Barrie would often stay with Doyle at his home. Among Doyle's books were some inscribed to him from Barrie. There was a signed portrait of Barrie on Doyle's wall. Barrie was a guest at ACD's wedding. Not only did they play cricket together on the Allahakbarries, they talked about writing together and in fact did collaborate, not very successfully, on an opera, "Jane Annie". When Barrie telegraphed Doyle for help, the telegram read, "Come at once if convenient—if inconvenient, come all the same." Barrie is known to have written three short pastiches of Holmes: "My Evening with Sherlock Holmes" (1891), "The Adventure of the Two Collaborators" (1893), and "The Late Sherlock Holmes" (1893).

Doyle and Barrie socialized at clubs such as the Idlers. Barrie joined the Authors' Club, where Doyle was also a member and eventually chairman. They both spent time at the Reform Club. They were both admirers of fellow Scottish writer Robert Louis Stevenson. They had been students at the same time at Edinburgh University, with Doyle graduating a year ahead of Barrie. Both of them had dealings with the American producer Charles Frohman, who was involved in the plays "Peter Pan" and "Sherlock Holmes". Both travelled to the United States to undertake speaking tours. Both travelled regularly to Switzerland.

And both, of course, created characters who never lived and so can never die. There are statues of Peter Pan in England, in Scotland, and around the world. There are statues, too, of Sherlock Holmes. Both appear in stained-glass windows and on postage stamps and live on, propelled by generations of readers, film viewers, and playgoers.

So then. How is Sherlock Holmes like Peter Pan?

There are obvious similarities. Both are flawed heroes, but despite those flaws, or maybe even because of them, they have found a way into the hearts and minds of generations. Holmes has a famous address: 221B Baker Street. Pan's is "Second star to the right and straight on till morning". Holmes has his Watson, Pan his Tinkerbell. For Holmes, The Woman is Irene Adler. For Pan, it is Wendy. Holmes battles Moriarty; Pan battles Captain Hook. And while Peter Pan has his lost boys, Sherlock Holmes has the Baker Street Irregulars.

Sherlock Holmes and Peter Pan have had parallel influences on the public since their creations. Scottish writers living in England wrote both. Since the first publication of *A Study in Scarlet* and *The Little White Bird* (where we have the first appearance of Peter Pan) both have remained in print and remain popular. W.S. Baring-Gould and Les Klinger wrote versions of an *Annotated Sherlock Holmes*; Maria Tatar of Harvard University wrote *The Annotated Peter Pan*.

Both Holmes and Pan appear in books but also in many other forms. Peter Pan, first introduced in *The Little White Bird* (1902), became well known through the play, "Peter Pan, or The Boy Who Wouldn't Grow Up" (1904), then *Peter Pan in Kensington Gardens* (1906), and eventually *Peter and Wendy*, later entitled just *Peter Pan*. Both have become Broadway musicals. Both have become straight plays. Both have become films and television shows. Both have been performed as ballets. Both have become animated Disney movies. Both are subjects of special collections and archives in American universities. Both continue to have international appeal. Literary pilgrims continue to travel to Baker Street and to Kensington Gardens.

And both, it seems, keep us young. Conan Doyle, in his preface to *The Lost World*, wrote:

> I have wrought my simple plan
> If I give one hour of joy
> To the boy who's half a man
> Or the man who's half a boy.

The Sherlock Holmes stories were certainly a part of Doyle's simple plan. He has kept generations of readers young at heart. If you have ever participated at a meeting of the Baker Street Irregulars or any of the many Sherlockian societies across the world, you will find many a man (and woman) who remains half a boy (or girl).

Alexander Woollcott (known to be a Sherlockian) wrote of Peter Pan fans that "the dearest friends of Peter Pan are among the oldest living inhabitants. Austere jurists, battered rounders, famous editors and famous playwrights, slightly delirious poets and outwardly forbidding corporation presidents, these are in the ranks of the devoted. You simply cannot recognize a Peter Pantheist at sight, but when you find him reappearing at each engagement you can begin to guess his heart is in the right place." That is a fairly accurate description of just about any Sherlockian gathering.

And Peter Pan is the boy who would not grow up. But because he refuses to grow up, he will also never die. We should have a Starrett poem for Peter Pan. Sherlock Holmes is like Peter Pan because he keeps us young. He keeps us wondering. He keeps us in the company of others who, no matter what age, are still young and wondering. We become the *puer aeternus* (eternal boy) who lives "Betwixt and Between". J.M. Barrie, through Peter Pan, will be forever linked with the joys of youth and the pleasures of childhood. A.C. Doyle, through Sherlock Holmes, will be forever linked with the mysteries of life and the complexities of logic and deduction.

"All children, except one, grow up." So starts Peter Pan. But there are many of us who are following his example. We do get older, but we never quite grow up.

Bob Coghill (Vancouver, British Columbia) is a retired teacher and archivist, a Baker Street Irregular, and a Master Bootmaker, renowned for introducing children to Sherlock Holmes. Since 2013 he has been travelling the world, meeting Sherlockians and adding friendships as he goes, but definitely not growing up.

FIGURES OF POP CULTURE

All was still and dark, save only
that brilliant yellow screen in front of us
with the black figure outlined upon its centre.

"The Empty House"

WORLD'S GREATEST

Batman

Mike Ranieri

Who is the world's greatest detective?

Well, if you do a Google search you may be surprised that the name which shares the top of the list—and sometimes dominates—is Batman, the black-clad character who made his comic book debut in 1939 and is now also known from television, film, and legend. Yes, "World's Greatest Detective" is among his monikers (others being the Caped Crusader, the Dark Knight, the Masked Manhunter, and, with Robin, the Dynamic Duo).

To be more specific, Holmes is referred to as the "Great Detective," being one of the first recognized detectives in fiction and arguably the most famous, while Batman holds the title "World's Greatest Detective" within the history of comic book lore. And as well as being the World's Greatest, Batman shares some other important characteristics with Sherlock Holmes. Indeed, Bill Finger, one of the creators of Batman, has admitted that indeed Batman was modeled, in part, after the man of Baker Street.

Holmes's deerstalker cap, inverness cape, calabash pipe, and magnifying glass, and even the silhouette of his profile, have become iconic identifiers of *the* detective. (Interestingly most of these were established by the American actor William Gillette, whose extremely successful portrayal of Holmes on the stage helped grow the character's fame worldwide.) Batman's cape and cowl, utility belt and bat symbol mirror these distinguishing features. Even Holmes's partner (sidekick), landlady, makeshift lab, index of collected data, martial arts training, disguises, and villainous archrival have equivalents in Batman's world: Robin, Alfred the butler, the Batcave, the Batcomputer, and of course The Joker. Even Batman's obsession with solving crime and righting wrongs to the exclusion of personal relationships mirrors Holmes's antisocial behavior and, as Holmes says in *The Sign of Four*, "My mind... rebels at stagnation... I abhor the dull routine of existence. I crave for mental exaltation."

There are a number of fine articles and essays that have compared the two characters. But what are the elements that have given these two characters such endurance? I believe there are two essential components.

The first is reader identification. In his book *The Great Detective: The Amazing Rise and Immortal Life of Sherlock Holmes*, Zach Dundas says that "Holmes appealed and appeals to audiences due to the idea that anyone could be him; the reasonable, surprisingly simple methods Holmes uses could, in theory, be mastered by anyone, especially since the public believed him to be real rather than fictitious." In *A Study in Scarlet* Holmes says, "If I show you too much of my method of working, you will come to the conclusion that I am a very ordinary individual after all."

Both men develop their skills through dedication and hard work. Like athletes they train themselves to be the best at what they need to do. As much as Batman is a superhero, he is just a human being who has put great effort into developing his abilities. We can marvel at an alien hero with "powers and abilities far beyond those of mortal men" but we can never really identify with one.

The second component is one that many authors or creators may not find appealing: the diversity of authorship. Wishing to extend the adventures of the character, even as Arthur Conan Doyle became bored with him, fans took to writing their own Holmes stories. From the very beginning, as the character grew in popularity (and thanks to the impotence of copyright laws at the time) plays and stories about Holmes were being performed and written by others.

Multiple authors who brought new ideas and new perspectives have directly been responsible for the popularity and longevity of the character (much to the consternation of the Doyle family estate, which never really understood this).

Of course, the same process is evident with most modern-day movie and television franchises. *Star Trek* and *Star Wars* remain popular because they have been taken over by professional fans. Batman and comics have always had many divers artists shaping and reshaping the characters to reflect their readers' times and moods. Holmes has been interpreted in many ways and in many genres: comedy, horror, sci-fi, historical, and so on. The latest modern TV adaptations—the BBC *Sherlock* and CBS *Elementary*—have revitalized the characters for today's audience and put Sherlockian fandom once again in the limelight.

It is true that Holmes has appeared in the comics, on his own and also teaming up with Batman. But what would a Sherlock Holmes tale have looked like if it had first been written in the style of a Batman comic book?

In the sitting room of stately 221B Baker Street, home of consulting detective Sherlock Holmes, a mystery is unfolding.

"Gosh, Holmes, what could it mean?" Watson scratches his pate.

"Tut, tut, old chum. We shall soon deduce the solution to this cryptic missive." Holmes removes his lens from a pouch on his belt and inspects the letter. "The paper is of a superior quality, and notice the particular hue—and there is a scent to it."

"Only a woman would send such dainty correspondence."

"Precisely, Watson. But not just *a* woman, *the* woman."

"You mean…"

"It seems that rumours of her death have been greatly exaggerated."

"But what of this confounded riddle?"

"It is a warning of impending doom, I fear."

Watson reads the letter aloud once more: "'I'm there once in a minute, twice in a moment, but never in a thousand years. Who am I?' If she wanted to alert us, she should have been explicit."

"Not if clarity would put her in danger. Still, the answer is elementary—it is the letter M!"

"You don't mean…"

"My old arch-nemesis, the nefarious Napoleon of crime, Professor Moriarty!"

Abruptly, a knock at the door and Mrs. Hudson enters the room. "Sir, I just received another post. It's from the commissioner of Scotland Yard. They require your service."

Immediately Holmes jumps to his feet. "Thank you, Mrs. Hudson. Come on, Watson. To the hansom cab—the game's afoot!"

Meanwhile, in an old abandoned tea factory in London's seedy East End, the fiendish Professor Moriarty, sinister scientist and madman of numbers, is gloating over the success of his latest dastardly deed.

"So, my corrupt cronies, it was my superior mathematical mind that devised this perfect plan to pilfer the precious crown jewels, the symbol of the monarchy. Ah, shiny-shiny, my precious, ha-ha, hee-hee!" rhapsodizes Moriarty to his admiring gang of villains.

"Hey, gov'na," says one of the Professor's dimwitted lackeys, peering out a broken window, "I sees a light in'a sky. It's the bleedn' shadow of man wif a pipe and a double billed cap, it is."

"It's the Holmes Signal, you fool!" cries Moriarty.

Suddenly the hideout door cracks and bursts open, and there, silhouetted by the light from the street, stand two heroic figures.

"So, it's Sherlock Holmes, the Piped Pimpernel, and his bone-headed bones, Doctor Watson. Come to defend queen and country, eh? You're too late! My plan is fool-proof!" taunts Moriarty.

"The only proof is that you're a fool, Professor, if you think you can get away with it!" challenges the undaunted Holmes.

"Give back England's legacy, you mathematician of mayhem!" shouts the good Doctor.

"Are you sure the return of jewels is all you require, Holmes?" Moriarty gestures to one of his contemptible cohorts lurking in the shadows. Coming into the light, he holds the figure of a woman with a burlap sack over her head. "Look who else came along for the ride." Moriarty tears the sack from her head.

"We are not amused," declares the regal captive.

"Holy pomp and circumstance," ejaculates Watson.

"You abominable filthy criminal," says Holmes with utter disgust. "If you hurt one hair on her royal head, I'll kill you all—I'll rend you limb from limb!"

"We'll see about that." Moriarty calls to his henchmen. "Fagin, Dodger, Sikes, get 'em, my fine felonious flunkeys. Get 'em or it's Scotland Yard's hoosegow for the lot of us!"

The Professor's gang of scoundrels stream out of every corner of the factory, rushing with evil intent upon our heroes. And so commences a royal rumble that tests the physical acumen of the Deductive Duo to their very limit. But Holmes, an adept bare-knuckle fighter, meets the challenge with gusto and precision.

"Take that, you rascally rogue," announces Holmes as he executes several blows to the jaw of an oncoming blackguard. SOCK! SPLAT! Another brigand swings at Holmes with a wooden club. Holmes ducks and then turns quickly before he can get his balance. "And here's one for you, you malicious miscreant." BIF! BAM! POW! "And one to the gut." OOOF! BLAP!

Holmes receives a vicious backhander from a slogging ruffian. But he responses with a straight left. KAPOW! And then a right. THWACK!

Watson, too, is in the thick of it. "Here's something I learned in Afghanistan, you gap-tooth goon," trumpets Watson. CRASH! BOFF! WHACK! An evil, pasty-faced brute with a harelip falls backward.

Suddenly two large blighters rush Holmes at once. Employing the ancient eastern technique of baritsu, he maneuvers and downs the knaves in one swift motion. ZOK! BIFF! ZZZZZWAP!

"Here's one for the honour of the Fifth Northumberland Fusiliers," shouts Watson. KRUNCH! KLONK! He delivers a crushing blow to a portly bounder who runs off in a daze.

Holmes's capabilities in singlestick combat are now apparent as he picks up his walking stick and dispatches the rest of the misguided minions—BONK! BOOM! EEE-YOW!—who fall to the floor unconscious.

"So, Moriarty, we've done fine work with your heinous hired hooligans," declares Holmes. "Surrender or I shall be forced to do the same to your own person."

"Holmes, you may have vanquished my men, but you'll never get me, do you hear! Stay back or the queen gets it." Moriarty now holds the queen in his grasp with a revolver pressed against her temple.

"Holy suffering sovereign!" ejaculates Watson.

But with speed and the precision of a skilled marksman, Holmes shoots his stick at the head of Moriarty. WHAMM!! Moriarty is struck between the eyes. He releases his grip and Holmes quickly wrenches the gun from his hand. And so our queen is rescued and falls into the arms of Holmes.

"We shall surely knight thee for such bravery," says the monarch as she raises her royal scepter.

"Please, Your Majesty, it is not necessary. The stability and safety of England is reward enough."

"Nonsense," says Her Majesty, but from the scepter there emits a noxious gas—choking both Holmes and Watson and rendering them helpless and insensible.

Sometime later… our heroes awake to find themselves trapped in a large perforated bag suspended by a thick rope over an immense porcelain bowl of water. But wait, what is that distinct aroma?

"Tea leaves is what you smell," chuckles Moriarty. "Ah ha ha, soon you will be dunked bodily!"

"Holy Earl Grey!" ejaculates Watson.

"You irreverent iconoclast! No self-respecting Englishman would dunk his teabag. The water must be poured slowly over the leaves at a precise temperature of 200 degrees."

"Bah! But where are my manners?" mocks Moriarty. "Shall I introduce you to our sovereign?"

The queen gazes up at the Deerstalker Dynamo and his faithful physician. But what is this? She's pulling at her face. It's a disguise!

"We've been betrayed, Watson, by *the* woman… *again*."

"Holy Victoria's secret!" ejaculates Watson.

"Come now, Sherlock, don't be so formal. Call me Irene *The Adder*, hisss," she hisses.

"Holy snake-in-the-grass!" ejaculates Watson.

"Oh shut up, you bombastic Boswell! Stop ejaculating all the time, hisss—"

"It's not too late to give up your life of crime," pleads Holmes. "Don't be seduced by this malevolent mastermind of malice."

"You forget, Sherlock, I'm an American and we're still pissed about that no taxation without representation business. And they're called potato chips, not crisps!"

"Enough flirtation, my dear, and on to important business," sneers Moriarty.

"Enclosed in this inescapable teabag, you will be lowered as the water reaches a deathly boil!"

"Holy third degree!" ejaculates Watson.

"Watson, that is getting a little annoying."

"Sorry, Holmes."

Can this be happening? Will Moriarty really teabag Holmes and Watson? Are our heroes to be steeped to death? Are they dued to be brewed? Is this the final problem? Their last bow? Unbelievable! If you care for the Inverness Caped Crusader and his Wordsmith Wonder keep hoping 'til tomorrow! Same Sherlockian time! Same Holmesian story!

Mike Ranieri (Toronto, Ontario) is a graphic designer and former actor who now directs amateur theatre. He is the current president of the Bootmakers of Toronto, the Sherlock Holmes Society of Canada, and is cohost of the Sherlockian podcast *I Grok Sherlock*.

HELPING THE CREATURES OF HOPE

Doctor Who

Monica M. Schmidt

How does one approach the impossible task of comparing two beloved heroes with incredibly rabid fan-bases without provoking anybody? This is the question that has been dogging me for months as I was given the arduous assignment of comparing the BBC television hero The Doctor (from the series *Doctor Who*) to the literary hero Sherlock Holmes. Because I am intimately familiar with both Arthur Conan Doyle's creation and the many versions of The Doctor, one would think it would be an easy assignment. But I recognized from the onset that the task is gargantuan, because one must understand the differences to appreciate the similarities.

While there have been many thousands of homages, pastiches, and parodies, the generally agreed upon Canon of Sherlock Holmes is the 60 stories written by Arthur Conan Doyle. The Sherlockian Canon was created by a single author over the span of 40 years. The same cannot be said of *Doctor Who*. The idea of canon in the *Doctor Who* creative universe (also known as the Whoniverse) is vast and sprawling. What began as a family-friendly BBC-TV show in 1963 now encompasses a television series spanning more than 50 years, several spin-off series, a number of tie-in movies, as well as hundreds of books and audio dramas (not to mention merchandising galore), all controlled and licensed by not a single author, but an overarching entity—the BBC. The Whoniverse continues to expand with every new script for the television series, audio drama, or book created by the dozens upon dozens of creative geniuses tapped by the BBC. So, the Sherlockian Canon is finite, whereas the Whoniverse is still growing.

As the creative universes are inherently different, so is character development within the established canons. Chronology problems aside, there is a fairly linear evolution of Holmes over the years, from a young man in his 20's considered a nuisance by Scotland Yard, to the seasoned and well-respected detective engaged by various European governments, to the retired old beekeeper. Holmes is always, at his core, the same man, and he becomes older and wiser with the passage of time. With apologies to the 10th regeneration of The Doctor, the evolution of that character is more "wibbly wobbly, timey wimey" and complicated.

The protagonist in *Doctor Who* is an alien—a Time Lord—whose potential lifespan crosses millennia and who can "regenerate" (take on new bodies and personality traits) several times across a full lifespan. Therefore, the character is ever-changing, as evidenced by the (so far) 14 faces that he is known by (to put it another way, the actors who have portrayed the various generations of the character on television). This is why The Doctor is seen an old, cantankerous professor in his first incarnation; a tall, curly-haired man with wanderlust big enough to match his scarf in his fourth; an attractive, geek-chic hipster in his tenth incarnation; and a blond woman in his thirteenth. With each incarnation comes a progression and regression of personality and traits, with some lessons previously learned to be forgotten and learned over again.

The adventures featuring Sherlock Holmes all take place between 1874 and 1914 and are largely set in England. Each of the stories is an essentially self-contained narrative that has a (mostly) satisfactory conclusion, and all the narratives are firmly planted within the realm of possibility. The fantastical and supernatural need not apply. While many of the *Doctor Who* narratives also take place in England, thanks to the TARDIS (a spaceship and time machine), the stories crisscross all of time and space, meaning that one adventure may be Victorian, but the next could occur on a space station orbiting a distant planet in a far-off galaxy. Narratives in *Doctor Who* are the very essence of fantastical and supernatural.

Some of the plots are limited to a single story arc, but there can be an overarching mythology in the show that carries plot threads across multiple episodes and seasons. Additionally, there are many subtle hints in various episodes and stories that call back references to previously told (or future, yet-to-be-told) narratives. In other words, it takes copious notes on a whiteboard with lots of zig-zagging arrows to try to make sense of plots and the timeline in the Whoniverse. So, while one could read any random Sherlock Holmes story from the Canon and have a pretty good idea of who Sherlock Holmes is and what is going on, with a few notable exceptions, knowing what is happening in any given story from *Doctor Who* depends heavily upon one's knowledge of the Canon up until that point.

The preceding paragraphs explain why many of my friends don't understand *Doctor Who*: understanding the structure of the Whoniverse, the development of the characters, and the story arcs of 50-odd years of storytelling across multiple mediums is a massive undertaking that can't be undertaken lightly. Knowing the world of *Doctor Who* essentially requires an immersion into the material for which most fans, most people, don't have the time or energy. It's taken me the better part of 15 years to feel like I have enough of a handle on the Whoniverse to write with some degree of authority, so I understand the reluctance for people to take the plunge into this fandom. In comparison, the Sherlock Holmes universe can be learned in a few short weeks of reading the 60 stories by Arthur Conan Doyle.

With these massive differences in authorship, canonical development, and character evolution, how can one argue that these two characters are alike? There are any number of shallow observations one could make about Holmes and The Doctor, ranging from their shared inquisitiveness and curiosity to their fondness and flair for recognizable costuming (the inverness and deerstalker for Holmes vs. the iconic outfits of each of the regenerations of The Doctor).

All surface-level comments aside, Holmes and The Doctor are arguably the best representations of the Ronin archetype. A Ronin is a wandering samurai [hero] with no lord or master. The Doctor is an alien being from a culture of infinite knowledge and power whose people could easily use their superior technology to be supreme overlords. But, instead, he stole the TARDIS from his people and mostly spends his time on Earth observing and assisting fragile, complicated, and messy humans—whom he refers to as "creatures of hope."

And while Sherlock Holmes is most assuredly human, he has an almost godlike power of observation and deduction which he uses, mostly, to help the little guy. Of the documented cases in the Sherlockian Canon, more than half feature Holmes helping the downtrodden, women, or the police (as compared to an aristocrat or government minister). Holmes and The Doctor operate independently of their established structural hierarchy for the betterment of humanity. And both have a shadow, or foil, who similarly operates outside of the establishment, but for selfish and personal gains (arch-nemesis Moriarty for Holmes and The Master in *Doctor Who*). The interactions with these foils indicates that despite the divergent universes and methods of creation, the characters have a similar ethical core: Holmes and The Doctor do good and act on the side of justice because doing so is the right thing to do. They are heroes that speak to the best of what we can find in human nature. Who, after all, is the alien?

Monica M. Schmidt (Solon, Iowa) is president of the Younger Stamfords in Iowa City and a member of the Adventuresses of Sherlock Holmes, the Hounds of the Baskerville (sic), and other societies. She works as a mental health counselor specializing in substance abuse.

WITH DOUGLAS IN CALIFORNIA

Zorro (Don Diego Vega)

Brad Keefauver

An expert swordsman, born of country squires, easily able to hide his skills beneath a disguise, and appreciative of his companion's gift of silence... there is not a word in that description that does not apply to Sherlock Holmes.

A character who brings a past era to life and had a streak of popularity in the 1920s... those words, too, could apply to Mr. Sherlock Holmes of Baker Street.

Yet all of that is the basic description of Don Diego Vega, also known as Zorro, who first appeared in *The Curse of Capistrano* by Johnston McCulley on August 9, 1919. Like Sherlock Holmes's, Zorro's popularity initially came from being serialized in a magazine, in this case a pulp magazine called *All Star Weekly*. Sherlock Holmes eventually figured in sixty novels and short stories by the same author; Zorro's original Canon numbered a nearby sixty-two.

And, as with Sherlock Holmes, the young movie industry was quick to grab the character up. By the time Eille Norwood stepped into the role of Holmes in England and, a year later, John Barrymore did likewise in America, Douglas Fairbanks had already portrayed Zorro in *The Mark of Zorro* (1920). The masked Californian was an instant hit.

When television began to broadcast to every home, there was Guy Williams as *Zorro* on ABC from 1957 to 1959, just as Ronald Howard was syndicated as *Sherlock Holmes* from 1954 to 1955. Indeed, one can almost find Zorro matching Holmes at every turn. In movie comedies, 1981's *Zorro: The Gay Blade* and 1975's *The Adventure of Sherlock Holmes's Smarter Brother* found both heroes with previously unknown siblings. In movie blockbusters, Antonio Banderas did two turns in 1998's *The Mask of Zorro* and 2005's *The Legend of Zorro* to match Robert Downey, Jr. in 2009's *Sherlock Holmes* and 2011's *Sherlock Holmes: A Game of Shadows*. The entertainment careers of these two heroes couldn't be more similar. Had Zorro been around in 1899, one almost has to wonder if William Gillette might not have picked up a sword and attempted to bring him to the stage as he did Holmes.

On the surface, Don Diego Vega's masked alter ego Zorro might seem more like Bruce Wayne's Batman than like Sherlock Holmes. And that's quite natural, as Zorro helped inspire Batman, both in reality and the world of Batman himself, whose parents were killed in an alley returning home from seeing Zorro on the big screen. But even Sherlock Holmes has been known to wear a simple black cloth mask and turn vigilante, as when he and Watson went out into the night to deal with Charles Augustus Milverton in the story of the same name.

And that Milverton moment is when we see how truly similar Sherlock Holmes and Don Diego Vega actually are.

Sherlock Holmes's career began in the 1880s, in the most civilized place on Earth. While his skill with a sword is admirable, and one that his fans love when an excuse to show it comes up in a movie or book, the sword was just not a useful weapon in dealing with gun-toting villains of Victorian England.

In Zorro's setting, however, California of the early 1800s, things were quite different. Firearms were still "one shot only" affairs and the sword still played a vital role in combat, as it did in the time of the Three Musketeers who are famous for swordplay, despite the fact their name describes their firearm use. A Sherlock Holmes of California's Spanish period would have been using a sword or whip much more than a gun, and so Zorro does.

While Don Diego Vega and Señor Zorro seem to have two different personalities, using the dual roles to hide in plain sight, it's easy to see that the attitudes of both personas suit Mr. Sherlock Holmes, given the sort of day he was having. Zorro, as a swordsman and strategist who gleefully knew he was the best at what he did, is very similar to Sherlock Holmes as a hero. Don Diego Vega, on the other hand, airily complaining of how hard it is to ride his horse a few miles, putting on a full show of being a carefree, lazy fop, looks a bit like the Baker Street detective as well. "I shall be as limp as a rag for a week," he moans at the end of *The Sign of the Four*, words that seem like they could have easily come from Don Diego. Was Holmes putting on a show for Watson, the way Don Diego Vega did for the townsfolk?

That scene comes as Sherlock pretends to have little notice or care about Mary Morstan's potential as a romantic partner, which Watson is all about, and there again we see a little Don Diego in our favorite detective. Don Diego Vega seemed to care nothing about women or romance. "I don't know anything about it," he would reply when pressed. "I never ran around making love to women."

"The fair sex is your department," Sherlock Holmes would tell Watson, expressing similar apathy. And yet when Holmes needs to court the maid Agatha (again in the Milverton matter), he seems quite adept at it. Did Sherlock Holmes drop into the role of worthless idler with not even the energy to find a woman attractive, as needed, in his interactions with even his friends?

It would be a very "Zorro" thing to do.

Both Vega and Holmes were tricksters in their way, heir to that long line of mythic figures going back to Loki, Coyote, and their like. Both men loved to tweak the noses of the official forces of their homeland, enjoyed their own cleverness a bit too much sometimes, and would shift their appearance as needed to accomplish their goals. And like the best tricksters of legend, Zorro and Sherlock Holmes both had a way of flipping a situation that looked like it was going one direction, to have it reverse to an entirely different result.

One could almost see Sherlock Holmes slipping into a Zorro role like a hand in a glove, were it not for one requirement for the job that we just don't have in Holmes's resume: how skilled he was as a horseman. We know he could drive a carriage and help groom a horse, but do we ever actually see him ride? It is hard to imagine him going through life in a horsey era such as the Victorian age, coming from country squires, and never once finding himself on horseback. Was he actually as good at it as he was with so many other things? It would seem a skill worth having for a case that took place in the country. Yet he and Watson always seem to be walking or taking a cart or carriage.

I suspect we should give him the benefit of the doubt on that one and say yes. If required to take up a Zorro role in defense of his countrymen, Sherlock Holmes would have certainly learned any horsey skills he was missing, if, indeed, he was missing any.

Don Diego Vega would have had a much harder time filling Holmes's shoes in a London consulting detective's business. But in at least one similar sort of adventure, Zorro did do a very "Sherlock" thing and exposed a local ghost as nothing more than a man-made plot. Of course, as with all Zorro titles, "Zorro Lays A Ghost" was a bit more direct than *The Hound of the Baskervilles*. The learning curve to be a Sherlock Holmes might have been a bit tougher on Don Diego than the other way around.

In considering these two fellows, Sherlock Holmes and Don Diego Vega, and the roles they played, it seems hardly enough to say that Sherlock Holmes was *like* Señor Zorro. Given the chance, Sherlock Holmes might have even *loved* taking on Zorro's job for a time, confronting villains head-on and playing them for the fool. It might not have stimulated his intellect enough for the long term, but for a while... for just a little while...

Well, perhaps Zorro's sword could have easily gone from its usual "Z" to curving its "swish-swish-swish" of the blade to make the mark of the letter "S." Any man who enjoyed shooting initials into a wall with a revolver, as Sherlock Holmes did, would certainly have enjoyed making Zorro's trademark initial on his foes.

Brad Keefauver (Peoria, Illinois) blogs under the title of "Sherlock Peoria," continuing a Sherlockian writing habit that began with a pastiche in a 1978 scion newsletter, and has woven through three books, numerous essays and presentations, and now a podcast he hesitates to admit to. The title of this essay is a phrase from *The Valley of Fear*.

THERE IS SOMETHING POSITIVELY INHUMAN IN YOU

Mr. Spock

Charles Prepolec

Who is tall, thin, and ascetic, has a sharp, striking profile, is physically strong, particularly in his long thin fingers, knows an exotic fighting style, is driven by logic, well grounded in the sciences, including chemistry, in strong control of his emotions, plays a stringed instrument, is always the smartest person in the room, finds guessing abhorrent, is largely asexual with little use for the softer emotions, was thought dead but returned to life, takes on a covert assignment in retirement, sports a goatee on one occasion, is called inhuman and cold-blooded by his Doctor friend, appears to read minds, is staunchly loyal to his friends, has his own views of justice, unexpectedly reveals he has a brother out of the blue, and has a name that starts with S and ends with K?

Got it? Well, of all the worthy characters and individuals in history, literature and mythology to make it into the pages of this book, surely there is but one who can claim the same sort of pop culture iconography and characteristics we associate with Sherlock Holmes. That figure is, of course, none other than the half-human Vulcan Science Officer of the starship Enterprise who first beamed into our televisions, hearts and minds, in the autumn of 1966: Mr. Spock of *Star Trek*.

While a green-blooded, pointy-eared, mixed species alien in a futuristic television series might not, at first glance, seem like the obvious choice, the characteristics I pointed out above are equally and inarguably true of both Sherlock Holmes and Mr. Spock. In some cases, the similarities are largely superficial, but in looking back at a 50-year history for Spock, the actor who portrayed him, and the work of the writers who developed him, with an eye on the impact of the character on pop culture and fandom, a much greater connection appears.

Superficial similarities between Spock and Holmes were noted fairly quickly in Sherlockian circles, with the earliest such commentary appearing in *Baker Street Pages* in December 1967 (a Sherlockian journal then edited by the esteemed, though much younger, editor of this very book), in a short article by Barbara Goldfield titled "Did Sherlock Holmes Have Pointed Ears?". A year later, no less a personage than SF/fantasy writer Poul Anderson, in an article called "The Archetypical Holmes" in the September 1968 edition of the *Baker Street Journal*, took note of the Spock and Holmes relationship, indicating that Spock was the latest incarnation of a Holmesian archetype. Anderson was so taken with Spock that he went so far as to say that Leonard Nimoy, who played Spock on *Star Trek*, "is the perfect successor to Basil Rathbone, and that you write to the networks and movie companies saying so." While a write-in campaign was certainly on the cards, it had nothing to do with having Nimoy play Holmes but was rather about saving *Star Trek* from cancellation.

That, however, is another story. In the meantime, others were also taking note, but the analysis was working in the opposite direction. It wasn't about Spock being like Holmes, but rather about Holmes actually being a Vulcan, as noted and excellently argued by Priscilla Pollner in "Was Sherlock Holmes a Vulcan?", first published in *Son of a Beach* (Spring 1970). That was just the beginning, based only on the 79 episodes of *Star Trek*'s original three-season run.

In that original television run we were introduced to the basics. Spock was born of a Vulcan father, Sarek, and a human mother, Amanda Grayson. The Vulcans, as a species, had embraced the path of logic and suppression of emotion, through meditation and training, as a means of moving their society away from violence and savagery. The goal was to function on a level of pure logic, without the distractions and diversion of emotional impulses. It's worth noting that Spock, and other Vulcans, are not without emotions, but choose to hold them in check, much like our hero. The Vulcans also embraced a strong belief in the benefits of cultural and racial diversity, symbolized by *IDIC* (Infinite Diversity in Infinite Combinations), pacifism, and veganism. Peculiarities of Vulcan physiology mean Spock is possessed of greater strength, superior hearing, an increased constitution, and the ability to go with less sleep and food than humans. He is also able to seemingly read the thoughts of others through a tactile process called the Vulcan Mind Meld. In terms of self-defence, he is capable of a unique means of rendering an opponent unconscious by applying a Vulcan nerve pinch. Another bizarre Vulcan oddity is the biological imperative to mate every seven years or die, which is a somewhat cruel situation for a species that tends not to express emotion.

Spock, being neither fully Vulcan nor fully human, was something of an outsider in either culture and found himself trying to understand and reconcile both sides of his heritage. To do so, he eschewed the traditional Vulcan educational route to the Vulcan Science Academy and instead opted to join Starfleet, resulting in an 18-year estrangement from his father. As a cadet, Spock was assigned to the U.S.S. *Enterprise* under the command of Captain Christopher Pike, under whom he served for eleven years, eventually becoming first officer and science officer by the time Captain Kirk took command. It is at that point that the five-year mission to "explore" and to "seek out" begins and the relationship with Captain Kirk and Dr. Leonard "Bones" McCoy comes into being. It is the friendship between these characters that drives *Star Trek*, much as the friendship between Holmes and Watson is crucial to the success of their canonical tales.

While the focus of my argument is that Sherlock Holmes is like Spock, I will suggest that Kirk and the good Doctor are also part of the package. Given that Star Trek gives us a triumvirate of friends, rather than a couple, the direct analogies can be awkward. However, Kirk, at times, can almost be seen as an extension of Spock's human side, the physical, the rash, the emotional, with the two individuals being so complementary that perhaps the two together might be more representative of the single Sherlock Holmes character. Most commentators, however, tend to see Kirk and McCoy as sharing or alternating in the Watson and Lestrade roles. In any case, the friendships are extremely strong, with each member of the trio incredibly loyal and ready to sacrifice themselves for the others.

Both Kirk and McCoy, though mostly the latter, repeatedly comment on how Spock's logic makes him seem cold, computer-like, insensitive and positively inhuman; observations also noted by our own dear Watson in regard to Sherlock Holmes, as when in "The Greek Interpreter" he calls him "an isolated phenomenon, a brain without a heart, as deficient in human sympathy as he was pre-eminent in intelligence." While the Kirk-Spock friendship appears closer than the Spock-McCoy relationship, it is Dr. McCoy who metaphorically, and quite literally, keeps alive the spirit of Spock at one point.

For both Kirk and McCoy, and everyone else aboard the starship *Enterprise*, Spock is always the voice of reason. He is the go-to guy when answers are needed, or a plan, or just a calculation of the odds of success. On more than one occasion, that reliance forces Spock to go outside his comfort zone and make educated guesses. While Holmes informs us that guessing is a habit destructive to the logical faculties, Spock simply indicates that "guessing is not in my nature." There are dozens of little character moments like that in the original run of the series that sync with Sherlock Holmes. Spock is soothed by music and plays a Vulcan harp, rather than a violin. The Vulcan nerve pinch might as well be a Baritsu move. The unique sense of justice that allows Holmes to burgle a house or allow a criminal to go unpunished in certain circumstances is illustrated when Spock defies Starfleet Command to effectively kidnap his disfigured former Captain, Christopher Pike, to return him to a place where he can live out his days without disability. Less charitably, Spock uses the romantic approach with an enemy female Romulan Commander to gain access to secret information harmful to others, basically having the equivalent of an Aggie moment. Watching the 79 original episodes, and the short-lived animated series that turned up after cancellation to cash in on syndication of the original series, will reveal far more than I can illustrate here, but all of it was certainly available to, and noticed by, the early *BSJ* commentators.

Then came the Great Hiatus and *The Return*. With the cancellation of *Star Trek* in June of 1969, aside from the 22-episode animated series that turned up in 1975, and the endless syndicated reruns of the original series, there were no new stories produced until 1979, ending a ten-year hiatus, with *Star Trek: The Motion Picture*. At that point we learn that Spock retired from Starfleet and returned to Vulcan to pursue a course of pure logic, much as Holmes retired from London life to focus on the writing of his magnum opus on detection. Spock does not keep bees in retirement, but like Holmes, he does take up active service when duty calls. As such, *Star Trek: The Motion Picture* serves as *The Return*, although things don't really hit their stride until the second film, *Star Trek II: The Wrath of Khan*, and the arrival of writer/director Nicholas Meyer on the scene.

Meyer, of course, as the author of the 1974 bestseller *The Seven-Per-Cent Solution*, and screenwriter of the 1976 film adaptation, is no stranger to Sherlockians. However, never having watched the show, he was a stranger to *Star Trek*. As such he recognized it as sort of "Horatio Hornblower in Space" and brought a classic nautical adventure sensibility to his film. Though not overt, one can find a couple of Sherlockian touches in the film. The villain, Khan, a revived character from the original series, plays a Moriarty-like nemesis role here. To be fair, it is as Nemesis to Kirk, but it is Spock who dies as a result of Khan's actions. In Spock's final scene with Kirk, as he's dying from radiation poisoning, he indicates a certain satisfaction in knowing that his death will save other lives, vaguely echoing the note that Sherlock Holmes left for Watson at Reichenbach. Later, during the funeral scene, Kirk says of Spock: "Of all the souls I have encountered in my travels, his was the most... human," tonally echoing Watson's description of Holmes as "the best and the wisest man whom I have ever known."

In the next film, *Star Trek III: The Search for Spock*, we learn that Spock's "essence" was transferred to Dr. McCoy moments before exposure to the radiation, and that the good Doctor was essentially keeping the spirit of Spock alive until it could be returned to his physical body. Spock is back to his usual self by *Star Trek V: The Final Frontier*, wherein he reveals that the rebellious Vulcan leading a political movement is his older (half)brother, Sybok. This comes as a surprise to Kirk, McCoy, and the viewers, since Spock has never mentioned having any siblings, much as Holmes surprised Watson with the news about Mycroft's existence.

With *Star Trek VI: The Undiscovered Country*, Nicholas Meyer is back in the director's chair, working from a screenplay he co-wrote with Denny Martin Flinn (author of two mystery novels featuring the grandson of Sherlock Holmes, *San Francisco Kills* and *Killer Finish*), and this time the Sherlock Holmes connection is made plain. When a Klingon chancellor is killed and the killer is thought to be aboard the *Enterprise*, Spock finds himself investigating and at one point declares: "An ancestor of mine maintained that if you eliminate the impossible, whatever remains, however improbable, must be the solution." The debate about whether Spock meant Sherlock Holmes or Arthur Conan Doyle has raged ever since. (Curiously, the line is also spoken by Zachary Quinto's Spock, but without the ancestor reference, in the 2009 *Star Trek* reboot.) In a syndicated 1991 newspaper interview, Meyer said: "The connection occurred to me because it seems to me that Spock is a very Holmesian character. Holmes describes himself as 'a thinking machine,' and Spock is always talking about logic. It seems to me he was a sort of sci-fi incarnation of Holmes."

In an odd bit of turnabout, in the second series episode of BBC *Sherlock* "The Hounds of Baskerville", when Benedict Cumberbatch's Sherlock trots out the "When you have eliminated the impossible" line, Martin Freeman's Watson responds with "All right, Spock, just take it easy," which suggests that in their world, Spock is the originator of the phrase. Interestingly, in the next episode "The Reichenbach Fall," Kirk's Spock eulogy from *Star Trek II: The Wrath of Khan*, is also paraphrased when Martin Freeman's Watson, at the graveside of Holmes, says: "You were the best man, and most human human being, that I've ever known."

Mind you, that isn't the only BBC *Sherlock* connection. I'd suggest that the character of Molly Hooper is largely modelled on Nurse Chapel, who was clearly infatuated with Spock, but largely ignored, in the original *Star Trek* series. Just as BBC *Sherlock* sprung an unlikely female Holmes sibling on us, *Star Trek: Discovery* gave Spock a previously unknown adopted sister.

As intriguing as those connections are, the most telling is not so much what was on screen, but in the viewer response. BBC *Sherlock* was a massive international hit, making stars of Freeman and Cumberbatch, and generating a huge and devoted fandom, which in turn started churning out reams of unofficial fan fiction, including a great deal of homoerotic Johnlock slash fiction. What many BBC *Sherlock* fans don't realize is that this was not a new phenomenon. Kirk, Spock, and *Star Trek* had been there before. As early as September 1967, as *Star Trek* began its second season, a fanzine called *Spockanalia* appeared and actor Leonard Nimoy was being swamped by fans at personal appearances. Within a few years, possibly as early as 1968, "The Ring of Soshern" by Jennifer Guttridge was privately printed and began changing hands on the fan circuit. Not only was it the first piece of Kirk/Spock slash, it was probably the first bit of fandom slash fiction about anyone. By the late 70s, the fanzine *Holmesian Federation* appeared, solidifying the connection between Holmes and Spock while also providing an outlet for unified fandom, but non-slash, fan fiction.

Lastly, no exploration of why Sherlock Holmes is like Spock would be complete without a few words about and from the actor behind the character: Leonard Nimoy. During the time of the Great Hiatus between the original series and the first film, Nimoy actually played Sherlock Holmes, both in a short educational film in 1975—*The Interior Motive*—and on-stage in 1976 in the touring production of the William Gillette play *Sherlock Holmes*. In 1978, he was the narrator of the documentary *In Search of... Sherlock Holmes*.

On playing Holmes, Nimoy said in the Chicago *Tribune* of May 9, 1978: "He's an asocial man, hardly your average 9-to-5 worker with a family. Instead, he's chosen a very special kind of life, and he has very little respect for most of the people around him who are also involved in his profession. He's an outsider, in so many ways—particularly in his relationships with women. Holmes is very much an alien, all right, and I felt that I could understand him the same way I understood Spock."

And, finally, the last word on the matter from Nimoy's 1975 memoir *I Am Not Spock*: "Perhaps Spock, with his superhuman intellect, is the greatest detective of them all."

Charles Prepolec (Calgary, Alberta) is a Baker Street Irregular, and freelance editor and co-editor of six Sherlock Holmes anthologies, as well as anthologies featuring Arthur Conan Doyle's Professor Challenger and Edgar Allan Poe's Dupin.

MAN, IT'S WITCHCRAFT!

Hermione Granger

Amy Thomas

"Oh, honestly, don't you two read?" This phrase comes from the first of J.K. Rowling's Harry Potter books, *The Sorcerer's Stone* (1997), where it is uttered by Hermione Granger; but it might well have come from the mouth of Sherlock Holmes. Similarly, Holmesian axioms such as, "It is a capital mistake to theorize before you have all the evidence. It biases the judgment," from *A Study in Scarlet*, read as though they might be Granger originals, straight from the mouth of the exacting purveyor of magic.

Surface similarities between a young girl in the 1990s and a Victorian detective may not seem immediately apparent, but upon further examination, the clever witch and the consulting detective have a great deal in common.

Holmes is a central character described through another's eyes. Save for a few occasions, the reader meets a Holmes who is filtered through the Watsonian perspective. Given that the Harry Potter series is told in third person, it may seem as though this is a point of major difference; however, it is almost completely a third person limited perspective, from the point of view of Harry himself. In practice, then, the Hermione encountered by the reader is usually filtered through Harry's eyes. The effect, in both cases, is that the reader understands and extrapolates a central character through another character's encounters and opinions.

The voluminous length of the Harry Potter series, as well as its focus on character psychology, provides for the development of Hermione as a character in detail and with a great deal of intricacy. Details of Holmes's domestic life and character traits are left to be gleaned mid-case, but this does not mean, in the end, that they are as sparse, in comparison, as they may seem. Sixty stories, including four short novels, provide ample material to form a picture of Holmes and his worldview, much as the seven books that comprise the Harry Potter series paint a complex picture of Hermione's character.

Hermione and Holmes both have largely unexplored backgrounds, arguably for similar reasons. Hermione's parents do not possess magical abilities, and Holmes's family, other than his brother Mycroft, apparently have no involvement with his own brand of deductive magic. The effect is similar in both cases: the reader is forced to take the characters as they are presented within the stories, without the kind of speculation that comes from elucidated childhood experiences.

Additionally, as a heartrending part of her wizarding destiny, Hermione must let go of her family. Ultimately, in *Harry Potter and the Deathly Hallows*, she is forced, by circumstances beyond her control, to make them forget she even exists. Holmes, too, leaves something behind, symbolically becoming a creature of the city, even though, according to "The Greek Interpreter," his family origins are in the country, an indication that he has likely relinquished a previous way of life. Beyond this, readers are told little of what shaped either character. In both cases, the special traits they possess isolate them from their families of origin but lead to the creation of new family units. Holmes becomes attached to Watson and Mrs. Hudson, Hermione to Ron Weasley and Harry Potter. As their stories spin out and become longer, more acquaintances and friends are added to the circles of both.

Differences in situation, gender, time period, and circumstances admitted, these characters display similarities in personality and the ways they view the world. Both are intelligent reasoning machines with loyal hearts. Both are also passionate about causes that affect their personal moral code. Hermione advocates for the plight of enslaved house elves, and, in *Harry Potter and the Goblet of Fire*, she takes justice into her own hands when she traps tabloid reporter Rita Skeeter and forces her to mend her libelous ways. Holmes similarly takes justice into his own hands on more than one occasion, notably when he lets Charles Augustus Milverton's murderer go free, believing justice has been served.

Magic might seem like the factor that firmly separates the witch Hermione from the eminently reasonable Holmes—but actually, Hermione uses magic very scientifically, and, at times, Holmes uses deduction almost fantastically. For Holmes, deduction is practically a superpower, although on its own, it does nothing. His assertion that "You see but you do not observe" in "A Scandal in Bohemia" is a reminder that it is the person who wields the observational ability who matters. Similarly, in Hermione's world, magic is a tool, but the witch or wizard who wields it determines its relative effectiveness. An early example of this occurs in *Harry Potter and the Sorcerer's Stone*, when Harry and Ron, who both possess magic, are nevertheless unable to perform the Wingardium Leviosa spell, but Hermione does it easily because of her superior technique. Others have the ability to do magic in the Harry Potter series, just as most people who appear in the Holmes Canon have some kind of basic deductive reasoning ability. Holmes's and Hermione's meticulous practice and attention to detail, as well as their heights of success, set them apart from others and bring them nearer to one another.

Throughout the stories in which she features, Hermione experiences prejudice related to her "mudblood" origins, the slur a reference to the fact that her family does not possess magic. Even as she excels as a witch and star student, she must contend with others' discrimination. Holmes experiences others' distaste related to his detection skills, although, as a white male, he is also part of a group that was highly privileged in the Victorian period. Both Holmes and Granger experience a mixture of prejudice and privilege, and both are widely lauded and derided by people in their stories.

Ultimately, both characters have something in them that takes them beyond the status of good character and all the way to hero. Hermione, an exceptional student, could spend her time simply studying, though her selection as a Gryffindor, the house associated with valor, hints at her other character traits. Additionally, Sherlock Holmes could have behaved more like his brother Mycroft and used his intellect in sedentary or exclusively academic ways. Instead, just as Hermione cannot resist fighting for her principles, Holmes cannot resist the lure of a case. Both appreciate the challenge, but for both, there is more to it than that. As Watson famously said of Holmes in "The Three Garridebs," he was possessed of "a great heart as well as of a great brain." In the end, Hermione's fight against evil, embodied primarily in the form of Voldemort, is more than a simple challenge; it leads her to risk her life to save her friends, and eventually her entire world, several times.

Perhaps the most important similarity between the two is that Holmes and Hermione become their best selves through friendship. Even though Hermione has no Watsonian narrator, her journey is shaped by and intertwined with the journeys of Harry and Ron, and she is seen through their eyes. Technically the cleverest of the three, she utilizes their humanity and ingenuity to help her develop into the most complete version of herself. Like Holmes with Watson, she flourishes by joining her wits with Ron's heart and Harry's selflessness. Years later, Harry and Ron still remain her supports even as she becomes the leader of the wizarding world. Just as Holmes is "lost without my Boswell," as he says in "A Scandal in Bohemia," so too are Hermione's destiny and character shaped by association.

Sherlock Holmes's influence is felt pervasively in English literature, but perhaps the greatest heroes always share some traits. After all, detective stories are mysteries. At the basic level, this simply means identifying and fixing problems in the world. As a protagonist, Harry Potter's journey is about coming of age under the shadow of destiny. In contrast, a version of Rowling's series with the clever, incisive Hermione as the protagonist might well have read much more like the Holmes tales, stories of her confronting and solving problems leading up to her courageous stand against the final problem that threatens her way of life. Holmes has his Reichenbach, Hermione the Battle of Hogwarts. Both survive their fights with honor and in so doing transform from character into legend.

Amy Thomas (Fort Myers, Florida) is part of the Baker Street Babes podcast, as well as the author of *The Detective and The Woman* series of novels featuring Sherlock Holmes and Irene Adler. She is a freelance editor and ghostwriter.

HOLMES IS IN THE HOUSE

Dr. Gregory House

Lyn Adams

"When you have eliminated the impossible, whatever remains, however improbable, must be the truth." —Sherlock Holmes

"It's never Lupus." —Gregory House, MD

In the 19th century, we were introduced to a consulting detective, the first one of his kind in the world, the brilliant Sherlock Holmes. In the 21st century, we meet an equally brilliant doctor who holds the lead position in the very first Department of Diagnostic Medicine at Princeton-Plainsboro Teaching Hospital, a unique assignment created especially for him—Dr. Gregory House.

Premiering in 2004, *House* quickly became one of the most popular television series of the decade. Although critics pointed out that Gregory House, portrayed by the talented British actor Hugh Laurie, was loosely based on Sherlock Holmes, some viewers may have been unaware of the connection between the two characters, at least initially. I will admit to being among those who didn't latch on to the series because of the clever allusions to Arthur Conan Doyle's creation. In fact, the opposite happened: House helped lead me to Holmes.

Prior to watching *House*, I was not yet a fan of Sherlock Holmes, having never read the original stories, though I was vaguely aware of certain details and images of the famous detective—deerstalker, pipe, cocaine—that have overshadowed the true essence of Holmes. Dr. House bears little resemblance to these ubiquitous images, so until critics of the show mentioned the connection between House and Holmes, I remained blissfully unaware of this clever screenwriting sleight of hand, and simply enjoyed the show for its superb writing and stellar cast, all wrapped around suspenseful medical cases with its fair share of human drama.

Sherlock Holmes is a complex character, and Victorian readers of the Canon latched on to his persona in a large part because he transcended their times. So too is Dr. House a unique character, more so than any doctor we've met before, with personality traits much like Holmes's but with a darker, edgier side, mirroring our more cynical society. House is a reflection of the times, a culture of narcissism, self-centeredness, telling-it-like-it-is regardless of how it might affect the listener, impatience at not only others' weaknesses but our own. In House, arrogance has been ratcheted up many notches, though it could be argued that it's partially to mask an underlying fear of failure.

With a keen intellect and almost unbelievable skills of deduction, House can diagnose not only his patients' ailments but also their personalities and lifestyles with just a cursory glance; he has a razor-sharp wit and off-the-chart mood swings, he is not one to make friends easily, in fact almost not at all save one, and prone to substance abuse. Any of this sound familiar? To those who know Sherlock Holmes, yes! Though House's personality traits are amped up to appeal to modern audiences, underlying them are the familiar Sherlock Holmes traits known so well to his devoted fans.

Before we delve further into the character of Dr. Gregory House, let's meet a very important person in his life, his best friend, Dr. James Wilson. Similar in many ways to the beloved friend of Sherlock Holmes, Dr. John H. Watson, Dr. Wilson helps humanize our protagonist, teaching him about relationships and societal norms, and perhaps just as importantly, does his best to prevent House from being arrested, imprisoned or killed.

As seen through the eyes of Dr. Wilson, here are some key characteristics of House, many that parallel those of Sherlock Holmes:

- A keen intellect—well, at least in House's fields of interest. But he can be woefully ignorant in current affairs. Except soap operas, he's an expert in those.
- Wit—very witty, and more often than not, very sarcastic. Very, very sarcastic. I have the scars to prove it.
- Misogynistic—actually, this character label is not wholly accurate, though it seems to be a consensus based on his lack of any long-term female relationships and his general disdain towards women. But there is much more depth there. He did have a few meaningful relationships in years past, but along with some deep familial issues, those failed relationships have left him scarred, hesitant to open himself up again.
- Drug addict—though House's drug addiction developed over time because of chronic pain brought on by an infarction in his leg, leading to muscle death, it has also become an emotional crutch of sorts, to go along with his actual cane, something to help dull not only physical pain, but the pain of tedium when there is a lack of any interesting cases. Some may use cocaine to dull such feelings of ennui; House's drug of choice is Vicodin. If I'm to be honest here, though House often blames his own cranky attitudes on his injured leg and

subsequent drug use, I can confirm that even before the infarction he could be a real jerk.

- Friendless—House actually does have friends, well, one friend to be exact—me—who remains loyal despite being treated as a whipping boy of sorts. Again, I have the scars to attest to that. Though he seems to enjoy consulting with me periodically, often to gain some much-needed insights into humanity, I'm also treated at times like a sidekick, or a mirror in which he can observe his own cleverness.
- Prone to laziness—House will literally jump at the chance to solve a juicy medical mystery, but then fall back into a state of apathy for days on end. TV soap operas are his preferred distraction when avoiding work. And stealing Coma Guy's food. I try to stop him, but he won't listen.
- Religious beliefs—simply stated, nil. It is a common belief that House is an atheist, and it's a title he often bestows upon himself. Yet, though he often mocks patients' religious beliefs, he reluctantly admits that evidence exists either way for there being a God. He simply chooses atheism for himself, as it's more comforting in its simplicity.

No patience for patients

"It is of the first importance," he [Sherlock Holmes] cried, "not to allow your judgment to be biased by personal qualities. A client is to me a mere unit, a factor in a problem. The emotional qualities are antagonistic to clear reasoning." —*The Sign of the Four*

"Treating illnesses is why we became doctors, treating patients is what makes most doctors miserable."—Gregory House, pilot episode, season 1

Gregory House displays incredible diagnostic skills that amaze patients and colleagues alike. Yet he insists he isn't interested in gaining their trust or respect; they are simply players in his game of puzzle solving. As Holmes will often do when clients enter his flat at 221B Baker Street, House can give a patient his diagnosis in mere moments, curtly dismiss them, then return to his office and willingly lapse into a state of self-induced apathy. However, when a case is brought to him that other specialists cannot solve, he will leap at the chance and go to sometimes life-threatening lengths—to both himself and his patients—to reach a diagnosis, determine eventual treatment, and ultimately bring about a cure. House at one point was willing to inject himself with his patient's blood, knowing it could kill him, to confirm that a transfusion was the cause of the symptoms. This incident is reminiscent of Holmes's attempt to solve the mystery of "The Devil's Foot," exposing himself, and Watson, to a deadly poison. House was even willing to sacrifice his pet rat Steve

McQueen for the greater good, to save the life of Dr. Foreman; it turned out that he didn't need to euthanize Steve after all, but as they say, it's the thought that counts.

What they did for love... or imaginary love

> "And yet the motives of women are so inscrutable.... How can you build on such a quicksand? Their most trivial action may mean volumes, or their most extraordinary conduct may depend upon a hairpin or a curling-tongs." Sherlock Holmes, "The Second Stain"

> "The most successful marriages are based on lies." Gregory House, "Maternity," season 1, episode 4

Though they often criticize women for their deceitful and manipulative ways, both Holmes and House can at times be very disingenuous towards women. In an attempt to glean vital information for a case against Charles Augustus Milverton, Holmes proposed marriage to Milverton's housemaid, then cruelly abandoned her once he had the information he needed. To the surprise, and concern, of his co-workers, House married a Russian immigrant, Dominika Patrova, in large part to irritate his former lover Dr. Lisa Cuddy, but ultimately so that Dominika could obtain a permanent resident green card, and quid pro quo, House would then have a live-in housemaid. Alas, the story does not end happily ever after, as is often the case when duplicity is involved. Just when they begin to develop true feelings for each other, Dominika discovers that House lied to her by destroying her green card letters of approval, in a misguided attempt to keep her from leaving him, and leave him she does.

A great heart as well as a great brain

> "It seemed to me that he [Sherlock Holmes] was more nearly moved by the softer human emotions than I had ever seen him. A moment later he was the cold and practical thinker once more."
> —"The Six Napoleons"

> "Humanity is overrated." —Gregory House, pilot episode, season 1

In the same way that House shows his human side in his personality flaws and drug addiction, so does he show he has a heart, and is capable of compassion. After he correctly diagnoses a young lacrosse player who is initially thought to have a terminal illness, thereby bringing about his cure, House appears at one of the young man's first games shortly after recovery, and quietly cheers him on with a look of almost paternal pride, but also profound sadness. He handles his cane as if mimicking the player's movements (perhaps he too once played lacrosse in his youth) and wistfully stares at the field long after everyone else has left, mourning the loss of his own mobility, and the drastic change to his life brought on by his injury.

Gregory House's final appearance in the series reminds us of what is most important in House's life: his love for his dearest friend, Dr. James Wilson. House fakes his own death—his own Reichenbach Falls—which ends his medical career, to be with Wilson during James's final months before his dearest friend succumbs to cancer. In truth, it wasn't a wholly altruistic act on House's part, as he was also dodging an inevitable jail term for a prank gone wrong that caused substantial damage to the hospital. Yet we tend to forgive that bit of self-centeredness when we understand the sacrifice House has made in order to be with his friend and help him navigate the dark, lonely road of terminal illness.

Though we are often shocked at Dr. Gregory House's appalling bedside manner, we can't help but admire him. He is human, just like us, and could have taken an easier road in life, one of simplicity and boredom, laziness and drug use. But despite his faults, he strives to use his amazing gifts of intellect and deduction to help others. In this respect, he is most definitely an incarnation of Sherlock Holmes.

Flawed as Sherlock Holmes and Gregory House may be, they are heroes. They may not be typical ones, unlike many of the lofty, glorified heroes we've encountered in life and literature, with high moral standards and deep compassion for humanity. But they are heroes all the same, in that they ultimately risk all to help others, and use their "superpowers" to bring about justice and healing.

In life and in literature, we will continue to meet other people and other characters who remind us of Sherlock Holmes. Through Dr. Gregory House, we are once again introduced to the Great Detective, or in my case, newly introduced, and very gratefully so, to the wisest and greatest man who never lived, and who will never die.

Lyn Adams (Livermore, California) is a neophyte to the world of Sherlock Holmes who enjoys chatting with fellow Sherlockians on social media. Her career is her family, but she works as a sales administrator to help support her book-buying habit.

PUTTING RIGHT WHAT WENT WRONG

Sam Beckett

Linnea Dodson

Sherlock Holmes is like… a lost time traveler.

Donald P. Bellasario, successful producer of *Magnum, P.I.* and *Airwolf*, wanted to create an anthology show. But those weren't popular, so he reframed the concept as a time travel experiment with no fixed setting and only two recurring characters. Sam (Scott Backula) would travel by "leaping" into the body of random Americans at any point between 1950 and 1980. Back in the future, Al (Dean Stockwell) would serve as exposition-ex-machina, feeding Sam data from a master computer and interviewing Sam's unwitting host. The result: *Quantum Leap*, a cult hit airing on NBC from 1989 to 1993.

The parallels between Sherlock Holmes and Sam Beckett are startling despite the century separating them. (So are the parallels between the smoking, drinking, ex-military Watson and Al, both men of great loyalty and enthusiastic multi-national love lives, but this is not their essay.)

Holmes and Sam are brilliant scientists and martial artists. Both are fluent in becoming someone else—Holmes as a master of disguise, Sam because his malfunctioning time machine forces him to live as someone else until he solves their problems. As the opening narration explained, "Dr. Beckett finds himself leaping from life to life, striving to put right what once went wrong."

Few things are more wrong than crime, so it's no surprise that many of the *Quantum Leap* stories dealt with foiling the same ventures Holmes worked to right: blackmail, robbery, kidnapping, even the occasional murder.

What is surprising is looking back at both sets of narratives and realizing that their respective creators weren't just telling thrilling tales of adventure. Doyle and Bellasario often used their heroes to champion feminist issues.

Oh, both had their missteps that are all the more glaring in the #metoo era. Holmes blithely breaks the law and the heart of Agatha the housemaid ("Charles Augustus Milverton"), while every man in "A Case of Identity" piles on poor Miss Sutherland—her stepfather gaslights her, Watson insultingly describes her, and Holmes laughingly refuses to tell her the solution to her own case. Sam's incredibly awkward attempt at encouragement in "How the Tess Was Won" is to assure Tess that women aren't just as good as men, they're better... at making babies. Patronizing consolation for a woman desperately trying to prove that she, not some putative husband or son, is smart enough, skilled enough, and strong enough to run her beloved ranch.

Yes, both narratives were a product of their times... but their times, they were a-changin'.

Woman's suffrage was a huge concern in Doyle's era. In Britain the years when the short stories were being written included the formation of the National Union for Women's Suffrage (1897), the Women's Social and Political Union (1903), the Women's March (1907), the hunger strikes (1909), forced feedings (1909), and the brutal Cat-and-Mouse Act (1913).

Quantum Leap came in the wake of Women's Lib, which in the United States had produced the Equal Pay Act (1963), Title VII bans on sex discrimination in employment (1964), legal contraception (1965), no-fault divorce (1969), Title IX bans on sex discrimination in education (1972), legalized abortion (1973), the Pregnancy [anti-]Discrimination Act (1978), the push for the Equal Rights Amendment (1982), and Geraldine Ferraro as the first Vice-Presidential candidate for a major party (1984).

So Doyle and Bellasario were creating light entertainment for societies roiling with reexamination of women's roles and rights. In response, although Doyle never mentioned suffrage and Bellasario mentioned women's lib just once, both creators repeatedly used their platform to illustrate why their male heroes thought it was important to side with women.

Doyle could have used any one of the plots from the *Adventures* as his first story for the *Strand*, including the one with the risible Miss Sutherland. He made the conscious decision to instead premiere with a beautiful, intelligent woman who not only foils Holmes, but beats him at his own games of deduction and disguise. In the stories, Holmes could have sympathized heartily with the King of Bohemia and Lord St. Simon, both done wrong by women. The king was being blackmailed by an ex-lover; the lord, through no fault of his own, had been stripped of bride, pride, and financial security. These were men that a middle-class British public could support. But Holmes mildly mocked them while expressing his admiration for the women. He even delivered a ringing defense of the runaway bigamous Lady St. Simon: "I cannot allow that there is any humiliation... I can hardly see how the lady could have acted otherwise."

Holmes could easily have upheld Victorian standards regarding moral failings. It was arguably Lady Eva Brackwell's own fault she had written compromising letters; even Holmes admits that Charles Augustus Milverton did not blackmail the innocent. Instead, Holmes accepts her commission to attempt negotiations with "the worst man in London" and when those negotiations fail, breaks into Milverton's house to steal what could not be purchased. This isn't just a one-time decision on Holmes's part either; in another tale, although less sympathetic, he's willing to help Lady Hilda Trelawney Hope secretly return the documents she stole to ransom her own compromising correspondence.

Quantum Leap was never going to cover dynastic marriage or the impecunious aristocracy. On the other hand, it was free to explore woman-centric themes inappropriate for Victorian sensibilities, such as stories about a single, pregnant teenager ("8½ Months"), sex therapy ("Dr. Ruth"), and the blunt "Raped." Blackmail, however, was as familiar to Bellasario as it was to Doyle, with nude photographs replacing letters in "Miss Deep South." Just as Holmes ultimately burned all the blackmail letters, it is Sam's job to end the photographer's career. (This episode also repeatedly reminds viewers not to equate beauty with stupidity. Sam's host is using prize money to put herself through medical school.)

Blackmailing women for impropriety is not the only plot point to have remained depressingly similar throughout the passage of time. In both Holmes's and Sam's worlds, women needed to work to survive—yet their careers were constantly being derailed by men. Violet Hunter's putative employer is insisting on controlling her very body—the length of her hair, the dresses she wears, where she might sit—in return for a suspiciously high salary. The owner of the employment agency ignores all these red flags, but Holmes fusses constantly that no sister of his should ever have accepted such a situation. In "Good Morning Peoria," Rachel Porter thinks rock-and-roll music will take her struggling 1959 radio station to the top. But one of the local businessmen so morally opposes rock that he slowly escalates from newspaper editorials through an advertising boycott and legal challenges until he ultimately physically attacks the station to literally silence the defiant Rachel. It is Sam's job to support her resolve—and use his advanced engineering skills to keep them on the air throughout the siege.

Holmes and Sam also need to rescue women who are facing a sexually hostile workplace, such as the already engaged Violet Smith fending off the polite advances of her employer and the impolite advances of his neighbor, or Sam-as-Samantha, literally chased around the office and forcibly fondled by a married man who expects physical thanks for promoting Samantha out of the steno pool. "What Price Gloria" was set in 1961, but aired a mere three years after the Supreme Court ruled in Meritor Savings Bank v. Winson that sexual harassment on the job was a form of legal discrimination. As with "Miss Deep South," Sam's job here is not to simply protect his host and her friend Gloria, but to ensure that the harasser never attacks again.

Staying home doesn't mean a woman is safe. Domestic abuse has continued unchanged from the 19th century into the 20th and through to the 21st. Britain's Matrimonial Causes Act of 1857 allowed a woman to sue for divorce in cases of extreme cruelty, but that recourse was only available to a woman who was wealthy, could find legal support, and wasn't killed for trying to escape. In reality, unchecked domestic abuse within marriage was so prevalent during the Holmesian era that Watson in "A Case of Identity" considers it commonplace: "'A husband's cruelty to his wife.' There is half a column of print, but I know without reading it that it is all perfectly familiar to me. There is, of course, the other woman, the drink, the push, the blow, the bruise, the sympathetic sister or land-lady. The crudest of writers could invent nothing more crude." Crude or not, Doyle's "The Abbey Grange" and *Quantum Leap*'s "Southern Comforts" have the hero helping a battered wife escape life-threatening violence, while "The Illustrious Client" and "Camikazi Kid" deal with them desperately trying to prevent an abusive marriage from happening in the first place. Sam is particularly motivated because he was unable to save his own sister. Katie Beckett may have had easier access to divorce than a Holmesian heroine, but "She was too frightened to leave and too ashamed to tell anyone," Sam confesses miserably to Al.

Yet it's not even descriptions of severe abuse that make for the most powerfully disturbing stories of both canons. That distinction lies with the plots detailing how women are accused of causing their own mistreatment. Every single woman in "Thor Bridge" is victimized and victim-blamed. Neil Gibson deliberately made his wife Maria's "life a misery to her"—while claiming that it was all her fault. ("I knew that if I could kill her love, or if it turned to hate, it would be easier for both of us. But... do what I might, she was as devoted as ever.") In the meantime, even Holmes has concluded Grace Dunbar was a homewrecker (Maria "was past her prime, which was the more unfortunate as a very attractive governess superintended the education of two young children.... If his wife dies, who more likely to succeed her?"). It's only when he discovers that Gibson had instead been harassing an employee who literally couldn't afford to lose her job ("others were dependent upon her, and it was no light matter for her to let them all down by sacrificing her living") that Holmes is willing to reconsider: "I don't know that anything she is accused of is really worse than what you have yourself admitted, that you have tried to ruin a defenceless girl who was under your roof."

Comparably, *Quantum Leap* has two wrenching episodes based on victim-blaming. In "Raped", everyone thinks Sam-as-Katie led her rapist on, is lying, or ought to be talked into dropping the charges against a popular athlete. Sam is there to bear the pressure as she is fired from her church job, is bribed to shut up, tries to find a lawyer willing to take the case, and must listen at trial as her rapist claims consent and the prosecution calls her too ugly for anyone to want to have sex with her. While Sam is handling all of that, Al is ensuring Katie-as-Sam gets trauma support. In "So Help Me God" it's a woman who has been accused of sexual violence, followed by murderous violence when her victim rejected her. Sam has leaped into the defense lawyer and plans to prove that Delilah killed in self-defense, but his work is made all the harder by his client being a poor black woman, the shooting victim being a rich white man, and the trial being set in 1957 Tennessee.

Neither Bellasario nor Doyle needed to be that controversial. There were plenty of exciting but socially safe stories in their respective canons. It was their decision to stray from the safe and conventional, just as it was their deliberate choice to use their masculine heroes to showcase plots illustrating feminine issues.

So yes, Sherlock Holmes is like Sam Beckett. Scholar. Scientist. Crimesolver. Fighter. Feminist. Leaping in from life to life, putting right what once went wrong.

Linnea Dodson (Baltimore, Maryland) is a technical writer and past Gasogene of Watson's Tin Box of Columbia, Maryland. She has also worked for Scintillation of Scions and delivered multiple panels at 221BCon. She has written about Sherlock Holmes, Doctor Who, gaming, mysteries, and feminism.

A FOREIGNER BY HIS ACCENT

Jonathan Quayle Higgins III

Vincent W. Wright

I know my choice for who Sherlock Holmes is like is going to sound a little odd, but I think I can explain it well enough to make some sense. To start, I have to admit that I was struck silent by this assignment. I had never really compared Holmes to anyone in any way. I had always compared everyone else to him. (I guess either way works, but my feeling was that we were to do the former.)

In fact, the only time I had ever done this was after reading a couple of stories where Holmes uses his skills to find clues in the woods and grass that no one else had found. It reminded me very much of indigenous North American trackers. I, being heavily of that blood, had oft heard tales of such things, and then saw those practices in movies and TV shows (which I know are not always accurate). And that represented the only comparison I had ever drawn for the Great Detective.

So, when I was contacted about participating I was thrilled, but a little nervous. I put a lot of thought into it and finally came up with my answer. To me, Sherlock Holmes is like... Jonathan Quayle Higgins III. You know, the guy from *Magnum, P.I.*?

Now, before you turn to the next chapter, hear me out. Growing up I had five television channels. Six, if the weather conditions were just right. The town I was in was so small it had no movie theater. My experience with most things British came in books. I spent a lot of time reading, but had no actual voice in my head for British folk except for cartoon characters or special guest stars on network TV shows.

When my aunt and uncle got cable we watched a lot of TV with them. While it wasn't actually on cable, one show I "discovered" was *Magnum, P.I.* (It was certainly on one of the channels we got, but Dad had control of the TV, so I don't recall ever watching it at home.) On *Magnum, P.I.* was an intriguing character whom one of the show's main players called Higgy-baby. Higgins, as he was otherwise called, was instantly my British voice. Everyone I read about afterward who was from England, or anywhere on the Isles, had a tone that was pure Higgins. He fascinated me, and at the time I doubt I understood the concept of an American doing an English accent. So, he was it.

This had to be about 1982. That was two years before Jeremy Brett began his role as Holmes, and at least five years before I found out about the Granada series. Thus, when a friend of mine loaned me his dad's copies of *The Annotated Sherlock Holmes* in about 1985, the voice in my head was from Higgins.

Now, it isn't easy to draw a lot of parallels between the two men, but I'll try.

- Both are British.
- Both are very intelligent.
- Both like dogs.
- Both have a mustachioed ladies' man as a "sidekick."
- Both have at least one brother.
- Both did sneaky work for the British government.
- Both can kick a little butt in one-on-one situations.
- Both carried a gun, but not all the time.
- Both have a last name that starts with H.

There might be more, but my guess is not many. In fact, Higgins has just about as many things in common with Dr. Watson, as does Dr. Watson with Thomas Magnum. But that's beside the point.

Now, I know there are going to be comparisons in here to lots of other candidates. My guess is there will be those who compare Holmes to Superman, or Michael Jordan, or Joan of Arc, or Harry Potter, or the Shaggy D.A. (You youngsters will have to look that last one up.) I will not, though. As I said, I have never really done that. Holmes has always stood alone in the pantheon of heroes and crime fighters. He was a calculating machine of the highest order, and no one could ever come close to him in any way.

So, let me reiterate: to me Sherlock Holmes is like Jonathan Quayle Higgins III because in a transitional part of my life Higgins was the voice of every British man, including Holmes... for a while. Whenever I see Higgins on TV, I am taken back to a time just before I discovered Holmes in a major way. And that discovery has set me on a path which has taken me to so many great places and introduced me to so many great people.

On a side note, I'd like to mention that just two days after I turned in my idea to the compiler of this anthology, the man who played Higgins, actor John Hillerman, died. Suddenly, he was everywhere. I was afraid someone else might take my idea and run with it. That turned out, of course, to be a foolish fear, as no one else had the same experience with Higgins/Holmes that I did. Still, people were being reminded of his contributions to the Sherlockian world, and his small, but beloved, place in our hobby.

During all of the hubbub about his life and death I remembered an episode of *Magnum, P.I.* called "Holmes Is Where the Heart Is," from March 1984. I found it online, watched it, and fell even more in love with my idea for this article. The connections linking the cast, plot, and trivia to Sherlockiana were fun to explore. It cinched my decision and helped convince me that perhaps someone would actually take the time to read and appreciate these 1,000 or so words. If this is you, thanks. I hope you've enjoyed my reminiscence.

Vincent W. Wright (Indianapolis, Indiana) is creator of the Facebook site Historical Sherlock and a member of the Illustrious Clients for more than 20 years. He has been hooked since discovering *The Annotated Sherlock Holmes* while in high school and seeing Jeremy Brett in the Granada series.

BUILT ON A DEEP LOVE

Dana Scully

Michelle Birkby

Of course you know Sherlock Holmes, but do you know Dana Scully? In 1993, a new television series, *The X-Files*, began. Fox Mulder (yes, Fox) an FBI agent, investigated strange and unusual happenings—UFOs, ghosts, locked room deaths, that sort of thing. He was partnered by Dana Scully, played by Gillian Anderson: a confirmed sceptic, a doctor also trained in physics. She was intelligent and logical, and she could look after herself. *The X-Files* became a massive cultural phenomenon, and Dana Scully became an icon for girls and women. I cosplayed as her myself sometimes.

Sherlock Holmes—it seems obvious at first—is just like Dana Scully, and vice versa. There are so many similarities. They're both scientists. Both are in a partnership. Both are coolly logical. And so on.

Well, no. Dana Scully is a proper scientist, with both a medical degree and a degree in physics. Sherlock Holmes, on the other hand, dabbles. He is a brilliant scientist, but never follows a fixed course of study. He has gone to university but doesn't seem to have a degree (perhaps because of whatever distinctiveness got him so talked about in college). Holmes is the perfect example of the Victorian dilettante scientist, who studies everything but never turned in a paper or passed an exam. Scully, on the other hand, works hard and is brilliant. She can perform surgery on children with severe problems, do an autopsy on an elephant, or write a paper on the theories of Einstein—but she always follows through. She never gets bored and wanders away. She passes the exams.

Sherlock Holmes's partnership with Watson is the cornerstone of his life. He states again and again that he cannot do without his Boswell. Dana Scully, comparably, has an intense partnership with Fox Mulder. She is seen, however, as the follower to Mulder. He is the one who charges into cases and makes the deductions, based on his esoteric knowledge of an immense treasury of weird facts. She, whilst being brilliant, is the follower.

Still, she can do without Mulder's leadership. She spends several years working alone as a doctor, and a while working with John Doggett.

Mulder, whilst important to her, is not necessary. She can survive without him. She can even investigate the strangest cases without him.

Holmes, on the other hand, rarely does without Watson. When his partner isn't around, Holmes misses him. All the joy of his brilliance goes out of him. Without Watson to be surprised and impressed, without Watson's literary skill to raise the science to art, Holmes feels… lifeless.

And let's not forget—Dana Scully is a woman. Holmes does not like women. Women are not to be trusted, not even the best of them. (This is, of course, before Holmes is completely defeated by a clever woman. Later on he says the impression of a woman may be worth more than the conclusion of an analytical mind.)

So, you see, Dana Scully and Sherlock Holmes are not that much alike. Except, perhaps, in some unexpected ways.

The first is faith. Perhaps that should be belief. Despite all their scientific training, despite every horrific thing they see, they believe in a higher power. Yes, both of them.

Mulder wants to believe. Mulder, however, will believe anything thrown at him: UFOs, werewolves, invisibility. His belief is without any kind of filter, or questioning, or quality control. Scully questions everything, but always wears a gold cross. She goes to church. She works in a Catholic hospital. She was raised a Catholic, and quietly, without fanfare or argument, returns to her faith in time of need.

Holmes—a believer? It's never mentioned, except once, in "The Naval Treaty", in the famous passage where Holmes says that deduction can prove that there is a Higher Power, and it is good, because what use is a rose, except as an expression of that goodness? For Holmes, God is proved to exist by a purely logical deduction. He has faith and belief of a sort, backed up by his own science.

And that relationship with their respective partners? Perhaps it's not so different. Dana Scully ends up sleeping with Fox Mulder and having a child by him. Holmes never slept with Watson (as far as we know). But both partnerships are built on a deep love. Mulder and Scully are bound together even before they declare their love, crossing boundaries for each other, risking danger for each other, standing by each other whatever happens. And Holmes? He declares he cannot love. Yet he refers always to Watson as "my Watson". He cannot do without him. Watson knows perfectly well that Holmes is the most important man in his life, perhaps the most important person, especially after his wife's death. He freely declares that it is his joy and his privilege to serve Holmes. Holmes, on the other hand, acts cool—yet when Watson is shot, Holmes is panic-stricken. Watson sees tears in his eyes and catches a glimpse of a great heart behind a great brain. It is a moment of revelation, and the feelings run as deep as Scully's for Mulder.

One last similarity. Dana Scully is a medical doctor, has a degree in physics, could do whatever she set her mind to. She decided to join the FBI. Sherlock Holmes, clever and learned, could similarly choose his own career. Both say they chose their path so they can distinguish themselves—but in fact, it's a craving for justice. In her work with Mulder—which does not bring her glory, quite the opposite—Scully wants to bring justice to people. Not always the law: she can ignore it, maybe not at first, but later her interpretation becomes fluid. Dana Scully has found herself in the world of the lost, the forgotten, the reviled and the disbelieved, and she, no matter what she herself thinks, brings them justice of a kind. They are listened to and fought for. Mulder chases the story, whilst Scully looks after the people.

For Holmes it is about justice, too. Much as he likes to say deduction is an intellectual exercise, he too helps the lost and the abused, the lonely and scorned. When the police won't help, he will. When family and loved ones conspire against someone, he gives them a way out. For him, justice is more important than the law: he will let a blackmailer's murderer escape the police because her cause was just.

At first glimpse Dana Scully and Sherlock Holmes seem superficially alike, but dig a little closer and they are very different. But dig still further and, at heart, they are actually the same. They have belief, they have a deep love, and they will fight for justice for all. They are both made of layer beneath layer beneath layer, twisting towards each other then away—but the final layer, of their deepest motivations, is the same.

Michelle Birkby (London, England) is the author of the Mrs Hudson and Mary Watson Investigations, *House at Baker Street* and *Women of Baker Street*.

THE BLOODHOUNDS

It seems to me that all the detectives of fact and
of fancy would be children in your hands.

"The Gloria Scott"

A TOUCH OF THE DRAMATIC

Eugène François Vidocq

Carlina de la Cova

Sherlock Holmes can be compared to many persons, both historically and contemporaneously, as the chapters of this book demonstrate.
An obvious example is Dr. Joseph Bell, Arthur Conan Doyle's mentor
at the University of Edinburgh. Other such figures include Charles Altamont Doyle, the author's father, and Edgar Allan Poe's C. Auguste
Dupin (although Holmes would detest the latter, as *A Study in Scarlet*
makes clear). Whilst it is tempting to write about Dupin, I argue here that
Sherlock Holmes is like the French criminal, turned detective, Eugène
François Vidocq (1775–1857).

Vidocq, born in Arras, France, has a rather colorful history, so colorful that it will not fit into this chapter. Often touted as a criminal who
turned to the good side by becoming a police informant, Vidocq led a
life far too complex, and some claim embellished, for the few pages that
have been dedicated to him in many English-language academic articles,
books, and blogs. By his early teens the Frenchman had resorted to a
life of crime. At fourteen he was a skilled fencer, often stealing from his
parents. He eventually fell on hard luck and joined a group of traveling
entertainers. By 1791, he had enlisted in the Bourbon Regiment. But
military life did not fit the young Vidocq; within four years he increased
his duel count and deserted. The Frenchman returned to his fugitive lifestyle, but thanks to his experiences with the previously mentioned traveling entertainers, was a master of disguise. This allowed him to easily slip
away from the police and the military.

After deserting, Vidocq engaged in illicit activity, experienced periods of imprisonment, and managed to escape incarceration twice through
his brilliant use of disguise. His stints in prison did little to tame him.
Vidocq remained a criminal and notorious womanizer (I will spare the
reader the illicit details, including a marriage he was conned into) who
became known in the underworld. Eventually, his criminal fame caught
up with him, making it difficult to remain in hiding even with a flair for
the dramatic. Somewhere along the way, in 1809, Vidocq flipped sides
and became a police informant. He utilized his criminal knowledge to

assist the French police in capturing crooks. Vidocq easily incorporated his keen ability for disguise into his work, which allowed him to fluidly move through prisons and the underworld acquiring intelligence and apprehending those on the wrong side of the law. In 1811, the former criminal organized the Brigade de la Sûreté ("Security Brigade"), which was the first plainclothes detective unit in the western world. Napoleon Bonaparte made the brigade a state security police force in 1813, renaming it the Sûreté Nationale.

Vidocq also founded Le Bureau des Renseignements (Office of Information) in 1833. Today criminal justice scholars consider it one of the first detective agencies in the west. Vidocq staffed and personally trained former convicts in both organizations, as they knew the hiding places and methods of criminals, as well as the underground networks in France. They were also aware of the danger involved in their law-abiding undertaking. Vidocq insisted that these operatives wear plain clothes, which did not attract attention in the nefarious environments in which they worked.

Despite Vidocq's success in law enforcement and reducing crime throughout the country, he continued to have trouble with the law. Ultimately, his reputation was damaged and French officials distanced themselves from him. They went so far as to silence his role in developing the Security Brigade, today's French National Police, before his death in 1857. Today criminal justice scholars recognize him as the "father of modern criminology" and celebrate his contributions to forensic science, which changed the way law enforcement agencies apprehended criminals.

This brief synopsis of Vidocq's life of course gives some hints about the similarities between this flamboyant French crime-fighter and Sherlock Holmes. By default, Arthur Conan Doyle most certainly knew of Vidocq. The Frenchman had published his exploits before Conan Doyle began writing his stories, gaining global notoriety before his death. His feats, described (and perhaps exaggerated) in his memoirs, inspired many literary authors, including Victor Hugo (*Les Misérables*), Alexandre Dumas (*Les Mohicans de Paris*), Émile Gaboriau (*Monsieur Lecoq*), and Edgar Allan Poe ("The Murders in the Rue Morgue"). The latter two are especially important as their creations, Monsieur Lecoq and C. Auguste Dupin, not only were heavily influenced by Vidocq's crime-fighting triumphs, but were the first to intertwine science and detection. Indeed, Poe is credited with creating the detective story genre. Most importantly for present purposes, however, these writers and their characters would heavily influence Conan Doyle in the creation and crafting of the Sherlock Holmes stories. Thus, in many ways, Sherlock Holmes is like Vidocq simply because the characters he is molded after were inspired by the great French detective.

On a personal level, both men had a French heritage. Through Holmes's maternal lineage he was related to the great artist Vernet. Whilst

Holmes was never a known criminal (despite acting underhandedly on a few occasions), he and Vidocq shared a love of crime-fighting. They also turned criminalistics into a scientific endeavor and were the first private detectives in their respective realms. Holmes considered himself the first consulting detective, but this may be a simple matter of semantics as Vidocq preceded him as a private investigator by decades. Like Holmes, his French counterpart was an expert fencer and skilled shot. However, Sherlock Holmes was truly like Vidocq in regard to introducing forensic scientific methods to crime-fighting. Both men knew the importance of shoe and tire impressions and their relationship to a crime. They paid close attention to these prints, ascertaining shoe type, height, directionality, tread, and other vital information. Vidocq went a step further, becoming the first criminal investigator to insist all impressions be cast with plaster of Paris. Today this is standard protocol; impression evidence is one of the core methods of crime scene analysis. Modern investigators, like Vidocq and Holmes before them, must assess and record all shoe and/or tire impression evidence, locate the entrance and exit points of a perpetrator, examine any trace evidence found in these impressions, and link them to a suspect.

Holmes's collection of Ms was a fine one, very much like Vidocq's. As the French detective had been a former criminal, he was familiar with the underworld and knew its major players. Vidocq saw the importance of recording criminal intelligence on descriptive index cards that included the names of criminals, their aliases, physical descriptions, modi operandi, specialties, previous crimes, history, unique characteristics, and known associates. Decades later Sherlock Holmes embraced this method, which gave him accessible intelligence on every criminal and notable person in Great Britain and beyond. However, Vidocq had the upper hand: by 1842 the Frenchman had collected information on 30,000 offenders, as noted in Clive Emsley and Haia Shpayer-Makov's 2006 volume *Police Detectives in History, 1750–1950*.

Both men were also highly observant, easily reading non-verbal cues in body language and observing the smallest details out of place on a perpetrator. Holmes and Vidocq especially valued undercover work as a means to gather evidence and build a case. Their respective French "art in the blood" and "flair for the dramatic" allowed them to utilize their theatrical training to ease into undercover roles. Holmes, like Vidocq, would change his posture, height, demeanor, ambulation, voice, accent, and gesticulations to fit the role he was playing. Multiple stories demonstrate how Holmes excelled at undercover work; in some instances he is unrecognizable even to Watson. What perfected both Vidocq's and Holmes's transformation in their chosen surveillance methods was the use of facial prosthetics to modify their features, walnut stain to darken their faces, coffee grain to create facial blemishes, belladonna to darken aspects of their face, fake blisters created from beeswax, dirt applied underneath the fingernails, and wigs, as well as additional make-up to create wrinkles. Whilst the Canon does not elaborate on whether or not Holmes dressed for his undercover roles down to his underwear, Vidocq apparently did. The Frenchman also carried items with him to rapidly change his appearance, including clothing and make-up.

Furthermore, "irregulars" were critical to the work both men did. Holmes had his "street arabs," the Baker Street Irregulars, whose eyes and ears were all seeing and all knowing. In many instances, they were an important intelligence gathering and surveillance network for the Great Detective that allowed him to know the behaviors, actions, and whereabouts of suspects. Vidocq also had his own band of agents, former convicts who were integral to his Security Brigade and Office of Information. Like Victorian London's street children, Vidocq's former criminals could effortlessly infiltrate the underground in their plainclothes attire and surveil suspects with ease, as they knew the criminal culture and spoke its language.

Thus, in many ways Sherlock Holmes is very much like Eugene Vidocq. Both men shared a similar heritage, excelled at fencing, were hyper-observant, knew the importance of record-keeping and data gathering on criminals, had a "flair for the dramatic," and relied on their respective irregulars. Most importantly, however, both men pushed criminalistics into a new scientific frontier, introducing many forensic science methods that now form the crux of the discipline. These include shoe and tire impression analysis, record keeping, behavioral profiling, and the importance of undercover work to build a case. Impression analysis, including locating the entrance, path, and exit points of a suspect at scene, is critical to crime scene analysis. As Vidocq did, impressions are now routinely taken with plaster of Paris. If this is not possible, they are recovered via photographs, removal from the scene, and electrostatic lifting. Records and crime databases also play important roles in linking individuals to a crime or identifying them. Lastly, some cases could not be built without modern day irregulars, which include informants and undercover operatives. Ultimately, modern forensic science owes a huge debt to Vidocq—as does Sherlock Holmes, whose very existence is tied closely to Vidocq's methods.

Carlina de la Cova (Columbia, South Carolina) is an associate professor of anthropology at the University of South Carolina, with research interests in forensic anthropology, Victorian medicine, skeletal health of the poor and marginalized, anthropology in the Canon, and Watson's suggestion that the human femur has an "upper condyle." She also serves as a deputy county coroner.

DOWN THESE MEAN
STREETS A MAN MUST GO

Inspector Edmund Reid

Vicki Delany

Sherlock Holmes and Dr. John Watson were not accustomed to regularly visiting the dark, damp, dangerous streets of the east end of London at the end of the nineteenth century. But that area was the habitual stomping grounds of Inspector Edmund Reid of the BBC TV show *Ripper Street*.

Although Holmes didn't often venture into Whitechapel and surrounding areas in the stories told to us by Watson, the fact is that he could make himself as much at home there as any resident, as much as Reid himself.

Ripper Street ran for five seasons from 2012 to 2016. The programme was initially cancelled after two seasons because of low ratings, but popular protest caused Amazon to agree to fund further episodes of the show. The story begins shortly after the Jack the Ripper murders of 1888 and centers around the police of H division on Leman Street in Whitechapel. The Reid character is based on the real Inspector Edmund Reid, head of CID at H Division at the time of the Ripper case. (As well as for his police career, Reid is known for being, at 5'6", the shortest man in the police department, and as a record-breaking hot-air balloonist.)

In *Ripper Street*, British actor Matthew Macfadyen (*MI5*, *Pride and Prejudice*) portrayed Reid as dedicated and stoic yet tormented by his failure to capture the Ripper and the loss of his daughter. (No ballooning was involved in the show.) The fictional Reid works out of the police station on Leman Street in Whitechapel and lives nearby. He is well known on these streets, and when later in the series he is "on the lam" he is easily recognized. His only method of disguise is to remove his iconic bowler hat and pull up his collar.

Holmes, by contrast, when venturing into the mean streets sometimes finds it necessary to put on a disguise so successful it fools even John Watson. In "The Man with the Twisted Lip", Watson comes across Holmes in Upper Swandam Lane (believed to be the real-life Swan

Lane). He describes the lane as "a vile alley lurking behind the high wharves... to the east of London Bridge." His destination is an opium den located "between a slop-shop and a gin-shop". Holmes is there on a case, of course, searching for one Neville St. Clair in an opium den which, he tells Watson, is "the vilest murder-trap on the whole riverside." He must disguise himself as, without the force of the law that Reid has, and lacking a troop of uniformed constables at his back, "Had I been recognized in that den my life would not have been worth an hour's purchase."

In "The Blue Carbuncle", Watson and Holmes don't venture into Whitechapel itself, but the pursuit of the origins of the jewel-containing goose take them through "a zigzag of slums" to Covent Garden Market. At that time the market would have been populated by not just food sellers, but large numbers of pickpockets, prostitutes, and beggars. Although Conan Doyle does not describe what they are wearing, clearly they attract no undue attention. (At least, until Holmes wagers "a fiver" that the goose is country-bred.) The men then go to Brixton Road, south of the river. Today that section of Brixton Road is a pleasant street lined with large trees and nice houses. It might have been so back in the nineteenth century, but a house that is also used as a goose-farm would not be the sort of home we associate with Holmes's usual upper-crust clients. But again, we see that Holmes is comfortable in the area.

Edmund Reid considers himself to be responsible for Whitechapel. By the end of the series, he won't even leave the district to visit his new grandchild. Holmes, as we know, travelled far more widely, not only within London but often to the "smiling and beautiful countryside." But London was the center of Holmes's world, as it was of the entire world of the time. As he tells Watson in "The Red-Headed League", "It is a hobby of mine to have an exact knowledge of London."

Based on the line already quoted from "The Man with the Twisted Lip", to the effect that Holmes was well known (and not at all favourably amongst the criminal classes) on Upper Swandam Lane, we can conclude that he was intimately acquainted with the meanest streets of London, much like Inspector Reid himself. Either Watson wasn't aware of this, or he chose for some reason not to tell his readers about such cases. It is therefore entirely possible that Holmes and Reid were acquainted. Reid was the sort of incorruptible, dedicated, detail-oriented police officer that Homes would have enjoyed working with. Might Holmes have even helped Reid in some small way with the Jack the Ripper case?

Sadly, we'll never know, as Watson chose not to tell us.

Reid and Holmes were both well ahead of others of their time in the new science of forensics. For example, Holmes first uses fingerprints in *The Sign of Four*, published in 1890. Reid, along with his morgue doctor Homer Jackson, use fingerprint evidence to make their case for the first time in the year 1893 (the date of the third season), but they are so far ahead of the rest of Scotland Yard that their evidence is sometimes not believed. (The fingerprint branch of Scotland Yard was first formed in July 1901.)

In their personal lives (or lack thereof) Reid is also very much like Holmes. Whereas Holmes is so dedicated to his work that he has no family, save a distant brother, and only one friend, Reid's focus on his job destroys his family and almost destroys him. In his pursuit of a case, before the show begins, he has taken his young daughter with him to serve as camouflage and she is lost; his wife can never forgive him, and she later dies of bitterness and grief. Reid's attempts at finding romance flounder on his obsessions. At the end of the show the job has become all he has.

Holmes and Reid are both identified by their headwear. In the Conan Doyle books, Holmes is never described as wearing a deerstalker, but the illustrations by Sidney Paget have come to define the way in which we picture him. Reid is never without his bowler hat and has to discard it as too identifiable when he is fleeing arrest at the end of the show's last season.

I believe Reid and Holmes would have liked each other and worked together well. Inspector Edmund Reid and Sherlock Holmes were very much alike. They were men of London through and through and equally determined to keep its people protected from the criminal element, sometimes to the exclusion of all else.

On a recent trip to London, I followed the footsteps of Homes and Reid to Whitechapel, Swan Lane, and some of the formerly less-savory parts of the East End, and I am confident that neither of those gentlemen would have recognized the modern streets—fancy restaurants and glittering bars, shops full of luxury goods, bright lights, towers of chrome and sparkling glass. In this, above all, Inspector Edmund Reid is very much like Sherlock Holmes.

Vicki Delany (Prince Edward County, Ontario) writes the Sherlock Holmes Bookshop series published by Crooked Lane Books, in which every book or piece of merchandise sold in the fictional store exists in the real world. She is one of Canada's most varied and prolific crime writers, a national bestseller in the US, the author of more than twenty-five novels of mystery and suspense, and a past president of the Crime Writers of Canada.

DETECTIVE, SPY, AND AUTHOR

Allan Pinkerton

Darlene Cypser

While they were born a generation apart, Sherlock Holmes and Allan Pinkerton, founder of the Pinkerton National Detective Agency, had some things in common. It is probable that they were both born in the United Kingdom. While many people think of Pinkerton (1819–1884) as an American detective, he was in fact born in Glasgow, Scotland. There are several theories as to the exact location of Sherlock Holmes's birth, but Dr. Watson has given us no reason to believe that Holmes was born outside of England.

Their formal educations differ substantially. In "The 'Gloria Scott'" and "The Musgrave Ritual," Holmes mentions being at university while Allan Pinkerton left school at the age of ten. Yet both Holmes and Pinkerton were primarily self-educated in areas relevant to the detection of crime. Watson recorded that Holmes's "zeal for certain studies was remarkable" and quoted Holmes as saying no man had ever brought the same amount of study to the detection of crime. Allan Pinkerton was also described as an avid reader.

Holmes and Pinkerton both had no thought of a career as a detective until someone else told them they had the skills to be one. Pinkerton had been a cooper (barrel maker) living in a small town near Chicago. At that time in his life, he was too poor to purchase hoop-poles and staves for his barrels, so he cut his own. One day while cutting wood on a little island in the Fox River, a few miles above Dundee, he saw signs that others had been occupying the island. He returned the following night and watched the men. The next day he contacted the sheriff and led officers to the spot. They found the men with a large supply of counterfeit coins and arrested them. This arrest brought Pinkerton a lot of attention, but he returned to making barrels.

Then in the summer of 1847, local businessmen asked Pinkerton to investigate a man they believed was passing counterfeit banknotes. Pinkerton was hesitant, saying he was a cooper, not a detective, but they pressed him and he agreed to help. He met the man and bought some counterfeit money from him. The man was arrested but escaped before trial. Despite the outcome, Pinkerton wrote that the incident scared counterfeiters out of the area for a number of years.

As recorded in "The 'Gloria Scott,'" Sherlock Holmes shocked Victor Trevor's father with his observations and deductions about the man's past. Old Trevor told the young Holmes that "all the detectives of fact and of fancy would be children in your hands. That's your line of life, sir," which Holmes told Watson was the first thing that made him think he could make a profession out of what had been "the merest hobby."

Pinkerton gained such a reputation after the counterfeiting cases that people kept calling on him to investigate other matters, and he finally decided to become a professional detective. He attributed the notoriety that propelled him into the detective business to "the country being new, and great sensations scarce." Sherlock Holmes, trying to establish himself in the midst of London, teeming with millions of people and numerous sensations, had a longer wait to make his name in the detective business.

Pinkerton was offered a part-time position as a deputy sheriff. Afterwards he became the first police detective in Cook County, Illinois, and a special mail agent for the United States Postal Service. Unlike Pinkerton, Holmes never worked for the "official police." Holmes preferred to work alone, aided only by the trusty Dr. Watson, and, when needed, the Baker Street Irregulars. He saw himself as a specialist who applied his special talents and knowledge to the case at hand.

In 1850, Pinkerton partnered with Chicago attorney Edward Rucker to form the North-Western Police Agency. When Rucker left to become a judge, Pinkerton created his own agency, the Pinkerton National Detective Agency. He worked alone at first but soon built a large agency of detectives, which even included a female bureau, an unusual thing at the time. Sherlock Holmes preferred to be seen as a gentleman consultant, and thought trivial cases were unworthy of his talents and better left to the official police. Pinkerton took a business approach and was willing to diversify when the need arose. In 1860, he created a uniformed guard service to protect meat-packing plants and other companies in Chicago.

Like Holmes, Pinkerton handled a variety of cases during his career, some of them remarkably similar to Holmes's. In *Criminal Reminiscences and Detective Sketches*, Pinkerton described a robbery method called "bank-bursting," consisting of renting a room or rooms above those occupied by a bank and tunneling into its vaults, or into the bank offices and then breaking into the vault, which is very similar to the robbery method used in "The Red-Headed League." Undoubtedly, Holmes read Pinkerton's books in his copious crime reading, and they assisted him in recognizing the scheme. As he tells Inspector MacDonald in *The Valley of Fear*, "It's all been done before." The creation of the League was a new twist on an old method.

Besides detecting criminals, Sherlock Holmes serves his country by retrieving stolen government documents and capturing spies. Watson records several such cases, including "The Bruce-Partington Plans," and

"The Naval Treaty." Holmes even comes out of retirement to capture the German spy Von Bork, in the adventure published as "His Last Bow." Pinkerton also served his country, though sometimes he exaggerated his work in this regard. Contrary to his claim in *Spy of the Rebellion*, he did not create the "United States Secret Service" during the 1861-1865 Civil War. There never was such an agency during the Civil War. Pinkerton provided intelligence services for General George B. McClellan for the Department of the Ohio and the Army of the Potomac. Pinkerton's service actually began before the start of the Civil War when he was hired by the Philadelphia, Wilmington and Baltimore Railroad to investigate a sabotage plot. During that investigation, he and his agents uncovered a plan to assassinate president-elect Abraham Lincoln, and Pinkerton himself escorted Lincoln safely to Washington.

Pinkerton and his operatives excelled at tracking men and collecting evidence, which made them especially good at counter-espionage, the same type of work that Holmes did for the British government. Pinkerton arrested a number of spies in Washington and the surrounding areas during the Civil War, including the notorious Rose Greenhow.

In the early 1870s, Pinkerton began writing books about his work including *Thirty Years a Detective*, *The Spy of the Rebellion*, and *The Molly Maguires and the Detectives*. Sherlock Holmes began writing early in his career, mostly on technical subjects. Holmes's early works included *Upon the Distinction between the Ashes of the Various Tobaccos*, *On the Tracing of Footsteps*, *Secret Writings*, and *The Dating of Documents*. Holmes also wrote a monograph on the *Polyphonic Motets of Lassus* (a type of music) while he was still in active practice. After he retired, Holmes wrote at least two stories of his own cases published as "The Blanched Soldier" and "The Lion's Mane." He also wrote the *Practical Handbook of Bee Culture*. In "The Abbey Grange," Holmes tells Watson of his plans to write *The Whole Art of Deduction* during his retirement, but no copies have yet been discovered.

Watson does not record whether Holmes ever met Allan Pinkerton or his sons William and Robert. However, in *Sherlock Holmes: My Life and Crimes*, Michael Hardwick postulated that Holmes worked with the Pinkerton Detective Agency in Chicago from November 1879 through August 1880 and that Allan's son William Pinkerton took him under his wing. It also would not be surprising to discover that Holmes, as his alter ego of Altamont, sought some assistance from the National Detective Agency during his time in Chicago preparatory to his counter-intelligence work that eventually netted Von Bork on the eve of the First World War as recorded in "His Last Bow."

Watson did write about two meetings in England between Holmes and Pinkerton operatives in *The Valley of Fear* and "The Red Circle." In the latter story, Mr. Leverton of Pinkerton's American Agency joins Holmes, Watson, and the London police for the finale. Holmes greets Leverton enthusiastically as "The hero of the Long Island cave mystery."

In *The Valley of Fear*, Holmes discovers that the victim (or perpetrator, depending on one's perspective) was Birdy Edwards, a Pinkerton operative who was living in England under the name of Douglas to avoid vengeance from the surviving members of the Scowerers gang, after he broke up their lodge and sent many of them to the gallows.

Thus, we find many points of similarity between the lives of these two great detectives. Sherlock Holmes respected Pinkerton's operatives and may have learned a few tricks from Allan Pinkerton's publications, if not from the man himself.

Darlene Cypser (Wheat Ridge, Colorado) is the Chief Surgeon of Dr. Watson's Neglected Patients (Denver). She has been writing and publishing a multi-book biography of Sherlock Holmes, beginning with *The Crack in the Lens*, followed by *The Consulting Detective Trilogy*, with its third part, *Montague Street*, expected in late 2018. She is an attorney and historian.

IS HE AT ALL HUMAN?

Dr. John Evelyn Thorndyke

Regina Stinson

Dr. John Evelyn Thorndyke was the invention of author R. Austin Freeman (1862–1943). Thorndyke is described by his creator as a "medical jurispractitioner" and, as such, is often asked by the police to examine the details of a case and to testify about his findings. Occasionally his lawyer friend, Mr. Brodribb, will ask Thorndyke to assist a client in trouble. On a few rare occasions, Thorndyke happens upon something that piques his interest and he begins an independent study of the matter.

The Red Thumb Mark, written in 1907, was Dr. Thorndyke's first case. Like Holmes, Thorndyke had just entered into an arrangement with his friend—in this case, Dr. Christopher Jervis—to share living quarters. Additionally, Jervis narrates a good portion of the Thorndyke tales and generally serves a role similar to that of Watson. Jervis also falls in love during the first story and eventually gets married. However, Thorndyke and Jervis continue to work together, and the wife is rarely discussed. The question of why Jervis frequently spends his nights at 5A King's Bench Walk (Thorndyke's residence in the Temple, London's legal precinct) is answered in *When Rogues Fall Out*, thusly: "As the circumstances of our practice often made it desirable for me to stay late at our chambers, I had retained there the bedroom that I had occupied before our marriage; and as these circumstances could not always be foreseen, I had arranged with my wife the simple rule that the house closed at 11 o'clock. If I was unable to get home by that time, it was understood that I would be staying at the Temple." (We are often left to wonder about the arrangements Watson had with his wife.)

There is no landlady, but Nathaniel Polton, Dr. Thorndyke's ubiquitous assistant, housekeeper, and cook, plays the role of Mrs. Hudson most adequately. The crinkly-faced Polton is an extremely gifted craftsman who, in addition to his housekeeping abilities, helps the doctor by creating necessary gadgets, preparing and testing evidence, and occasionally playing an active role in tracking down a suspect. Thorndyke finds Polton's help invaluable and treats him as his equal in spite of the fact that Polton is in absolute awe of the doctor. In the novel *Mr. Polton*

Explains (1940), we discover the circumstances under which the two met and the explanation of Polton's devotion to Dr. Thorndyke.

As might be expected, since Dr. Thorndyke works as a medico-legal practitioner, his relationship with the authorities is more congenial than that between Holmes and the constabulary. There is a Lestrade-like character in the person of Inspector Badger; however, the police generally have great respect for Thorndyke's superior powers of observation and deduction. Like Holmes, Thorndyke is happy to allow the police to take all the credit.

There are several instances where Thorndyke seems to be channeling Holmes. Compare Thorndyke's words from *The Red Thumb Mark*, "It has just been borne upon me, Jervis, that you are the most companionable fellow in the world. You have the heaven-sent gift of silence," to Holmes's proclamation in "The Man with the Twisted Lip": "You have a grand gift of silence, Watson. It makes you quite invaluable as a companion." In "The Stranger's Latchkey," someone asks Jervis about Thorndyke, "Is he at all human?" In the same story Jervis tells us: "This explanation, like others, was quite simple when one had heard it," which is reminiscent of "Every problem becomes very childish when once it is explained," from "The Dancing Men."

Thorndyke, like Holmes, is extremely reticent about his investigations until he is ready to reveal his conclusions. He does, however, seem to have faith in Jervis's reasoning abilities that is somewhat greater than Holmes has in Watson's: "You have these few facts that I have mentioned. Consider them separately and collectively, and in their relation to the circumstances. Don't attempt to suck my brain when you have an excellent brain of your own to suck" ("The Moabite Cipher").

In "An Anthropologist at Large," Thorndyke is asked to examine a gentleman's hat in such a way that it is obvious his client has read "The Blue Carbuncle": "I understand," said [the client], "that by examining a hat it is possible to deduce from it, not only the bodily characteristics of the wearer, but also his mental and moral qualities, his state of health, his pecuniary position, his past history, and even his domestic relations and the peculiarities of his place of abode. Am I right in this supposition?" Although Thorndyke cautions his client not to expect too much, since hats have a way of changing owners, his examination of the hat proves that it could have fit no one other than the person for whom it was made.

Since Dr. Thorndyke is an officer of the court, he is required to abide by the law and doesn't often have the opportunity to let the guilty party go free, as Holmes sometimes does. In the instance of "Mr. Pottermack's Oversight," however, Thorndyke is never called upon officially to become involved. He is simply curious about some circumstances and begins his own investigation, the end of which allows him to grant the so-called "guilty party" his freedom. In this case, the victim was more despicable than his killer.

One of the unique things about the Thorndyke tales is the author's invention of the inverted mystery. The crime is explained to the reader at once, and the criminal is known at the beginning of the story. The fascination is in watching how Thorndyke examines the evidence, tests his theories, and draws his inferences. Using the data collected, the doctor is able to discover how the crime was committed and who did it, which he either proves with evidence or traps them into admitting. Freeman, the author, performed many experiments himself before writing the stories so he could have an exact knowledge of what Dr. Thorndyke would need to do. The long-running television series *Columbo* employed the inverted mystery technique to great advantage.

Amongst the many similarities between the Thorndyke and Holmes stories are a palimpsest ("The Moabite Cipher"), the Italians of Saffron Hill ("The Aluminium Dagger"), a gold pince-nez ("A Message from the Deep Sea"), Trichinopoly cigars (*The Red Thumb Mark*), and a Duchess of Devonshire hat ("A Message from the Deep Sea"). In addition, in "A Sower of Pestilence," Jervis makes this statement: "Our friend seems to think that you are one of those master craftsmen who can make bricks, not only without straw, but without clay," which is reminiscent of Holmes's statement in "The Copper Beeches": "I can't make bricks without clay."

Freeman wrote 22 novels and 40 short stories about Dr. Thorndyke between 1907 and 1942. The series can be considered somewhat contemporary with the Holmes Canon, and one of the stories, "The Moabite Cipher," is contained in the anthology *The Rivals of Sherlock Holmes*, edited by Hugh Greene. Two of the stories, "A Message from the Deep Sea" and "The Moabite Cipher," were adapted for a British TV series of the 1970s also entitled *The Rivals of Sherlock Holmes*.

Regina Stinson (Royal Oak, Michigan) is a Baker Street Irregular, a member of the Adventuresses of Sherlock Holmes and of the Hounds of the Baskerville (sic), as well as founder and long-time Gasogene of the Ribston-Pippins. She also makes and sells Sherlockian jewelry and gifts (etsy.com/shop/ArtfulPippin).

THE DOCUMENTS IN THE CASE

Lord Peter Wimsey

Al Shaw

Lord Peter Wimsey is like…

The present subjects of discussion are Sherlock Holmes (first appeared 1887, as readers of this volume will know) and Lord Peter Wimsey (first appeared 1923, in the novel *Whose Body?*, to be followed by a series of novels and short stories all written by Dorothy L. Sayers). Initially, to compare them efficiently, I was tempted to use the standard two-column list method. List A, all the Lord Peter attributes; list B, all the Holmes attributes. Thus, "See how similar they are?"

I soon realized that comparing a British lord and mama's boy to the fiercely independent, middle-class English gentleman of an earlier generation could not be achieved by a terse, coldly calculated, Sherlockian list of facts. This parallel review must be examined with warmth and affection for both characters. Thus, for the most part, I will simply discuss Wimsey's attributes and behaviors and let the similarities fall where they may.

Right from the outset, Lord Peter Wimsey mentions Holmes, or being like Holmes, multiple times, even in the first story. ("A grey suit I fancy, neat, but not gaudy… suits my other self, better…. Exits the amateur of first editions… enter Sherlock Holmes…. Makes me feel like Sherlock Holmes…. Perfectly simple, Watson," says Lord Peter, and that is just for starters.) It seems quite evident that Lord Peter keenly admires Holmes, or his techniques, and aspires to emulate the Master. "You know my methods, Watson."

Did you know that Wimsey smoked a pipe? ("There it is, Parker," said Lord Peter, pushing his coffee cup aside and lighting his after-break-fast pipe, addressing a policeman brother-in-law.)

In the series of Lord Peter Wimsey's adventures, he continues to grow and age, as the stories are presented. Many earlier cases are mentioned in passing. Some are detailed, but some are never expounded upon.

Let us pause a moment to examine Lord Peter's roommate, so to speak—more precisely his manservant, valet, caretaker if you will: Bunter. It is Bunter who finds a flat near Piccadilly Circus for them to share, after returning from service in World War I. Bunter does the actual dirty work in crime solving. Bunter photographs crime scenes and collects fingerprints. He follows suspects and checks alibis. Bunter comments on the progress of their cases.

But there are other considerations, other salient points, about Lord Peter Wimsey throughout the Wimsical canon (yes, I just said that). Lord Peter is a well-dressed British gentleman—the younger brother of a duke, indeed—although he's a bit of a dandy.

Wimsey served in the War, from 1914 to 1918, and was wounded. He was saved by his orderly who, it turns out, is none other than Bunter. After the war, his nerves were shot (PTSD, as it would now be called), and he was sent home to recuperate. He continued to live with, and with the support of, his employee, partner, and friend, and they became a crime-solving team. (Wimsey gets on well with some police, but feels, pretty much, that they are boobs and knaves.)

Lord Peter Wimsey is a ladies' man who has, and has had in the past, several affairs. But all this is eventually put behind him when he meets a woman accused of murder, Harriet Vane (*Strong Poison*). He marries her and settles down (*Busman's Honeymoon*).

It is revealed to us that Lord Peter plays cricket (*Murder Must Advertise*) and is fond of both hunting (*Clouds of Witness*) and fishing (*The Five Red Herrings*). In the latter tale, he takes time out for a fishing holiday in Scotland.

As I reached this point in my Wimsical research, something began to feel askew. I started to feel an uncomfortable itch where I could not scratch. That little finger was poking at some undefinable part of my brain. I am sure by now you, too, fine reader, are beginning to smell a Sumatran rat. The more I ruminated, the more my suspicions were aroused.

I decided that I would, after all, make a list.

Lord Peter Death Bredon Wimsey…

- admires Sherlock Holmes
- tries to be like Holmes
- ages through the years
- refers to cases not told
- smoked a pipe
- is a British gentleman
- dresses well
- sees the average police as ineffective, at best
- enjoys hunting and fishing
- served in the War
- was wounded and saved by his orderly
- suffered a nervous collapse
- was sent home to recuperate
- shares lodgings with his crime-solving partner
- is a ladies' man
- married the woman he met on a case

It was at this point that the itch turned into a fiery brand. I was dumb-struck with a bolt of metaphorical lightning that flew around the room and hit me between the eyes. How could I have been so dense? It was staring me in the face the whole time. I saw, but clearly I did not observe. I am sure that you, my dear reader, saw it for what it was, from the very outset.

It was most elementary.

Lord Peter Wimsey is not much like Sherlock Holmes at all. He is like... Dr. Watson!

Al Shaw (Chicago, Illinois) is a Baker Street Irregular and has been a member and officer in many Sherlockian societies, including Hugo's Companions and the Hounds of the Baskerville (sic). He creates still life cards and calendars from his collection of pipes and Sherlockiana. He extends thanks to Dino Argyropoulos, Brenda Rossini, and Claudine Kastner "for keeping me on Peter's Path."

THE HEROES OF BAKER STREET AND WEST 35TH STREET

Nero Wolfe

David Marcum

Sherlock Holmes has been my hero for more than forty years, and Nero Wolfe has been my second favorite "book friend," as my son used to call them when he was small, for nearly as long. To me, Holmes and Wolfe will always be linked, as I will explain. Certainly they're often mentioned, along with others such as Ellery Queen and Hercule Poirot, as the best of the Great Detectives. But on the surface, there are more differences than similarities. But only on the surface.

Setting aside their greatly contrasting appearances, as well as the different tones provided by the narrators of their adventures, the stories about these two characters occur in different countries and different eras. Holmes's canonical adventures took place mostly in England and mostly during the reign of Queen Victoria, while Wolfe's published cases—narrated in a long sequence of books beginning with *Fer-de-Lance* in 1934—are nearly always set in New York City, spanning the decades from the 1930s to the 1970s.

There are distinct personality differences between the two of them. Holmes is more prepared to share his deductions than Wolfe, and their approaches to solving a case are rather different. Holmes dashes about, while Wolfe has the pieces of the puzzle brought to him. In Holmes's first published narrative, *A Study in Scarlet*, he amazes his new friend Watson (and amuses the police) when "he trotted noiselessly about the room, sometimes stopping, occasionally kneeling, and once lying flat upon his face." Watching Holmes investigate for the first time, Watson commented that he "was irresistibly reminded of a pure-blooded, well-trained foxhound as it dashes backwards and forwards through the covert, whining in its eagerness, until it comes across the lost scent." Can anyone who read this, and recalls all the other energetic aspects of Holmes's methods, be immediately reminded of Nero Wolfe?

In fact, if one had to describe Wolfe, the initial response would be a figure resembling Mycroft Holmes rather than his brother Sherlock, both in behavior and in physique. Additionally, any description of Wolfe found in the Corpus, as the body of Wolfe narratives is conventionally known, would be much more critical, and humorous as well, than anything that Watson would write. The lens through which we see Nero Wolfe is Archie Goodwin, one of the greatest narrators to be found anywhere, period. Archie knows that Nero Wolfe is unique and amazing, but it doesn't keep him from describing things exactly as he sees them—including stating that the heavy-set Wolfe weighs a seventh of a ton, and specifically listing all his idiosyncrasies and foibles. Archie, by way of his literary agent Rex Stout (himself a noted New York Sherlockian), paints an amazing picture of Wolfe that isn't easily forgotten.

What immediately comes to mind when considering Wolfe are all of the Mycroft-like aspects: The physical description, certainly. Both men abjure physical activity. (Mycroft is described as doing nothing but walking from Pall Mall to Whitehall and back each day. Wolfe sets up a dart board in his office for exercise—although he refers to the darts as "javelins.") Both Wolfe and Mycroft have a preference for using others to carry out tasks that they would prefer to avoid. In "The Bruce-Partington Plans," Sherlock Holmes says, "Why do you not solve it yourself, Mycroft? You can see as far as I." "Possibly, Sherlock," replies Mycroft. "But it is a question of getting details. Give me your details, and from an armchair I will return you an excellent expert opinion. But to run here and run there, to cross question railway guards, and lie on my face with a lens to my eye—it is not my *métier*." Those words could have been said just as easily by Nero Wolfe.

Sherlock Holmes tells Watson that Mycroft's routine consists of traveling every morning from his lodgings in Pall Mall to his work in Whitehall (where he sometimes *is* the British Government), and then back to the Diogenes Club, located just opposite his rooms. Nero Wolfe carries this to an even greater extreme, adamantly trying to hold to the policy that he never leaves his house on West 35th Street in New York for anything related to business. (This doesn't always work out, resulting in some of Wolfe's greatest adventures—along with Archie's most gleeful descriptions of his boss's ever-increasing irritation and inconvenience.) Additionally, Wolfe maintains a very fixed schedule, with meals at set times, and work in his plant rooms on the roof of the building from 9 to 11 and 4 to 6 every day but Sunday. Although not canonically stated, one can imagine that Mycroft might also keep to the same sort of rigid time-table.

Of course, Wolfe's rules are frequently violated, often to his frustration and the reader's amusement. But then it must be recalled that in his few canonical appearances, Mycroft—who is often pigeon-holed as being completely locked into his routine—moves about more than we might recall. After Holmes and Watson visit him in "The Greek Interpreter," his first appearance in the Canon, he beats them back to Baker Street, where he is waiting to provide additional information. Then, in

"The Final Problem," he makes an unrecognized appearance as a "very massive driver wrapped in a dark cloak" who drives Watson from the Lowther Arcade to Victoria Station. Finally, in "The Bruce-Partington Plans," he and Lestrade visit Baker Street to seek brother Sherlock's assistance. Clearly, Mycroft travels around more than what is expected from someone who is described as having such a fixed orbit. (Of course, Mycroft's true activities as the head of the British Secret Service, and the fact that he's more active than he seems, have been explored to a much greater degree in countless post-canonical narratives.)

Nero Wolfe is also much more willing to move about than might be initially recalled by the casual reader. On several occasions, the sedentary and house-bound Wolfe gives hints of his energetic youth, when he was lean, athletic, and active, before he chose to give it all up. As he states in *Over My Dead Body* (1940), "I carry this fat to insulate my feelings. They got too strong for me once or twice and I had that idea. If I had stayed lean and kept moving around I would have been dead long ago."

We know that Wolfe was an espionage agent before, during, and after the First World War. He may have ended up as a Mycroft-like figure in his New York brownstone, solving mysteries—a distasteful necessity in order to fund his life—from his specially-constructed chair while his agents "run here and there" to obtain information, but in his youth, Wolfe was clearly much more akin to Sherlock Holmes.

Even during his later Mycroft-like years, as related in all of those Archie-narrated novels and novellas published from 1934 to 1975, Wolfe showed glimpses of more decisive and active Sherlock Holmes-like behaviors. In *Fer-de-lance*, Wolfe kills a particularly nasty snake with a beer bottle. (Sherlock Holmes similarly repelled a snake with only a cane in "The Speckled Band.") In *Over My Dead Body*, Wolfe again uses a beer bottle and his quick reflexes to dispatch an enemy—but this time a dagger-wielding assassin rather than a reptile. In *The Black Mountain* (1954), Wolfe and Archie travel *incognito* to Montenegro, a land much associated with Wolfe's mysterious past, where they are trapped by a bad man in an abandoned fortress high in the mountains. Wolfe and his opponent faced off with knives—clearly a skill that a stunned Archie was not expecting, and once more a hint at intriguing aspects of Wolfe's background. One is reminded that Sherlock Holmes was able to defend himself upon numerous occasions, such as when facing opponents like Woodley in "The Solitary Cyclist" and Professor Moriarty above the Reichenbach Falls in "The Final Problem."

Wolfe has his own Moriarty in the form of Arnold Zeck. Over the course of three brilliant books—*And Be A Villain* (1948), *The Second Confession* (1949), and *In the Best Families* (1950)—Wolfe came ever closer to the New York version of the Professor, who sat motionless in his own web of crime. Finally Wolfe, showing the same resourcefulness as Sherlock Holmes during the Great Hiatus, vanishes, not even telling Archie, his closest confidante, where he has gone. He returns, brilliantly disguised as the thin and unappealing Pete Roeder, showing that he could assume another identity and fool his biographer quite as easily as Holmes had often done. In fact, he is so changed that Archie didn't recognize him at all. (Wolfe's extended ruse as Roeder is reminiscent of Holmes's two-year impersonation of Altamont; each persona was crafted to penetrate the organizations of their respective enemies.) Together, Wolfe and Archie destroy Zeck through a clever ruse, even as Holmes and Watson trap and defeat Colonel Moran in "The Empty House."

There is much more that is similar between Holmes and Wolfe than is initially noticed. Holmes is famous for deductions, and Wolfe is known to make them as well, such as in *The Red Box* (1937), when he explains how someone had seen the contents of a poisoned box of candies. Holmes is often impatient with lesser mortals, and in *The Second Confession*, Wolfe states, "I am congenitally tart and thorny." Each has somewhat distant attitudes toward clients, women, friends, and people in general—but nevertheless they exhibit great loyalty and courtesy when appropriate. Both men have strong working relationships with the police and have earned their grudging respect. And Holmes and Wolfe are each strongly associated with the buildings in which they live—so much so that 221B Baker Street and Wolfe's West 35th Street brownstone have almost become additional characters in the Canon and the Corpus.

I cannot conclude this essay without mentioning a Holmes-Wolfe connection that has been wide-spread for more than half a century—the theory that Wolfe is Holmes's son, by way of Irene Adler, following a meeting between Holmes and Irene in Montenegro in 1892, while Holmes was in hiding during his Great Hiatus. Bernard DeVoto first began pondering about Wolfe's background in *Harper's* magazine (July 1954). This line of thought was continued by John D. Clark in the January 1956 *Baker Street Journal*. The speculation was only encouraged when Rex Stout wrote to the *BSJ* editor in response to Clark's essay: "As the literary agent of Archie Goodwin I am of course privy to many details of Nero Wolfe's past which to the general public must remain moot for some time. The constraint of my loyalty to my client makes it impossible for me to say more now."

The idea that Wolfe was Holmes's son continued to gain traction, and it was finally codified in William S. Baring-Gould's influential biography *Sherlock Holmes of Baker Street* (1962). Since then, Wolfe as Holmes's son has become a very popular and accepted idea with a number of Sherlockians and Wolfeans... including me. I first read Baring-Gould's biography of Holmes before I'd even read all of the Canon, in the mid-1970s when I was around ten years old. When I learned that Holmes and Irene Adler had a son, I wasn't surprised—although it was several years before I figured out exactly who this strangely named Nero Wolfe actually was. Over the years, many additional stories have elaborated upon the idea, such as John Lescroart's *Son of Holmes* (1986) and *Rasputin's Revenge* (1987). The idea was also featured in the book and film *Sherlock Holmes in New York* (1975), and I myself have "edited" a number of Watson's manuscripts that further prove and reinforce the Holmes and Wolfe father-son connection.

Once one begins to look for Holmes-Wolfe connections, they are easily found—and too numerous for this short essay. A good starting place is in the Wolfe adventure *The Rubber Band* (1936), in which Archie Goodwin mentions that a Sherlock Holmes portrait hangs over his desk in Wolfe's office. This Holmes portrait can be seen in opening moments of the film versions of both *Nero Wolfe* (1979, based on the 1965 book *The Doorbell Rang*) and *The Golden Spiders* (2000, from the 1953 novel).

Of course, Literary Agent Rex Stout continued to fan the flames. In "The Great O-E Theory" (*In the Queen's Parlor*, 1957), Frederic Dannay and Manfred Lee, doing business as Ellery Queen, recount how they were at a book signing with Stout in October 1954 when theories of Wolfe's background were first starting to surface. They asked him about the origin of the name Nero Wolfe—which is of interest to all Wolfeans, since Wolfe himself implies several times that it isn't his true identity. After some thought, Stout revealed another brilliant connection—the same placement of *O* and *E*, the vowels in each of their names: *shErlOck hOlmEs* and *nErO wOlfE*.

As the popularity of both Holmes and Wolfe continues to grow with each passing year, their relationship will be noticed and accepted by new generations of readers. And with the various connections between the two being reiterated and reinforced—by people like me, in whatever forum I can find—the links of the association will only grow stronger.

David Marcum (Maryville, Tennessee) has collected thousands of traditional Holmes pastiches including novels, short stories, radio and television episodes, movies and other items. He has written many such stories himself, and edits the continuing *MX Book of New Sherlock Holmes Stories*. He is a civil engineer.

THE MARROW OF THE MATTER

Hercule Poirot

Marina Stajić

Sherlock Holmes took his last bow during the most terrible August in the history of the world. He predicted the coming of an east wind, such a wind as never blew on England yet. Over the next four years, that cold and bitter wind blew mercilessly over the world. In 1916, two years after Holmes retired, the east wind brought to England a number of refugees from Belgium, including a retired member of the Belgian police force. His name was Hercule Poirot. After he settled in England, Poirot established a long, illustrious career as a consulting detective and private investigator, documented in more than 40 books by Agatha Christie from *The Mysterious Affair at Styles* (1920) to *Curtain* (1975).

Holmes would have been about 62 years old at the time Poirot arrived in England. Poirot's origins are vague, but he is thought to be an elderly man in his early British cases. Indications are that he and Holmes are about the same age.

> And yet, my dear Watson, there is so very close a connection that the one is extracted out of the other. —*The Hound of the Baskervilles*

Profession and age are not the only things Holmes and Poirot have in common. They brilliantly applied the science of deduction to solving cases, yet were willing to let Scotland Yard inspectors take credit for the solution since the satisfaction of successfully solving a case was to them a greater reward than any public applause. They undertook cases with little or no monetary reward simply because the problem involved interested them. Modesty was not among their virtues. They were self-confident, vain, conceited, egotistical, sensitive to flattery, and occasionally rude and arrogant. Both are known for misquoting Shakespeare and enjoying classical music. They even chose a similar occupation after retirement from careers as consulting detectives: Holmes took up beekeeping, Poirot cultivated vegetable marrows.

The most striking similarity between Holmes and Poirot is surely their companions, friends, and biographers, namely Dr. John H. Watson and Captain Arthur J.M. Hastings. Dr. Watson and Captain Hastings resemble each other even more than the two detectives do. Both have a British military background and are war invalids (Watson of the second Afghan war and Hastings of the Great War). At the time they started their partnership with Holmes and Poirot, neither had kith or kin in England. Watson and Hastings occasionally shared London lodgings with Holmes and Poirot. As biographers, both narrate adventures in the first person and are slow to see the significance of clues. They see, but do not observe. They are not themselves luminous, but they are conductors of light. Watson and Hastings are chivalrous gentlemen with a weakness for the fair sex. Both eventually got married (Watson more than once, Hastings once) and subsequently became widowed.

Taking into account all the above, one may deduce that Sherlock Holmes is not *like* Hercule Poirot. He *is* Hercule Poirot.

When you have eliminated the impossible, whatever remains, *however improbable*, must be the truth. —*The Sign of the Four*

Impossible, many will say, pointing immediately to the striking difference in the physical appearance of Holmes and Poirot, particularly to the difference in height. Holmes was six feet tall while Poirot was hardly over five feet four. But is it really impossible?

The impossible is eliminated by the fact that Sherlock Holmes was a master of disguise. Watson tells us in "The Blanched Soldier" that Holmes had at least five small refuges in different parts of London, in which he was able to change his personality. His various disguises range from Captain Basil in "Black Peter" to a Nonconformist clergyman in "A Scandal in Bohemia" and an old woman in "The Mazarin Stone." We know additionally that Holmes "would have made an actor and a rare one" and that "the stage lost a fine actor" when he became a specialist in crime, as well as that "his very soul seemed to vary with each fresh part that he assumed." Obviously, Holmes was able to act young when he may have been as old as 45 ("Charles Augustus Milverton") and act old when he was just 34 (*The Sign of the Four*).

Acting as a man of his own age would be easy. Acting as a much shorter man, naturally, would present a challenge. However, I draw your attention to Holmes's disguise as an elderly, deformed, hobbling bibliophile in "The Empty House." After shocking Watson by his dramatic reappearance, Holmes stated that he was glad to stretch himself since "it is no joke when a tall man has to take a foot off his stature for several hours on end."

Holmes chose an additional interesting disguise for his new persona. Hastings first describes Poirot in *The Mysterious Affair at Styles* as an extraordinary-looking little man whose head was exactly the shape of an egg, always perched a little to one side. He is very proud of his moustache, very stiff and military, and devotes a lot of time to grooming it. He considers the growing of the moustache to be an art. He dyes his hair black. Later in life he admits to Hastings that he wears a wig and a false moustache. Poirot's native language is French, but he speaks it rather like a stage Frenchman, while on occasion speaking perfect English. However, he considers the use of broken English "an enormous asset" in order to appear more foreign. Generally, his appearance and behavior are so exaggerated that he gives the impression of a caricature. Did this effective disguise resemble the real Hercule Poirot? Holmes may have encountered Poirot during his visit to Brussels ("The Final Problem"). It is also possible that a real Poirot never existed and that is why his origins are so vague.

"We balance probabilities and choose the most likely. It is the scientific use of the imagination." —*The Hound of the Basker-villes*

Further inconsistences are more easily explained. Holmes's and Poirot's methods of investigation are not identical. Deductive reasoning and "little grey cells" are used by both, but Holmes is far more physically active. In his early British cases, Poirot applies "Sherlockian" methods of case investigation (examining footprints, fingerprints, cigar ash, and the like). Several references to Sherlock Holmes are made throughout Poirot's cases. For example, he compares one of his own observations in "Murder in the Mews" to Holmes pointing out the curious incident of the dog in the night-time. When asked in "Yellow Iris" if he is "really some kind of Sherlock Holmes" doing "wonderful deductions," he replies: "Ah, the deductions—they are not so easy in real life. But shall I try?" References are also made to Watson. He paraphrases Holmes: "I have my methods, Watson.... Obvious, my dear Watson." (No, he never says "Elementary, my dear Watson.") Hastings uses the same words when asked for his own deductions. Poirot and Hastings even jokingly refer to Hastings as being Watson.

However, Poirot eventually becomes more of an armchair detective. Let us not forget that Holmes was in his sixties when he reappeared as Poirot, an age when his physical prowess would have declined. Watson tells us in the preface to *His Last Bow* that Holmes was "somewhat crippled by occasional attacks of rheumatism" during his retirement years. So, perhaps inspired by his brother Mycroft, he became more of an armchair detective. The minimized physical activity also made it easier for a tall man to pretend being short. Reducing his height must have become increasingly harder as Holmes aged. In *Curtain*, Poirot's last case, physical activity was minimized to the point that Poirot is seen only in bed or in a wheelchair or being carried by his valet.

Why didn't Holmes retain his friend Watson as his Boswell? One likely reason is that Watson was two years older than Holmes and on occasion felt "rheumatic and old," as in "Lady Frances Carfax." Therefore, he wouldn't have made an ideal partner in the investigations of the aging Holmes. Instead, Holmes chose Hastings, some 30 years younger, as a companion and assistant in his investigations. Another reason for abandoning Watson may be similar to the one Holmes had during the Great Hiatus, that he didn't want to reveal his latest disguise to his enemies (and he must have created several after capturing Von Bork) and chose to keep it a secret even from Watson. It is also possible that Watson declined further partnership since he was busy with continued writing and publishing of Holmes's adventures. Or, it could have been a combination of all three.

On the personal side, both Holmes and Poirot had *the* woman in their lives: Irene Adler and Countess Vera Rosakoff, respectively. If Poirot was Holmes, it is evident that, later in life, the versatile detective found another woman of dubious and questionable memory who beat him by her wit (the details are in the novel *The Big Four*).

Some Sherlockians argue that the lack of Sherlock Holmes's obituary is a proof that he is still alive. On August 6, 1975, *The New York Times* did publish Hercules Poirot's obituary. Does that mean that Sherlock Holmes died at the age of 121? Of course not. He just retired one more time and happily continues to raise bees and, having improved his knowledge of practical gardening, to cultivate vegetable marrows.

> Each may form his own hypothesis upon the present evidence, and yours is as likely to be correct as mine. —"The Empty House"

Marina Stajić (New York, New York) is a forensic toxicologist. She is an Adventuress of Sherlock Holmes, a Baker Street Irregular, a member of the Sherlock Holmes Society of London, an honorary member of The Sherlock Holmes Society of France, and a member of several other societies. She is a passionate Yankee fan and lives with two fabulous felines, Altamont and Sigerson.

A WHOLE LOT OF DETECTIVE STORIES

Nick Charles

Angela Fowler

When I say that Nick Charles is like Sherlock Holmes, I do it knowing that they're completely different in every possible way.

Well, perhaps not every possible way. They're both amateur detectives with adoring, erstwhile companions, and they both skate the margins of social class and respectability. How they're different lies in their status in the detective genre. While Sherlock Holmes is the first serialized detective and the originator of many of the detective tropes, Nick Charles is the amalgam and a parody of all the tropes that came before him.

First, some background. Nick Charles and his wife Nora were wildly popular during the 1930s and 40s, but they haven't quite had the longevity of Sherlock Holmes and Dr. Watson. Nick and Nora Charles were introduced in *The Thin Man* (1933) by Dashiell Hammett. It was a departure from Hammett's usual fare: Nick may have been a hard-boiled detective in the past, but now he is retired and happily settled down with his wife Nora, her fortune, their dog Asta, and enough alcohol to make one weep for their livers. Nick and Nora became household names with a six-film series that spanned 1934–1947, starring William Powell and Myrna Loy.

While the Nick Charles of the novel is like Sam Spade in retirement, William Powell created a retired detective who's urbane and sophisticated. He's introduced demonstrating what rhythm a martini should be shaken to: "The important thing is the rhythm. Always have rhythm in your shaking. Now a Manhattan you shake to fox-trot time, a Bronx to two-step time, a dry martini you always shake to waltz time." He similarly waltzes through the drama and murder around him, all the while drinking, trying to stay retired as a detective, and cracking wise with his wife.

Nora, on the other hand, pratfalls spectacularly into the film, the wire-haired terrier Asta dragging her into the bar where Nick was mixing drinks. She proceeds to match him drink for drink:

> Nora: How many drinks have you had?
> Nick: This will make six martinis.
> Nora [to the waiter]: All right. Will you bring me five more martinis, Leo? Line them right up here.

Nick and Nora together are the epitome of *joie de vivre*. While drama and mystery play out around them, they react by playing, by making wry comments, and above all by enjoying themselves and each other. They're what is still a rarity in media: a married couple who truly enjoy being around each other. When Nora ribs Nick about a pretty girl he was talking to, he says his type is "only you, darling: lanky brunettes with wicked jaws." When reporters ask Nora if he's working on a case, she responds, "Yes, yes! A case of scotch! Pitch in and help him." At one point, the two are threatened by an armed gangster in their bedroom, and Nick punches Nora to get her out of the way of the bullet. When she comes to, she exclaims, "You darn fool! You didn't have to knock me out. I knew you'd take him, but I wanted to see you do it." When Nora remarks that she read Nick got shot five times in the tabloids, he responds, "It's not true. He didn't come anywhere near my tabloids."

It takes quite a bit of restraint not to begin quoting the movie the moment an essay about it begins. While the plots are often thin and the mysteries not all that interesting, the true magic of the Thin Man movies lies in Nick and Nora's relationship to what happens around them, and we mainly get that through their dialogue and physical tomfoolery. (In one particular scene, Nick and Nora playfight quietly while a policeman is on the telephone.) The mystery seems to be more of an excuse for Nick and Nora to make jokes. The movies are comedies with a detective in them, often throwing together heaps of genre conventions that would have been old hat by 1934, all played for laughs.

So, then, what does this have to do with Sherlock Holmes?

There are a few ties between Charles and Holmes, besides the fact that they're both detectives. Dashiell Hammett based Nick Charles on himself, a former Pinkerton detective (Nora was based on Hammett's long-time romantic partner, playwright Lillian Hellman). A Pinkerton detective was featured in Doyle's last Holmes novel, *The Valley of Fear*. William Powell, most famously associated with playing Nick Charles, began his film acting career as one of Moriarty's henchmen in the 1922 silent film *Sherlock Holmes*, starring John Barrymore as the detective. And to demonstrate that the connection is no coincidence, in the first Thin Man film, Nick and Nora cheekily call each other Sherlock and Watson as Nick finally, officially takes the case.

Nora is not entirely Nick's Watson, as she's less of a Boswell and more of an enthusiastic instigator. She most fulfills the Watson role during her less-than-successful forays into solo detection. Nick usually tries to keep her away from danger, even sending her in a taxi to Grant's Tomb at one point (she assures him that she's getting a copy made for him), but Nora is tenacious. However, her attempts usually backfire, leading her to variously get arrested, follow the wrong lead, nearly get attacked by a mental patient, and get stuck dancing with a lothario. These instances bear striking similarities to Watson's disastrous attempts to investigate in *The Hound of the Baskervilles* and "The Solitary Cyclist." Nick, like Holmes, is always there to pull his companion out of the soup.

And then there are their unconventional methods as detectives. Sherlock Holmes's primary method of detection is listening to people and creating narratives out of small details. He may claim that he uses deductive reasoning, and people may remember him wandering around with a magnifying glass checking for fingerprints, but he solves most of his cases by inductive reasoning, or ascribing meaning to details based on probability. He also builds narratives as he observes more details, often reciting these narratives to the amazed criminal.

Nick Charles follows similar methods, though those methods are certainly affected by the more cynical world he inhabits. In other words, everyone that Nick talks to lies. He acknowledges this in Hammett's novel: he has to take everything with a grain of salt and sift through the lies for a glimmer of truth. In the films, most of Nick's detection comes from listening to the lies and finding inconsistencies. In fact, he gathers everyone for a "parlor room scene" in each film just so they can keep talking and he can catch someone in just the right lie. The first two films—*The Thin Man* and *After the Thin Man*—memorably reveal the unlikely murderer through this method. One tiny detail, one innocuous comment, leads Nick to, like Holmes, confront the murderer with a narrative of his crime, and that usually leads to a desperate shoot-out with said murderer.

The difference between Holmes and Nick Charles, though, is pretty significant, and it lies in their respective places in the genre of mysteries and detective stories. When Nora, in both the novel and film of *The Thin Man*, laments that Nick won't take the case, Nick offers, "Tomorrow I'll buy you a whole lot of detective stories." In a way, Nick is a whole lot of detective stories. He's a combination of all of the trappings of detective stories, only now with a parodic twist and a happy ending.

Sherlock Holmes and his early adaptations originated the tropes of the detective character and story. He's an amateur and a gentleman, separate from the official police even when he's working with them. He's an artist and connoisseur of crime with an eccentric personality, which often puts people off their guard around him. While not all detectives who came after him are exactly like him, every detective follows his model in some way: the strange methods, the eccentricity, whatever. The structure of the Holmes stories influenced what came after as well, with the focus on methods and the detective's penchant for keeping the reader in the dark until the final reveal.

Now let's jump forward in time a few decades. Agatha Christie, Dorothy L. Sayers, and a whole host of writers have made the detective genre an institution, establishing such tropes as the "parlor room scene." In the meantime, the detective story is mixing with the spy thriller and pulp crime stories to produce the hard-boiled detective, which Dashiell Hammett partially originated. The detective then becomes working-class and leaves his amateur status behind, as well as the parlors and dinner parties of their more high-class predecessors. These detectives would spawn the film noir genre after World War II, recasting the detective as the moody arbiter of justice in a world that otherwise lacks any.

Nick Charles somehow embodies all of those traditions. The novel establishes him as the working-class son of a Greek immigrant (his father changed their name from Charalambides). While the first film leaves out his immigrant origins (and the fifth film *The Thin Man Goes Home* replaces this back-story with a middle-class rural father), most of Nick's friends are lower-class or even criminals he's sent to prison, a contrast to Nora's high-class upbringing and associates. He's flippant about his former career as a detective, but we get the impression that he's lived hard and dangerously before he married Nora, as he's well aware of the dangers and wishes to shield Nora and eventually their son from them.

On the other hand, Nick's marrying rich allows him to be the amateur detective, hobnobbing with the elite and only solving murders when he's dragged in, usually by his adventure-loving wife. The low class social circle and Nora's more "respectable" friends and family often clash, throwing the elite in with gangsters and former criminals. While Holmes associated with people across a wide social spectrum, from royalty to street urchins, the Thin Man films bring them to one dinner table to comedic effect. As Nora says, "Will you serve the nuts? I mean, will you serve the guests the nuts." And, as in most of Holmes's resolutions, the murderer is usually from the more "respectable" crowd.

In sum, Nick Charles is a performance. Aware of all the detective tropes (one film establishes that he used to read the very detective stories he offered to get for Nora), Nick plays the detective and makes sure he has a captive audience. Part of this is the nature of the film and William Powell's portrayal: the Nick of the novel still speaks and acts like a hardboiled detective, but William Powell plays Nick as an urbane, tipsy showman. He's not just performing for the camera, though; Nick sets the dinner party reveal in the first film as a performance for Nora, asking her beforehand if she wants to watch him catch the murderer. Through the dinner party, he continually checks in on Nora, cheekily letting her know she can pull out when things get too rough. Nora sticks it through, of course, and later she becomes more integral to the performance of the final reveal, offering warnings for what's coming next and even a meta-commentary to Nick's parents in *The Thin Man Goes Home*.

So Nick Charles is a character made up of often contradictory detective tropes, performing the detective for an audience well versed in detective fiction, in films that are more comedies than mysteries. While the films never go for all-out parody, they're certainly light-hearted takes on well-worn genre conventions that saw their beginning with Sherlock Holmes. Of course, even Holmes, ever theatrical, performed his detection for Watson, setting up his final reveal just as carefully as Nick does. Perhaps, then, after decades of detective stories, Nick Charles is just like Sherlock Holmes after all.

Angela Fowler (Montgomery, Alabama) is an instructor at Auburn University Montgomery whose PhD dissertation was on "Arthur Conan Doyle and British Cosmopolitan Identity: Knights, Detectives, and Mediums." She is the host of the podcast Through the Pages of Sherlock Holmes.

HEARING IT ALL OVER AGAIN

Jimmie Lavender

Ray Betzner

It is a winter's evening on Portland Street in Chicago. As dark descends and the snow piles up outside, amateur detective Jimmie Lavender and his assistant Charles "Gilly" Gilruth sit before the fire and discuss death and detectives. The firelight highlights the shock of white hair that "lay like a heron's feather in the dark masses" on Lavender's head.

"How many letters would you say the alphabet contained?" asks Lavender with cheeky pleasure.

"Shall I say that there are still only twenty-six?" Gilly fires back.

"Precisely!" he says. "Twenty-six—and out of them we have composed some half a million words, all different, which we call the English language."

After declaiming for a bit on physics and medicine, Lavender returns to murder.

"It is the same with crime and crime solutions. In spite of the number and variety of crimes committed, the principles involved are actually very few." And Lavender is off again, recounting how he was able to solve a crime that Chicago's best police detectives found baffling.

It might not be Sherlock Holmes lecturing Dr. Watson on "The Science of Deduction," but the concept is the same. The learned detective is schooling his faithful friend in the theory that helps him do what others cannot: solve bewildering crimes. And the friend is amazed and amused, perfectly willing to hear once again the stories he has lived through or learned about whenever Lavender wanted to ruminate.

"I am never so happy as when I am hearing it all over again," Gilly enthuses. "Carry on, Jimmie. I'm listening!"

For the better part of 20 years, from the 1910s through the 1930s, Lavender and Gilly carried on together, solving the high life crimes of Chicago. It's a city where well-to-do matrons accidently kill their boytoy lovers and the occasional gangster interferes with the pleasures of the foolish and rich. In a city where lawlessness was legendary, Lavender was on the side of justice, that blind-folded lady whose robe keeps slipping off her shoulders.

Lavender reflected the experiences of his creator, Vincent Starrett. Best-known today for Sherlockian masterworks like *The Private Life of Sherlock Holmes*, "The Unique Hamlet" and the sonnet "221B," Starrett's early career as a crime reporter for various Chicago newspapers opened up the real-life world of jealousy, lust, and anger that fueled people's bad behavior. By day he reported on crimes. By night, he committed them at his typewriter.

Soon he quit the newspapering business and, just as Arthur Conan Doyle had done when he gave up medicine several decades before, decided to make his way in life as a writer. Starrett's range was eclectic and wide. He wrote stacks of poetry, book reviews, and Sunday features, and soon made a name for himself as a glimmer among the city's literary stars like Ben Hecht, Charles MacArthur, and Carl Sandburg.

The most consistent sellers for Starrett were his Jimmie Lavender stories. "It was my trick of plot that sold my early stories and made it possible for me to make a precarious living for many years as a writer of detective stories," Starrett explained in his memoir, *Born in a Bookshop*.

Truth be told, the solutions were often hard to swallow.

Take, for example, Lavender's most famous locked room mystery. The solution turned out to be this: After the bad guy was shot, he stuffed a hanky in his fatal wound, made his way back up the street, up the elevator, into his apartment, and down to the hall to his home office where he locked the door, sat down at the desk chair and then died.

Without anyone noticing.

Possible? Yes. Probable? Not hardly.

Jimmie Lavender (Starrett thought of him "James Eliot Lavender," but only in his head) borrowed his name from a Chicago Cubs baseball player who spelled his first name the usual way. Starrett deliberately changed the spelling to "Jimmie," thereby driving copy editors crazy for the next several decades.

Unlike Holmes, who would throw himself on the carpet to hunt out tobacco ash or stray bits of string, Lavender would more often stand stock still in the center of a busy room and watch. Just watch. In this way he would see things that others miss, identify the cracks in a theory that did not hold together, and find the solution others failed to recognize.

Like Holmes, he tended to see these things because he was looking for them. Case in point: In *Recipe for Murder*, Lavender knows that while a woman has shot a gun at close range at her philandering husband, the gun did not fire the fatal shot. No. Lavender realized—by not accepting what everyone thought was true but looking for the alternative—that someone else also fired a gun at the exact same time, and that was the shot which killed the cad.

Lavender's talents were well known in Starrett's imagined version of Chicago. An amateur consultant in crime who preferred his books and cozy quarters, Lavender responded when the upper crust called him in to bail out a wayward wife or ne'er-do-well son. But Lavender was just as comfortable with the working class and preferred their company, truth be told. The rich paid his bills, but the cops and reporters were people he could talk to and trust, at least a bit. He also had the respect of the city police. Like Holmes, Lavender was happy if he solved the case and the police got the credit, so long as the guilty person was nailed for the crime. Detectives therefore called him "Jimmie" and invited him to roam about crime scenes as you would invite your Uncle Gene over to watch the big game on your new TV.

And then there is his roommate and ally, Gilly. Although he occasionally proved useful in an investigation (Gilly was a master at getting fingerprints off a surface that would stymie a crime lab detective), Gilly's two most important functions were to be a sounding board for Jimmie, and to add a little comic relief. This he often achieved through his lecherous thoughts regarding the attractive females in the case. As it was for Watson, women were Gilly's department.

"She was enormously attractive. My pulses, as usual in such circumstances, beat more quickly. Whatever else Albert J. Penfield might have lost, I reflected, he was still a lucky stiff," Gilly says after meeting the missus. Later on, Mrs. Penfield learns her lover has been killed. "Then she screamed and keeled over into my arms. It was my good fortune to be standing just behind her." Heh.

Re-reading the stories today gives a good lesson in plotting and pace. Events move quickly and Starrett's newspaper background taught him economy of words. Besides, Starrett didn't want the reader to pay too much attention to the details. It's a situation he acknowledged decades after writing the last Lavender story. "My problems were ingenious, often fantastic, and Jimmie Lavender solved them very deftly, I think. His deductions were sometimes pretty fuzzy, however, and I can see now that he was very fortunate in bringing some of his cases to a successful conclusion," Starrett said.

The downside to this is that it leaves the reader curiously dispassionate about the detective and his pal. There are more than 50 Lavender short stories, just about the size of the Holmes Canon, but we learn very little about the detective and care even less. There's no smarter brother, no love interest, no arch-nemesis pulling the strings to Chicago's evil doers. And because the Lavender stories turned up in a variety of publications, each was a self-contained story, independent of what came before, and promising nothing of what would come after.

Starrett's friends, who were editors at the various pulp magazines based in Chicago, accepted his work readily enough, and his name features frequently during this period on the covers of pulps like *Short Stories*, *Wayside Tales*, *Mystery*, and *Real Detective Tales*. At the start, Starrett was young and full of ideas. "I enjoyed writing detective stories and not because they were the easiest stories to write," he said in his memoir. "Nothing is harder to write than a good detective story. And I had some grand ideas in those days before I had really learned *how* to write."

Short story writing is also hard work, and over time, Starrett wanted something that would pay better and get him off the pulp hamster wheel. Unlike Conan Doyle, who took Holmes from novels to short stories, Starrett worked the other way around. At first, he thought he could put Lavender in a novel, but that didn't work out and he created new detectives. Walter Ghost and Riley Blackwood made appearances in detective novels that made a ripple upon publication but faded soon enough. Starrett hit it lucky just once, in 1935 with *The Great Hotel Murder*. He sold the same story three times: first to *Redbook* magazine, then in novel form, and finally as a film plot. Then he grabbed the Hollywood money and his wife and went on a world tour.

More than two years later, he came back to Chicago to find his money had run out and no one cared about Jimmie Lavender or his type of puzzle stories. The hard-boiled school was now all the rage, and Starrett knew his time as a mystery writer had passed. He reinvented himself as a Chicago book columnist, and as "The Last Bookman," a role he would keep for the next four decades.

But Jimmie Lavender was not completely forgotten. Newspaper syndicates wanted fodder for Sunday magazines in the 1940s and 50s, and a few of the Lavender stories were recycled. *Ellery Queen's Mystery Magazine* picked up a few more of the tales to keep Lavender's reputation alive. A cheap anthology of Lavender stories, *The Case-Book of Jimmie Lavender*, was published by Gold Label Books in 1944, and reprinted by Bookfinger in 1973, one year before Starrett died.

In Starrett's dedication to the anthology, he thanks the baseball player who loaned his name, the editor who first accepted the Lavender stories, and "Ellery Queen who revived them." Then he thanks one other: "To Dr. John H. Watson, formerly of Baker Street, London, who wrote the original prescription."

Wherever he went, whatever Starrett wrote, Sherlock Holmes was never far.

Ray Betzner (Thorndale, Pennsylvania) has been involved in the Sherlock Holmes world for 40 years. He is a member of the Baker Street Irregulars and Comptroller of the Kennel for the Sons of the Copper Beeches in Philadelphia. He writes about Vincent Starrett at www.vincentstarrett.com.

THE SHERLOCK HOLMES OF IRAN

Sadeq Mamqoli

Navid Farrokhi

The emergence of crime fiction in the West has been affected by such factors as the spread of science, the invention of electricity, the theory of Darwin, autopsy science, the philosophy of positivism, industrial and mechanical civilization, the expansion of urbanization, and other things. In the Middle East, however, the situation was not the same. The necessary prerequisites that led to crime fiction in the West were not yet available in a country like Iran, so it is not surprising that the initial Iranian crime stories were only written after Iranian writers became familiar with translated crime novels. *Sadeq Mamqoli: The Sheriff of Isfahan or Sherlock Holmes of Iran* (1925) is a novel by Mirza Kazem Khan Mosta'an. Some literary scholars consider this book to be the first crime novel in Iran, and without a doubt, Sadeq Mamqoli is the first detective. As the title suggests, the author was clearly inspired by Sherlock Holmes.

There is a background of connections between Sherlock Holmes and Iran (formerly called Persia). The Holmes adventures are set during the golden age of the British Empire, when vast territories around the world had been covered by British economic and military forces. Sherlock Holmes's job as consulting detective spanned from 1880 to around 1914. But there is a famous gap during 1892–1894. In this period, although Holmes is supposed dead in England, actually he travelled eastward disguised as a Norwegian explorer named Sigerson. "I travelled for two years in Tibet... I then passed through Persia," he says in "The Empty House."

And this is not the only hint of Persia. There are other evidences, too. Holmes "keeps his tobacco inside a Persian slipper," according to three different stories. And Holmes says to Watson at the end of "A Case of Identity": "You may remember the old Persian saying, 'There is danger for him who taketh the tiger cub, and danger also for whoso snatches a delusion from a woman.' There is as much sense in Hafiz as in Horace, and as much knowledge of the world." Hafez (usually so spelt) was a poet whose works are considered a pinnacle of Persian literature. Hafez's poems were first translated into English in 1771 by William Jones. Nevertheless, there are doubts about the authenticity of this quote and its connection to Hafez.

The first translation of a Sherlock Holmes story into Persian was *London Police* (1904), based on *A Study in Scarlet* and translated by a Qajar prince called Abdol Hossein Moayed-Aldole. Although the translation was from an Arabic source, it's close to the original text. A more serious attempt was made the next year. *Book of Sherlock Khoms* (1905) was translated by Mir Ismael Adollah-zadeh. Again, the source wasn't in English, as the translation was done from Russian to Persian. Book of Sherlock Khoms contains three short stories: "The Golden Pince-Nez," "Charles Augustus Milverton," and "The Reigate Puzzle." The most notable point about Abdollah-zadeh's translation is a reference in the book's introduction. The word "memoir" in the title *The Memoirs of Sherlock Holmes* had made Abdollah-zadeh think Holmes was a real person, and he wrote a few lines describing Holmes's sharpness and courage in solving London crimes, as well as his dedication to his country.

Edward G. Browne (1862–1926), a British orientalist, in the fourth volume of his *A Literary History of Persia* (1920) mentions Abdollah-zadeh's translation of Sherlock Holmes: "Before leaving this subject I must at least mention a Persian translation of three episodes in the career of the immortal Sherlock Holmes, translated from a Russian version by Mír Isma'íl Abdu'lláh-záda.... Holmes in passing through a Russian medium has been transmuted into Khums or Khúmis." Browne considers the translator's prose completely fluent: "The adventures are narrated in the simplest possible style, and would form an admirable reading-book for beginners in Persian."

About two decades after the early translations from Arabic and Russian, another translation was published. *The Extraordinary Adventures of Sherlock Holmes, the Famous English Policeman* (1927) was translated by Colonel Mohammad Hossein Jahanbani. The source of the original text is not certain, but using words like "Baker Strasse" gives a hint of the German language. Jahanbani says in the introduction of the book that the author (Doyle) shows the "fictional detective" and his adventures as "believable" and with "reason and deduction." *The Extraordinary Adventures* includes six stories and is more like modern Persian prose.

Since the 1950s, the Sherlock Holmes books have been translated several times from the original English text. The writer of this paper is also a translator of canonical stories into Persian.

Holmes's stories became popular among Iranian readers, and it was natural that the Iranian writers were also influenced by him. The first wave of Iranian crime novels was accompanied by political changes in Iran. In fact, early detective stories of Iran were influenced in terms of the overall features and capabilities of Sherlock Holmes. The greatest example is a fictional character called Sadeq Mamqoli, who figures in only a single novel, *Sadeq Mamqoli: The Sheriff of Isfahan or Sherlock Holmes of Iran* by Mirza Kazem Khan Mosta'an.

Mosta'an's detective story was written and published about twenty years after the first translation of the Sherlock Holmes stories. The first edition was published by Shargh Publication and ran to 160 pages. It was later reprinted by Fahm Press Office, and in recent years, there have been several other new editions, most recently (2017) from Mania Honar. *The Sheriff of Isfahan* is recognized by literary researchers as the first modern detective story from Iran.

The Sheriff of Isfahan is, of course, the story of a sheriff named Sadeq Mamqoli. The atmosphere of the book is quite similar to the stories of *One Thousand and One Nights* and other ancient stories, and it features a surprise ending—though there are no traces of magic and fantasy elements, for Sheriff Mamqoli solves the case with the help of his own intelligence and reasoning methods. He also likes to admonish criminals to change their way of life.

But he continues to feel disappointed that he has not been able to solve a few mysteries in the past. At the beginning of the novel, Sadeq Mamqoli is tired of working on a kidnapping case: while he is a master of footprint techniques, he cannot find the traces of the kidnappers. A letter comes to Mamqoli in which he is told that if he wants to arrest the kidnappers, he should go to a local castle. When he goes to the fort, he is imprisoned by a black man who is serving someone else. Later, the reader finds out the servant is the agent of a woman named Khan Kuchak. This woman, who has a boyish appearance, proves to be a young girl who is the head of an underground group that has arisen to avenge the tyranny of the central government. The book is clearly an indirect, sarcastic critique of the Qajar dynasty that ruled Persia from 1785 to 1925.

The Sheriff of Isfahan is a bright example of how Iranian authors tried to develop Persian detective novels by imitating foreign works. Other crime and detective novels from that period were full of prolonged speeches from the characters, especially those about the status of traditional societies, and lacked remarkable mysteries. Mosta'an was obviously inspired by stories about Sherlock Holmes, as evident even in the title of his story, and the result was an attempt to create Persian detective fiction that uses the native space of Iran well and acceptably, and lets its plot unfold very simply. It remains one of the most successful examples of the detective genre in Iran, and Sadeq Mamqoli deserves to be called the "Sherlock Holmes of Iran."

The stories and characters have some similarities which can be mentioned here:

Both works can be considered as a sub-genre of crime fiction.

Mamqoli and Sherlock both can learn many details about the past and personal life of a person through his or her appearance.

It seems that neither Mamqoli nor Holmes has any particular affinity for their families. Neither of them talks about their spouse, or their child, or even their parents (though in Holmes's 56 stories and 4 novels are some tiny points about the Holmes family).

- Both of them are experts in disguise.
- Although Mamqoli and Holmes both have weird characters, they do not look unrealistic. In the Holmes stories, his face, body, and thoughts are discussed in more detail. For example, we know Holmes is tall, plays the violin, and is not interested in literature, philosophy, astronomy, and politics. However, in the only work in which Sadeq Mamqoli takes part, this kind of information is not revealed.
- Both detectives have assistants. Watson is always with Holmes and narrates his adventures. In *The Sheriff of Isfahan*, Mahmoud somehow plays the role of Mamqoli's assistant, and he consults with him. But since he isn't always with the detective, he can't be the narrator of the story.
- Both detectives do not believe in metaphysics and try to solve the mysteries by using logical reasoning.
- Both detectives pay attention to the smallest things. Mamqoli's sharp observations can be matched to Holmes's. For example, in a dark basement in which a candle has burned down, the amount it has burned is used as a measure for the passage of time.
- Mamqoli and Holmes both have informants and spies in the city. Holmes organized the Baker Street Irregulars to spy for him, and Mamqoli uses Mahmoud and an old woman to do the same. Mahmoud even pretends to sell sweets to spy on the neighborhood.
- There is a suspense element in both stories.
- Both detectives work in large cities, Holmes in London and Mamqoli in Isfahan, Iran's third largest city, with a population today of 1.7 million.

However, Sherlock Holmes appears as a consulting detective, but Sadeq Mamqoli is an official detective.

Navid Farrokhi (Tehran, Iran) is an enthusiast of Sherlock Holmes and translator of canonical stories into Persian, as well as an author and historian of detective fiction. He has a master's degree in computer engineering from the Amirkabir University of Technology.

BODY LANGUAGE

Special Agent Dale Cooper

Brian and Derrick Belanger

March 30, 7 p.m. Have just finished reading about Sherlock
Holmes in *The Hound of the Baskervilles*. I believe Mr. Holmes
is the smartest detective who has ever lived, and would very
much like to live a life like he did. It is the Friends School belief
that the best thing one can do in life is to do good rather than do
well. I believe that in Mr. Holmes I see a way to accomplish this.

This passage is taken from *The Autobiography of FBI Special Agent
Dale Cooper: My Life, My Tapes*, one of several media tie-ins to the
original run of the TV series *Twin Peaks*—a quirky detective series created by director David Lynch and writer Mark Frost. It focused on an
investigation into the murder of high school homecoming queen Laura
Palmer by Special Agent Dale Cooper (played perfectly by actor Kyle
McLaughlin). The show, which originally ran on ABC in 1990–91 and
returned for a season on Showtime in 2017, also involved elements of
horror and the supernatural.

What is fascinating about the quote is that Cooper is referring to
Sherlock Holmes as an actual historical figure. The book itself is written
by Mark Frost's brother Scott Frost, who seems to share Mark's passion
for the Great Detective (Mark Frost wrote two Sherlockian novels, *The
List of Seven* and *The Six Messiahs*). Is it too much of a stretch to assume
that the world of *Twin Peaks* is the same world where Holmes and Watson once solved their own mysteries a century earlier? And if so, how
much more of a stretch is it to view the adventures of this unorthodox
Special Agent as the continuing saga of Sherlock Holmes, the latest link
in a chain connecting Holmes to Solar Pons, Nero Wolfe, George Smiley,
and the rest?

Using unconventional methods of deduction, relying on otherworldly irregulars, fighting criminal masterminds with his own loyal companion by his side—Agent Cooper's actions in *Twin Peaks* clearly show that he is indeed a modern-day version of his boyhood idol. Take, for example, Cooper's powers of observation, narrowing his focus on seeming trifles to reveal their importance. In the series' pilot episode, Cooper is summoned to Twin Peaks after Laura Palmer, the beloved high school sweetheart, is found murdered, her body lying by a riverbank, wrapped in plastic. During the investigation, Cooper and the local police watch a recent videotape recording of Laura having a picnic with her friend Donna. At one point Lucy, the police receptionist, tells Agent Cooper and Sheriff Truman that she overheard two of the suspects discussing a biker. Cooper tells Lucy and Truman that he already knows that a biker is involved. He pauses the video and zooms in on Laura's eye. It is here, reflected in her eye, that we see the image of a motorcycle.

The following day Agent Cooper, along with his partner Sheriff Harry Truman, interviews Josie Packard, the young owner of the Packard Sawmill. After the interview, Cooper asks Truman, "So, Harry, how long you been seeing her?" The Sheriff is surprised and asks, "How did you know?" Cooper answers matter-of-factly, "Body language," to which Harry pauses and says "Jeez, Louise." One could almost hear Cooper saying, "Elementary, my dear Truman."

The Sheriff perfectly fits the role of Watson to Cooper's Holmes. He admits as much in one interchange when he tells Cooper, "You know, I better start studying medicine." Cooper asks, "And why is that?" Truman responds, "Because I'm beginning to feel a bit like Dr. Watson." Sheriff Truman assists Cooper as an officer of the law working in tandem with a federal agent not only to solve Laura's murder, but also to clean up the criminal element in Twin Peaks. We never know if Truman's sidearm is a trusty Webley, but it is there to back up Agent Cooper when the two stop a drug trafficking ring. Sheriff Truman displays extreme loyalty to the FBI agent throughout the series, and in *Twin Peaks: The Return* we learn that he never gave up searching for his friend after Agent Cooper mysteriously disappeared from Twin Peaks following the events of season two's finale.

There is also a Mycroft-like character assisting Agent Cooper: his boss, FBI Regional Bureau Chief (and later, Deputy Director) Gordon Cole. Both men have memorable appearances in their canons—assigning cases to our heroes, conveniently updating them with pertinent information, and providing much-needed assistance above what the local constabularies can provide. Both Cole and Mycroft also care about their charges, Mycroft's devotion to Sherlock being familial, while Cole's relationship with Cooper is more of a friendship formed out of professional respect. Most importantly, both Cole and Mycroft are authority figures in their respective governments, entrusted with secrets. At first, the pair appear to have relatively small governmental roles. Mycroft is said to be an auditor for some government departments in "The Greek Interpreter," but in "The Bruce-Partington Plans" we learn he has a much larger role in his position: "sometimes he *is* the British government." Cole's role develops in a similar vein. We first see him as no more than Cooper's boss, but we later learn he is actually the creator of a secret FBI division entrusted with the Blue Rose cases. These cases concern the safety of no mere country, but rather our entire world and dimension.

While Cooper has Truman as his Watson and Cole as his Mycroft, he also has a Moriarty-like foil, an older Special Agent by the name of Windom Earle. Mark Frost has stated that Windom Earle was deliberately created as a Moriarty character to play against Cooper's Holmes. Both Moriarty and Earle are evil geniuses bent on obtaining power no matter the cost. Moriarty wants to control the London underworld, and Earle wants to tap into the power of the otherworldly Black Lodge, a mystical realm in which resides creatures we might call angels and demons. Fortunately, both plots are thwarted by the great detectives—Moriarty losing his life by going over the Reichenbach Falls, and Earle by losing his soul to the demonic entity Bob. Sadly, in the process of thwarting their enemies, both Cooper and Holmes seemed to sacrifice themselves.

Seemed is the key word. One of the great joys of both *Twin Peaks* and Doyle's canon is that both of these series returned, after an absence or Great Hiatus, to the delight of their fans. Doyle famously killed off his beloved creation, having grown weary of the Great Detective. *Twin Peaks* was abruptly canceled on a cliffhanger ending with Cooper trapped in the extradimensional Black Lodge, replaced by an evil doppelganger. During their hiatuses both detectives reappeared, but sadly for fans it was in stories which occurred before their heroes' respective demises. Holmes appeared in *The Hound of the Baskervilles* and Cooper in the theatrical film prequel *Twin Peaks Fire Walk With Me*. Fortunately, Doyle saw fit to revive his Great Detective and had him return from his Great Hiatus after four years abroad. Cooper's fans had to wait much longer, a full 25 years, for their hero to emerge triumphant and restored to life.

One aspect of both men's personalities that is often overlooked is that they share a deep reverence for nature. Agent Cooper's very first impression of Twin Peaks is his sense of wonder for the woods surrounding the town: "Never seen so many trees in my life. As W.C. Fields would say, 'I'd rather be here than Philadelphia....' Got to find out what kind of trees these are; they're really something." Later, when he meets with Sheriff Truman for the first time, Cooper explains that as an FBI agent, he is taking charge of the investigation. Then, a boyish excitement comes over Cooper and, steepling his fingers, he can't help asking "Sheriff, what kind of fantastic trees have you got growing around here?" The Sheriff tell him that they're Douglas firs, leaving Coop wide-eyed and thoughtful. Then it's right back to business, with Cooper asking Truman for a copy of the coroner's report.

Compare this incident to the scene in "The Naval Treaty" where Holmes abruptly breaks away from his investigation to state not only how much he admires flowers, but even goes so far as to say he finds evidence of the Divine in them: "He walked past the couch to the open window and held up the drooping stalk of a moss-rose, looking down at the dainty blend of crimson and green. It was a new phase of his character to me, for I had never before seen him show any keen interest in natural objects," and so on.

Not all connections between the two detectives are quite as clear as the ones noted above. An argument could be made that there is a very un-Holmesian side of Cooper, and that is the side which follows the guidance of his dreams and its inhabitants, surrealistic creatures which contact Cooper with cryptic subconscious messages. However, upon a closer examination, one sees that Cooper is actually following the unconventional methods of Sherlock Holmes. After all, when the creatures speak to Cooper in visions, he analyzes these messages in a very logical way. Take for example, his analysis of the dream where the spirit of Laura Palmer (if it is Laura Palmer) whispers the name of her killer to him. Cooper cannot remember precisely what Laura tells him, but he does remember some actions of a little man whom he encounters in his dream. The "man from another place" dances, and at one point tells Cooper that the chewing gum he likes is coming back in style. An average person would probably have discounted these aspects of the dream as random ephemera, but Cooper keeps these details tucked away in his brain attic to revisit again and again. These obscure clues eventually have a great significance to the case, and help Cooper uncover the true identity of Laura Palmer's killer.

A final connection between the two men which makes them all the more endearing is that despite their almost superhuman abilities, their astute powers of observation and brain attic storage space, both men are still fallible. They both make mistakes, sometimes fatal ones. Holmes's most famous error is underestimating Irene Adler in "A Scandal in Bohemia"; however, possibly his worst was underestimating Moriarty in *The Valley of Fear*. This leads to the murder of fellow detective Birdy Edwards as he attempts to flee to America. Early in his career, Cooper makes the mistake of being manipulated by Windom Earle, who deliberately orchestrates Cooper into falling in love with Earle's wife Caroline. Cooper is unable to prevent Earle from subsequently killing Caroline, wounding Cooper in the process, and nearly driving him mad with grief. Cooper's greatest failure, however, would be allowing himself to be trapped in the Black Lodge while his doppelganger took his place for a quarter century, building a criminal empire of death and destruction. Fallible heroes indeed!

Sherlock Holmes and Special Agent Dale Cooper share many traits. They are both agents of the law fighting the corrupt and villainous. Both have loyal, sometimes unusual allies in their crusade against evil. Both also are continuations in the long line of great detectives, a line that will continue into the future as more detectives like Holmes and agents like Cooper take up the sword of justice.

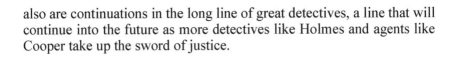

Brian Belanger (Manchester, New Hampshire) is a publisher, editor, and illustrator noted for co-founding Belanger Books LLC (belanger-books.com) with his brother, author Derrick Belanger. He illustrates the popular *MacDougall Twins Mysteries with Sherlock Holmes* young reader series, in addition to designing covers for MX Publishing, the largest publisher of Sherlock Holmes material in the world.

Derrick Belanger (Broomfield, Colorado) is an author, educator, and publisher known for his books and lectures on Sherlock Holmes and Arthur Conan Doyle; his books include *Sherlock Holmes: The Adventure of the Peculiar Provenance* and a two-volume anthology *A Study in Terror: Sir Arthur Conan Doyle's Revolutionary Stories of Fear and the Supernatural*. He is a middle school language arts teacher.

THE OTHER ARTFUL DETECTIVE

William Murdoch

Wilda R. Thumm

In Canada we have our own version of a clever detective who uses unorthodox, for the times, methods: none other than Detective William Murdoch, as portrayed in the CBC TV series *Murdoch Mysteries*, also shown on an American cable network as *The Artful Detective*.

The opening episode of the series, broadcast in 2008, is set in the year 1895, in the city of Toronto, and subsequent episodes carry on through the early years of the twentieth century. The adventures are set in the same general time period as Sherlock Holmes's cases, and in a large urban setting: Toronto was then Canada's second-largest city (it is now the largest) and bears some resemblance to Holmes's London, the largest city in the United Kingdom.

And just as the Sherlock Holmes character comes to us from the mind of a writer, so the character of William Murdoch, portrayed for television by Yannick Bisson, is based on a series of novels written by Maureen Jennings, the first being *Except the Dying* (1997).

Like London's great detective, Murdoch believes that each crime is an intricate puzzle that can always be solved (well, almost always). Murdoch's approach to solving crime is very familiar to readers of the Canon. Both detectives are prone to periods of introspection and deep thought, and do not often share their thoughts as they unwind clues, preferring to wait until the picture is complete. Both are able and willing to mix it up physically when required, while preferring to employ more cerebral methods. Indeed, both detectives possess a brilliant intellect, as well as a passion for justice, and both work in a methodical fashion. Both can be described as pioneers of innovative investigative technology, and tireless advocates for justice.

As we are all well acquainted with the cases of Sherlock Holmes, so we are well acquainted with some of the methods used not only by Holmes, but also as it turns out, by William Murdoch. Both use leading edge technology and science, to the amazement of police officers (in the case of Murdoch, other police officers), criminals, witnesses, complainants, and anyone else involved in the case. As does Holmes,

Murdoch uses fingerprints (referred to in these stories as finger marks), blood testing, surveillance, and trace evidence collected at the scene of the crime. Both detectives are also adept at solving codes and ciphers. Both are committed to furthering the science of solving crimes; science and technology are heavily relied on to make links between clues, find more clues, and eventually solve the mystery.

Holmes normally has his faithful sidekick, Dr. John Watson, along on a case. We don't find an exact parallel in the *Murdoch Mysteries*, but there is a similar theme. Constable George Crabtree is a loyal and enthusiastic member of the team, who does not always grasp the intricacies of Murdoch's methods, much as the beloved Dr. Watson is often mystified by Holmes's methods and deductions. In an interesting twist, Murdoch's superior, Inspector Brackenreid, seems to function most often in the role of an assistant. Even though Brackenreid is the higher ranking officer, he is as mystified by Murdoch's methods as is Crabtree, and quite content to good-naturedly let Murdock take the lead on a case, to be amazed at the methods and results, and to bask in the glory of solved cases, without trying to take the credit.

Even though Holmes can normally solve cases quickly enough to be described from beginning to end in a short story, he does occasionally become entangled in a case that requires a much longer time to present; thus we have four novel-length cases as part of the Canon. Similarly, Murdoch normally solves his case in the length of a single episode, but occasionally, as in the case of "The Book of Jackson", which takes seven episodes to resolve, things don't move along that quickly, and the detective must slog on for a longer period of time.

Interestingly, the Canadian detective interacts with both Sir Arthur Conan Doyle and Sherlock Holmes (well, sort of with Holmes). We are not the only ones who recognize the linkages between Holmes and Murdoch; the writers of the TV series do also. In episode 4 of season 1, very early in the series, Murdoch actually teams up with ACD to solve a case. It turns out that ACD is Murdoch's hero and he welcomes the opportunity to work with him on a real case. In a nice touch, the name of this episode is "Elementary, My Dear Murdoch".

The encounters between Murdoch and Holmes are more complicated. In episode 4 of season 6, titled "A Study in Sherlock", we are first introduced to a young man who has suffered a trauma and has taken on the persona of Sherlock Holmes. He does actually believe that he is Holmes: he dresses like Holmes and has obviously done an extensive study of the character of the great detective, which he displays in both mannerisms and methods. As it turns out, "Holmes" and Murdoch work well together, as they approach cases in a similar methodical, evidence-based fashion. It is clear that Murdoch understands the situation, and he interacts with the delusional young man as if he is indeed Sherlock Holmes. He treats him as a colleague and accepts his help, while clearly, as viewers can see, not actually believing. They solve the case together, and part as successful colleagues. We next meet "Holmes" in episode 4 of season 7, titled "The Return of Sherlock". Here we have a new situation, and a similar interaction between and collaboration between the two detectives, one a professional, the other an amateur.

Sherlock Holmes often has a tongue-in-cheek approach; with a twinkle in his eye he throws out a double entendre with the best of them, or manipulates an un-cooperative person, as he does with Lord Mount-James in "The Adventure of the Missing Three-Quarter". He delights in challenging Watson, in a friendly way, to follow or anticipate his deductions. In a similar fashion, Murdoch takes a sardonic view of the obviously lesser skills and techniques of his fellow officers, never being unkind or condescending, but obviously well aware that his colleagues do not follow his methods or understand the science behind them.

Holmes and Murdoch are both foci for dedicated, passionate fans. ACD tried unsuccessfully to kill Holmes off in "The Final Problem" but was compelled by public opinion to rescue him from this untimely death. Fortunately for future generations of readers, he pulled this off nicely. Analogously, although the Murdoch series was well received from the beginning, it was slated to end after five seasons. In September 2011, the production company Rogers Media announced that it would not be continuing the series. However, it continued to be renewed, one season at a time, and has completed eleven seasons, the latest being released in October of 2017. Current fans will have their Murdoch, as earlier fans would have their Holmes.

To be sure, Murdoch is not simply a created-in-our-modern-day Holmes There are differences. Murdoch is a devoted Roman Catholic, reflected in the fact that he regularly genuflects over the body of a murder victim; his faith is an important aspect of his daily life. Holmes's views on faith are a little less clear. There is indirect support for Holmes as an atheist in *A Study in Scarlet* and "The Retired Colourman". However, there is also support for his belief in a deity based on the Bible. In "The Naval Treaty", Holmes waxes eloquent on the goodness of Providence as evidenced by flowers, and in "The Boscombe Valley Mystery" he makes reference to an afterlife, complete with a higher power sitting in judgement. We can deduce from the faith-based references in the Canon that Holmes does have some faith, which makes this another point of commonality for the two detectives, even though it marks Murdoch as a person in his own right, not just a copy of Holmes.

There are other points of difference between these two detectives. They include the fact that Murdoch is clearly in love with Dr. Julia Ogden, while Holmes has no romantic interests throughout the Canon. Murdoch is something of a dandy, always impeccably turned out, while Holmes appears well groomed, but not overly concerned with his appearance. We are well acquainted with Holmes's dalliances with cocaine when he has nothing to otherwise occupy his intellect. Murdoch displays no such disposition.

I suggest that the small differences in the characters and habits of Holmes and Murdoch, as noted above, do not outweigh the many and much stronger similarities. The defining characteristics of both detectives are their probing, scientific approach to their work and their passion for justice. Here we have two detectives, one a consulting detective, one a member of the Toronto Constabulary, whose world views are so closely aligned that I am indeed confident in asserting that Sherlock Holmes is like William Murdoch.

Wilda R. Thumm (Guelph, Ontario) joined the Cesspudlians of London in November 2015 and the Bootmakers of Toronto in January 2016. She is a retired accountant, currently working towards a degree in sociology and history at the University of Guelph; she is also a Trekkie, and loves to travel.

SOMETHING RECHERCHÉ

So strange and unexpected that we stood for
a moment staring at it in amazement.

The Hound of the Baskervilles

PROFESSIONAL THINKER

Alan Kay

Bonnie MacBird

Alan Kay is often called "The Father of the Personal Computer," and his group at Xerox PARC (Palo Alto Research Center) developed the graphical user interface, which is the face of computing today. He coined the terms "personal computer" and "object-oriented programming," and his early design of something he called the "Dynabook" envisioned the laptop/tablet of today twenty-five years in advance. He's won many awards, including three that are considered to be the "Nobel" in their respective fields of engineering, technology, and computing: the Draper Prize, the Kyoto Prize, and the Turing Award. The latter, named for Alan Turing, was for Kay's "ideas at the root of contemporary object-oriented programming languages" and "for fundamental contributions to personal computing."

Alan Kay is also my husband of thirty some years. His similarity to my favorite fictional character is a source of delight, frustration, and fascination, and I'd love to share it with you. (When I told him I was writing this, he said, "Hey, I'm nothing like Holmes! I'm not depressive! I don't take drugs!") True. But please humor me, because Sherlock Holmes is like computer scientist Alan Kay in some significant respects.

Professional thinkers. First of all, most people would say that "thinking" is what everyone does. A car is a car, right? But there are Model Ts and there are Ferraris. There's Watson, you, and me… and there is Holmes. And Kay. Like anyone who practices a highly developed art form—music or writing, for example—people who are paid to think may start with talent, but have honed their ability over years through multiple processes: skill building, stocking the "brain attic," and development of an aesthetic which informs the thinking. Not to mention a serious work ethic.

Here are a few things that set such "professional thinkers" apart:

Slow vs. fast thinking: In contrast to normal people, both men seem quick. They astound in casual conversation. Move the subject into their fields and you cannot surprise them. But—and this is key—when approaching their work, neither man settles for the *first good idea*. Instead they take their time. In order to solve a problem that others cannot, both men know that finding *the right question to ask* is essential. Defining the actual problem. Neither man cleaves to the first solution that appears. In computer science, this is one meaning of the term "late binding."

Says Sherlock Holmes in "Silver Blaze": "It is one of those cases where the art of the reasoner should be used rather for the sifting of details than for the acquiring of fresh evidence. The tragedy has been so uncommon... that we are suffering from a plethora of surmise, conjecture, and hypothesis. The difficulty is to detach the framework of fact— of absolute undeniable fact—from the embellishments of theorists and reporters. Then... it is our duty to see what inferences may be drawn and what are the special points upon which the whole mystery turns."

Alan Kay similarly differentiates between *news* (the facts that reporters spout, sometimes accurately) and *"the new"* (actual "new ideas, events or information"). It's a sorting process. Most people ready, fire, aim. Holmes and Kay take their time aiming first.

Historically informed. Just as Holmes criticizes the police detective who hasn't studied crimes and criminals ("There's nothing new under the sun"), Kay wonders why new systems designers waste time and resources coming up with worse designs than those that have existed before. ("Why reinvent the flat tire?") Colleagues who don't do their homework or know what came before are a pet peeve of both men.

Those brain attics. Sherlock Holmes's and Alan Kay's well-stocked "brain attics" appear idiosyncratic. Chinese tattoo designs (Holmes) and optical illusions (Kay) might not seem to relate to detection and computer science respectively, but of course they do, along with many other arcane facts and subjects. Both men have stocked those shelves with purpose but also with surprising eclecticism. Kay thinks of this material (mostly acquired through reading) not so much in terms of answers, but as "grist for the mill" in problem solving.

It's my view that Watson in "The Five Orange Pips" woefully misrepresents Holmes's areas of expertise. His famous list begins with philosophy, astronomy, and politics, all marked at zero. But no! Holmes is far too literate to merit this assessment. His Goethe quote (in the original German, no less) in *The Sign of the Four* puts this argument to rest in a single stroke. Kay is equally well-read. While other philosophers are more to his taste, here's a Goethe quote he likes: "We should all share in the excitement of discovery without vain attempts to claim priority."

Which leads to the next point of similarity...

Modesty. Both Holmes and Kay take pride in their well-honed process, but despite acclaim are essentially modest men. Holmes turns down a knighthood and generously shares credit for solving his cases. Kay never gives a talk without extensive attributions regarding the work of those who came before, and including his team members as well. He is universally respected for this. Neither man seeks publicity.

Logic, but also art. On the surface, Holmesian deductions or inductions and computer science seem to be entirely based on logic. Casual readers and even some deeper fans emphasize the "thinking machine" aspect of Holmes's methods. But the intuitive leaps, pattern recognition, and emotional intelligence are artistic in nature.

Didn't Holmes aim to write *The* Art *of Detection*? Perhaps this aspect of the Great Detective is best characterized in his famous "art in the blood" aphorism in "The Greek Interpreter." He and his brother Mycroft share what he claims are inheritable gifts (and modern neuroscience bears this out) which elevate them above mere logicians. As Watson describes it, it's a temperament thing, and mostly a blessing. Alan Kay credits similar gifts, but also serious art training (music, theatre, and visual arts) for his own abilities. He's often described as a polymath, and believes that most science owes as much to art as to logic.

Pragmatic work in the service of the greater good. Sherlock Holmes skulks around back alleys and the underworld, solving sordid and often bloody crimes with the immediate aim of an arrest, but also with the lofty purpose of creating a safer, more just world. Alan Kay's work alters the way ones and zeroes are put into service in new systems, designing new ways for humans to interact with machines, but with the larger goal of amplifying human gifts.

Both know *why* they are doing what they do. Both are men of deep purpose, aiming for a better world.

Musicians. Both men are gifted "amateur" musicians whose music sustains them. Holmes plays the violin to think, to relax, and (simulated once) to catch a criminal. Kay played jazz guitar throughout high school and college, later discovered the organ, and like Holmes, plays his instrument frequently for respite, refreshment, and mental "reset." Both men are discerning and enthusiastic concert goers but play their own instruments privately, with only their closest companions allowed to listen.

The Asperger question. Both Holmes and Kay might be described as "on the spectrum" of autism, sometimes referred to as Asperger's syndrome—a name that may be falling into disfavor with revelations that the researcher it is named for had close Nazi connections during World War II. Some Holmes fans dispute his identification with this syndrome, as our fellow can certainly turn on the charm when he so chooses. Likewise, Alan Kay gives public lectures filled with humor, and is very warm and funny in person.

But both Holmes and Kay can miss social cues, leaving the impression that their understanding of human emotion arrives more from study than feeling. Or perhaps they are simply occupied "elsewhere." Both occasionally receive a *sotto voce* suggestion from their closest companions.

While non-Aspergians shift easily from discussing their work or key interests to friendly chit-chat, neither of these men does so with any relish at all. For both, small talk is anathema.

They each have intense, very specific side interests (for Holmes these include Sri Lankan Buddhism, boxing, bees, those motets; for Kay, the Red Sox, baroque music, women's basketball, cooking).

Also a bit on the spectrum is the shared ability to hyper-focus and work to exhaustion, and a remarkable, almost obsessive engagement and expertise in their chief topic.

However, both Holmes and Kay have many more interests than most Aspergians display. They share a great sense of humor, and both easily navigate any social situation that is actually required. Therefore, I think that if this condition is present, Kay and Holmes could be said to be on the very, very mild end of the spectrum.

Blind to class, race, and age, but not ignorance. Holmes is an equal opportunity consultant, never spurning a client or colleague for class, race, or age. These things are similarly invisible to Kay. But neither man suffers fools gladly, and willful ignorance is intolerable to both.

The love of cozy. Sherlock Holmes lounges about 221B Baker Street in his dressing-gown, frequents the baths, and clearly enjoys his creature comforts. Alan Kay, too, is fond of soft leisure wear, in his case sweat-pants and a sweatshirt and fleece-lined slippers from L.L. Bean. Both alternate extreme expenditures of energy (Holmes on a case, Kay on a multi-city lecture and consulting trip, both on a deadline) with sloth-like downtime, usually prone, garbed for comfort.

Neither Holmes nor Kay cares who sees them in these clothes. Both refer to themselves as "lazy," though people who know them would disagree.

Theatre. If the theatre lost a great actor when Holmes turned to solving crimes, then it lost another contributor when Alan Kay stopped doing set design and incidental music for theatre, which he adores.

Parcheesi is never afoot. Neither Sherlock Holmes nor Alan Kay is interested in spending time on cards, parlor games, or the like. For both, their work is what is most fun. They are both happiest when the game is afoot, but their preferred games never include dice.

Affinity for children. Holmes displays a gentleness and consideration for children. Kay's entire career has been devoted to creating a system that children can use to learn critical thinking skills. Neither has children of their own, but both understand kids, notice individual differences, and show great empathy in their presence.

The need to reduce 'noise.' Sometimes Holmes needs to sequester himself for a serious bout of thinking. So, too, Alan Kay will "hole up" to ponder and dissect a problem, brooking no interruption. Their respective companions understand this and don't, generally, take offense.

Private. Both men have a very small circle of people to whom they are close. Holmes has zero desire to "overshare" and few really know the full man. Can you imagine Sherlock Holmes on Facebook? No way, and you won't catch Alan Kay posting there, either.

Optimists. Despite their unromantic view of human nature, and Holmes's occasional depressions, a key similarity is that both men are essentially optimists. As Kay once put it, scientists generally think positively. Otherwise, they wouldn't take on the really hard problems.

In "The Naval Treaty," Holmes and Watson arrive in London by train, passing what Watson sees as a depressing row of buildings. Holmes sees something else. They are schools to educate the poor, and he says: "Light-houses, my boy! Beacons of the future! Capsules with hundreds of bright little seeds in each, out of which will spring the wise, better England of the future."

And perhaps the best-known Alan Kay quote is this similarly buoyant epithet: "The best way to predict the future is to invent it."

Finally, if all this hasn't convinced you that Sherlock Holmes is like Alan Kay, there's this: they both love dining at Simpson's on the Strand. QED.

Bonnie MacBird (Los Angeles and London) writes Sherlock Holmes novels for HarperCollins. *Art in the Blood* and *Unquiet Spirits* are the first two in her series, with *The Devil's Due* now in preparation. She is a member of the Baker Street Irregulars, ASH, and many other Sherlockian societies.

WITH A LITTLE HELP FROM MY FRIENDS

The Beatles

Ashley D. Polasek

"Come, Watson, come!" he cried. "The game is afoot."
"Where are we going, Holmes?"
"To the toppermost of the poppermost, my dear Watson."

Devotees of Sherlock Holmes have spent over a century scrutinizing his every minute characteristic, but we really have only Holmes's recollections of a few pre-Watson cases to suggest what his early career was like. Given his relatively mature abilities in *A Study in Scarlet*, we might be forgiven for assuming that he emerged with skills and reputation intact, ready to chart his own course. But in "The Musgrave Ritual" Holmes himself tells Watson, who may be guilty of the same error, that Watson "can hardly realize… how difficult [he] found it at first, and how long [he] had to wait before he succeeded in making some headway" in his profession.

Looking back over the span of fifty-odd years, millions make the comparable and equally mistaken assumption that when an up-and-coming pop group from Liverpool released its first album in 1963, the band's earth-shattering success had been a foregone conclusion. But as Holmes did not emerge like Athena from Zeus, fully formed and assured of his eventual mythic standing, no more were the Beatles assured of theirs.

By first establishing the similarities in the raw assets and distinctive approaches shared by the world's greatest band [Fight me!] and the world's greatest detective, I hope to demonstrate that the former is an apt analog for the latter. By then exploring a particular—and by no means inevitable—confluence of circumstances and resources necessary to catapult the Beatles to success, I believe we may gain a more complete understanding of what the early career of Sherlock Holmes must have looked like as he charted a similar path.

We are led to our misguided faith in the inevitable success of both the Beatles and Sherlock Holmes by the sense of innate genius present in both. The Beatles displayed brilliance in both music and poesy. All four Beatles picked up music early, from John Lennon's start on the harmonica at seven and Paul McCartney's start on the piano around the same age, to George Harrison's fevered dedication to teaching himself guitar from the age of fourteen. Ringo Starr beat a drum for the first time at thirteen and "never wanted anything else from there on." Their passion to learn and develop their musical talents overrode every practical consideration. "I would often sag off school for the afternoon," admits Paul, "and John would get off art college, and we would sit down with our two guitars and plonk away." (*The Beatles Anthology*, 2000)

Playing and singing aside, the genius of the Beatles is in their songwriting. The partnership of Lennon/McCartney published nearly 200 songs, and unlike most composing teams, which include a composer and a lyricist, John and Paul both wrote music and lyrics; often, especially in their early years together, they produced true collaborations while sitting "eyeball to eyeball," as John put it. George, too, was a composer and lyricist, contributing over twenty songs to the Beatles catalogue, some, such as "Something" and "While My Guitar Gently Weeps," among the best the band recorded.

It is easy to draw a connection between this incredible concentration of musical and songwriting talent and Holmes's faculty of observation and his ordered, logical mind. From "The Greek Interpreter," we infer that he and Mycroft made their shared talent for observing trifles into a regular game, which we can only assume they played as youths. We know also that Holmes displayed a considerable talent for reasoning when he was still in school, having developed a reputation among his peers for his "habits of observation and inference."

At least as important as innate ability are the uncanny similarities in the Beatles' approach to their vocation and Holmes's approach to his. Perhaps the most important distinctive attribute in the Beatles' approach is their consummate synthesis of musical styles. While their contemporaries imitated the hits of Elvis Presley and Chuck Berry, The Beatles absorbed not only those hits, but also more obscure artists and diverse styles; they infused their rock 'n' roll with Country-Western, R&B, and the distinctive sounds of black American girl groups, like the Shirelles, whose "Boys" the Beatles covered on *Please Please Me*, gender notwithstanding. As they developed, they fearlessly blended other styles—blues, folk, Indian, show tunes, classical, hard rock, and easy listening, among others—into their music, ultimately producing a totally new foundation for rock 'n' roll that would influence everything that came after them.

Another key to their approach was their refusal to conform to the expectations of the industry. In the early 1960s, as Beatles historian Mark Lewisohn notes, "there *were* no bands like the Beatles. Three guitars and drums, all three front-line guitarists singing lead and harmonies, a group who wrote their own songs—it was simple, direct, and not done." (Mark Lewisohn, *Tune In: The Beatles: All These Years*, vol. 1, Crown

Archetype, 2013) Rock 'n' roll groups also weren't called anything like "The Beatles." Early in their pursuit of a recording contract, they were advised to name a leader and rebrand themselves in the standard mode: "Someone and the somethings", à la Bill Haley and His Comets. They were also advised to select a name without such unpleasant connotations. On both counts, they refused.

In their determination to become successful on their own terms, the Beatles also refused to temper their personalities or create tailored public images. They spoke in regional Liverpudlian accents and shared a wry, bawdy sense of humor. They enjoyed being outrageous. "We've always disliked the phony 'star image'," George said in a 1964 interview. "We'd much rather be ourselves. We always came out as ourselves, and we thought, 'If they don't like us how we are, then hard luck.' And they did. People like natural better, I think." Acting naturally would become a hallmark of their success.

Holmes's unprecedented approach to detection is strikingly similar. In *A Study in Scarlet*, Holmes's knowledge is eccentric enough that even in actively cataloguing his interests and activities, Watson cannot identify Holmes's profession. Like the Beatles, Holmes builds a singular expertise out of diverse influences. He knows the hits, as it were, of police work, but he also has an encyclopedic knowledge of the history of crime, has studied geology, chemistry, and anatomy, practices martial arts, and is adept in stagecraft, which sets him not only apart from, but above his fellows. And like the Beatles, this amalgamation—not merely detection but the whole art of detection—influences everything that came after.

Just as the Beatles refused to conform to the standard model of an early 1960s pop group, Sherlock Holmes is unconcerned with conforming to the standards set for a Victorian gentleman, as he "loathed every form of society with his whole Bohemian soul." Just as the Beatles refused to be rebranded to suit the industry, so Sherlock Holmes invented his own professional title—the world's only consulting detective—to encompass the job he created for himself, rather than applying his talents to the existing policing infrastructure.

With so many attributes in common, the Beatles' early years, particularly from mid-1960 to the release of their first album, *Please Please Me* in March 1963, might tell us much about the likely nature of Holmes's early career. John, Paul, George, then-drummer Pete Best, and, eventually, Ringo, honed their stagecraft through five seasons in various seedy, often dangerous clubs along the notorious Reeperbahn in Hamburg, Germany. They logged 918 exhausting hours on stage in their first two seasons alone, playing eight-hour sets long into the night, and living in squalor. This hard slog was crucial in sharpening their skills. "We went in young boys," said John of the experience, "and came out old men."

In late 1961, the Beatles had finished their first two seasons in Hamburg. They were enjoying local and regional success and were brought to the attention of Brian Epstein, then 27 and managing his family's Liverpool music store. Brian was immediately and entirely enthralled: "I never thought that they would be anything less than the greatest stars in the world," he said often, and he set about leveraging his business contacts and his finances to get them there. As their manager, he was tireless in his pursuit of their success. He sought bookings, publishing rights, and the holy grail of a recording contract. Most importantly, embedded in his devotion was a determination to see the Beatles to stardom on their own terms. Brain was the champion the Beatles needed.

He managed to sign the Beatles with George Martin on EMI's Parlophone label in June 1962. Martin was a seasoned professional; he produced his first hit for the label in 1952, had enjoyed sustained success with classical and novelty records, and had been head of artists and repertoire since 1955. Initially unimpressed with the Beatles' unpolished sound, Martin was obliged by various circumstances to give them a contract to record six sides—three singles—in their first year. Martin released their first single, "Love Me Do/P.S. I Love You" unenthusiastically, and was surprised at its sustained success in the charts—it peaked at 17 in the UK. Crucially, not only was he willing to admit his mistake, he risked his resources and his reputation on a bold, unconventional decision: he would produce a Beatles LP. "No one else operated as he did," Mark Lewisohn declares; "he was a maverick experimenter, following instincts where others played safe... and now he'd invest his expertise in the Beatles, to find out what they could make together" (Lewisohn again). In their early collaboration, as the Beatles began to produce more complex music, they leaned heavily on Martin's expertise. In their later years, as they became more confident and accomplished in the studio, they felt they had outgrown him in many ways, but he was nonetheless an essential guide for the band.

Sherlock Holmes seems a solitary genius, and it is easy to cite Watson as the sole individual who somehow connects him to the outside world. Certainly, Watson is essential to Holmes's legend, but if there is anything the Beatles' early years demonstrate, it's that genius is not enough. If *A Study in Scarlet* is Holmes's *Please Please Me*—the first great success that propels his career—then he plainly needed help to get there: Holmes must have had considerable support before Watson came along.

We can only speculate as to where that support came from. Holmes acknowledges in "The Musgrave Ritual" that "now and again cases came [his] way" in his early years, but judging by just how tenaciously the Beatles developed their craft over hundreds upon hundreds of stage hours before ever stepping into a recording studio, it seems evident that there were considerably more early cases than we realize—cases that served as Holmes's Hamburg. Perhaps Holmes inspired the love of an unknown benefactor who, like Brian Epstein, had the means and acumen to support him and worked tirelessly to bring the young genius the fame he knew he deserved. Perhaps an older, experienced tutor at university saw his unique potential and, like George Martin, invested his time and staked his institutional reputation on publicly launching his career. Or maybe Mycroft took on that role, charting the same mentorship trajectory as Martin. One of the first statements Watson ever hears from Mycroft is that he "expected to see [Sherlock]... to consult" him on a case on which he thought the younger Holmes "a little out of [his] depth," but because of the sedentary limitations of his "own métier," like Martin, his young protégé outgrew his abilities and influence.

We can be certain, though, that like the lads from Liverpool, Holmes's success was not as assured as hindsight suggests. Without practicing their craft in clubs in Hamburg, without the financial backing and indefatigable devotion of Brian Epstein, and without the professional and creative guidance of George Martin, the Beatles' very first album, let alone their world-conquering triumph, would have been impossible. Having eliminated the impossible, we must therefore conclude that improbable as it may seem, without similar practice and aid, Sherlock Holmes could never have gained even enough success to share rooms in Baker Street and thus meet the friend who would write him into immortality. We must all be grateful that such practice and aid did precede the good doctor, for a world without *The Hound of the Baskervilles* would be as bleak as a world without "Hey Jude." I couldn't bear to live in either.

Ashley D. Polasek (Anderson, South Carolina) holds a PhD in the study of Sherlock Holmes on screen and is a member of the Baker Street Babes, the Adventuresses of Sherlock Holmes, the Sherlock Holmes Society of London, the Diogenes Club of Washington, D.C., the Curious Collectors of Baker Street, and the Sons of the Copper Beeches.

LIKE A FOLK TALE CHARACTER

The Third Little Pig

Gayle Lange Puhl

Through a series of circumstances that surprise even me, I appear to have become an "expert" on Sherlock Holmes and folk tales. A Sherlockian since the mid-1960s, I decided in the late 2000s to begin writing short stories featuring Mr. Sherlock Holmes and his Boswell, Dr. Watson. Needing a template on which to build my original ideas, I chose fairy tales, nursery rhymes, adages, and folk tales.

I resolved on three major requirements: the stories would continue the original Holmes and Watson adventures in the correct Victorian and early Edwardian time period and with the best rendering of Dr. Watson's writing style that I could deliver; there would be no magic (fairy dust, talking animals, mythical monsters), only logic; and there must be a crime for Holmes to investigate.

Those rules made writing the tales interesting. How would you write the story of Cinderella with no fairy godmother? Little Red Riding Hood with no talking wolf? Jack and the Beanstalk with no magic beans? It was fun, and over the course of jotting down my short stories I have managed to produce 27 tales and counting.

Nursery rhymes and folk tale characters are universal. Such tales, based on stories handed down from the distant past by oral traditions, are known from Russia to Africa, from South America to Iceland, from Asia to Australia. They are kin to more modern children's stories, such as *Alice's Adventures in Wonderland* and *The Wind in the Willows*. Frequently they are a child's first literature, the first beloved night-time stories offered by parents, and the first moral lessons offered to young impressionable minds.

The themes of most folk tales cover three points. Good and bad morality is first. The good is rewarded and the bad is punished. Little Red Riding Hood disobeys her mother by talking to a stranger. She is then nearly eaten by the wolf, who has gobbled up her grandmother. Her disobedience is redeemed only by the huntsman, who suddenly appears, kills the wolf and frees Red and her grandmother from his stomach. The wolf is punished by being killed by the huntsman's axe.

Second, each story, in the form in which we now know it, encourages the upholding of middle-class values. Cinderella is reduced to scrubbing floors and running errands for her horrible step-sisters by her evil step-mother. But she never loses her sweetness and her belief in herself. Her fairy godmother gives her a dress, glass slippers and transportation to the ball. When she arrives, it is her own noble nature that allows her to behave as a princess amid all the lights and dazzle, to carry herself with dignity and to impress the prince with her natural abilities. Contrast that to her two social-climbing stepsisters, who vie vulgarly for the prince's attention and manage to make fools of themselves. When Cinderella is forced to leave the ball at midnight she makes no complaint about the loss of all her gifts and the coach and horses.

Back home with her scrub brush, she avoids bringing wrath down on her head by not mentioning her part at the ball. That shows her intelligence. She knows that if her stepmother found out she was the mysterious woman who caught the prince's attention she would throw Cinderella down into a dungeon or do something worse. When the prince shows up to test the women of the house to see if their feet fit the glass slipper left behind at the ball she sees her chance. When she is finally quizzed by the prince she pulls out the one bit of incontrovertible proof, the missing mate of the original shoe. The ugly stepsisters are married off to the butcher and the baker at the castle and, in the original story, the evil stepmother is forced to dance at Cinderella's wedding in a pair of red-hot iron shoes until she collapses and dies. The moral is that every-one has a prince out there and that fulfillment is found in marriage. That was considered a happy ending at the time.

And thirdly, folk tales are fashioned to teach lessons or demonstrate values important to the culture. With Little Red Riding Hood, the mes-sage is not to talk to strangers. Cinderella teaches that a sweet, kind girl will meet her Prince Charming and her oppression will end with happi-ness.

The characters in folk tales follow certain patterns, but pipe-smoking detectives are rare. In the world of folk tales, one can't cross a running stream without stumbling over a talking fish, the third son of a poor miller out to make his fortune, or a shepherdess searching for her lost sheep. The nearby dark woods are populated with dozens of helpful yet vindictive old crones, bands of evil robbers, and dogs with eyes the size of saucers. Overhead, enchanted swans fly toward distant magic castles. One is lucky not to be trampled by the hooves of mighty steeds ridden by questing princes just walking from one poor tailor shop to another.

Then there are the villains. Dragons, ogres, wicked witches with cauldrons, nasty stepmothers, and selfish kings with their own agendas to fulfil are staples of folk tales. Every time one tries to cross a bridge there is a troll to deal with. Every fourth story has a giant or a big, bad wolf.

The victims can be unusual. A prince is enchanted into a frog, a beautiful mermaid trades her fins for a pair of legs, a wooden puppet has the wish to be a real boy. Numerous children of both genders, lacking adult supervision, wander into all kinds of danger. Kindly grandmothers and simple townspeople can find themselves caught up in the adventures. It must be hard to breathe with a black pudding attached to one's nose, the result of a careless wish. Crashing giants falling from the skies can be a real pain to clean up.

While the hero of a folk tale can vary from a meek little tailor to a simple shepherdess to a third son of the king, there are certain qualities evident in each protagonist. Here are a few:

The hero must have courage. Facing dragons in whatever form they take is not for the meek. A hero can have doubts about his abilities, but his confidence must be fortified with strong doses of determination, focus, perseverance, and dedication.

The hero must have loyalty. The story of Jack and the Beanstalk has a hero who was a thief and a rogue, but his ultimate goal was to make a better life for his hard-working widowed mother.

The hero must have honesty. If he made a promise to bring a fresh rose to the princess in the middle of winter, that rose must be obtained. A vow carelessly given or ignored is the surest way to find oneself chained and forgotten in a dungeon or turned to stone on the terrace of an evil sorcerer.

And, not least, a hero must be responsible. Undertaking a quest only to be distracted by the first pretty wench or a keg of beer at the nearest tavern is a blueprint for failure. That lack of character explains why so many first and second sons never return to claim the kingdom, mill, farm, fortune, or beautiful princess [delete as applicable] while the third, underrated son succeeds.

Well, Sherlock Holmes bears all those fine qualities, most of all in the story titled "The Final Problem." He has courage, with which he faces Professor Moriarty alone at the Falls of Reichenbach in "The Final Problem." He has loyalty, seeing the trap ahead but allowing the Professor's trick to separate himself from Watson in order to protect the doctor. He has honesty, telling Watson when they discover Moriarty has eluded the police that the doctor should abandon Holmes at once and return to England. "You will find me a dangerous companion now, Watson. This man's occupation is gone. He is lost if he returns to London. If I read his character right he will devote his whole energies to revenging himself upon me. He said as much in our short interview, and I fancy he meant it. I should certainly recommend you to return to your practice." He has responsibility, admitting to Watson that "if I could beat that man, if I could free society of him, I should feel that my own career had reached its summit, and I should be prepared to turn to some more placid line in life."

Which folk tale character, out of the hundreds available, could ever reach such heroic heights as these, to stand as the Great Detective's companion in equality?

I think it is The Third Little Pig.

The timeless story is well known. Three Little Pigs are sent out by their mother to make their way in the world. The First Little Pig builds a house of straw, the second one a house of sticks, and the third a house of bricks. He warns his brothers that a house made of bricks is the best protection against wolves. They laugh at his warning, but he still protects his brothers.

The Big Bad Wolf comes along, well-known for preying on the countryside. He is hungry and he knows pigs are delicious. He tells the First Little Pig to "Open the door and let me come in or I'll huff and I'll puff and I'll blow your house in!" The First Little Pig refuses, saying "Not by the hair of my chinny-chin-chin!" The Wolf lets loose and destroys the house of straw. In some versions the First Little Pig runs to the Second Little Pig's house for safety. In many versions he doesn't make it past the Wolf.

The Wolf deals with the Second Little Pig and his house made of sticks in the same fashion. The end result is the same, with the First and Second Little Pigs either eaten by the Wolf or rooming with their brother in the brick house.

The Third Little Pig, when confronted by the Big Bad Wolf, also refuses to surrender. The huffing and puffing do not work, however. The brick structure holds firm. The Wolf must take another tack.

Three times the wily Wolf makes appointments to meet with the Third Little Pig outside the brick house in order to ambush his prey. Each time the Third Little Pig outsmarts him and remains safe. If his brothers have escaped the Wolf earlier, they remain safe as well.

Out of frustration the Big Bad Wolf becomes desperate. He climbs to the roof of the Third Little Pig's brick house and attempts to climb down the chimney. The Third Little Pig stokes the fire and places a large pot of water on the flames; when the Wolf comes tumbling down and lands in the hot water a lid is slammed down on top of the pot and the Wolf is boiled to death. The Pigs call in the neighbors and have a feast.

Like Sherlock Holmes, the Third Little Pig has courage. He faces up to the Big Bad Wolf when challenged. He is determined to outwit the Wolf after traps are set out to capture him. He never runs away.

The Third Little Pig shows loyalty to his brothers, sheltering them in some stories, avenging them in other versions.

The Third Little Pig is honest. He believes his brothers when they report the Big Bad Wolf's attacks. He admits the danger the Wolf presents to him. He doesn't try to gloss over his situation or wish it all away.

The Third Little Pig is responsible. He builds his house of bricks. He knows he cannot surrender to the Big Bad Wolf and survive. He realizes that it would not be enough to just evade its clutches. He must kill it and end the terrorizing of the neighborhood for once and all.

There are many heroes in the folk tale world. I chose the Third Little Pig to compare to Sherlock Holmes because he fights the Big Bad Wolf not just to save his own life and the lives of his brothers, but to remove a danger to the countryside. He sees the bigger picture and responds for the greater good. Sherlock Holmes, on the cliff beside the Reichenbach, does the same.

Gayle Lange Puhl (Evansville, Wisconsin) has been a Sherlockian since 1965. She is a member of the Adventuresses of Sherlock Holmes and several other societies, two of which she founded. She hosts the radio show "Holmes World" on WADR 103.5 FM (janesvilleradio.org) and has written more than two dozen short stories that blend Sherlock Holmes with nursery rhymes and fairy tales.

THE DOCTOR IS IN

Lucy Van Pelt

Steve Mason

When the editor invited the authors of this collection to choose a historical or fictional character of which Sherlock Holmes reminds them, I am sure many of them had to ponder over their decision. Not me.

Fifty years ago I read my first story of the Canon, *The Hound of the Baskervilles*. ("50 years ago you say... but Steve, you are only in your forties." Oh, the miracles of hair coloring.) When I was a lad of seven, I discovered my father's copy of *The Hound* while staying at my grandparents' house in Indiana. I stayed up over two nights reading the entire novel. Of course, many of the terms and phrases zipped right over my head. But I was able to quickly understand the book focused on a bad guy, a very mean dog, and a great hero. As I found the other stories in the Canon, this hero reminded me more and more of another fictional character, one I read about on a daily basis. This was none other than Lucy Van Pelt of the *Peanuts* comic strips by Charles M. Schulz.

So, now that you have finished laughing, rolling your eyes, and wondering, "What is he smoking?" (no, that's still illegal in Texas), allow me to present my case with observations and clues I have contemplated through the years, after which you shall be able to determine your own conclusion.

In *A Study in Scarlet*, Sherlock Holmes proclaims himself to be the only consulting detective. People in trouble come to him for advice and to solve their issues. Lucy Van Pelt describes herself as the only sidewalk psychiatrist, first showing her skills in a comic strip that appeared in March 1959.

If you close your eyes, you can easily conjure your own image of the sitting room at 221B, where clients visit Holmes to express their concerns and ask for assistance. You should also be able to easily bring up the image of Lucy's psychiatric booth where her clients seek help. Holmes places his clients in seats so that he may see them in the proper light; Lucy strategically seats her clients on a stool so she has the higher position.

Holmes does not pat the clients on the hand and tell them everything will be fine. Many times he is blunt, critical, and non-empathetic. Likewise, Lucy does not patronize her clients, but will be very harsh in her judgment of them. When Charlie Brown tells her that he has feelings of depression, she simply states, "Snap out of it."

In "Thor Bridge," Holmes declares that "My professional charges are upon a fixed scale. I do not vary them, save when I remit them altogether." Lucy also charges the same price for each client, 5 cents, unless she waives (remits) the fee entirely (which is seldom).

To Sherlock Holmes, Irene Adler is "the woman," the only woman to best him. Even in *Elementary* and the BBC *Sherlock*, Sherlock admits his judgment fails him when it comes to Irene. To Lucy, Schroeder will always be "the boy" who causes her to do crazy things, such as joining the baseball team (she is lousy at baseball) just to be around Schroeder. Many times, her judgment is askew due to her unrequited love for him.

In "The Greek Interpreter," Sherlock acknowledges Mycroft, his older brother, as his superior in observation and deduction. Annoying to the younger Holmes is Mycroft's laziness, his preference for staying at his club or in his own apartment instead of doing actual field work. Sherlock cannot resist the slight jabs of his brother, but quietly expresses a genuine love for him. Lucy once admits that Linus, her younger brother, is one of the smartest people she knows. Linus regularly annoys Lucy, with either his blanket-carrying or his obsession with the Great Pumpkin. Lucy constantly criticizes her brother, but expresses a genuine love for him. On one occasion, when Lucy demands to know what she has to feel grateful for, Linus replies, "Well, for one thing, you have a brother who loves you." Lucy immediately bursts into tears and hugs Linus. She brings a blanket to cover Linus while he sleeps in the pumpkin patch; later, she carries him home and tucks him into bed. In both situations, love between siblings is very subtle but unmistakably present.

In the BBC *Sherlock*, the detective recognizes himself as a "highly functioning sociopath," admitting he has a few personality or social issues. Lucy freely concedes to being crabby, and even a "fussbudget" (a fault-finding person), including not playing well with others.

Several times Watson comments upon Holmes's vanity. In *The Sign of the Four*, Watson notes that "More than once during the years that I had lived with him in Baker Street I had observed that a small vanity underlay my companion's quiet and didactic manner." Lucy once proudly points out, "I never made a mistake in my life. I thought I did once, but I was wrong."

Holmes refuses to clutter his mind with useless facts, such as what rotates around what (*A Study in Scarlet*), because it hinders his ability to solve cases. Lucy ignores the minutiae of life, even once claiming, "Snow comes up from the ground!"

Holmes consistently criticizes Watson's writings, and states that he could do a better job himself in chronicling their cases. In a few cases, Watson challenges Holmes to chronicle his own adventure ("The Blanched Soldier"). Lucy consistently reads and criticizes Snoopy's writings. In one strip, she can't decide if his writing is simply "awful or terrible." Many times, she proclaims that she could be a better author, if she simply cared enough to try.

Watson described Holmes as "cat-like" in his love of personal cleanliness (*The Hound*). Lucy constantly berates Pigpen for his poor personal hygiene as she herself is fastidious in her grooming habits. Once, she even points out that Pigpen's filth should lead him to seek out not a psychiatrist, but an archeologist.

Watson reports repeatedly that Holmes goes into moods of depression: "He was bright, eager, and in excellent spirits, a mood which in his case alternated with fits of the blackest depression." Lucy admits to being crabby on a regular basis, and in a "blue mood" for much of her waking time.

In "The Man with the Twisted Lip," Holmes is first seen in a blue dressing gown. Christopher Morley theorized that Holmes was partial to this gown, and wore it so often, it ultimately faded to purple and then to mouse (gray) color. From the first time Lucy appears in color, a blue dress adorns her figure, until she switched to pants in the 1970s.

Most Sherlockians believe Holmes yet lives because no London newspaper ever printed his obituary. In theory, Holmes would be approximately 164 years old. Lucy first appeared in 1952 as a very young child, 3 to 4 years old. Sixty-five years later, she is still only 8 or 9 years old. She will easily outlast us all.

In "The Naval Treaty," Holmes refers to schools as "Light-houses... with hundreds of bright little seeds in each." Lucy could be one of those bright little seeds. In Latin, the name Lucy means "bringer of light."

Holmes has one primary antagonist: Professor Moriarty. Holmes is willing to sacrifice himself to rid society of London's greatest villain. Lucy has her one primary antagonist: Charlie Brown. She consistently tries to knock him off the pedestal as the most likeable person in the neighborhood.

Holmes believes in law and justice. In *The Valley of Fear* he states that "I go into a case to help the ends of justice and the work of the police." At times, he dispenses his own brand of justice by bending or breaking the rules, such as breaking and entering, letting criminals walk, or suppressing evidence. Lucy constantly ensures that others follow the laws of the neighborhood, policing her own street; however, she also is willing to bend the rules. The most notable example is pulling the football away every time Charlie Brown tries to kick it, even at the cost of the school football team's win during homecoming.

Holmes endures the torment of a canine in the most popular story of the Canon. Lucy endures the torment of a canine throughout her childhood, including slurps on the nose that cause her to exclaim, "I've been kissed by a dog! I have dog germs! Get the hot water, get some disinfectant, get the iodine!"

Sherlock Holmes is the most portrayed literary "human" character in film and television, seen on screen some 260 times and played by more than 75 actors. His stories and novels have been translated into over 100 languages, and his image is instantly recognizable worldwide. *Peanuts*, in which Lucy is one of the primary characters, is the most popular and influential comic strip in history. There are 17,897 individual strips, making it "arguably the longest story ever told by one human being." At its peak in the 1970s and 80s, *Peanuts* ran in more than 2,600 newspapers, with a readership of 355 million in 75 countries, and was translated into 21 languages. Each of the characters is recognizable worldwide.

The final evidence I offer in support of my contention arrives more directly from Charles M. Schulz. In one of his biographies, as well as a *Washington Post* article, Schulz admits that in high school he became a fanatic of Sherlock Holmes. He would go down to the five and dime store to buy big blank books of paper, and he would fill the pages with highly-detailed illustrations to accompany pastiches which he had created. He would share the stories with his best friend, Shermy, who was the basis of an early *Peanuts* character. Later in life, Schulz explained that his creation of Lucy van Pelt in 1952 provided an edge to the comic strip. Louanne van Pelt, a former neighbor in Colorado Springs, inspired Lucy's name. Schulz explained Lucy was based on his first wife, as well as one of his favorite childhood fictional characters.

In short, I promised to present a case for similarities between Holmes and Lucy van Pelt. I consider that these observations make a solid case for Lucy being based on the Master. Their personalities, actions, and characteristics are similar enough to meet the theme of this book.

Steve Mason (Denton, Texas) has been an avid reader of all things Sherlockian since he was seven years old. He is the president (Third Mate) of the Crew of the Barque Lone Star, as well as the communications chair for the Beacon Society. He is also part of the team responsible for the Baker Street Elementary comic strip.

ONCE YOU HAVE ELIMINATED SIX IMPOSSIBLE THINGS

Alice

Resa Haile

At the beginning of Lewis Carroll's 1865 classic *Alice's Adventures in Wonderland*, Alice is bored. She has an active mind and nothing to fix it upon. She also feels rather lazy. She is sitting on the river bank on a hot day while her sister reads, and Alice doesn't know whether it would be worthwhile to get up from her boredom to make a daisy chain. Fortunately, a mystery presents itself to her—a White Rabbit in a tearing hurry, looking at his pocket watch (which had been in his waistcoat) and muttering about being late.

Of course, daisy chains and boredom and the heat are all forgotten. Alice is after this unusual rabbit in a heartbeat. She follows him, right down the (non-metaphorical) rabbit hole.

> "I followed you."
> "I saw no one."
> "That is what you may expect to see when I follow you."
> ("The Devil's Foot")

Alice's first foray into tailing a suspicious character has mixed results. The White Rabbit doesn't seem to have caught her at it and later even mistakes her for his maid (perhaps his eyesight is not very good) without her ever having to don a disguise. On the other hand, she does lose him early in the game.

Alice is quite young here, about seven. (A few months later, in *Through the Looking Glass and What Alice Found There*, she is seven and a half and is advised by Humpty Dumpty to forget about the half.) Presumably, she was born about 1858. Several birth years have been theorized for Sherlock Holmes; 1854 is the most popular, and 1861 is well argued for by Laurie R. King. Accordingly, Alice and Sherlock would have been children at about the same time—or at least, depending on the chronology used, quite close in age.

Alice and Sherlock Holmes are both curious, observant, and easily bored. Although Holmes doesn't enter his underworld through a rabbit hole, he nonetheless is led to it by curiosity, and, like Alice, he attempts to fit in with its denizens as he goes about his quest for knowledge, his pursuit of the solution to the mystery.

> "Come, let's hear some of your adventures."
> "I could tell you my adventures—beginning from this morning," said Alice a little timidly: "but it's no use going back to yesterday, because I was a different person then."

Like Alice, Sherlock Holmes has adventures. After the first eight accounts of his cases, only four will make it to print during Watson's lifetime without "The Adventure" as the beginning of the title. These four begin variously with "The Hound," "The Disappearance," "The Valley," and "The Problem."

Hares appear to be more in Alice's line than hounds, but she deals with several problems in Wonderland and the Looking Glass world, the location of the 1871 *Through the Looking Glass* sequel. They are two separate places, it would seem, to which Alice disappears from her everyday world. And if Wonderland is not a valley, Alice still arrives there by traveling down. If Alice becomes a different person in her journeys to the underworld, Holmes also travels in many guises.

Indeed, a famous Sidney Paget illustration of Holmes and Watson in a train compartment is reminiscent of one of Alice by John Tenniel. Alice's compartment is a bit more crowded, but she sits on the same side as Holmes does in the other picture, and opposite her, with legs crossed in the opposite direction of Watson's, is the gentleman dressed in white paper.

As with the Sherlock Holmes Canon, there are not many recurring characters—Alice's sister, who plays Watson on one of those days when he relaxes and reads a book, only hearing about the adventure later, and Alice's cat, who is not exactly Mrs. Hudson but does do most of the cleaning mentioned.

Holmes looks at outward signs to draw his inferences. He enters "into the region of probabilities and choose[s] the most likely. It is the scientific use of the imagination, but we have always some material on which to start our speculation."

> [Holmes] picked [the hat] up and gazed at it in the peculiar introspective fashion which was characteristic of him. "It is perhaps less suggestive than it might have been," he remarked, "and yet there are a few inferences which are very distinct, and a few others which represent at least a strong balance of probability. That the man was highly intellectual is of course obvious upon the face of it, and also that he was fairly well-to-do within the last three years, although he has now fallen upon evil

days. He had foresight, but has less now than formerly, pointing to a moral retrogression, which, when taken with the decline of his fortunes, seems to indicate some evil influence, probably drink, at work upon him. This may account for the obvious fact that his wife has ceased to love him." ("The Blue Carbuncle")

Years before Holmes is deducing the state of Henry Baker's marriage from the state of his hat, and at the same time when Holmes would have been a child himself, Alice is not too timid to draw inferences from the state of a duchess's temper based on the proximity of pepper, and she extrapolates from these inferences, although she neglects to balance the probabilities properly.

Alice was very glad to find her in such a pleasant temper, and thought to herself that perhaps it was only the pepper that had made her so savage when they met in the kitchen. "When I'm a Duchess," [Alice] said to herself (not in a very hopeful tone though), "I won't have any pepper in my kitchen at all. Soup does very well without—Maybe it's always pepper that makes people hot-tempered," she went on, very much pleased at having found out a new kind of rule, "and vinegar that makes them sour—and chamomile that makes them bitter—and—and barley-sugar and such things that make children sweet-tempered. I only wish people knew that: then they wouldn't be so stingy about it, you know —"

Some of her deductions may be a bit faulty, but if Sherlock Holmes is the detective fully formed, Alice is the detective in chrysalis.

Like Holmes, she is tactful:

[The Gnat says:] "That's a joke. I wish you had made it."
"Why do you wish I had made it?" Alice asked. "It's a very bad one."
But the Gnat only sighed deeply, while two large tears came rolling down its cheeks.
"You shouldn't make jokes," Alice said, "if it makes you so unhappy."

Alice moves among royalty. In the Looking Glass world, the royals are chess pieces, the Red and White Kings and Queens. In Wonderland, they are playing-cards: the King and Queen of Hearts are in charge of the trial of the Knave of Hearts, who has been accused of stealing the Queen's tarts. (This is rather a famous case.) A letter, which later turns out to be a poem, is brought into evidence.

"Please, your Majesty," said the Knave, "I didn't write it, and they can't prove I did: there's no name signed at the end."

"If you didn't sign it," said the King, "that only makes the matter worse. You must have meant some mischief, or else you'd have signed your name like an honest man."

There was a general clapping of hands at this: it was the first really clever thing the King had said that day.

"That proves his guilt, of course," said the Queen: "so, off with—"

"It doesn't prove anything of the sort!" said Alice.

Like Alice, Sherlock Holmes stands up for the wrongly accused. Holmes is also familiar with royalty, and, although he has royal clients on occasion, he is not cowed by them. (Alice may have an advantage here in that she is in one of her too-tall phases.)

Of course, in this instance, the King of Hearts knows something that Alice does not, that no one is ever executed, despite the Queen's frequent orders. The King routinely pardons them all. In this, the Queen of Hearts becomes like the theoretical Mrs. Rucastle in "The Copper Beeches," whose fancies must be humored (fancies that involve the cutting off of hair rather than heads).

There is much to investigate in these strange worlds, and Alice, as has been noted, is a curious girl. She is also a very logical child, and she attempts to apply logic to her encounters, which sometimes doesn't work because the laws of logic are different there, and, conversely, sometimes doesn't work when the inhabitants catch her out in flawed logic.

Talking to the flowers, Alice misses a deduction about the ground (flowers don't usually talk because the ground is so soft they go to sleep, but here the ground is hard) and is insulted by a Violet (perhaps genus *de Merville*).

"I never saw anybody that looked stupider," a Violet said, so suddenly, that Alice quite jumped; for it hadn't spoken before.

In the Looking Glass world, Alice becomes a pawn whose goal is to become a queen. This is the world where the White and Red Queens live. Holmes, of course, believes that excelling at chess is "one mark of a scheming mind" ("The Retired Colourman"), which is not an argument that he did not excel at chess himself—quite the opposite, in fact. As Holmes will later do, Alice deciphers cryptic writing. She listens to a recitation of a poem about a murderous Walrus and Carpenter, who lure young oysters away to eat them up. The Walrus weeps over the oysters, but he also eats more of them. Holmes will later dream in delirium— or pretend to ("The Dying Detective")—about oysters overrunning the world. (At least the Walrus and the Carpenter are doing their part to prevent this.)

"How often have I said to you that when you have eliminated the impossible whatever remains, however improbable, must be the truth?" (*The Sign of the Four*)

Alice tries to eliminate the impossible, but where she travels, the impossible cannot be eliminated.

> Alice laughed. "There's no use trying," she said: "one can't believe impossible things."
> "I daresay you haven't had much practice," said the Queen. "When I was your age, I always did it for half-an-hour a day. Why, sometimes I've believed as many as six impossible things before breakfast."

And Holmes, despite his occasional exhortations to "cut out the po-etry," is quite as poetic as Watson and as imaginative as Alice, as this passage from "A Case of Identity" shows:

> "My dear fellow," said Sherlock Holmes as we sat on either side of the fire in his lodgings at Baker Street, "life is infinitely stranger than anything which the mind of man could invent. We would not dare to conceive the things which are really mere commonplaces of existence. If we could fly out of that window hand in hand, hover over this great city, gently remove the roofs, and peep in at the queer things which are going on, the strange coincidences, the plannings, the cross-purposes, the wonderful chains of events, working through generations, and leading to the most outré results, it would make all fiction with its conventionalities and foreseen conclusions most stale and unprofitable."

It is perhaps fitting to end with "A Case of Identity," as the *Alice* books follow the trajectory of their very young heroine's becoming herself, the beginning of a journey to adulthood. She doesn't "gently remove the roofs"; she knocks them down—and at her age, Sherlock Holmes probably did, too.

Resa Haile (Janesville, Wisconsin) is a co-founder of the Original Tree Worshippers and of the Studious Scarlets Society. She has been published in *The Baker Street Journal*, *NonBinary Review*, and the previous anthology, *About Sixty*. Her current Sherlockian projects include co-editing an anthology and writing a spinoff.

SINGULAR DREAMS

Elon Musk

Ian J. Bennett

I can imagine the great man ensconced comfortably in his cottage on the Sussex coast: walking out in the warm sunshine of the morning to tend his apiary, strolling over the downs with a stop for a quiet drink at the local inn, burning a light late into the night working on his magnum opus, *The Whole Art of Detection*. A Victorian man of singular vision, shaped by his time, but dreaming of a future where the investigation of crime by his methods leads the world to a better tomorrow, prolonging his time to complete his destiny and sharing that vision so the rest of us may profit by it. A man with a dream, bringing it step by step into reality.

The Elon Musk of his time.

Musk, you say, the billionaire designer behind Tesla and SpaceX? You just don't see it? But you will.

I think of them first in their youth, in the earliest incarnations of the men they will be become. Both had a childhood that was less than ideal. In Musk's case we know about the early bullying that he endured in his youth. On one occasion he was knocked down a flight of stairs and kicked unconscious, ending up in hospital. We don't know very much about Holmes's childhood, but we can try to apply his methods to draw a picture. He makes no mention of his parents to Watson, and indeed he is even reluctant to tell Watson very much about his brother Mycroft. Why this reticence about his past? What might have occurred during this formative period of his life that brought him down the path of detection? What keeps him away from discussing his early years and his family? Surely it could have been nothing positive.

A few tidbits about his late teen years are available to us as Watson discusses the earliest cases of which his friend keeps a record in his battered tin box. We know Holmes left for university and made only one friend there. Even this meeting was "accidental," as Trevor's dog managed to bite him severely on the ankle and lay him up in bed for a few days. How did the other boys at school, and college classmates, regard this unusual, tall, thin youth with his strange ways and "powers"? It's not hard to imagine that Holmes could have been subjected to merciless bullying in respect of his oddness. As with Musk after him, the early days of Sherlock Holmes surely cannot have been happy ones.

"You never heard me talk of Victor Trevor?" he asks in "The Gloria Scott". "He was the only friend I made during the two years I was at college. I was never a very sociable fellow, Watson. I was rather fond of moping in my rooms and working out my own little methods of thought, so that I never mixed much with the men of my year. Bar fencing and boxing I had few athletic tastes, and then my line of study was quite distinct from that of the other fellows, so that we had no points of contact at all."

Surely, the other boys knew of Sherlock Holmes and his remarkable gifts and had seen them demonstrated. Reginald Musgrave tells us so when he says, "But I understand, Holmes, that you are turning to practical ends those powers with which you used to amaze us?" But did those other boys regard those powers with friendly or scornful amazement?

As for Holmes's reticence about his brother, we know that Mycroft is a busy and important civil servant, but such positions were not overly well compensated. No man of Holmes's time could afford to live as Mycroft did—especially to maintain his Diogenes Club membership—on the salary afforded by Her Majesty's Government. Surely then, Mycroft lives well because he has access to other funds, and those are assuredly from family sources. As the oldest, Mycroft would certainly have received the estate of his parents into his keeping upon their death, but perhaps he was not as generous as he could have been in his support for brother Sherlock. Perhaps some lingering bitterness exists between them which stems from this time? Here we find more evidence of the scars and damage done in early life. Sherlock can't even afford rooms without taking on a flatmate. What might have passed between the two brothers?

Both young men, the Victorian detective and the contemporary inventor, grew up singular and somewhat solitary in early life. Both had to overcome hurdles placed in their path towards social acceptance. Both were known for their unusual gifts: Holmes for his powers of observation and deduction, Musk for his computer programming. Musk sold his first video game when he was just 12 years old. While his peers lived in the real world, Musk lived in his computer screen, watching the lines of code and seeing the bigger picture that would emerge from what to others might have seemed incomprehensible. All those strings of text would form a game for others to enjoy and wonder at, the magic of computer programming. And the other boys had seen Holmes's remarkable gifts demonstrated. How they must have gasped when Holmes showed his remarkable powers even in their nascent stages of development. What did they think when the demonstration was concluded, and was that thought always complimentary? I suspect those unique capabilities marked Holmes and Musk out as "odd" or "strange" and perhaps that goes some way to explaining why there are so few friends from those early days.

So we find two young men, standing out from the crowd, teased, bullied, with a lack of close friends and feeling alone in the world, but determined to make their own way, on their own terms. Each showed a singular vision for achievement. With Holmes we see it in in the creation of what would become his magnum opus, *The Whole Art of Detection*, a methodology so comprehensive in its scope as to make crime useless, since detection of the criminal was almost certain to occur. Musk, a century later, moves on from his programming beginnings to the incredible task of establishing a permanent colony of humans on Mars in order to ensure the preservation of the human race for all time and protect it from extinction level events on the home planet. Best known for his work with Tesla automobiles, Musk has now become a serial entrepreneur. PayPal, Tesla, SolarCity, and SpaceX all sprang from his fertile brain. Will future humans look into the night sky above Mars and point at a tiny shining dot that is Earth? What an achievement that would be.

About Holmes's labours we know little, since the Master has yet to complete and release his work, but surely we can deduce from his cases how Holmes intended his compendium to benefit law enforcement in the future. The title, *The Whole Art of Detection*, could hardly be more ambitious! Imagine the benefit to society if the greatest detective of all time could encompass in one work everything he learned about the skills and knowledge required to bring criminals to justice. What will be the effect of gathering together all those monographs about enigmatic writing and the analysis of tobacco ashes and the use of disguise (undercover cops wait anxiously for that one), and the utilities of dogs? Criminals will be unemployed and police forces will shrink as crime becomes impossible! What an achievement that would be.

Everything that is done or created has to be done first in the imagination. That is the fertile ground where dreams and ideas first gestate, later to burst into fruition and full flowering in the real world. In the mind of Sherlock Holmes, dreams of detection grew into practical application of skills to fight crime and solve the unsolvable through the use of scientific method to realize the truth. Where would we be today if we had not had the example of his amazing career to lead and inspire us? His methods of crime scene investigation have grown into the CSI (Crime Scene Investigation) and SOCO (Scene of Crime Officers) who today work crime scenes in minute detail to uncover every forensic clue. Holmes beat bodies to investigate bruising of corpses; we have the famous "body farms" where scientists learn how bodies dissolve and break down after death. There is a straight line between them, and it commenced with the work of the man from Baker Street.

We wait still for Sherlock Holmes's great book, just as we wait for Musk's vision to carry humans far into the night sky to their ultimate landing on Mars. Given Musk's previous record of success, there is every reason to believe his dream will also come to fruition so that one day, humans will live and work on another planet. The latest launch of the

Falcon Heavy rocket by his company SpaceX brought us one step closer to this reality.

Two visionary dreamers, with two singular dreams, yet to be fully realized but with great promise. That's why Sherlock Holmes is like Elon Musk.

Ian J. Bennett (London, Ontario) is a retired school administrator and burgeoning curmudgeon. A member of the Bootmakers of Toronto and the Cesspudlians of London, he divides his time between visiting his grandchildren and being an international man of leisure.

THE STAGE'S GAIN

Peter Cushing

Joanne Chaix

Is Sherlock Holmes like an actor who remains famous for his Sherlock Holmes? An interesting metadrama question, is it not?

Let us start by quoting our dear Dr. Watson from "A Scandal in Bohemia": "It was not merely that Holmes changed his costume. His expression, his manner, his very soul seemed to vary with every fresh part that he assumed." Indeed, we must not forget that Sherlock Holmes is a consummate actor in his own right. Even beyond the many roles he takes for the sake of his cases, the detective has always had something of the actor, as we classically imagine the profession. He is inconstant, passionate, has a proclivity for disguises and a flair for the dramatic. "You'd have made an actor and a rare one," says Inspector Athelney Jones in *The Sign of the Four* after such a performance. Just the night before he was hanged, Old Baron Dowson is said to have added that "what the law had gained the stage had lost" (as recounted by Holmes himself in "The Mazarin Stone").

For background to this short article, I owe a lot to Tony Earnshaw and his masterful book *An Actor and a Rare One* (Scarecrow Press, 2001), the most comprehensive work on Peter Cushing as Sherlock Holmes, and to Peter Cushing himself and the written words he left us, most notably in his *Complete Memoirs* (Signum, 2013). But since it would be highly unfair to Earnshaw to simply summarize his work, I will try to bring my own point of view on the complex relationship linking the great Peter Cushing and the most celebrated detective in the world. Also, contrary to Earnshaw, I am chronologically a Holmesian literary fan first and a film buff second, which, I hope, might bring a new perspective to this question.

As Cushing himself has said (in the *Sherlock Holmes Review*, 1987): "I've never copied any actor. I was never influenced by the way Rathbone—who played Sherlock Holmes superbly—approached the character. I tried to reflect Conan Doyle's impression of the character. And, of course, whatever part an actor plays, his own personality must come through. You can't help that." So, the tricky question to ask oneself is how much of our own perception of Holmes has been influenced by what we have seen interpreted of him on screen as well as in other media.

I am now 30, meaning I was only six when Peter Cushing passed away in 1994. I never had the chance to meet him or see him in person. Yet he was the one who introduced me to Sherlock Holmes on screen in my childhood years through the brilliant Hammer film *The Hound of the Baskervilles* (1959). I was already an avid reader of detective novels and Sherlock Holmes in particular.

My grandparents had recorded (sadly in French, obviously) the Hammer masterpiece and, as I sat watching it for the first time on their old TV, I remember thinking "Ah. It's him. It's really him." I had yet to even see Sidney Paget's illustrations, and Basil Rathbone was not popular on French TV anymore. Cushing really was my first Holmes. That is why, through all the descriptions of the famous detective gathered haphazardly through the short stories and novels, I could not imagine him differently. That did not change until I saw Jeremy Brett on TV.

Conversely, Holmes may have been my first introduction to Peter Cushing, an actor I would soon come to love dearly. (I honestly cannot recall if first I saw him as Holmes or in *Star Wars*, but the period was much the same.) So I would say that, as far as I am concerned, Sherlock Holmes made a very good Peter Cushing.

The Hound of the Baskervilles, produced by Kenneth Hyman and Anthony Hinds and directed by Terence Fisher, was an ambitious project, the first full-colour adaptation of Conan Doyle's iconic tale, and remains well known and well loved. The story, while widely popular, has the peculiar aspect of featuring a largely absent Holmes. It means that, whenever Holmes appears, he must be memorable and true to the mark. Cushing delivered, thanks in part to the strong partnership he had with Fisher, a Hammer regular, just like him, and to the writing of Peter Bryan, veteran Hammer camera operator, who made his writing debut on this film. Though it differs significantly from the Canon (especially when it comes to Miss Stapleton's role), its atmospheric and distinctly Hammer ambiance offers a powerful influence on the future of Holmes in films and TV. Cushing himself insisted on the deerstalker, correctly convinced that, as with the pipe, it was an element the public associated with Sherlock Holmes. He would later mostly set those props aside when he prepared for the 1968 BBC series, wanting to get closer to Paget's work and to Canon Holmes.

As a teenager who read mostly in French and had little access to Holmesian resources, I had yet to immerse myself in the extensive works of analysis and research about the detective. I could only count on my own imagination and memory, my own passion for Sir Arthur Conan Doyle's beloved and hated Sherlock Holmes. So Cushing's age when he was playing the role (he was 46) did not affect me, nor did the myriad of differences between books and adaptations.

For a very long time afterwards, Holmes was Cushing and Cushing was Holmes in my head. If Cushing and Holmes had one vital thing in common, it was the hunter gleam in their eyes. I also liked to link their thin, angular faces, their hands, their demeanour and even their noses, though the last is considered a difference by Holmesian scholars: the original Holmes has a "thin hawk-like nose" which Cushing lacked. It is also true that, while Sherlock Holmes is tall and gaunt, Cushing was dwarfed by Christopher Lee's Sir Henry in *The Hound*. But there is something about Cushing's form that is very Holmesian, thin and sinewy, hence this detail did not shock me either. Cushing accompanied me while I was growing up, from the celebrated Hammer horror films of my Gothic aesthetic passion, to *Star Wars IV* and his chilling role as Grand Moff Tarkin. Cushing's Van Helsing has also that scientist aspect I imagined when thinking of Holmes in his makeshift lab in his 221B dwelling.

Every time I saw Cushing on screen, I thought to myself how otherworldly he was, how intelligent his eyes looked, how he could be both cold and warm, sarcastic yet genuinely open. All those traits can be found here and there in Holmes Canon, hinted at sometimes, plainly shown in others. They are what makes Sherlock Holmes so remarkable, aside from his deductive abilities. Afterwards, I realised of course that Cushing bore a physical resemblance to Paget's work (except mayhap the nose), which he studied and used, although he found that the camera's light "exaggerated the icy blueness of his eyes". It served him well, nonetheless. So, in my opinion, Cushing's role brought him close to what Holmes is in many respects.

What about Peter Cushing as a person? Chapter 1 of Earnshaw's book starts with a quotation from Cushing himself in a conversation with David Stuart Davies in 1992 about Sherlock Holmes: "He's the most devilish, difficult part to play. It's difficult to make him not irritating mannered and insufferably conceited." I am fairly certain that this was and still is a concern for every actor who ever took on the part. Jeremy Brett's Holmes, with its eccentric mannerisms, is not without its charm, and he brought to his Holmes a warmth and gentleness that is greater than Canon Holmes ever shows, while Benedict Cumberbatch still wholly embraces the "insufferably conceited" aspect of his character, for example.

Cushing himself was an ardent reader of Holmes and a fan of Sir Arthur Conan Doyle, as Earnshaw is quick to remind us. I invite you to read the Appendix 2 of *An Actor and a Rare One*, titled "The Canon According to Peter Cushing", to fully realise how much the actor loved the Canon and was an Holmesian at heart.

Would Sherlock Holmes have gone and seen his alter-ego's films and plays? Watched him on TV? Listened to his radio dramas? It is hard to say. We know Sherlock Holmes has very little interests outside of his work. The young Peter was also selective in his studies, excelling in the dramatic arts. Yet, Holmes loves music and has an appreciation for every person who excelled at their work, and Cushing definitely excelled. He was conscientious to a fault, as his extensive notes and sketches on the script (about his character and costumes) prove. For the BBC series, he adopted a strict regimen to match the detective's wiry, iron constitution. He also took a three-month retreat to study the fifteen scripts and compare them to his collection of books about Holmes and his collection of original *Strand* magazines. Cushing's love and knowledge of the character appeared most exemplary when he added a line about Holmes's stance on his fees from "Thor Bridge" to the script of *The Hound*.

It is not impossible to imagine that, had Holmes and Cushing met, they would have shared a deep respect for one another. And perhaps a few notes.

One thing that definitely separates the two brilliant men is Cushing's boundless love for his wife, Helen, whereas Holmes has a less than appreciative view of the feminine gender and, in the Canon at least, never married. (We even learn from his own lips in "The Devil's Foot" that he has never loved.) Nonetheless, the way Helen Cushing, through her own streak of stubbornness and competences, helped her husband thrive and become famous inevitably reminds us of a certain doctor's devotion to his friend and the way his notes bring Holmes some measure of celebrity.

Another difference is the boisterous laughter Cushing possessed in real life, which would be far from the dry chuckle traditionally associated with our favourite Baker Street resident. And of course, from all accounts (including that of the Cushings' secretary, Joyce Broughton) Peter Cushing was a sweet, humorous and generous man, while Holmes, who has a "strange and occasionally offensive" humour about him ("Lady Frances Carfax"), also abhors emotions and is wont to avoid forming friendships. Cushing, on the other hand, never hid his love for his friends (Christopher Lee is a prime example, as mentioned in Cushing's memoirs). Cushing also admitted himself, in his usual humorous manner, that smoking a pipe would put him on the brink of nausea.

So is Sherlock Holmes like Peter Cushing? Not really. At least, not completely. "For Sherlock Holmes, acting was a means to an end, never a goal in itself," says Curtis Armstrong in his playful article "An Actor and a Rare One" in the *Baker Street Journal*, 2007. He would have made a convincing Cushing, no doubt, even playing the lover as he did in "Charles Augustus Milverton". But Cushing was not a solitary soul. Helen's death devastated him. His own retirement was spent with Joyce Broughton and her family, fighting cancer with their love and his passion for art, far from bee keeping. And, of course, I agree when Armstrong says that "A life in the theatre would never have done for [Holmes]. It simply wasn't enough of a challenge."

Yet, there is an undeniable link between them, a closeness between fiction and reality when it comes to Sherlock Holmes. He has been made alive by the heart and soul of every Holmesian, old and young, in the world. Cushing was born in 1913, a little after the detective left for retirement in Sussex, and between 1959 and 1984, he played Holmes a total of seventeen times. He was a passionate soul to carry Holmes's adventures through the ages.

Joanne Chaix (Paris, France) is a freelance writer, translator, and International Relations and Asian-Japanese studies consultant. She is an active member of the *Cercle Holmésien de Paris*.

THE DOLL AND ITS MAKER

Arthur Conan Doyle

Daniel Stashower

"I suppose I am Sherlock Holmes, if anybody is," Conan Doyle once remarked, "and I say that the case for Spiritualism is absolutely proved." This is a remarkable statement in that—for many readers, anyway— it somehow manages to embrace two contradictory extremes. On the one hand, Conan Doyle makes an uncommonly direct acknowledgment of Sherlock Holmes, the most perfect reasoning and observing machine that the world has seen, as an expression of his own character. On the other hand, however, he presses his famous creation into service as a means of advancing his own views on Spiritualism. For many of the author's admirers, this presents a paradox of a three-pipe order.

Spiritualism, which Conan Doyle often described as "the most important thing in the world," is the belief that it is possible for the dead to communicate with the living through an earthly conduit, known as a spirit medium. Conan Doyle believed wholeheartedly in this "new revelation," as he phrased it, but it's clear that Sherlock Holmes felt otherwise. "This agency stands flat-footed upon the ground, and there it must remain," the detective once remarked. "The world is big enough for us. No ghosts need apply."

On this point, it would seem, Sherlock Holmes is decidedly unlike Conan Doyle. Even if we set aside the full-throated endorsement of Spiritualism, however, Conan Doyle's statement is no less remarkable. We are not accustomed to hearing the author associate himself so closely with his famous creation. Indeed, for much of his career Conan Doyle appeared to hold Sherlock Holmes at arm's length, in keeping with his belief, often stated, that the great detective existed "on a different and humbler plane" from his other works. In an interview with *The Bookman*, published in May of 1892, the 32-year-old Conan Doyle was asked to explain "how on earth he had evolved, apparently out of his own inner consciousness, such an extraordinary person as his detective Sherlock Holmes."

The author gave an emphatic reply: "Oh!" he exclaimed. "But, if you please, he is not evolved out of anyone's inner consciousness. Sherlock

Holmes is the literary embodiment, if I may so express it, of my memory of a professor of medicine at Edinburgh University." This will be familiar ground for many readers. The story of Dr. Joseph Bell as the model and inspiration for Sherlock Holmes is widely travelled largely because Conan Doyle himself insisted upon it over and over again. For the benefit of *The Bookman*, he gave several distinctly Sherlockian examples: "I am not quite sure whether this man is a cork-cutter or a slater," he recalled Bell as saying. "I observe a slight *callus*, or hardening, on one side of his forefinger, and a little thickening on the outside of his thumb, and that is a sure sign he is either one or the other."

Privately, in a letter to Bell himself, Conan Doyle made the point even more forcefully. "It is most certainly to you that I owe Sherlock Holmes," he wrote, "and though in the stories I have the advantage of being able to place him in all sorts of dramatic positions, I do not think that his analytical work is in the least an exaggeration of some of the effects which I have seen you produce in the out-patient ward." And finally, in 1924, Conan Doyle repackaged the story for posterity in his autobiography *Memories and Adventures*, describing the circumstances that inspired him to try his hand at detective fiction:

> I felt now that I was capable of something fresher and crisper and more workmanlike. Gaboriau had rather attracted me by the neat dovetailing of his plots, and Poe's masterful detective, M. Dupin, had from boyhood been one of my heroes. But could I bring an addition of my own? I thought of my old teacher Joe Bell, of his eagle face, of his curious ways, of his eerie trick of spotting details. If he were a detective he would surely reduce this fascinating but unorganized business to something nearer to an exact science. I would try if I could get this effect. It was surely possible in real life, so why should I not make it plausible in fiction? It is all very well to say that a man is clever, but the reader wants to see examples of it—such examples as Bell gave us every day in the wards. The idea amused me.

As a result of these and other exaltations of Bell's genius, we are left at times with a sense that Conan Doyle was little more than a genial stenographer who happened to be present when Sherlock Holmes sprang into being. One suspects that Conan Doyle himself, who often regarded Holmes as a "workmanlike" exercise of his apprenticeship, would not have objected too strenuously to the notion if it directed more attention to books such as *The White Company* and *Sir Nigel*, which he considered to be "more serious literary work."

Even so, as he readily acknowledged, "it was still the Sherlock Holmes stories for which the public clamoured, and these from time to time I endeavoured to supply." And from the beginning, whenever interviewers arrived to spend "A Day with Dr. Conan Doyle," as *The Strand*'s Harry How did in August of 1892, they were eager to discover traces of Sherlock Holmes. "I found him totally different from the man I expected to see," How admitted. "There is nothing lynx-eyed, nothing 'detective' about him…. He is just a happy, genial, homely man; tall, broad-shouldered, with a hand that grips you heartily, and, in its sincerity of welcome, hurts."

"Never trust to general impressions," Sherlock Holmes would tell us. Though Conan Doyle insisted that he possessed only limited powers of observation, he was often called upon to assist in the unraveling of mysteries, both large and small, in the assumption that he would be able to shed light where others had failed. Three of these cases—the "horse-maiming" accusations against George Edalji, the wrongful imprisonment of Oscar Slater, and the disappearance of Agatha Christie—command special attention. In all three cases Conan Doyle involved himself in a very public way, gaining a reputation as a "paladin of lost causes." His efforts on behalf of both Edalji and Slater would have a dramatic impact, with lasting consequences.

It could be argued, however, that none of the three cases presents a pure showcase for "the science of deduction"—they are, perhaps, more a series of tales than a course of lectures. In the Edalji case, Conan Doyle concluded early on that the young lawyer's poor eyesight rendered him incapable of the crime of which he stood accused, a conclusion that owed more to the author's medical training than his detective instincts. In the Slater case, Conan Doyle made effective use of his fame and influence to draw wider attention to a miscarriage of justice, amplifying the work of men such as William Roughead and William Park alongside his own conclusions. And during the celebrated disappearance of Mrs. Christie, Conan Doyle interceded not as a detective but as a spiritualist, placing one of the missing woman's gloves in the hands of "psychometrist" named Horace Leaf, a man said to be able to receive psychic impressions from physical objects, in the hope that Leaf would be able to "call up in his mind thoughts, feelings, and even visions," much like a bloodhound catching a scent. Though his efforts in these cases drew headlines such as "A. Conan Doyle Is Detective in Real Life," the author himself was more restrained. "I was called upon to do what I could," he remarked in his memoir, but nowhere does he describe these efforts as detective work.

Fiction has given us many cultural touchstones, but we do not always pause to wonder what attributes they share with their creators. We take it as an article of faith that Edgar Rice Burroughs was not raised in the African jungle by Mangani apes, that Walt Disney was not a mouse, and that J.K. Rowling is not a boy wizard. As Conan Doyle once wrote, responding to a rhymed criticism of his detective:

> So please grip this fact with your cerebral tentacle,
> The doll and its maker are never identical.

Nevertheless, it is a high tribute to the power and enduring fascination of Sherlock Holmes that we so often seek out his models and inspirations, and look for the traits in common with his author. It is undoubtedly true that there would be no Sherlock Holmes without Joseph Bell. The same could easily be said of Edgar Allan Poe, whom Conan Doyle regarded as the "master of all," along with other literary influences such as Émile Gaboriau and Robert Louis Stevenson. But in looking for the external clues—the thickening on the outside of the thumb, or the shiny patch at the knee of the trousers—we occasionally overlook the creative synthesis that took place when Conan Doyle drew these disparate strands together into a tangled skein. Perhaps no one understood this better than Dr. Joseph Bell himself. Though Bell would come to relish his identification with the famous detective, he was always quick to reflect credit back onto his former student. "Dr. Conan Doyle has, by his imaginative genius, made a great deal out of very little," Bell told a journalist, "and his warm remembrance of one of his old teachers has coloured the picture." Once again, Bell's observations are correct: what was vital had been overlaid and hidden by what was irrelevant. Or, to return to the moment at which we met him, Sherlock Holmes is a reagent precipitated by Conan Doyle, and by nothing else.

"I have done five of the Sherlock Holmes stories of the new Series," Conan Doyle told his mother at the close of 1891. "I think of slaying Holmes in the sixth & winding him up for good & all. He takes my mind from better things." This unguarded comment tells us a great deal about the author's ambivalence towards his famous creation, but in his final years Conan Doyle was able to strike a conciliatory note: "I have not in actual practice found that these lighter sketches have prevented me from exploring and finding my limitations in such varied branches of literature as history, poetry, historical novels, psychic research, and the drama. Had Holmes never existed I could not have done more, though he may perhaps have stood a little in the way of the recognition of my more serious literary work." One is tempted to leave it there, but I have always been struck by a remark made privately in a letter to editor Greenhough Smith while Conan Doyle was at work on *The Lost World* in 1911. "My ambition," he wrote, "is to do for the boys' book what Sherlock Holmes did for the detective tale. I don't suppose I could bring off two such coups. And yet I hope it may."

It is an admirable sentiment, although, yet again, one is irresistibly reminded of the words of Sherlock Holmes: "How small we feel with our petty ambitions and strivings in the presence of the great elemental forces of Nature!"

Daniel Stashower (Bethesda, Maryland) is a member of the Baker Street Irregulars, the author of *Teller of Tales: The Life of Arthur Conan Doyle*, and the co-editor of numerous other Sherlockian works.

BEHOLD THE MAN

Jesus Christ

Laura Sook Duncombe

Humility is not high on the list of Sherlock Holmes's many virtues, but even he would be surprised to find himself compared to Jesus Christ. "In a modest way I have combated evil," he says in *The Hound of the Baskervilles*, "but to take on the Father of Evil himself would, perhaps, be too ambitious a task." To a Christian, it seems ill-advised at best and doomed at worst to attempt to draw parallels between the two men. No doubt many will find the topic blasphemous and reject the present essay out of hand. However, to many other Sherlockians, Jesus Christ is just another legendary character with no particular special significance, and the topic is no more intriguing than any other in the collection.

It is my hope that all Sherlockians, whether Jesus Christ is their Lord and Savior or just another myth, will find this essay enjoyable. The structure is simple: as Christians believe in a Holy Trinity, this essay will explore a trinity of similarities between Jesus Christ and Sherlock Holmes. Although there are many superficial connections between the two men—the fact that neither ever married, for example—these three main points will serve to illustrate the important parallels in the lives of the Master and the Messiah.

The idea to compare the two men is not entirely new, of course, and could perhaps be traced back to Monsignor Ronald Knox, a young tutor at Oxford who wrote and presented a satirical paper eventually published as "Studies in the Literature of Sherlock Holmes" in 1911. Tongue-in-cheek, Knox addressed the published stories of Sherlock Holmes—incomplete then, but eventually to grow to 60 tales, almost as many as the 66 books of the Bible—with techniques that had lately come into vogue for the study of Biblical texts. He was comparing Canon to Canon, and by implication comparing the central figure of the one collection to the central figure of the other, though he did not go so far as to point out the resemblances that now follow.

The first way in which Sherlock Holmes is like Jesus Christ is that he is, like Jesus Christ, both ordinary and extraordinary. Jesus Christ was born in a stable and raised a carpenter's boy, and never traveled more than two hundred miles from his home town. Yet he also, the texts assure us, turned water into wine, cast out demons, and raised people from the dead. His humanity made his miracles all the more remarkable. No floating spirit was Christ—he was a flesh and blood man, who ate and slept and laughed and cried. Sherlock Holmes, too, was a man born into a normal family, though in his case an upper-class one. He had to attend to all the mundane vagaries of life: paying rent, attending musical performances, even occasionally taking ill. In addition to these tasks, which his friend Dr. John Watson did also, he also did what Watson could not do—what nobody else could do. Sherlock Holmes witnessed things ordinary people missed. He connected stray strands of evidence and wove them into a rich tapestry of truth. His rare mind allowed him to perform miracles, of a sort: diagnosing one's profession by a crease in the sleeve or the state of a marriage by the disrepair of a hat.

Both men are firmly rooted in the everyday world, seemingly compelled to operate in it although they have abilities that place them high above it. Sherlock Holmes and Jesus Christ are two men who, rather than turn their backs upon their fellow men who do not share their gifts, dedicated their lives to aiding mere mortals in need. Their methods were different, but their mission was the same. Each was devoted to making the world a better place in the best way he knew how.

Jesus Christ, so the Gospels say, rose from the dead after three days. Sherlock Holmes was a little bit more tardy about it, lollygagging among the dead for three years before triumphantly unmasking himself to a gobsmacked John Watson. But both men died (or were presumed dead) and then came back to life to complete the work they had left unfinished. For Jesus Christ, the work was the fulfilment of ancient prophecies and the beginning of the Christian church. For Sherlock Holmes, it was taking down Col. Sebastian Moran and returning to stalking the streets of London, searching for answers.

Clearly the circumstances of the two deaths could not be less similar. It must be acknowledged that Sherlock Holmes did not actually die at all; he only staged his own death to deceive Moriarty's henchmen who were out to kill the detective at the Reichenbach Falls. Jesus Christ was nailed to a cross outside Jerusalem and publicly ridiculed until he succumbed to his injuries. And while Sherlock Holmes spent his "death" wandering through Europe and Asia, Jesus Christ descended into Hell. Even John Watson could conclude that the deaths of these men were of entirely different natures. Still, although the circumstances were strikingly different, it is a small club indeed made up of men who have risen from the dead, and both Sherlock Holmes and Jesus Christ are members of that club.

Finally, both of these men share a characteristic that is at the core of who they are: each existence greatly increases the happiness of the people who believe in him. Jesus Christ's followers started a religion that bears his name. Christianity has endured for over two thousand years and is the largest religion in the world, with over two billion followers. While

Sherlock Holmes's followers cannot boast of as long a tenure or as many adherents, the great detective has amassed quite a number of acolytes since his introduction to the world in 1887 in *Beeton's Christmas Annual*. People do not congregate weekly to celebrate Sherlock Holmes as they do Jesus Christ, but Watson's Tin Box of Ellicott City, Maryland, meets once a month, and many other Sherlockian societies gather approximately as often. The rituals that unfold at each meeting, though different, are in some sense sacred to those who participate. And in both groups, one of the finest benefits of these meetings is the fellowship that blossoms among the believers.

Many people do not believe in Jesus Christ. For that matter, many people do not believe in Sherlock Holmes. But for those who do believe, either in "the Great Game" or in the Holy Gospels, great solace and comfort come from that belief. This is not to say that Sherlockians revere Sherlock as a deity—although it is certainly possible that some do. It is not *what* one believes about these men that matters, but *that* one believes. Christians and Sherlockians share a belief in something larger than themselves, and that belief brings, for the believers, order out of chaos, light out of darkness, the improbable out of the impossible. This gift that each man gives to those who believe—the gift of an anchor to cling to in times of trouble—is what truly unites the disparate pair. Sherlock Holmes is like Jesus Christ not because of who he is, but for what he means to those who love him.

Laura Sook Duncombe (Tulsa, Oklahoma) is a past Gasogene of Watson's Tin Box (of Maryland) and an author and lawyer who lives with her husband and son. When not immersed in Sherlockiana, she enjoys feminism, musical theater, and *Star Wars*.

INDEX

CPSIA information can be obtained
at www.ICGtesting.com
Printed in the USA
LVHW090335201118
597694LV00001B/6/P

9 781479 441082